# LION OF JUDAH

# VICTOR OSTROVSKY

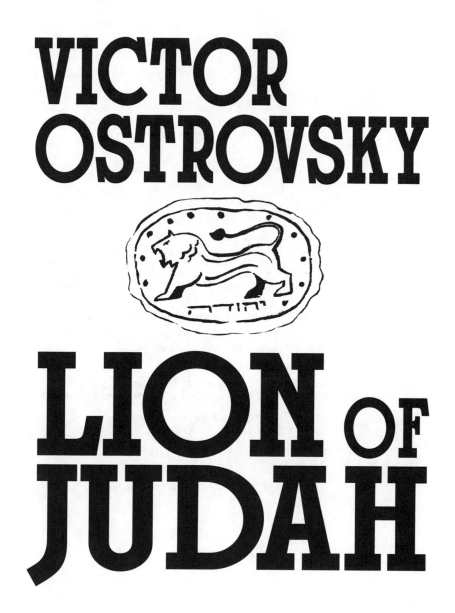

# LION OF JUDAH

St. Martin's Press
New York

**Library of Congress Cataloging-in-Publication Data**

Ostrovsky, Victor.
Lion of Judah / Victor Ostrovsky.
p.   cm.
ISBN 0-312-10016-7
1. Political crimes and offenses—Israel—Fiction.   2. Government
investigators—Israel—Fiction.   3. Intelligence service—Israel—Fiction.
I. Title.
PR9510.9.O85L56      1993
892.4′36—dc20        93-23124        CIP

First published in Canada by Stoddart Publishing Co. Limited

First U.S. Edition: September 1993

10  9  8  7  6  5  4  3  2  1

*To Bella, my wife, my love, my ally
and our treasures,
Sharon and Leeorah*

# 1

KARL PRESSED the 9-mm Luger to his cheek. The cool
steel had a pleasant, soothing effect in the hot room. A crumbling
log was still glowing in the fireplace, and the few shots of schnapps
he'd downed only made him sweat more.

Karl Reinhart was a tall, slim man in his early forties. He stood
at the window, wiping the sweat off his forehead with the back of
his hand, ruffling his neat, fair hair. He was studying the elegant
nineteenth-century palace across the street. The decaying building
with the impressive facade had been his realm until recently. Now
it was only a sealed, forlorn East German relic as gray as the
autumn sky above it, but it represented all that was familiar for
him and his colleagues in the East German Ministry of State
Security, better known as the Stasi. He had spent almost twenty
years of his life in that old building, and from its underground
vaults of files, he had drawn his power.

His lavish apartment, next to the German-Soviet friendship
house, was one of the perks that had come with the appointment
to head Department C/5, responsible for Coordination of Liberation
Activities: in layman's terms, the Stasi officer in charge of main-
taining terrorist organizations around the world.

Karl squinted as his breath fogged the cold windowpane, blurring his view of the colorless scene. He was still puzzled by the way things had been allowed to happen. Until several days ago, he and his comrades had been in control and then abruptly it was over. The demonstrators, or citizens' committee, as they called themselves, had seized the building. With his source of power gone, all Karl could do now was the "honorable" thing. There was no turning back.

No one would miss him, and it seemed to be the appropriate way of saying farewell to his crumbling world. The call he'd been expecting had come several hours earlier. A former colleague informed him that sometime this evening they would be coming to take him in for questioning. Him: Stasi Colonel Karl Reinhart. There was no doubt the glorious reign of the Stasi was over.

He turned from the window, carefully inspecting the room. Everything was as he wanted it to be found. Next to him, on the smoked glass tabletop, was an almost empty bottle of schnapps. Behind the sofa was a cardboard box filled with documents stamped TOP SECRET in blazing red.

Karl had foreseen the end several months earlier, when the demonstrations had brought no retaliation. East German Chairman Erich Honecker had gotten cold feet. For weeks now in Stasi headquarters they had been burning files that could incriminate not only themselves, but thousands of agents around the world. Everyone seemed to be caught up in the frenzy, either destroying or sending to Moscow truckloads of intelligence treasures that they'd spent a lifetime gathering.

Karl was jolted back to the present by a loud knock on the door. *"Moment, mal!"* he called out, giving his voice a drunken slur.

At that moment Johan's foot slid off the sofa to the floor with a thud. The room's other occupant was oblivious to what was going on.

*"Polizei hier!"*

"Go to hell!" Karl yelled back.

The knocking on the door intensified into pounding. The frustrated police outside were still unaware that they were dealing with a reinforced door. Karl knew it would take quite a while for them to force entry, and by then they would find him dead.

He walked closer to the door and shouted, "Long live the German Democratic Republic!" The pounding continued, as Karl walked over to the sofa. He cocked the Luger and, turning to the door, cried, "Fuck the lot of you!" then pulled the trigger. Several seconds of silence followed the gun blast, then the men outside started to pound at the door more vigorously.

Killing yourself was not an easy task, Karl thought, especially if you wanted to start a new life afterward. His papers, conveniently placed on the dresser in the bedroom, all had Karl's name, but the photo was of the man who seemed to be asleep on the sofa, were it not for his splattered brains and the back of his head now almost completely missing. Indeed, he had been asleep when Karl placed the gun in his mouth and fired.

This vagrant *Auslander*, or foreigner, known to a handful of other street people as Johan, was almost identical to Karl in build. Bringing the man up to the apartment in the almost abandoned building whose tenants, former Stasi officials, were seeking refuge from Moscow to Beijing, was much easier than Karl had at first anticipated. And once he'd gotten Johan hooked on his large stock of schnapps, he'd become a frequent visitor, so that everything just fell into place.

In addition to being displayed as Karl on the papers in the bedroom, Johan's photo was to be found in every file that bore Karl's name in the building across the street that had been his headquarters. Once the police broke in, they would treat this as an open-and-shut case of suicide and no further investigation would take place. Karl was nothing if not a thorough and meticulous man. Over several weeks, he had carefully positioned all the elements of his plan.

Now he pulled a lever inside the fireplace, using a heavy oven mitt so as not to burn his hand. Part of the fireplace back wall spun open, revealing a rope ladder that extended down into the shaft behind it. Once on the ladder, Karl used a second lever to return the back wall to its original position. The existence of the shaft and its secret entrance was revealed to him by his predecessor at C/5. He, too, had no idea why or who installed it, but said it might just come in handy one day. How right he was.

In less than three minutes Karl reached the bottom of the shaft. He climbed a narrow staircase leading from the basement to the back entrance, emerging into an alley behind the building. Several police cars drew up to the curb as he walked out into the street. Firefighters with axes had also arrived in an antiquated fire truck and were now striding into the building. People had stopped on the sidewalk to watch the commotion, but no one paid any attention to Karl, who simply melted into the crowd.

Some two blocks north and several minutes later, Karl arrived at the Hotel Krantz, where he had checked in the previous day using the name Franz Toller. The real Toller was at the bottom of the Mulde River just outside Wurzen, but he wouldn't be found for several days, if at all, and Karl would be far away, regardless.

"I would like to check out, please. Toller, my name is Franz Toller," he told the desk clerk, placing his key on the counter.

Reluctantly folding the sports page of the local paper, the man looked over his glasses at Karl. Then he stood up, opened a large drawer, leafed through a bunch of cards, and pulled one out. "Weren't you supposed to leave tomorrow, Herr Toller?" the man inquired, looking at Karl again.

"So, what about it? I'm checking out now. You get the bill ready and have someone bring my luggage down. I'll be in the lounge having a drink." Karl's authoritative tone of voice preempted further questions.

Several hours later, at the wheel of Toller's dark blue Mercedes, Karl noticed tiny droplets of blood on the cuff of his shirt. Peering hard into the rearview mirror, he saw several tiny marks on his face, too, although those looked like shaving nicks. So, the bastard didn't just splatter the sofa, he thought, wiping at his face with his hand.

Karl arrived the following morning at 0730 in Hamburg. He parked the car in an empty lot on Domstrasse, about three blocks from the Rathaus Market, leaving all of Toller's belongings and papers inside. He wiped the wheel, as well as all other places he had touched, clean of fingerprints, and taking only his overcoat, walked toward the market. Once he walked away from the car, no connection could be made between himself, Toller's car and the naked, faceless body that might be found later in the Mulde River. The cord was severed. Karl was free.

Karl rented a car using his new identity, and drove to the Hotel Kempinski, where he had reserved a room for one night. He had prepared this particular identity, and kept it secret even from his compatriots. He became an American citizen with a spacious Fifth Avenue apartment overlooking Central Park in Manhattan. The apartment had been bought by the Stasi, but he had totally erased all records of the transaction. There was a handsome sum in Karl's U.S. bank account, and he also had some holdings in France.

But the real treasure awaited him in his New York post office box. While Karl and his colleagues had been destroying the Stasi files in Leipzig, he had managed to smuggle out most of his agents' files, selecting only those who had no idea for whom they were working and so were unaffected by the fall of East Germany. With that assortment of well-placed agents around the world, whom he could activate at any time — in addition to the international terrorist network he had helped create — Karl possessed a potential bonanza.

Paris would be his next stop, and then New York. For the next few months, Karl planned to lie low and analyze the world scene, assessing the value of his equity in what was now being called the New World Order. He was on his way to becoming a capitalist. And, as a professional, he knew he would be a very rich one.

# 2

**DAMASCUS**
**SEPTEMBER 5**
**1700 HOURS**

SHABY TARIK TALAAT, a short, fleshy gentleman in his late forties, emerged from the Syrian High Command building into the hot September afternoon, his deeply trenched face unnaturally pale. He had no doubts about the information he had just acquired, though it was quite by chance that he had attended this particular briefing.

Ahamed Dayeb, head of the Office for National Security, had been sick for several days, and his deputy, who was Shaby's boss, had been called away to Al-Hasakah in Eastern Syria on an urgent matter, leaving Shaby to represent the most powerful office in the security services at a highly sensitive briefing. Shaby had been treated with great respect and shown information to which he would not have been privy under normal circumstances.

From the moment the presentation had started, it was clear to Shaby that he had stumbled upon a treasure trove, and he had made up his mind at that moment to take it for all it was worth. He would sell the information one piece at a time. This was much better stuff then he had ever gotten before. He knew it was worth a fortune. First he would send them a taste of what he had, then he would squeeze them for every additional bit. When the meeting had adjourned, he had been the first one out of the conference room.

Now he walked briskly down the stairs leading from the ornate, colonial-style building to his black Peugeot 504, parked at its reserved spot. As he drove out of the compound, an armed sentry saluted him.

Damascus, with its narrow streets, is not a city for fast driving, but one where skillful maneuvering is essential. Anxious as he was to get home, Shaby nonetheless kept a steady pace along the crowded inner-city streets, crossing through the covered bazaar of Midhat-Pasha to El Malek. Then, passing the central government offices and the new buildings of the Ministry of Education, he emerged onto the traffic-jammed Faruk El Awal Boulevard.

The heat was not letting up, even though temperatures were lower than usual for that time of year. Shaby was sweating profusely, his thin white cotton shirt sticking to his skin. He knew full well that the act of transmitting information on a secret communications device was punishable by death. An end that would not necessarily come quickly if he were caught. It was only his fantastic appetite for the good life that helped him calm down the fear of what he was about to do.

Driving almost instinctively while his thoughts drifted — calculating, manipulating, assessing — Shaby didn't hear the muezzins high in their minarets against the dusty yellow sky, summoning the faithful for afternoon prayers. The air was heavy with the smell of meat charring over open charcoal pits. He found it incredibly hard to concentrate. He wanted badly to get out of Syria. He hated it here. Life here was boring, dull. He had a desire for the glitter of Europe: the sounds, smells, the women. Especially the women.

He parked the car haphazardly in his parking stall beneath the apartment building. The small, squeaky elevator cage's climb to the ninth floor seemed to take forever. When it finally came to a bouncing stop, Shaby rushed out as if he expected it to leave then and there on its final plunge back down the dark shaft.

There were four apartments on his floor, two on each side of a long, dim corridor. When he reached his apartment door, he looked around nervously. It was time to check if the small piece of rubber he had placed between the door and the jamb was still there. Once sure he was alone, Shaby drew a business card from his shirt pocket. His sweaty hand was shaking as he placed the card in the space between the door and the jamb.

"If the piece of rubber you placed there is gone, it means someone opened the door in your absence. That means it's time to split," Brad, Shaby's contact, used to say. "If it's still there, your place is safe." Every day Shaby expected the worst. He held his breath again today as he slowly moved the card up the slot.

He could feel the piece of rubber in place. He was relieved; he was going to live one more day. Moving quickly, Shaby returned the card to his pocket and opened the door with his key. Out of the corner of his eye, he saw a movement and froze in the doorway. Exhaling loudly, he realized it was only the living room curtains, blown inward by the hot wind outside. Frantically he bolted the door and slid the chain into its slot. Still he felt uneasy. A feeling of impending doom hung over Shaby like a menacing cloud.

For the first few months he thought he'd get used to the covert activity — that it would become second nature, something he could live with. But it hadn't worked out that way at all. And now fear was gaining the upper hand, pressing hard against his chest and making every breath painful. Today he was going to break from his schedule and transmit early. It was an option he had never before used. Brad always told him to do it only in extreme circumstances. As far as Shaby was concerned, this was it.

The transmission procedure had to be done fast. Shaby stepped into the bedroom, removed the lamp from the mahogany night table, and placed the table upside down on the bed. Then he pulled a two-inch pin from a fold in his wallet and inserted it into a tiny cavity at the base of one of the table legs.

"Unless you knew its location, there's no way you'd ever see it," Brad had bragged.

With the pin deep in the cavity, Shaby pressed it with his thumb. There was a dull click and the inner section of the table popped out revealing three small black instruments, each in a separate recess. One of them, the transmitter, resembled a calculator, with a small keyboard and several additional red and yellow keys and a single blue key. The other two instruments were the same size as the "calculator," about four inches long by two and a half inches wide, and no more than half an inch thick.

Shaby sat there for several seconds collecting his thoughts. "This is the most dangerous stage of the operation, with all the equipment exposed. Don't waste any time. Just move!" Brad used to say. "Get this over with fast. Once it's all back in the table, you're safe, so move it!"

The words rang in his ear as if Brad were right there, leaning over his shoulder, sternly instructing him. He quickly picked up the "calculator" and turned a small knob on its back. He had to do that every time he transmitted. The knob's function had something to do with changing frequencies, but it was not totally clear to Shaby how it worked. All he knew was what Brad had told him: that it was very important he not forget to turn the knob one notch to the right before each broadcast. Next, he keyed in the message. That, too, was a wonder to Shaby. He could key a message as long as two hundred words and the small black box would condense it and send it in a single short burst to wherever it was going, making its detection practically impossible. His message read:

From Shaby

1. New terrorist team setting up in Europe.

2. Team to be led by a pro-Syrian Palestinian officer nicknamed FOX x FOX.

3. Planning activity soon.

4. Ex East German Stasi assisting in operation (said to have a mole in the Mossad).

5. Will have more information in several days.

6. Coming out to Europe soon. Will contact to confirm.

7. Want confirmation on bonus for information.

8. END x END.

He pressed the blue key, and the words ran across a small crystal screen above the tiny keyboard. Satisfied that the message was clear and complete, he returned the "calculator" to its recess in the table, then he connected it with a thin black wire to the second unit and pressed a yellow key. At that point the small "calculator" began coding and compressing the message, preparing it for transmission. Next he removed a small coil attached to the third instrument and, as he uncoiled it, walked out through a pair of French doors, onto a small semicircular balcony.

He attached the wire he had uncoiled to the ornate cast-iron railing, which would act as an antenna. Standing there for a moment, he could see most of Damascus through the haze of the sultry afternoon. In the distant west lay the soft, yellowish shadows of the Anti-Lebanon Mountains, with Mount Hermon looming over them, its white crown like a huge tidal wave frozen in time. Shaby looked back into the room. The green light on the instrument flickered, signaling that the transmission was ready, and Shaby quickly returned. He leaned over and pressed the red key. The burst transmission lasted less than a second.

His first transmission was over. Now he had to wait for two long minutes until the green light went on, at which point he would repeat the transmission.

"Just to make sure it's been received," Brad had explained. Shaby waited.

A loud slamming sound shocked his adrenalin-charged body like a splash of cold water. Instantly he was drenched in sweat. Shaby couldn't move. He was terrified and still shaking when he realized it was a neighbor's door that sounded so close through the paper-thin walls. He hit the red key and the second transmission was over. Then he moved immediately to recoil the wire and place everything back in the table. A faint click signaled that all was secure.

With the table back in its place, Shaby slumped onto the bed like a stringless marionette. His thoughts drifted as he lay back, to a different place, a different time, yet not so long ago. A time that seemed like a part of another life. Rome. He'd give anything to be back there. He thought of Carolyn, with her soft, milky skin and long, honey-colored hair. The vision of her perfect, yielding features caused a twinge in his groin. He couldn't remember if they'd ever left the room during the two weeks. Or the bed, for that matter. Except for his training sessions with Brad, it had been a single, long whirlwind of pleasure.

Strange, he thought, how the mind wanders at times of such tension, and fragments of the past become startlingly clear. Shaby wiped his sweaty forehead with the back of his hand. There was nothing to do but wait. He was not out of the country yet. The cold hand of fear still had a clenching grip on his chest, and death was silently stroking the back of his neck.

# 3

**MOSSAD HEADQUARTERS, NORTH OF TEL AVIV**
**SEPTEMBER 5**
**1745 HOURS**

"ANYTHING NEW?" asked Arik, a six-foot-two burly man. His almost transparent complexion was emphasized by curly black hair and a fuzzy black beard. He and a younger companion had just entered the decoding room on the fourth floor of the five-story Pentagon-shaped concrete building that houses Mossad head-quarters. The building nestles in a small aspen grove behind a large shopping center on the highway to Haifa, not visible from the main road.

The decoding room smelled of fresh paint, stale coffee and cigarette smoke. Its harsh white fluorescent light seemed to rob everything of its color. It was a depressing place.

"No, just the usual garbage," replied the balding forty-year-old man, glad that his replacement was here to relieve him. "How is it outside?"

"Just like a public toilet. Hot, stinking, and humid. I hate when it gets like this."

"I guess in here it's only stinking. Who's your shadow?"

"He's a new member of our crew," Arik said, placing a large hand on his slim companion's shoulder. The two looked like father and son. "He'll be replacing Avy once he learns the ropes."

"Where are you from?" the balding man asked, gathering up his things in preparation to leave.

"Paratroopers," the newcomer replied, not really paying much attention to the conversation. He was more interested in the wall-to-wall computer equipment.

"What the hell is wrong with this country?" complained the bald man. "Whenever you ask a guy where he's from, he gives you his military background." He turned to face the new man. "Look, my boy, and listen carefully. I'm from Petah-Tikva. That's where I live. Now, slowly," he was pronouncing every syllable as if speaking to a toddler, "don't rush this. Where are you from?"

"Leave the kid alone," Arik said. "I remember your first day after the familiarization course." He made a face, dropping his mouth open and widening his eyes in a parody of bewilderment. They both started to laugh, then Arik turned to the replacement. "Don't pay any attention to the old bugger. He only looks intelligent."

"Natanya," the young man said, as if he had just awakened.

"What?" the balding man asked, still laughing.

"I'm from Natanya."

"Good for you. Smart answer. I knew you could do it." Then, turning to Arik, comically distorting his face, he said, "A smart kid you got here. With those brains, I guess Avy will be out of here in what . . . two years? Of course, if he's here to replace Avy, he'd better have a brass cock or he'll wear his out." The two veterans burst into laughter again, and even the rookie smiled, although he didn't completely get the joke.

"Is there any coffee?" Arik asked as he knelt by a small corner table. On it a large chrome kettle surrounded by an array of colorful coffee mugs were the only things in the room that hinted of human inhabitants. Not waiting for a reply, he said to the young man, "When we're in this decoding room, you don't touch any of the instruments. And don't leave my side except to use the washroom. Is that understood?"

Somewhat taken aback by this sudden flow of instructions from Arik, the newcomer shot back, "Yes sir," in a military fashion.

"No 'sirs' around here," Arik snapped, "but I do like your attitude." He was still hunting for coffee. "Now, this room is where we receive coded communication from Mossad agents in all target countries."

"Do you know what target countries are?" the balding man asked sarcastically.

"Sure," replied the young man, sounding somewhat offended. "Arab countries are target countries." He looked to Arik for approval.

"Aren't you leaving or something?" Arik asked the balding man who was now at the door. Then he looked at the rookie. "Yes, you're right," Arik said, his head now in the small cupboard, searching for the coffee.

"Isn't there any coffee left?" Arik demanded of the balding man.

"I don't know, I drink tea."

"Well, looks like I'd better call down for some."

"Good luck," he said, and seemed about to leave. Then, noticing that the time sheet hanging by the door wasn't signed, he asked Arik, "Could you sign in so I can leave? It's getting late, and the world awaits me." He made a comical flourish with his hand.

Arik signed his shift in, officially taking over the watch. Then he dialed the so-called cafeteria, which in fact was nothing more than a room with a television and a large coffeepot, lighting a cigarette while he waited. When the phone was finally answered, he could hear loud music and laughter in the background.

"Buckingham Palace," said a voice.

"Hey, Avy," Arik said, "get off your butt and bring me some coffee. The bastards didn't leave any and I'm starting to dry up."

"Could you wait for a couple of minutes? I'm setting something up for us with some chicks from the computer pool."

"Okay. I'll wait," Arik said reluctantly, "but it better be worth it." He put down the receiver. "Well, my boy," he turned to the rookie, "we might as well get some work done." Arik rolled his chair across the gleaming white floor and punched in his personal code, gaining access to the computer. "Let me have it," he said, speaking to the computer. "What do you have for me from the land of the dead?"

"The land of the dead?" the newcomer asked, puzzled.

"Target countries, my boy, we call them the land of the dead. People calling from there are much closer to death than any of us. I know they don't teach you that in the academy."

"Gotcha," the rookie said, placing a chair next to Arik and lighting a cigarette.

"All messages coming in have been translated in diffusion," Arik went on, taking his tutorial role very seriously.

"What do you mean by diffusion?"

"It means that the translator gets the words out of sequence and for more than one message at a time, so in fact he is translating individual words, but not getting to read the message. Then the computer reassembles the messages and transfers them to us. All messages received here have been sent by burst communication. Do you know what that is?"

"Sure."

"So everything's clear to you up to this point?"

"Yes."

"Just remember," Arik said, staring directly at the rookie, "people are risking their lives to bring in this information. There is no room for error here, do you understand?"

The young man was nodding, eyes wide open.

Arik went on, running his fingers through his thick beard. "If more than one message comes in at the same time, who do we handle first?"

The rookie raised his shoulders questioningly

"That's why we have a smart computer." Arik now smiled. "Agents are ranked by importance, and receive a value code."

"Who ranks them?" The rookie was showing interest.

"Don't they teach you anything at the academy? They're ranked by the research department, based on the quality of their information. The computer can identify the agent by his name and rank him according to value. It brings the messages to the screen based on a compilation that calculates the agent's value as well as how long the message has been in the system."

Arik was not sure it was totally clear to the rookie, but the boy would have to wait, he thought, as messages started to come in. Arik read the first few reports. He pointed at the screen and said, "This one is from an agent in Beirut reporting the new location of a PLO officer." Arik dealt with the message directly on the screen, using a special light pen. The letters on the screen were white and the background was blue. He separated the information, highlighting sections of the report, then pointed the pen to icons on the screen that transferred the highlighted sections to their destination in various departments of the Mossad. Moving on, he next read naval information from an agent in Tripoli, Libya.

At 1820 the screen suddenly changed color to a pulsating black and red that alternated two messages in large yellow letters: CODE BLACK. ENTER SECURITY CLEARANCE.

The rookie froze, a cigarette halfway to his mouth.

"You!" Arik turned to him. "Don't ask questions. Just do what I tell you!" A low beeping sound was coming from the computer. "Get down to the cafeteria and stay there. I'll call you later and tell you what to do, now move."

"But, . . ." The rookie was on his feet.

"You're not cleared for this, so get the hell out of here. I have work to do." Acting on reflex, he typed in a code. Once he pressed the return key, the printer started to cough out the message. It was from Damascus. Arik stared at the blinking square at the bottom of the screen. There was a small star in it, which indicated an unscheduled transmission. The agent's scheduled time was also flashing on the screen: from 2000 to 2100 hours. He was almost two hours early. Arik peered intently at the screen. "Shit," he hissed, "I hate it when they do this! Why couldn't he call on his regular timetable?" He walked over to the printer, opened the cover, and tore out the printed message. One look told him it was extremely hot. He'd better do this one by the book.

Arik picked up the point-to-point scrambler phone and waited for someone to come on the line. The scrambler made everyone sound flat and metallic.

"Yes?" asked a man's husky voice that Arik couldn't recognize.

"Activate red flare and notify driftwood."

"And?" the voice asked calmly.

Arik was in no mood for games. "And fuck yourself."

"The same to you, big boy, but I need the code."

Realizing his mistake, Arik said, "Sorry, code two oh three five nine one three." Once he had hung up the scrambler, he reached for the internal phone. He had to get the rest of the team up there. This was more than any one man could handle. The room that doubled as an emergency conference room at the other end of the decoding room would be full of top brass in a very short time. The communications department he had just activated on the scrambler was already busy calling the people who had to respond to the bombshell that had just arrived from Damascus.

There was no sign of Avy, though he'd very soon be needed to assist. Arik dialed the cafeteria, and the phone rang several times before it was picked up.

"Yeah?" a sleepy voice mumbled.

"Where's Avy?" Arik shouted into the receiver.

"How the hell should I know? Am I his keeper? That new guy, Avy's replacement, has just walked in, though."

"Listen to me," Arik said in a stern voice. "Find Avy and bring him here on the double. Do you understand? Tell the new guy to go home."

"What the hell is going on?" The voice was still groggy.

"I'll tell you later. Now, look for Avy in the quarters. He might be with a girl. Get him up here!"

"Okay. Take it easy. I'll get him."

"If you don't find him in the next ten minutes, get your ass up here without him. I need you here to handle the incoming messages. Even with Avy we'll be short if things get hectic."

"I'm on my way."

Ten minutes later, a tall, slim fellow in his late twenties entered the decoding room just ahead of Mark, Arik's boss. He nodded to Arik and whispered, "I couldn't find Avy." With that, he turned around to acknowledge Mark.

Although Mark was head of the department, like everyone in the Mossad, they were on first-name terms. "Okay, I'm here. What's it all about?" Mark headed directly for the coffee tray.

Arik grabbed the paper he had taken out of the printer and handed it to him.

Mark stood by the coffee cabinet reading the message. "Oh, shit!" he growled. "Did you transfer or paraphrase this to anyone?" he demanded, staring at Arik. Mark was a well-built man, standing almost as tall as Arik, slightly on the heavy side but still quite athletic. His voice was deep and rasping. He turned his eyes back to the paper as he waited for Arik's response.

"No," Arik said. "I called a red flare and notified driftwood. I got one printout," he pointed to the sheet Mark was holding, "and the message never came up on the screen. I sent the new man we had here away before I got the printout."

"Is there anyone in the conference room yet?" Mark asked.

"No, you're the first."

Mark plucked a handleless mug decorated with colorful balloons from the coffee table. "Where the hell is the bloody coffee?" he barked, clearly angered by the unthinkable omission.

"I'll send him to get some," Arik said, staring at his friend who was already on his way to the door. "The jerks from the previous watch didn't leave any."

"I'll be in the conference room," Mark mumbled half to himself.

"No damn coffee. You *know*, coffee is right up there with cigarettes, sex, and the *International Herald Tribune*."

With Mark out of sight, Arik called to his friend who was about to leave again. "Wait! Don't look for Avy now. Just get the bloody coffee, then we'll look for the bastard."

In the conference room, Mark had read the message for the sixth time. He was seated at the head of a long oval table that could accommodate twenty with comfort. The computer terminal next to him was linked to a large screen behind him. Next to him were several telephones and an intercom set.

As Mark was about to turn on the computer, Mousa walked in. Dark-haired, he was about five foot ten and built like a brick wall. As deputy director in charge of Security, Mousa was the most powerful man in the Mossad after the director. Although he had started his career in the rival General Security Service known as the Shaback, Israel's internal secret police service, Mousa had managed, at the age of fifty-five, to reach the top command circle in the Mossad, Israel's equivalent of the CIA. Being a close personal friend of Avraham, Mossad's director, hadn't hurt him much either.

"How the hell did you get here so fast?" Mark asked. "Don't you live in Ramat Hasharon?"

"Yes, I do, but I was here when the call came, over at the Jordanian desk in Research."

"In that case, what took you so long?" Mark teased, smiling.

"I'm glad to see you're so amiable during a red flare. Can we look at what's going on here?"

Mark handed him the communiqué. Mousa read it, then sat down next to him. After reading it again, he stared at Mark for several seconds before scanning it a third time. He placed the paper on the table in front of Mark and asked in a low voice, "Who else has seen this?"

"Except for Arik and myself, no one."

"Good," Mousa said in relief. "Let's keep it that way."

"What are you talking about?" Mark panicked. "The place is about to be swarming with people who were called in for red flare, and you want me to keep this a secret? What am I supposed to say to everybody? Sorry, there was a mistake. Go home. Forget about this?"

"Take it easy. That's not what I meant," said Mousa, trying to stay calm. "I want you to tell them everything except the identity of the agent."

"What about Amos? How can I keep it from the head of Operations?"

"I don't think you're listening to me," Mousa said, starting to lose patience, his thick eyebrows slowly becoming one long, angry line. "I don't give a shit about Amos. Do you understand me? This is an order." He looked at his watch. His voice was calm again. "You'd better get Arik in here and tell him to keep this to himself. Tell him to reprint the message deleting the agent's name."

Mark immediately called Arik on the intercom. There was no point in arguing with Mousa. When Arik entered, Mark held up the printout. "You're not to discuss this message with anyone except Mousa and myself. Is that clear?"

"Yes."

"Now go back to the decoding room and print a new copy of the message, deleting the name of the sender."

"I can't alter a message. It's against regulations," Arik countered. "It's not our message. You're the one who keeps telling me that and . . ."

"Just do as you're told!" Mark snapped. "There's no time to screw around. I'll deal with the procedure. You just do it. Move, man!"

"Okay, okay," Arik said, hastily leaving the room.

"Now," said Mousa, nodding his head in the direction of the

computer screen. "Bring the agent's file up on the computer and tell me who his recruiting officer was."

Mark turned on the computer and, after entering his clearance number and typing several requests, said, "Natan. Natan Stone." After typing in another request, Mark turned to Mousa, puzzled. "The damn computer won't tell me where Natan is."

"That," replied Mousa, smiling sarcastically, "is because he is working in Al, and that is out of your clearance range."

Mark leaned back in his seat. He knew of the Al department, which handled activities in the more sensitive places such as the United States, where the mistake tolerance was zero. Certain top case officers were assigned there and it was out of the jurisdiction of anyone but the director himself.

"Turn the damn thing off!" Mousa ordered. "I'll handle it later. I want to talk to him before we do anything. Let's just ride this meeting through, okay?"

Mark nodded.

# 4

## MOSSAD HEADQUARTERS
## SEPTEMBER 5
## 1940 HOURS

THE MEETING was about to begin. Mark, still seated at
the head of the table, was eyeing the computer screen to his left.
On Mark's right was Amos, a tall, pale, restless fellow in his early
fifties, who wore gold-rimmed glasses. Amos was deputy director
in charge of Operations. Under his command were a string of
stations located in Israeli embassies around the world, in which
some thirty-five katsas, or case officers, worked clandestinely,
recruiting agents — mainly in Europe and mainly Arabs — who
would in turn supply information from Arab countries, where
Israelis had limited access. These stations abroad were supported
by a series of geographical desks located at Mossad headquarters
so that all in all, Amos ran what amounted to the Mossad's largest,
and probably most important department. Even so, Amos lacked
Mousa's clout.

At the other end of the table sat a husky man whose ball-like
head perched squarely on his shoulders. He had no visible neck,
as though his head had been whacked into place. This man was
the night duty officer from the Planning department, also known
as "the Providers" since they were called upon to solve logistical
problems relating to operations. This department could be trusted

to get anything anywhere at any time, from money to transport planes. There was seldom a situation where they could not supply the demand, and when an emergency meeting was called, they came, in case they were needed.

Mousa, seated next to Amos now, looked bored as he waited for things to get started. He kept himself busy by cutting a sheet of paper into little squares, hoping to elicit a stupid remark from the duty psychiatrist seated nearby.

"Could you read the message, please?" Amos grumbled restlessly, stubbing out his cigarette and immediately reaching for another. Then, realizing his pack was empty, he reached for Mark's and withdrew one, tossing the pack back onto the table. The group had been in the room for less than twenty minutes and already the air was thick with smoke.

Mark turned to Mousa. "Well, I guess we've waited long enough for the others. We'll start without them, and then fill them in." Mousa nodded.

"Headings and coding all confirmed," Mark said in a dry, mechanical voice as he stared at the paper before him. "The message was clean, there were no distress calls, and the style is confirmed as original. To sum it up, this is what it appears to be. Now, wh —"

Amos cut in, his normally pale face flushed. "Mark, d'you really think you're talking to a bunch of kids here, or what?" His voice was sharp, angry. "Cut the crap and get to the message, for God's sake. I assume you'd have checked all that nonsense before we got here, so get to the point. It's late."

Mark stared at Amos with clear dislike. As he was about to answer, Arik walked in, carrying a tray of coffee mugs. "Compliments of Clandestine Communications," he said, smiling as he placed the tray on the table, and walked right out.

Mark leaned forward and began to read as everyone else started to fix their coffee. "One," he said and cleared his throat, "a new terrorist team setting up in Europe. Two," he paused, waiting for everyone to be quiet, "team to be led by a pro-Syrian Palestinian officer nicknamed Fox. Three, planning activity soon." Mark took a deep breath and glanced around the table. They were all listening now. "Four, ex-East-German Stasi assisting in operation, said to have a mole in the Mossad. Five —" A commotion started around the table then, as everyone seemed to be speaking at once.

"Quiet!" Mousa roared. "Quiet, I said! What the hell is going on here? Let the man finish."

"Did you say 'mole'?" Amos asked, creasing his reddish forehead, his glasses dropping to the end of his nose as he stared at Mark.

"I'm just reading what it says." Mark answered calmly, then went on. "Will have more information in several days. Six, coming out to Europe soon. Will contact to confirm. Then he goes on to speak about a bonus he wants. That's it." Mark tossed the paper onto the table in front of Amos as if to say, check it out yourself.

Amos stood up, raising his hands in bewilderment. "That's it? Nothing else?"

Mark, trying hard to put on an innocent face, said, "That's it."

"Who is the agent, Mark? Who the hell is the bloody agent?" Amos demanded.

"That information isn't available at the moment," Mark replied.

Like a shark smelling blood, Amos went in for the kill. "When you people called this meeting, you proclaimed a red flare for driftwood. Is that correct?" He paused, a sardonic smile playing on his face.

Mark nodded.

"Now, correct me if I'm wrong," Amos continued, "but a red flare is called when information comes in on an imminent terrorist attack." He took another puff from his cigarette. "And driftwood means that the agent was recruited, and is handled by, the Rome station," he said, glaring at Mark as he slammed his hand down hard on the table, making the coffee mugs jump. "That's my jurisdiction!" He took a deep breath and lowered his voice to a hiss as he spoke slowly, skewering Mark with his eyes. "Will you please repeat to me what you just said about the availability of the agent's name?"

"I'm sorry," Mark said. "I can't give you the name."

"I hope you've covered yourself well, Mark, because I'm coming after you personally with everything I have. Before we go any further, I'll give you one more chance." He straightened up as he said, "Are you going to tell me who the agent is? Or give me a reason — and it better be a good one — why not?"

Mark looked at Amos with hate in his eyes. "I know you're a big shot," he said, "and you can kick me all the way to the Milan station, where you'll make sure I remain a clerk until I retire. You've told me that more than once. But as long as I'm head of this department, you will not tell me what to give you and when. Now *sir*, what you have is what you'll get, and nothing more."

"Well, well, what do we have here?" Amos asked, smirking, "Did you go out and rent some balls or something? I don't have the time for your games, Mark. Do you have the original message in Arabic?"

"No, but I can guarantee the quality of the translation."

"I'm sure, but with something this important, I'd like to see it."

"No problem," Mark said, pressing a button on the intercom. "Arik?"

"Yes?"

"Get me the Arabic original of the message."

"I have to go get it from Translation on the first floor, if there's someone there now."

"Okay. Get it and bring it to me."

"I'm on my way," Arik said.

A moment later Avy entered the room, with a mug of coffee in his hand, and walked over to the young man with the large black book. The young man readily gave Avy his seat and he took it silently, nodding a small hello to Amos.

Mark noticed the nod. He knew Amos was Avy's patron, and that was his main reason for getting rid of Avy.

Ignoring Amos, Mark took a mug of coffee from the tray. He sipped from the top, trying to avoid the floating coffee grains.

"As of this moment," Amos proclaimed, "this communiqué is no longer under the jurisdiction of the red flare forum. This is my department's problem, so we'll reconvene in my office in, say, ten minutes." Amos pushed his chair back and, turning to Mark, he said, "Have the boy bring me the copy as soon as he gets back. You can go home. And you," he said, pointing at the night duty officer, "call your boss. This is out of your league."

"Wait just one stinking minute," Mousa growled, his voice low as he drew out every syllable. "I don't agree that it's out of the forum yet." He leaned back in his chair, looking very relaxed. "The creation of a new terrorist unit, and a direct warning regarding an unspecified imminent terrorist attack, plus talk of a possible mole can hardly be regarded as your private property. How do you figure it's yours, Amos? Please explain. I don't seem to understand."

"The message came from an agent," Amos retorted. He hadn't expected Mousa's interference, and was slightly off balance. "Information from an agent is my responsibility, and therefore it's my jurisdiction. You know the rule as well as I do. If it's your dick in the fire, you're the fireman."

"I'm sorry, my friend, but I don't agree with you," Mousa persisted. "We still need to discuss this with the specialists at Research who handle the terrorist scene, so we can put this in the proper perspective. Also, Counterintelligence has to be brought in. So just cool it, okay?" Mousa smiled at Amos. "Don't misunderstand me. If you want to go, you can. After all, this is still a free country. But as far as taking over the situation, as the saying goes, 'no bears and no forest,' so forget it. This is, however, going to move up to the commanders' forum."

"This isn't your call, Mousa," Amos said, moving toward the door. "This has nothing to do with you."

"When it comes to the security of operations, personnel, or

installations — and the way I see it, all are in danger at this moment — it sure as hell is my call!"

"This is going to cost you!" Amos stated, staring hard at Mark as he walked out of the room.

"What the hell was that all about?" the neckless man asked. He glared at Mousa, who rose from his seat.

"That, my friend, was playing it by the book," Mousa replied. "Now, you, get your boss." Then he turned to Mark. "Get the head of Counterintelligence in here now. Fill him in, then call Research. They need a handle on this, too. I'll be in my office. Call me once you've briefed them. Meantime, put out a call for a top forum."

"Doesn't a call for top forum have to come from the director's office?" Mark asked, sounding a bit distraught.

"I'll talk to the chief and fill him in. You just make sure everyone gets here. Okay?"

"Sure, okay." Mark was tired. His confrontation with Amos had apparently drained him. It wasn't every day that an administrative officer such as himself confronted a field officer, let alone the top field officer.

Mousa left without another word, leaving Mark alone in the conference room.

Mark called Avy back in and instructed him to summon the commanders' forum, a name for an emergency meeting of all the department heads, in the director's office. After he placed several of the calls himself, he sat back and read the communiqué again. It could be a trick of Syrian intelligence, he mused. He clicked the agent's file onto the computer again and faced the large screen which lit up in a bluish haze marked by glowing white letters.

Mark sat there for almost an hour reading the file. The information this Syrian bastard code-named Foul Play had given them over the past two years was phenomenal, he thought to himself. He then turned to the keyboard and typed in a request for the agent's operational information. A few seconds later the color of the screen changed to red with yellow letters. At the top of the screen appeared the word *Operation*.

Mark read. *Recruiting officer: Natan Stone (Kid)*. Mark knew Natan, although mostly by reputation, as an attack case officer. He was stationed at the time in Brussels, but could recruit anywhere. Foul Play's recruitment operation had started in London and was wrapped up in Rome. It looked like a beautiful piece of work. Not surprising, considering Natan's reputation.

Because Arab agents are recruited mainly in European countries but end up working in their homelands, they officially belong to, and are serviced by, the station they were recruited through. In this case, it had been Italy's Rome station. But because the recruiting officer no longer worked in that station and no transfer of agent had taken place, Mark knew there was plenty of room for Mousa to maneuver.

Mousa picked up the phone even before he was seated behind his large oak desk one floor below the Clandestine Communications room. This phone was a secure point-to-point which connected him to a secure operator, who would in turn obtain whoever he requested. "Get me Kid," Mousa instructed, giving the operator Natan Stone's code name.

"He's not in the building," said the voice on the other end. "I'll have to locate him. Do you want me to call you when I do? Or should I give him a message?"

"Connect him to me when you get him. It's urgent."

"Okay," said the voice, and the line went silent.

## 2155 HOURS

WHEN THE phone on his desk rang, Mousa cleared a spot in the ashtray with his cigarette and placed it there before he answered. With the receiver to his ear, he leaned back in the big black leather chair. "Hello?" he said.

"Mousa?" Natan said.

"Hello, my friend," said Mousa, smiling. "I need you. When can you get here?"

"What happened? Is everything okay?"

"There seems to be a problem with one of your children."

"Was he caught speeding?" came a worried question as Natan used the code for a captured agent.

"No, I don't think so. Look, when can you be here?"

"About an hour, an hour and a half."

"When you get here, go to Amir's office. You know where that is?"

"Do you mean the Amir that I went to school with?"

"That's the one. Wait for me there, and don't come into the main building. I'll explain everything when I see you."

"No problem," Natan said and hung up. Mousa turned his chair to face the large world map with the logo of the Mossad charter airline. Mousa was glad the officer was Natan. At forty-three, he was one of the Mossad's best case officers. Mousa was proud of him, as he liked to think that he had taught Natan most of what he knew. Years back, when Mousa had headed the Mossad academy, less than 500 feet from where he was seated now, and Natan had been his best student, the young man's only real fault had been his big mouth. It had also been his biggest asset.

# 5

## MOSSAD HEADQUARTERS, DIRECTOR'S OFFICE
## SEPTEMBER 5
## 2320 HOURS

TEN DEPARTMENT heads were seated around a long, dark Formica-topped conference table set perpendicular to a large mahogany desk. They had been there for about ten minutes, awaiting the head of Mossad. Amos was seated closest to the director's desk on the right-hand side; although there was no formal seating arrangement, everyone knew Amos felt he had title to that particular seat. Next to him sat a big man whose smile looked more like a frozen twitch: he was head of the so-called "Providers."

On his left was the head of Research, nodding from side to side as he read the communiqué. His white hair and slightly hunched back underlined the fact that he was the oldest department head. Next to him was Mark, and then the deputy head of Technology, whose boss was in the hospital, making him acting head at the moment. The young man was sloppily dressed and seemed transfixed by a technical manual he had propped in front of him.

Across from him, Mousa was having a low-pitched conversation with the head of Masada, a well-built, distinguished-looking man, the only one present who wore a suit. Masada's function was to send Israelis under deep cover on special missions into Arab

countries, and to carry out what was considered the most dangerous work in the Mossad. As a department, it was totally separated
from the rest of the Mossad: a microcosmic Mossad within the
greater body.

This man was also the caretaker of a special unit within Masada
that answered only to the director of Mossad, the chief's so-called
praetorian guard. This unit's code name Bayonet or in Hebrew,
Kidon, was appropriate to its tasks, one of which was carrying out
assassinations. One seat closer to the director's desk sat a small
insignificant-looking man who was staring at the ceiling and
waving his hand before his face in a vain attempt to clear some of
the heavy cigarette smoke away. The head of Psychology, he was
the only nonsmoker in the room. Next to him was the head of
Counterintelligence, a strange-looking man of five foot two with a
bald head and a huge bulbous nose. He was going over a thick
computer printout, highlighting it with a yellow marker, while
shielding the pages with his arm from the head of Liaison, who
kept craning over to try and read the pages. Liaison handled
relations with other intelligence agencies around the world, relations that could provide the so-called soft pillow for the field people
to fall back on in case of a screw-up in the field. He was a very
handsome man, but his rather blank expression made one doubt
his intelligence.

Just as Avraham Alon, the Mossad director walked in, the
whistle of the Haifa-bound train shrieked its signal at the crossing,
some 500 yards east of the building, as if it had announced him.
Dressed in short khaki pants, sandals, and a light green golf shirt,
Avraham was the antithesis of his predecessor, who had always
been regarded as foppish. That was not the only difference, however. While Admony had been meek and lacked presence, Avraham
was the boss in every sense of the word. As he reached his seat,
he placed a copy of the communiqué in front of him on the table,
alongside a pack of cigarettes.

Short on ceremony, Avraham glanced around at his subordinates to make sure all were attentive before he spoke. "I assume you have all read this by now," he pointed to the communiqué.

They all nodded. "We're not going to have a symposium about this today." Avraham paused as Oren, his aide, entered the room, taking a chair by the door. He prepared to take notes.

Avraham went on, "What we have here is extremely serious. On the one hand, a possible mole — and I emphasize *possible*. At the same time, we're told of the threat of an imminent terrorist attack." He turned to the head of Counterintelligence. "What did you find out since we had our little talk?"

"Well," said the little man with the big nose, clearing his throat. He seemed nervous and being new at his job didn't help. "From what I can see," he leafed through the printout, "there is no way we could have a mole in the Mossad."

"How can you be so sure?" Avraham demanded.

"Well sir, as you know, we conduct lie detector tests with every person in the Mossad at least once every six months. And with the field personnel even more frequently. Since we've seen no evidence to the contrary, I must conclude that there is no mole." He hesitated, then added, "Unless . . ."

"Unless what?" Avraham said abruptly, leaning forward.

"Unless he's been a mole for less than six months or he's somehow managed to avoid the tests."

"So," Avraham pointed to Oren, wanting to make certain his aide was taking down his remarks. "Counterespionage will start testing immediately and I want you personally," pointing at the little man who was busily wiping his forehead, "to ensure that everybody, and I mean *everybody*, takes a test." Avraham lit a cigarette and turned to Amos. "I want you to instruct all stations to start questioning every agent they have about this Fox, who's supposedly leading the terrorists. All other operations are to be stopped until after this is cleared."

Amos was nervously tapping his matchbox. "What about operations where we have contacts going on at the moment? I can't just pull the men off."

"You'll freeze all activity," Avraham raised his voice slightly. "If there's something critical, you'll clear it with me personally on a case-by-case basis. Is that clear?" Avraham had never liked Amos, referring to him behind his back as the pompous ass. He hadn't liked him when he had been head of Operations with Amos as his deputy, and he didn't like him now.

"Okay. But I want to protest the fact that the name of my agent — the one who sent this communiqué — is being kept from me." Amos's face was flushed, and his lips looked pale blue.

"I hear you," Avraham said. "But I've decided that this whole affair will be handled by a special task force. The way I see it, locating and eliminating the new terrorist team and the mole are linked and they'll have to be handled consecutively. I want everyone to give Mousa, who will be running the task force, priority over everything else. He will get most of his manpower from Masada, so as to keep his operation contained as much as possible."

With that, Avraham was back on his feet. Glancing swiftly around the table, he said, "Are there any questions?" There was total silence in the room. "One more thing," Avraham said then. "I'm sure that Shaback's director would be more than happy to run to the prime minister with this story about a mole in the Mossad, to make us look bad. I want it understood that this is not to get out at any cost. If it does I'll personally find the leak. And trust me," he smiled cruelly, "it will be a black day for the perpetrator."

He turned to the head of Masada. "You and Mousa stay here. I want to talk to you." The two men resumed their seats. Avraham sat back and switched his interest to a file he withdrew from a drawer in his desk, signaling that the meeting was over.

Once all the rest had left, Avraham went to sit next to the two. Clearly, this was not going to be a formal conversation.

"I want you to get me that mole," said Avraham with a rare intensity. He seldom showed such anger. "We're paralyzed until we can get the bastard. You said you had some sort of plan?" he asked Mousa.

"I'm not sure you could call it a plan, more like a course of action."

"Spit it out."

"I've called Natan in, but I'll need your approval for that. He's in Al."

"Okay. And?" Having given orders that made his whole organization grind virtually to a halt, Avraham was now understandably impatient.

"I want to team him up with a Kidon unit and funnel all the information received on the matter to him. That way he'll be able to move, once we've established the location of the terrorists. But no one outside the Kidon unit will know about it."

Avraham leaned back, inhaling deeply. "Why Natan?"

"He's Foul Play's recruiting officer. Besides, I trust the man."

"What do you think?" Avraham turned to the head of Masada.

"I agree with him. I've already told Amir to expect Natan. Amir is section head for one of the three Kidon units," the man explained. "I told him that Mousa will be coming over with instructions. I have only one concern."

"Which is?" asked Avraham.

"We've never had a case officer work directly with a Kidon team before. They're not really compatible. The Kidon is both a special and specialized unit, and they're not used to working with outsiders."

"Look," Mousa interjected, "I personally trust Natan, and he was an officer with the naval commandos. If anyone could work with them, it's him. Besides what other option do we have?"

"Okay." Avraham got up. It was clear he had made up his mind. He turned to Mousa. "Get them together and find these terrorists before they do any damage. I want to be informed every step of the way. And I want to be able to call off anything, at any stage. Is that clear?"

"Sure is." Mousa smiled.

"One more thing," Avraham was halfway back to his desk. "The first priority is the mole. We get terrorists every day, but I want this mole." He pointed a finger at Mousa. "Whatever it takes. Understand?"

Mousa headed directly for Amir's office in Masada's headquarters, just off the sunken concrete yard in the center of the complex, on the second underground level.

When Mousa arrived, Natan was already seated on a small sofa in the corner of the office, browsing through a magazine. Amir was talking to Mark about some postcards pinned to a cork board behind his desk.

"Well, hello there, Mousa," Natan said, clearly glad to see his mentor and old friend.

Of average height and medium build, Natan had black hair that was turning silver at the temples. While his tanned, square face with its strong chin made him look tough, his light green eyes were soft. Natan was one of those men who always appeared neat, even when he needed a shave, as he did now. It was said that he was the sort of person men wanted as a friend and women longed to love. His friends in the Mossad knew him as low-keyed, yet someone who could still be outspoken when defending a cause. He had a passion for his work. He wore a pair of faded jeans and a white T-shirt.

Mousa grabbed Natan's outstretched hand and shook it with both of his. "How are you, Kid?" He always used Natan's code name when they spoke in a secure area, as the one who had originally chosen it for him. "It's been a long time."

"I guess," said Natan. "What's new?"

"Nothing, really. If only I didn't get older each year, everything would be just fine." Everybody laughed.

"What's the score, anyway?" Natan asked.

"Well," Mousa looked at Mark and Amir. "Didn't these guys fill you in?"

"No," Natan said.

"Was I supposed to fill them in?" Mark was clearly uncomfortable.

Mousa took a deep breath. "No harm done," he said, seating himself on the edge of Amir's desk. He proceeded to give a full account of the day's events, starting with the communiqué from Damascus.

Mark, who knew the story up to the point at which he had left the meeting, nodded in approval until Mousa reached the part he had not been in on. Mousa summed up, saying, "This is where we stand at the moment. Avraham wants this handled in isolation from the rest of the Mossad, because it's obvious from the information at hand that we're up against a bloody mole."

"Just a minute," Mark interrupted. "You're reaching the conclusion that there's a mole when that's not known yet. Until we see some evidence, we should keep an open mind. Remember what the boss said. We're not sure."

"What's the harm in assuming there's a mole?" Amir asked.

"The assumption would involve us in a witch hunt." Mark looked at him darkly, then sat down and lit a cigarette.

"Well," Mousa said, "we on this task force are going to assume there is one and that's that." He got up and walked over to the coffeepot in the corner, helping himself to a cup. "I won't rest, and neither will you, until we get our hands on him." He turned back to face his small audience, grim-faced. "We will receive as much operational support as we need. Avraham has granted us unlimited resources, so we can start immediately.

"Natan, you'll run the operation in the field. You're on loan to us from Al effective immediately. I'm in charge of this operation. Mark will coordinate communications, and Amir will represent Masada and supply the manpower. For starters, he'll place his Kidon team at your disposal. Now, before we go any further . . ." Mousa paused as he took a seat again next to Natan.

"Just one minute," Natan interjected. "This is not my cup of tea. I work alone. I recruit agents." There was no hesitation in his voice.

It was clear he was unhappy with what was said. "I am a case officer, I've been trained to do one thing, and that is make contact and recruit agents and I am good at that."

Mousa raised his hand, nodding his head with a smile at Natan. "I know exactly what you trained as and I also know what you are capable of. The bottom line is I want you to do this, and I know you can. That is what I told the chief, now are you going to make me a liar?"

Natan was shaking his head in disbelief. There was no point arguing with Mousa. Mousa went on staring directly at Natan. "About Foul Play." He paused. "Would you be able to tell from his message if he was being run by the Syrians?" There was silence at first, and then Natan spoke.

"No. If they were running him, he'd play it straight with them. After all, he wouldn't want them to hang him."

"Didn't you guys set up some code system so that he could give you a warning?" Mousa persisted.

"Yes we did, but if you're asking me if I could be absolutely sure he would use it to warn me, the answer is no." Natan turned to Amir. "What's your accessibility to Damascus?"

"Why do you ask?" Mousa cut in.

"We need to observe Foul Play's apartment building before, during, and after his next transmission. That way, we can see if he's being watched, coerced, or whatever."

"I can get a man there in about forty-eight hours," Amir said, addressing Mousa.

"You mean you don't have anyone there now?" Mark asked.

"Not someone I could contact. Don't forget my man is not an agent. He's a combatant — one of ours. We send people in only as we need them. Besides, how would we communicate with him?"

"Like we do with agents," Mark said. Natan nodded in agreement.

"What? Are you people crazy? We're not talking about some stinking Arab agent here." Amir started pacing the room. "If you need anyone in there, we'll have to send someone. But I can't clear that." He turned to Mousa. "You'll have to clear it with my boss."

"I'll get you whatever you need," Mousa said. "Do you people realize what we're dealing with here?" He paused as all three turned toward him. "We have a mole up our ass. Someone who could be giving the enemy everything. Who knows how many agents he has already burned? What assets do we have out there? How many are actually liabilities?"

He lit another cigarette. "There's one more thing I want to make crystal clear to all of you. From now on, we're a team. We'll work, trust, and back each other. And if anyone here says anything whatsoever outside this circle about what's going on here, I'll personally cut off his balls. And if you think I'm kidding, try me!" He turned to Natan. "What sort of game do you think this bastard agent of yours is playing?"

"Well, if he's playing it straight, and I think he is, he has a lot more information than he is letting out."

"What do you mean?" Mark asked.

"This guy is crazy about making a buck, and he's a fairly good poker player. All he'll show us up front is an appetizer, then he'll hit us for the big bucks. But if he plays this too close to the vest, it could all blow up in his face.

"I think," said Natan, "we'll have to go in there and get him out, just to see what he's got. But first, we must be sure he's on the level. The only way to do that is to observe him in such a way that no one there will know we're looking."

Amir nodded. "Okay. When exactly do we need this surveillance?"

"Next Thursday. He transmits on Thursdays."

"We'll work something out," Mousa confirmed. "Meantime, Amir, you take Natan to his new office tomorrow, and I'll meet you there.

"See you tomorrow, Kid," he said to Natan. "It's good to work with you again. Brings back some memories."

Natan grasped Mousa's outstretched hand. Mousa spoke to Mark. "Just deliver a copy of every communication to me as it comes in. Is that clear?"

"Yes, sir!" Mark said, making a mock salute.

"Enough with the jokes, Mark. This isn't the least bit funny."

"Okay Mousa, relax. It will be done just right."

"Remember what I always told you," Mousa said to Natan. "Use your imagination. After all, by way of deception thou shalt do war." Not waiting for a reply, he left the room.

Mark shook his head, smiling wanly. "Sometimes he can drive you up the wall, but at least he's honest. See you guys tomorrow." And with that he left.

Once Mark was out the door, Amir asked Natan, "Care for a drink?" He opened one door of a walnut cabinet, exposing a large selection of bottles.

"Now that's impressive," Natan said. "I'll have a tequila, please."

"How do you take it?"

"Just pour it into a glass. Forget all that nonsense with the salt and the lime."

Amir handed Natan the drink.

"Thanks," Natan said, and raised his glass. "Here's to Foul Play, a man who throws stones from a glass house. May he get out of there in one piece."

Amir raised his glass. "I'll drink to that."

He sat down opposite Natan, who said, "You know, as things stand at the moment, there is no lead we can pull in, so until someone comes up with one, or Foul Play comes out of Syria, we're going to be mostly twiddling our thumbs."

"That's fair, we'll just wait and see." Amir said. "Meantime, tell me, what do you know about a Kidon team?"

"Not much, only what everybody knows, which is not much. I mean I know what they do and so forth, but that's all. Why?"

"Since you're going to be working with them, I wanted to know how much I have to tell you, that's all. Anyway, let's meet tomorrow and go over to that new office of yours that Mousa was talking about."

"How do I get there?"

"I'll take you there. You can't bring your own car into the base anyway."

"Okay. Where shall we meet?" asked Natan.

"Where do you live?"

"About two blocks from the Sheraton hotel."

"How about the lobby of the Sheraton, then? Say, at 1300?"

"You've got yourself a date," agreed Natan.

The steamy night air was oppressive, and there was a faint smell of burning wood, probably from a beach party some kids were having somewhere over the sand ridge to the west. The silence was only occasionally broken by the hiss of a car speeding by. Natan left the compound, waving to the sentry in the glass booth, and crossed the highway to the country club grounds on the other side. He was heading for his car when he noticed a hooker in the nearest bus shelter. She was wearing a tight miniskirt and had a scarf wrapped around her breasts. When she saw him, she opened the scarf, revealing her breasts.

"Wanna fuck, sweetie?" she called out in a heavy Russian accent. "For you, anything for only forty shekels."

"No thanks," he answered, not slowing down.

"What the hell, twenty!" she shouted as he reached his car.

He waved to her as he spun the car around toward the Haifa road, where he turned south, heading for Tel Aviv. Just for a moment he thought of another lady of the night, though she seemed far away now.

Her name was Francesca, and she'd been working the Piazza Navona in Rome. She was beautiful and he'd been looking for a woman. He'd taken her to a nearby hotel, where she'd demanded the money up front. When he returned from the bathroom, he found her lying on the bed, naked except for a black garter belt and stockings. It had been one hell of a sight, since she had quite a body. He totally bewildered her as he sat next to her, gently stroking her breasts, telling her he wanted to hire her for several weeks to keep a client happy. The client must not know that she was a pro. She would move to a small but elegant apartment that Natan would provide and play the lady . . . up to a point. She would pretend to fall for the man and move into his hotel for two weeks, to make sure he was happy. How had he put it? "Something the guy would never forget."

Then he'd renamed her Carolyn.

# 6

THE DRIVE across the city was slow, as was the trip on the Petah-Tikva road that took them through the religious orthodox neighborhood of Bnai-Barak.

"So where exactly is this new office of mine?"

"It's in the Kfar Sirkin military base," said Amir. "You know the place, don't you?"

"Sure. I took my officers' course there. I thought they'd turned that base over to the Matkal reconnaissance unit."

"That's true, but the base is huge. They have most of it, but tucked away in a small corner, you'll find the special training and living facility of our Kidon unit."

"I always liked this place," Natan said, as they approached the base. He rolled down the window and took in a breath of air. "Don't ask me why. It could be the smell of the eucalyptus trees, I don't know."

At the base gate, a soldier wearing a white helmet and carrying a Galil assault rifle peered straight into the car. Amir presented a certificate giving him free access to all military bases without exception. The soldier opened the black and white barrier. The car passed through and onto a narrow road bordered on both sides by giant eucalyptus trees that created a long, shady tunnel. After turning onto a dirt road they passed an old airstrip and an abandoned control tower. Finally Amir slowed the car as they approached a second gate. This time they were scrutinized by a soldier in a bulletproof vest and full combat gear, who compared Amir's license plate to a list he had on a black clipboard. Then he checked ID's. Amir had to punch a code into a small keyboard by the gate. When it opened, he sped through onto a gravel road. Minutes later they reached a small parking lot.

Amir parked next to a large glass door that seemed totally out of place at the entrance to what looked like an old British-style hangar with an arched tin roof. Its high bare walls were dull tan while the bottom portion, up to about five feet, was whitewashed — just like all the trees on the base. The lime in the whitewash prevented insects from climbing the trees.

"I hope we're getting close?" Natan said, a hint of sarcasm in his voice.

"Close, but not there yet." Amir held the glass door open for Natan. They entered a small room with what looked like an elevator door at the other end. Amir headed for the door and spoke into an intercom next to it. "It's A two two eight." A few moments later the door slid to one side, revealing a glassed-in compartment. Amir stepped in, turning to Natan. "You wait here. When this light turns green —" he pointed at a small light on the intercom that was currently red " — state your name and enter the compartment, okay?"

"No problem."

Once inside, Natan looked around. "You mean I have to go through this every time I come in?"

"I'm afraid so, my friend, but look on the bright side. So does everybody else." Amir chuckled. "Follow me. I'll take you to your new office. Mousa's waiting." Amir led the way down a narrow, well-lit corridor. At the end he opened a gray door and entered, with Natan right behind. A glass wall overlooked a large, well-kept lawn surrounded by a dense eucalyptus grove, all completely secluded by a high wall behind the trees. The room was dominated by a large oak desk facing the door. Behind it was a huge black leather chair.

The sound of a flushing toilet drew their attention to a door across the room. As the door swung open, Mousa emerged, smiling broadly. "Well, well, I didn't expect such a reception. After all, I only pissed."

"Hi, Mousa," Natan said. "What's new?"

"Oh, several things happened since we met, but there's no rush to talk about them. How about something to eat?"

"Come to think of it, I am hungry. I hope we don't have to go out for food. Getting back in will take all day!" Natan chuckled.

"No, no," Amir said. "There's everything here. We even have an excellent chef. I'll have some sandwiches sent in and you can have a larger meal later."

"Sounds great," Natan said.

Once Amir was out of the room, Mousa grabbed a chair and sat next to the desk. Pointing to the black leather chair behind the desk, he said, "Have a seat, Kid. It's your office."

"I hope you're not trying to impress me with all this," Natan said, sitting behind the desk. "You know I won't spend much time behind a desk if I can help it. Anyway, let's have it."

Mousa lit a cigarette and threw the pack across to Natan, who drew one out for himself. "Look in the drawer in front of you," he said. "There's a file there." Mousa waited until Natan took out the tan folder. "We found a lead to the pro-Syrian Palestinian that Foul Play mentioned in his communiqué."

"You mean the Fox?" Natan asked.

"Exactly. The guys over at the PLO section in Research ran it through their computer and the name Fox popped up in another file."

"What do you mean?"

"The file that came up was of a Palestinian who's worked for someone called the Fox."

"Wasn't there a file on the Fox himself?"

"No. Nothing is really known about him."

"So this is the file of a man who worked with him," Natan said, opening it.

"That's correct. The people over at Research say this man is believed to be working with this Fox, acting as his liaison with several Palestinian cells in Europe."

"What's their source for this?"

"It's from a listening device the Danish Secret Service had placed for us in a Palestinian's home in Copenhagen. It seems we have more luck in this case than brains," Mousa said.

"Sounds like that song about the girl who knew a man who knew a girl who danced with the prince." They both laughed.

"Well for the moment," Mousa said, "this is all we've got. So we'll have to make the best of it."

Natan nodded. "I was thinking," he said, "through Liaison, could you get from the German Secret Service, some information on Stasi officers who were connected to Middle East affairs — to the terrorist world in particular? You see," he put down the file, "I believe the Stasi officer Foul Play heard about must already have had some contact in the Middle East, in order to land in with the Syrians after the collapse of East Germany."

"I've already asked for that," Mousa said, "but it seems the Germans don't really have a handle on these things, as far as the Stasi is concerned." Mousa drew on his cigarette. "The only thing we got from them is a promise for several files that might fit that profile. Actually, they did say that one who would have been a match, unfortunately — or maybe fortunately — killed himself when they came to arrest him."

"So you'll be bringing me those files?"

"Sure."

Natan paused, "I'd also want the file of the one who killed himself, okay?"

"I'll see what I can do." Mousa wrote something down in a small notebook he carried in his shirt pocket.

"Let's just get this straight," Natan said, picking up the file again. "This Halim Nafsy is the contact man for Fox, who's running the new Palestinian terror unit mentioned by Foul Play?"

"Yes, and we have a location on this Halim. He's now in Piraeus." Mousa got up and started to pace the room. "I want you to promise me that you won't do anything without consulting me first. I want you to get my clearance to fart. We're going to play this one by the rules."

"What rules? We don't have any rules. You told me yesterday to use my imagination and all that crap. What was that all about?" Natan looked Mousa straight in the eye.

"Our rules," Mousa answered. "Hell, you know what I mean. Think free but report to me and yes, be treacherous — but against the other side. Just remember, if you mess this up, I'll have your own Kidon team come after you. And, Kid, I'm not kidding!"

"Don't worry. I'll hold your hand every step of the way."

"Now with that out of the way, what's your first step going to be?"

"I want to find out what this Halim character is up to."

"Let me just remind you what our primary goal is."

"There's a terrorist act being planned. I'll try my best to stop it," Natan said, looking through the file.

"That's what I thought you'd say." Mousa shook his head in disapproval. His voice was getting louder. "The main objective is the mole. Do you understand what the hell I'm saying? I want the bastard, alive if possible. The terrorists are only the lead. I'm not saying don't get them. But, if there's a choice to make down the line, it's the mole I want."

"I don't have a lead on the mole." Natan was hissing. He was not going to take any abuse, not even from Mousa. "And it appears we might have a lead on the terrorists." He paused, leaning back in his seat. "So what exactly is your point?"

There was a knock on the door, then a tall man in a light khaki uniform entered, carrying a large tray of assorted sandwiches, coffee, and tea.

Amir walked briskly in behind him, sitting down next to Mousa. He turned to the man in uniform. "Thanks. Tell everyone to be in the green room in about thirty minutes." Then he turned to Natan. "I'll take you to meet your team when you're ready."

"I'm on my way now," Mousa said. "I promised the little woman I'd take her to the matinee at the Tsavta Theater. It's one of those plays where the poor Palestinian gets a bad deal and everybody is supposed to feel sorry for him." He got up, holding a sandwich in one hand. With the other, he gave Natan a card. "You can reach me through this number at all times. Is there anything more you need from me now?"

"No, not that I can think of at the moment."

Mousa nodded, waving his sandwich at them. "See you soon."

Natan turned to Amir, a certain urgency in his voice. "I need maps of Greece and a list of the people I have to work with. I want to know what each of them is good at and what sort of cover they can take."

"Well, we'll be meeting them all in few minutes in the lounge," Amir replied. "We call it the green room. But before we go, let me fill you in on a few things. This is not like any other unit you have worked with in the Mossad. These people have no knowledge regarding the rest of the Mossad, just as Masada combatants don't. You see, they also do a lot of work inside Arab countries and if they get caught, we know they will probably be made to reveal whatever it is they know. So the less they know, the better it is for all concerned."

"I assumed that much," Natan said, clearly unimpressed by what Amir was supposedly revealing to him.

"In addition to that, they are a self-contained unit. You will not assign different jobs to different people. Instead, you will hand your requests to the commander of the unit and he in turn will bring you the results. You can ask how he intends to carry out your instructions. In fact, you'll have to approve them anyway. What you can do is recommend something or ask for it to be done in a specific way. If he agrees that it's feasible — always considering the safety of the team first — he will proceed in the way you recommend." Amir walked over to the big window behind Natan. Looking out, he went on, "If, on the other hand, you insist they do something that could put them in extreme danger, you will have to get Mousa to have the director overrule their commander." He turned to face Natan. "Any questions?"

"Not at the moment," Natan replied.

"I will repeat some of what I told you in front of the team," he smiled, "just so we don't have any misunderstandings. Let's go, then." Amir headed for the door.

There were fourteen men and women seated in the lounge, engaged in numerous conversations. Some were standing by a loaded buffet at the far end of the room. None of them paid any particular attention to the new arrivals.

"Everybody, listen please," Amir said, standing in the center of the room with Natan. "This is Natan," he said, placing his hand on Natan's shoulder. The room fell silent, with all eyes on the new-comer. "And this," Amir went on, "is the team, my friend. You will refer to team members by number, beginning with one." He pointed at a tall man in his early thirties, who stood and nodded. "And ending with," he indicated a short, broadly built man in his twenties, "number fourteen."

The team members were all quite young. No one seemed to be over thirty-five. They all wore light khaki uniforms with no tags or markings. "I know you think it's quite extraordinary," Amir continued, addressing the team, "that we've brought in an outsider, but this is an extraordinary situation. This team, effective immediately, is to carry out this man's operational needs. But," he said, speaking to Natan now, "you must remember several rules. First and foremost, you are not to discuss any of your previous or present operations with this team. For reasons I've already explained to you. Is that clear?"

Natan nodded.

"Second," Amir continued, this time addressing the entire room, "the normal command chain won't change. Natan will request all operational activities from Number One, who will decide how to carry them out. Third, information gathered in this operation won't be transferred into the regular computer. Instead, it will be entrusted to Natan for use at his discretion." He paused for a minute, then said, "I guess that's all. I'll be going now, and I'll be back on Sunday."

Amir and Natan walked together to the door. "Take good care of them, Natan. And by God, let them take care of you. They're very professional. Oh, and you should get into khakis yourself."

"Sure," Natan said. "What about transportation? I mean, when I want to get out of here?"

"Don't worry about it. Whatever you want, just ask Number One. He'll get it for you."

"One more thing, was that a voice-recognition system when we entered?"

"Yes," Amir smiled, "and your voice is already logged as you probably guessed. Now, can I please get the hell out of here?"

"No problem," Natan said. "See you Sunday."

He stood outside the green room for several minutes, smoking a cigarette. This operation was a totally new experience for him. The Kidon team was something he'd only heard about, usually discussed very circumspectly. The people he was about to work with had killed as a team in cold blood, which was something quite foreign to Natan. He had also killed in his time, more than once, but it was in the heat of battle, which somehow seemed very different to him. It suddenly occurred to him how absurd it was to justify one style of killing over another. The fact was that the enemy was a soldier who, like himself, was ready to die the moment he put on the uniform. Natan straightened up, placing the thoughts behind an unseen veil in the back of his mind. Some other time, he would handle it. Now it was time to get things moving.

The introductions were cursory at best. The nine men and five women were clearly not eager to get acquainted with Natan. When the introductions were finished, Natan asked Number One to come to his office for a briefing. After giving Number One a short summary of what they were after, with no explanation of how the information had been obtained, or reference to the bigger picture, Natan handed the man a page out of the file, pointing out that Halim's address hadn't been confirmed for a week or so.

"It's possible," Natan said, "that he's no longer there. But he's the only link we have at the moment to the terrorists, so it's vital to find him and consider how to bring him in."

None of this fazed Number One. "Why don't I just send a small team to case the address and see if Halim's still there? If he is, they'll learn his routine. Otherwise, we'll start a search for him. That way we can plan ahead without losing time."

"Sounds good."

"They can be ready to go in an hour or two," Number One told him. "I'll need your written approval."

Natan nodded and after Number One left, he cleared it with Mousa, also saying that he should not expect him to call about every minor detail.

"It's up to you," said Mousa. "If it turns out later that you should have asked, it's your ass in the sling."

Number One returned twenty minutes later. "Three of my people will be leaving on a flight to Vienna in about two hours," he told Natan. "A foreign office courier, traveling on a separate flight, will carry their documents in the diplomatic pouch and leave it for them in a designated locker at the airport. Once they exchange IDs, they'll be on their way to Athens on the first available flight."

"Don't you know which flight?"

"It may change, and in any case, they won't all be together. Two are going as a couple. The third will travel separately. Once they get to Athens, they'll call in. If this Halim is found, they'll await orders. Is there anything else you need at the moment?"

"I'd like to get out of here," Natan said, handing him the written directive he'd prepared.

"There's a car outside for you." Number One gave him a folded khaki uniform and a small beeper. "In case we need you."

"Thanks. I'll see you tomorrow, then."

# 7

BY THE NEXT morning, Number One had confirmed that Halim was still at the address. "It's a small apartment overlooking the Torkolimano Harbor Yacht Club in the southeast corner of Piraeus. The apartment is registered to a shipping company. I think it's a safe house."

"What makes you say that?"

"It's a hunch."

"Okay, what if I want him snatched and brought here?"

Number One raised a blue file he was holding in his hand and said, "It's quite simple. We bring a small yacht to the club, we spike his ouzo, and to the sound of the bouzouki, we load him onto the boat and away we go. Actually, that would be easier than what we had to do with Vanunu. I mean, the trip is shorter and the man is sitting right there on the waterfront, ripe for the picking."

"Sounds good to me, but don't put the cart in front of the horse. Before we take him, I want to know what he's up to. Only if we see that he's not doing anything will we bring him in, to try and get something out of him. But if he's living in a safe house, then he must be part of some operation, so we'd better sit back and let the bigger fish come in first."

"It's your call," Number One said.

"What's in the file?" Natan asked.

"It's a set-up plan for Athens. We have one for almost every city in the world." Number One handed the file to Natan.

"That sure saves a lot of time."

"Yes."

"I want you to think of a plan," Natan said as he was glancing over the file, "in case we do decide to take him. That way we'll be ready on short notice."

"But I just suggested a plan you said was good."

"I know, but there's only one hitch . . ."

"There's always a hitch," shrugged Number One.

"It has to be foolproof. We can't tolerate even the slightest mistake. Because if we blow it, we'll tip off our main target and then we'll never get him."

"Well, for starters, we can install a bug in his room and hook onto his phone line at the same time. We can probably do it today if he goes out. We can get in and out of there in minutes."

"I see," Natan said. "So, when do we leave?"

Number One smiled. "You're not going anywhere. I mean, you can go wherever you please, but you're not going with us."

"What the hell do you expect me to do?"

"Sit here with Number Nine and wait to hear from us. I'll fill you in every step of the way and you'll give your approval if necessary."

As a combat officer for many years, Natan knew that no field commander wants brass on his back in the field. There was little he could do there. And he had to admit to himself that he would have a far better perspective of what was going on from where he was. Always depending on how accurately Number One reported to him. "Fine," Natan said at last. "So how are you going to keep me informed?"

"I'll be talking to you by phone." The man smiled at Natan's surprised expression. "Don't worry. It'll be scrambled. In two days, I'll have a yacht in the harbor as a control center. For the time

being, though, several of us will be in Athens at the Hotel Grande
Bretagne, and the others at the Hilton. After all, we'll be posing
as a bunch of rich Canadian tourists."

At about 1800 on Sunday, a beeper signal summoned Natan and
Number Nine to the communications room.

"Well, hello there," came a voice from the speaker on the
communications console. The voice had a metallic quality from the
scrambling process.

"Number One?" asked Natan.

"How soon they forget," came the reply. "Yes, this is he. We have
your man under surveillance. We placed the bug last night when
he went to the Plaka district for a good time."

"So, did you get anything yet?"

"Not much. He came back at about oh two hundred with a
hooker, and she stayed there until early this morning. I can only
tell you he's very loud when he fucks, and I have the tapes to prove
it. But there was nothing more, except for a message that arrived
around eleven hundred. It was delivered by a regular messenger
service, but we have no idea what it was. Your man left the
apartment right after that and made a phone call from the restaurant on the ground floor of his building."

"I thought he had a phone in the apartment," Natan said.

"He does, but he seems to be taking precautions when it comes
to the phone. No other precautions, though. I mean, if you gave me
the word, I could have him in your office tomorrow."

"Don't even think about it."

"Just kidding. Don't panic. What I did was to place a small device
on the restaurant phone line. Fortunately, the bloody telephone
cable runs through the washroom in the back of the establishment,
so it was easy."

"What did you get on that one?"

"Not much yet, since he's not the only one using that phone. We
have plenty of Greek on tape, though. He did make a call to a local

number, but there was no answer." Natan could hear someone in the background speaking to Number One, who then said, "Wait a minute! He's in the restaurant again. I'll have to call you back." With that he hung up.

Natan lit a cigarette. Then he started to tap the lighter on the table, as if to make time go faster. The ring wasn't even complete before he had the receiver to his ear.

"Okay," Number One said, "we have something. Halim talked to someone in Paris. They spoke in Arabic. I have the number, and you might want to have it checked through the computer. They didn't use names in the conversation. The man from Paris said he'd be coming to Athens in two days — that's the tenth — and Halim suggested he stay with him, so he wouldn't have to register in a hotel."

"Anything else?"

"That's about all. What do you want me to do next?"

"Nothing more than what you're doing now. Let's just hope things go on this way. We seem to have been very lucky so far."

"Well, you can call it what you like. The way I see it, luck has very little to do with this. Anyway, we'll lay low for the time being. The yacht will be here tomorrow, and then we'll have an open line to you. We'll get you some photos of the place and of the new guest when he gets here. I hope he's a big fish. It might be worth bringing both of them in."

"I hope we don't get into trouble with the government here, when it seems the policy is to get Palestinians out of the country."

There was a loud silence on the line.

"Okay," Number One said finally, "we'll wait and see. Meantime, would you put Number Nine on the line? I want her to receive a fax for you with that Paris number and a partial transcript of the conversation. If there's anything you need, you can reach me here at all times. Just have Number Nine look after it. So long, amigo."

Natan handed her the phone and headed back to his office. Things were starting to fall into place. And no matter what Number

One said, this was luck, all right. Something was about to go down, and he had a front row seat.

Amir and Mousa dropped in later that evening. Mousa was extremely pleased with the developments, though Natan could sense tension from him. When they were alone for a few minutes, Mousa started in again on the importance of getting the mole.

"We've got to get clean or we won't be able to make a goddamn move. We're not built for a mole. You know our need-to-know factor is worth shit. It seems that with Mossad people, everybody needs to know."

"I agree, but there is absolutely nothing we can do but wait. I mean, we're working this lead, and until Foul Play comes out or sends us more information, there's nothing we can do."

"So you say, but can you imagine what would happen if the Shaback got wind of this problem?"

"Mousa, I can only do things one step at a time."

"I know. I guess I'm just worried about what we're going to find out. I mean, I know practically everybody in the Mossad personally and one of them is a traitor. Someone I'm sure I trust. Hell, this whole thing stinks."

# 8

DAMASCUS
SEPTEMBER 10
1045 HOURS

KARL SAT in a deep, ornate armchair across a large mahogany desk from his Syrian employer. As head of Active Operations in the Muchabarat, the Syrian intelligence service, Fuad had an office very similar in decor to that of his boss, the head of the service, whose office was only several steps away. Fuad, as right hand to the chief, was one of the most powerful people in Syria.

At five foot two and 140 pounds, he was far from physically impressive, but it didn't take long in his presence to realize the scope of this small man's ability. At the moment, his bright, beady eyes were scanning Karl's face, as if to compare the man's words with his expression. Indeed, Fuad bragged to his friends that he could tell from a man's expression whether he was telling the truth, or even if he had some hidden agenda for telling the truth. His subordinates told of a case where Fuad saw in a man's face that he was lying and without hesitation shot him in the head, right there in his office. Some would even point to a slight discoloration on the wall to show where the bullet had penetrated. It all added to the reputation Fuad sought.

"And why, exactly, do you need to know the reasons for our

request?" he asked Karl. "We handed you a list of people we want out of the way, as it were, and we expect you to deal with it. We're paying you quite handsomely, so I don't see why you need to know any more than that."

"Well, sir," Karl said, leaning slightly forward, "you see, I've been handling such affairs for a very long time with my special section —"

"If I'm not mistaken, you don't work for that outfit anymore. Am I right?" There was sarcasm in Fuad's voice. "And I'm still not sure you can be completely trusted. You'll have to give me time and prove yourself."

"I can accept that, although I did hand you several of the Zionist agents, if you recall. But I must still insist that you at least tell me the results you want from this activity."

Fuad stood and went over to the arched window that looked out on the inner yard of the compound. With his back to Karl, he asked, "How much more specific can I be? I want these people dead, out of the game, *finito, kaput*."

"Fine, but whom do you want to be blamed? After all, you don't want the finger pointed at you, especially now that you're looking for room on the American lap." This time there was a hint of sarcasm in Karl's voice.

There was no reaction from the little man. He simply turned to Karl and said, "Just get the job done. Didn't you start setting up a certain Palestinian group?"

"Yes, I did."

"Well, where's the problem?"

"I can't guarantee that it won't all point back to Damascus."

"Wait," Fuad said. He picked up the phone and placed a call, clearly to someone higher up, although few were above him. After a short conversation, he hung up and turned to Karl. "What we want you to do is quite simple. The blame is to fall on the Israelis."

"I thought as much," Karl said, smirking.

"Good, then you have no problem."

"Not really, as long as you understand we'll have to use the Palestinian team as a decoy. In which case they will become expendable and will be eliminated during or right after the operation."

"Well, I'll have to get back to you on that," Fuad then hesitated for a minute before he said, "but for the moment, yes, that should be the approach."

"What about your man Nazir, or as you call him, the Fox? I mean, I have been working with him for a while. He's the one organizing the Palestinians for me."

"What about him? Is he giving you any trouble?"

"No, not at all. But if the team's eliminated, it's quite possible that he will be, too."

"Proceed as you see fit to obtain the goals we have indicated. I will get back to you regarding the Fox."

Karl placed both hands on the desk in front of him and said, "If we're going to sacrifice the Palestinian team, I'll have to use a backup team from my old network in Europe to guarantee completion."

"Are you talking about the people on the list you gave me for clearance?"

"Yes."

"Well," said Fuad, "do so. They are on the payroll already. We might as well get some use out of them. Will there be anything else?"

"No, I don't think so." Karl got up and walked to the door. He turned to nod a farewell, but the little man was once again reading his reports.

# 9

**KFAR-SIRKIN
SEPTEMBER 10
1515 HOURS**

NATAN WAS totally immersed in a pile of papers he had
on his desk when his beeper went off. He had been trying to deduce
a pattern from activities carried out by East German backed
terrorists. While there was even more information on these activities in Mossad archives than he had anticipated, the only common
denominator seemed to be the lack of one. "Shit!" he muttered, as
he tossed a file back into a cardboard box and headed rapidly for
the communications loft.

When Natan got there, Number Nine handed him the phone.

Number One was on the line to tell him that the yacht was now
in place at the Limini Marina and Yacht Club. From the cabin
window, the balcony of Halim's apartment was clearly visible, and
its red canvas awning made it even easier to spot.

"Halim's friend has just arrived. At the moment they're eating at
the restaurant downstairs. We got several good shots of the pair. Now
we're hoping they'll go back upstairs so we can hear them, too."

"Can't you put someone next to them in the restaurant?"

"No!" Number One exclaimed adamantly. "I can't burn someone
like that. It's too early in the game. We'll have to wait until they
go up, and hope for the best."

"I still think you should have someone there. Why not burn one person and use him later in an out-of-sight position?"

"It's your call. I can have someone in the restaurant, in less than five minutes. But when he comes out, we'll all be on our way home. Now, what will it be?"

"Your options stink," Natan growled.

"Sorry, man. Listen, once they go up to the apartment, I'll patch the line directly to you. That way, you'll hear the conversation in real time. The line is secure, so there's no problem."

"Oh, yes, there is," Natan insisted. "I don't understand a word of Arabic."

"Number Nine does. She'll translate for you simultaneously. Just turn on the intercom and you'll both pick it up through the speakers. We should be back to you within the hour, so please stand by." He hung up.

"Would you like me to get you something from the kitchen?" Natan said to Number Nine. She was really quite beautiful, and he found it difficult not to stare at her.

"No, thanks. I'm on a diet," she smiled at him.

"You're kidding me, right?" He took the opportunity to look her over. "As you are now, you're probably in constant danger of other women wanting to kill you."

She was laughing now. He waved his beeper as he headed back to the stairs. "Call me if they come back before I do. I'm definitely not on a diet."

Fifteen minutes later, the beeper went off again. Natan got back to the communications loft and learned that Number One and several of his team members were watching from the yacht as the two men left the restaurant and crossed the street to the water's edge, where they were now standing, looking at the boats in the marina.

"They're looking directly at me. They're leaning on the railing and peering over at the boat right next to ours. I don't like it. It's too close." His voice was low now, as if he were afraid the two men on the dock could hear him.

"Can you hear what they're saying?" Natan asked.

"No. Who would have thought they'd come to the boat? Are you sure you don't want me just to bring them home? I could, you know."

"We've been through that one before. But, dammit, I'd like to hear what the fuck they're talking about."

"Wait," Number One said. "Halim is motioning toward the apartment building. They're turning back and heading for the restaurant. If they go back there, I'll send someone in because . . . no, wait, they just passed the restaurant and . . . yes, they're going back home. They should be in the apartment in about three minutes, so I'll switch you to the listening device there. If you want to tell me something, just talk. I can hear you. Okay, I'll start you now." There was a click, and then silence. In the background they could hear a steady, monotonous noise.

"What's that sound?" Natan asked.

"It's probably an alarm clock," Number One replied. "We put the listening device under a small dresser and later, Halim put something ticking on top."

There were several more minutes of silence with only the clock ticking away, creating an eerie, tense mood, as if the whole scene was unreal. They heard a key turning in the lock and a sudden burst of voices. Number Nine began a simultaneous translation.

"Would you care for some coffee?" Halim asked.

"Please, with some cardamom, if you have any," his guest answered.

"Of course."

Dishes rattled next, and Natan heard running water.

"Help yourself to some baklava," Halim suggested. "It's almost as good as the one Tarif makes in the Casbah at Nablus."

A few more minutes of silence was interrupted by loud sipping sounds as the two took in the hot, sweet coffee.

"This is really good," the visitor said, "and the baklava is excellent, too."

"I told you. Thank Allah there's much of what a man longs for in this country."

"Don't get too comfortable here, my friend. After all, our brothers are suffering and it's up to us to help them. We should be wary of the comforts that will turn us soft so that we lack the strength to lift the sword when the time comes."

"You're right, but what can one do while waiting to act? There is so little activity on our behalf and now, with the talk of peace, what are we to do?"

"Forget the peace. Forget it. It is not our job to handle that. We must not lose sight of the real enemy, the one who has stolen the lands of our ancestors from under our feet with only our women there to protect it, while we fled like cowards. Yet now there are some of us who want to talk to the killers of our brothers and negotiate with them. We must act to kill those who come to us dressed in sheep's clothing, when underneath they point a saber at the heart of our nation."

"So, what should we do?"

"Have you checked this place to see if it's clean?"

"Do you mean for listening devices and things?"

"Yes," said the guest, starting to lose his patience.

"Who would put something here? Nobody knows about this place."

"That's not the point. I told you to check. Did you?"

"Of course I did." Natan could hear Number One and his men laughing on the other end.

"Things are coming together," the visitor said. "What I want you to do is gather our men. Are you in contact with them?"

"Yes, they're all in Cyprus, waiting. I speak to them every other day."

"Here is a list of apartments just like this one. I want you to fill them with provisions. Once you've done that, you are to call the men from Cyprus and house them in the apartments. There are five apartments in all for them. Do not bring them to this one, we'll keep it as the control center. Each group is to stay apart from the others and members should not even speak to each other on the street. I'll be calling in a niece of mine to be a go-between for all of you. She'll stay here with you, and you'll look after her."

"All this will cost a lot of money. Where will I get it?"

"I'll give you fifty thousand dollars in a day or so, before I leave. As soon as you have the money, you must start organizing every-thing, then wait for my orders."

"What are we supposed to do?"

At that, Natan leaned forward: a reflex action, for if the visitor answered this question, they'd have made a major step forward, with very little effort.

"What's the matter with you?" the man's voice was angry now. "Don't you know better than to keep asking me this? You will be told in time. You and your men have trained in every combat and demolition technique possible. There should be no job that you people can't do."

"I didn't mean it that way . . ."

The visitor seemed only to be getting angrier. "What does it matter what it is you're to do? Is there something you would not do?"

"No, Nazir, my brother. Whatever the Fox tells me, I will do, and so will all the others. I can assure you that on my mother's grave."

"Never, ever call me that again. Do you understand?" The man was clearly very angry.

Natan almost sprang out of his chair at the word Fox, realizing that here was the head of the operation — in the palm of his hand. He knew they had him!

The temptation to tell Number One to grab him was overwhelm-ing, but Natan knew it was possible that the Fox was not really running the show. If that was the case and they grabbed him one minute too early, they could blow the whole thing.

"Let's hope you remember that," continued Nazir. "I wouldn't want to be the one to have to teach you a lesson." He paused and there was only the ticking of the alarm clock on the dresser. Then he spoke again.

"I'll be staying here with you for a few days, Halim. Then I'll give you the money and let you set things up the way we planned them. I'm hoping to have time to take a small vacation on one of the islands. That way, I can rest and not have to look over my shoulder all the time."

"What can I do for you meantime? Have you made your travel plans already?"

"No, I haven't. I'll wait and see. It all depends on some information I'm expecting from a friend. One more thing, while I'm away, my niece will probably contact you, saying that Nazir sent her. She's reliable and she speaks English, French, and Arabic. Just make sure she has everything she needs, and I'll fill her in when I come back. We'll talk more about this later."

At about 1900, the two decided it was time to go out on the town for some dinner and entertainment.

"They left the building and are now hailing a taxi. We know pretty well where they're going, so we won't follow them," said Number One.

"That's fair," Natan said.

"Ah, by the way," said Number One. "They've just now picked up a taxi."

# 10

CLIMBING THE stairs to the communications loft after breakfast, Natan enjoyed watching Number Nine come into view. Her hair was gathered in a long ponytail held in place with a wooden pin. Then he saw her long, smooth neck. He could feel the warmth in his chest as he stared at her firm, pointed breasts holding up a short T-shirt. And by the time he was admiring her legs in a pair of khaki shorts, she was looking at him. She seemed to be amused. Embarrassed, he forced himself to look away.

"Don't you eat breakfast?" he asked.

"I do," she replied, laughing. "I had mine about an hour ago."

"What's happening with Abdul and Costello?"

"They're asleep. They came in at about oh two thirty. Apparently Halim got drunk and Nazir wasn't thrilled with him. At the moment, all we're getting from the apartment is snoring."

Natan had brought along the translated transcripts of yesterday's conversations between Halim and the Fox and was going through them, to make sure he hadn't missed anything.

The phone rang and Number Nine handed him the receiver. It was Amir.

"Well, how are things in the loft?"

"Very well," said Natan. "It seems we have more luck than brains."

"Speak for yourself," chuckled Amir. "Is everything okay with Number Nine? Are you in love yet?"

Natan was smiling. He could understand what Amir was talking about. "If there is nothing specific you want, buddy, I'm going to hang up."

"Just wanted to know all was well. See you later." Not waiting for a response, Amir hung up. Natan handed the receiver to Number Nine and went on with his reading.

About an hour later Nazir began complaining about Halim's behavior in the nightclub they'd gone to, and the fact that he got drunk. Halim explained that he'd wanted to bring back the two girls they'd met. He thought they'd all have had a grand time.

Nazir got angry at that. "They were hookers, *ya maznun* (you crazy). What is it with you? Don't you know about all the diseases they have? Besides, what kind of man are you that you have to pay for a fuck? I should get paid, not pay," he said, and went on about it tediously.

"But . . ." Halim finally managed to break in, "but in training, they told us to use prostitutes for sex. That way we wouldn't get into a relationship that might jeopardize whatever operation we were involved in."

"Well, that's okay for you, then. As for me, I'll have a tourist. I mean, what could be better? She's here today and gone tomorrow. And when I screw an American, I feel even better."

"In that case," Halim said, "why don't you get yourself an Israeli? You'll be having fun and fulfilling your duty, too."

The two seemed to find that notion extremely amusing.

Natan was starting to coordinate the information he had so far. He wanted Nazir badly, but first he must be sure the man had all the answers. There was still time, as Nazir was not going anywhere. Natan hoped his prey would get fat with information, and then just when that information was about to turn into action, they would pluck him away, so as to leave not a trace.

Nazir's voice was loud now. "I'm going to take a shower, then I must make a phone call."

"If he leaves, I want to know where he's going," said Natan. "Are you set up for that?"

"We'll watch him from a distance, but if he starts to take defensive measures, to check if he's being followed, we'll let him go. I don't want to burn a man yet."

"Okay." Natan said.

For several hours, very little information came in. Natan had returned to his office and was eating a sandwich when Number Nine transferred a call to him.

"Starting to feel at home?" asked Number One, sounding even more metallic than he did upstairs.

"It's about time you called. What's going on?" Natan was impatient. Having to sit back and run things from a distance was starting to take its toll on him.

"Not much actually. We tailed Nazir when he left the apartment this morning. He made no attempt to see if he was being followed."

"What did he do?"

"He went all the way to the center of Athens to make his phone call. The call lasted about twenty minutes. He used the OTE office on Omonia Square — it's like a post office where they have lots of pay phones. There was no way for us to listen in on the conversation, nor could we get the number he called. Then he went for a walk. He appeared to be in a good mood. After doing some window-shopping, he had lunch. Would you like to hear what he ate?"

"I think you can skip that," said Natan, "unless of course you think it's relevant."

"Not really. So that's it for the moment."

"Keep me informed," Natan said, and hung up.

Natan went to the kitchen and made a fresh pot of coffee to take to the loft. Number Nine smiled at him as he poured two cups. He lit a cigarette and sat down.

They sat there quietly for about an hour, listening to the hypnotic ticking of Halim's clock and some Arabic music from the transistor radio he'd left on.

"The two clowns are coming back," said Number Four from the yacht. "You should be able to hear them in about two minutes."

"I'm listening," said Natan.

They said very little that was of interest to Natan until finally Halim said, "I'm going down to the restaurant. Would you care to join me?" His voice was low, his tone unhappy.

"What's with you? You sound like someone cut off your dick and fed it to the dogs."

"No *ya afendy*. It's that I feel I've offended you in some way. Otherwise, I can't understand the way you're treating me after all I went through."

"*Yah ebkeh alek bekah* (I'll cry a cry for you). Stop behaving like a baby. You're a man and I'll treat you like one. If that means talking harshly to you, then I'll do that. Remember, we're not members of a country club. We're freedom fighters that the whole world wants to get rid of. But we're our people's only hope of freedom. Stop moping and go have something to eat. I'll join you in a few minutes."

"Okay."

"Get someone into the restaurant!" shouted Natan into the receiver.

"I have a man wired and ready," Number One said.

"If he makes a call, can you get the number?"

"Yeah, and if it's long distance, it's even easier. He has to get the operator to connect him. All we need to do is listen and he'll read out the number he wants."

"Great!" Natan was getting anxious.

"My man is in position."

"Are they there yet?" Natan asked.

"They just left the building." There was a moment of silence, then Number One said, "They're in the restaurant. I'm signaling my man to go in."

"Does that mean we'll have one less for the rest of the operation?" Natan inquired.

"Not necessarily. He has a beard. He can get rid of it if he has to come in close to these two sometime later. Or if worst comes to worst, we'll swap him for Number Nine. Granted, he's not as gorgeous, but he can do the job."

"Okay," Natan smiled at Number Nine as he went on, "can you see into the restaurant from where you are?"

"No, it's fairly dark inside and we're in the bright sun. It's difficult to see."

"Will you pass on the transmission to me?"

"No. He's wearing a recording device. We'll just have to wait for him to get out. He can beep me, though, with another device, if our man goes to the phone. That one, you'll hear."

There was nothing for the next twenty minutes, then came a loud beep.

"He's going for the phone," said Number One.

Seconds later, Natan and Number Nine heard Nazir dialing then speaking to the international operator. The call was directed to a suburb of Beirut known as the Muslim section. After the second ring, a husky voice that seemed to growl blossomed into a joyful welcome once he recognized Nazir. It was clear from the tone Nazir was talking to relatives. After the required niceties, in which Nazir blessed them and was blessed with unending health and guidance from the Lord, he apologetically asked for Latifa.

She must have been waiting by the phone, because she answered almost immediately. The conversation was short and to the point. Clearly, the arrangements had been discussed with the girl before. Her voice was soft and although Nazir had spoken Arabic to her at first, they now spoke English. Natan concluded that they did not wish to share the information they were discussing with the others in the room.

"Well, my dear," Nazir said, "a man will bring you here to me within three weeks at the most, so be prepared."

"Don't worry. I will do as we have agreed," she promised.

"What did you tell them you were going to do?"

"I told them what you suggested. That you've arranged for me to study at the Sorbonne in Paris." They bade each other farewell in Arabic.

"Did you get the number?" asked Natan.

"Yes. It came across loud and clear. I'll give it to Number Nine and she can get you the address from our computer."

Number Nine gave it to Natan for future reference.

Very little was learned from Nazir and Halim's conversation in the restaurant after the phone call. However, they knew that there was a plan that Nazir would not elaborate on. Its timing depended in some way on the peace talks. That in itself was very sketchy as there were several bilateral negotiations taking place simultaneously in various places around the world.

In not revealing details of the plan to Halim, yet explicitly confirming his knowledge of those details, Nazir had signed his own death warrant. Now Natan knew the goose was plump and ready for the plucking. It was time to bring him in.

As it turned out, Number Five was burnt in the restaurant, since Halim had eyed him the whole time Nazir was on the phone. At first Number One had him shave off his beard, only to conclude that he would still be identifiable due to his physique, so Number Nine would have to replace him.

Natan placed a call to Mousa, advising him that he was going to mount an operation to bring the Fox in, because he was worried that one of the clowns as he put it — especially the Fox — might leave the scene, resulting in an empty trough and a very thirsty horse.

## 1715 Hours

"Okay," said Natan in a low voice, "now you can show me what you're really worth."

"And how, my friend, can I do that?" asked Number One.

"We're going to bring Nazir in."

"Now you're talking."

"We'll have to take him in such a way that he won't be missed, and then somehow return him after getting what we want out of him. You see, the man can't just up and disappear forever . . ."

"It's not that simple," Number One interjected.

"Are you telling me you can't do this?" Natan asked, sounding surprised.

"No. Not at all."

"What then?"

"I want to point out the difficulty of letting him return and keeping his experience from his colleagues. Unless he's returned dead, of course. And then there's the time frame for his return. It can't be more than twenty-four hours from his departure. That is, if you want it to look genuine. We might be able to extend it slightly, but it should be thought of in terms of hours, not days."

"I think you're right on both counts."

"We have to get someone closer to him, someone who could latch on to him," Number One said.

"And how do you propose doing that?"

"It seems, from what they were saying, that he's going off today to try and find a woman to bring back to the apartment. I might just be able to help him out there. Once I know where he's going, I can plant someone before he arrives. That way, he won't suspect anything."

"Are you suggesting that one of your women go to bed with that shitball?"

"Not exactly, but we need someone near him and there's nothing better on such short notice."

"Isn't it against regulations to place one of our women in that kind of situation? I thought you had to get someone from the outside for that," Natan said.

"It's against regulations to force her to go to bed with someone, but if she has to do it to protect her cover, then it's her call to make," replied Number One.

There was something twisted in what Number One was saying, but not having worked with a Kidon team before, Natan was not about to pass a moral judgment.

"Okay," Natan said. "You do it your way, but I want to know what you're up to as you proceed."

The main problem was that Nazir had made it very clear to Halim that he was going out alone this time. So he had no reason to tell Halim where he was going, leaving the team and Natan with no idea either. But the woman would have to be inside before Nazir arrived so that he would feel confident that meeting her was by chance, not a setup.

"I'm going out around nine," Nazir said. "Could you stay at a hotel tonight? I want to be undisturbed."

"Yes, yes, of course. With pleasure," Halim told him.

"Here — for your expenses," Nazir said, apparently handing Halim a substantial sum of money, as the man virtually purred his thanks.

"Can I accompany you to the city?"

"No, no," Nazir chuckled. "I'll get a cab."

At 1800, Number One reported in to Natan. "I've arranged it so that the woman will be able to wait for him at his destination tonight."

"How?" asked Natan, impressed.

"It takes about half an hour to get from Piraeus to downtown Athens at that time of night," said Number One. "We're going to block Koumoundourou Street — the street the apartment building is on — to cabs at about twenty forty hours. At the same time, we'll have a cab waiting in the street about half a block from the apartment building. Our man will hold the cab, telling the driver he's waiting to pick up a friend. When our man sees Nazir heading for the street to find a cab, he'll pay his off and let it go, telling the cabby he's not going to wait any longer. That cab will then be the only one in the area, so it's pretty likely Nazir will pick it up. We'll have a second cab set up similarly for backup just in case."

"Set up?"

"Our so-called passengers will plant a small bug in both cabs. Something simple that you just place under the seat. We'll activate the one in the cab Nazir takes and find out where he's going. We'll then call the woman, who will be waiting in a car somewhere quite central, give her the location, and she'll get there ahead of him. Then it's up to her to make the contact."

"Why don't you just get a couple of cabs, and have one of your men drive him? Instead of blocking the streets and all that?"

"Where am I going to get a cab that we could drive? Besides, what's the big deal in blocking a couple of streets?"

"Okay, okay, but what if he leaves the cab at one point and walks to another?"

"We'll still be on him, so we'd move the woman to him. It wouldn't be as clean, but it would probably still work."

Natan was satisfied. "So, I'll be here. I have to go for a meeting, but I'll be back to listen in on it."

"Sorry," said Number One, "but with one of my people in direct contact with someone regarded as dangerous, I won't be able to keep you informed all the time. Why not take the night off and let me get on with it?"

Natan hesitated. He was reluctant to let go, but he knew Number One was right. "Will do," he said finally.

"Thanks," Number One acknowledged.

Number Five arrived shortly after Natan had hung up. A big, heavyset man, he was in a foul mood. He'd had to shave off his beard, a longtime companion, only to find it was for nothing when he was sent back from the field to replace Number Nine.

"I'm going off for the night," Natan told him. "I'll be back tomorrow morning, but if anything significant happens, call me at once, no matter what the time is. And be sure to call me when Nazir returns to the apartment."

Natan thought about the Kidon team as he took the new road leading to the Glilot intersection. What a world, Natan mused as he passed the large tennis center, its parking lot full. Here, people were having a good time; out there, the team was taking risks, setting up the first stage of the trap, homing in on a target who didn't yet know he was a dead man. When he had been a naval commando, Natan often came back from missions where he'd lost a friend, only to find that, on the streets of Tel Aviv, it was business as usual. It was a strange feeling, living in two distinct realities, but not really knowing which one you belonged to. He was still shrouded in thoughts as he parked his car at the main lot of the Country Club Hotel — one of several residential premises the Mossad leased.

He stood for several minutes by the entrance to one of the two-story apartment units as dusk settled slowly, the sky cloudless and glowing along the horizon. Natan hoped this was not going to be a long session. He was looking forward to dinner that evening with his ex-wife Hanna, whom he missed very much. At the same time, he wasn't particularly comfortable about this night's hiatus from the Athens operation. He was in no mood for bullshit, that was certain.

Natan rang the doorbell. He saw someone at the door's peephole and, a moment later, Mousa drew him inside.

"Well, well, don't you look sharp," Mousa greeted him, commenting on his tie and blazer. Natan was well known in the Mossad for regarding anything more than a T-shirt and jeans as work clothes.

Natan smiled. "I'm taking Hanna out for dinner."

"Hey, you don't have to explain to me. As far as I'm concerned, you could be in a tuxedo. Whatever makes you happy."

Natan followed Mousa into the living room where they joined Amir and Mark, who were both eager to know what was happening.

After handing Natan a beer, Mark motioned for him to sit. "Are we alone?" Natan asked, gesturing toward the stairs that led to the bedroom on the second floor.

"Definitely. Don't worry," Mousa grinned. "I might have a guest arriving a bit later, but there's plenty of time. So, give us a rundown on what's happened and we'll take it from there."

Natan gave them a short summary of events. He made a point of not elaborating, as no one really wanted to hear all the tactical details. "The next stage will depend on what we achieve tonight, so that's where we stand for now," he concluded.

"Well then," Mousa was speaking through a mouthful of peanuts, "everything seems to be in order." He went on chewing as he took a large manila envelope from a drawer in the sideboard. "Here, I think these photos might interest you." He handed the envelope to Natan, finally swallowing the peanuts and wiping the back of his hand across his mouth.

Natan extracted an aerial photograph from the envelope and stared at it for several minutes before asking, "Is this Damascus?"

"You sure know your geography," Mousa replied.

"What's this about?" Natan was still staring at the photo.

"That's Foul Play's neighborhood. Remember you wanted to have him checked out?" Mousa paused, looking at Natan like a parent about to give his kid a candy.

"When was this taken?" Natan asked.

"Sometime this morning. You see the small x over there?" Mousa leaned forward and pointed at the mark on the photo. "That's where a combatant will be parking a car sometime tomorrow morning. He'll hold a parking spot that the 'Providers' said would be the best place from which to videotape Foul Play's building."

"I still don't understand what you hope to achieve by that," Mark muttered, almost inaudibly.

"What's the matter with you, Mark?" Mousa asked. "Do you have a mental block or something? I told you that if the man has fallen and is now being activated by the Syrians, we'll be able to see if there's any surveillance around his place before he comes in — *if* he comes in at all. For all we know, he might be transmitting from the Syrian high command. If we are to pursue this, we have to be certain he's not playing games with us."

"So, how do we get a video out there? I don't believe Masada will allow their man to place a camera in enemy territory." He gave Amir an inquiring look.

"There won't be any need for that. The U.N. will do it for us," Amir smirked. He and Mousa started laughing.

"Okay, okay," Natan put the photo on the table, "what's the plan?"

Mousa sat back in his chair. "We'll have a combatant place a rented car in the spot marked on the photo. He'll put the car keys in a post office box in downtown Damascus. Two of the U.N. men we recruited a while back to do deliveries for us into Syria and Lebanon will be setting off tomorrow morning on a scheduled run. While these guys have a terrific time tonight with a couple of chicks in Haifa, our people will install the video camera in their jeep. I think they said they'd place it in the headrest, but it's one of those tiny jobs, and the main equipment will be installed underneath the vehicle. It can apparently record about seven to nine hours, which is far more than we need. As far as our U.N guys know, their job is to collect the keys to the rented car, place a fairly large sum of money inside it, and leave it in a parking lot on the other side of town. That will be done on Thursday around noon, one day after they arrive in Damascus. They'll leave their jeep in the space vacated by the rented car."

"What if they drive off with both vehicles? After all, there are two of them."

"They'll be told that their jeep must stay in that spot as a sign that the rented car has been moved according to plan. And they are to leave the jeep there until the following morning."

"But if the tape runs for seven hours, by the time they get there, won't it have run out?" Natan asked.

"The people from Technology solved that one. The video will be activated by a short transmission from the military communication unit eight two hundred on Mount Hermon." Mousa paused. "So, Natan, everything's already in place, but is there anything you'd add?"

"Not really. I have no problem with it. Go ahead."

"Great," said Mousa. "I'm happy you see it that way. Of course, there are several more technical details we have to work out, like retrieving the equipment from the jeep; after all, it will be much harder to do once it's back in the U.N. compound in Naharia."

"Won't that burn the combatant once the rented car is found — if anything goes wrong with the U.N. people?" Natan asked, slowly sipping his beer.

"It probably will, but he's not going back after this one," Amir told him.

"What's going to happen to the money you're leaving in the car?" Mark wanted to know.

"Well, I guess the U.N. guys might take some. Or maybe not. What can I tell you? Expenses." Mousa lit a cigarette, shrugging.

"What about the combatant?" Natan turned to Amir. "You said he's out of the game after this job."

"He's going back to Switzerland after Damascus — just to get his things and close the business in an orderly fashion. But he won't be going back into a target country. He should be home and out of the bush in about three weeks."

"That's a shame. I sure hoped he'd be left there for the full four years," said Mark, yawning and stretching.

"Why is that?" asked Natan.

"Mark's having a thing with the guy's wife," said Amir, "and from what I hear," he smiled at Mark, "a good thing. But I guess all good things must come to an end."

Natan tried to keep his voice low. "You're kidding, of course. I mean, there's no way you people could be talking seriously!"

"What the fuck's the matter with him?" asked Mark, surprised at his reaction.

"You are serious," spat Natan in shock. "You bastards, you send people out to risk their lives in the most dangerous job there is. They do it with patriotism and courage — and you, their so-called superiors — repay them by fucking their wives."

He jumped up and stood staring down at Amir. "What happens if you want to keep the woman because you really like what you're getting? Do you get the poor bastard to fuck up? Do you see to it that he ends up buried in some unmarked grave in a foreign land so you can go on with your little game?"

Mousa turned to face Natan. "I think you're looking at it the wrong way. Consider this. The woman is alone for almost eight months at a time. If she's lucky, she maybe gets a weekend with her man once or twice a year. What we do is give her what she wants and, mind you, *needs*. This way, she doesn't have to go looking God-knows-where. When her husband comes home, there's no chance he'll find out, so all is well. And she doesn't end up running off with the milkman."

"How very neat. Tell me, is that the way you handle all the wives? I mean, you wouldn't want to leave anybody out. And is it only people working in top level who get to do this job — or do you hire outside help?"

"It's a lot of work alright," said Mark, laughing now, "but someone has to do it."

"Look," Mousa interrupted, "I agree it's not the best way to do things, but that's the way it's done here. You can't tell me this is the first time you've heard of it."

"No, but I always figured it was just a story, like the one where we say we did the Entebbe raid."

"Not very funny," said Mousa. "You're out of line, Natan."

"And you're disgusting." Natan walked to the door. "You can reach me through the installation if you need me." He stormed out, slamming the door behind him.

"What's with him?" Mark was stunned. He turned to Mousa. "Do you think he'll talk?" He hesitated. "You know what I mean."

"And what would he say? And who would he say it to? Look, Natan is okay, he just has this sort of moral code when it comes to married women. He's still one of us." Mousa was getting restless. He looked at his watch.

"I hope to God you're right," Mark said.

Mousa smiled at him as he said, "Thank God I'm an atheist."

"I have to go to my office for a couple of minutes," Amir said. "There's something I owe Natan, after his performance tonight."

Amir and Mark walked out to the parking lot in silence. When they reached their cars, Mark turned. "I hope you're not planning to screw up the operation just to get back at Natan for talking to us that way, Amir. After all, he does have a point, when you think about it."

"I would never screw an operation for personal reasons, Mark. But I might just screw a person for operational reasons. And anyway, I don't agree that he has a point. You know as well as I do that we don't force people into things. If a woman said no, that would be that. Come on, they enjoy it just as much as we do, so don't *you* start on me. Go on home, Mark, and if there's nobody else with your wife when you get there, have a good time."

"That's not funny."

"Have I touched a raw nerve? I *am* sorry." There was mean sarcasm in Amir's voice, and something even more unpleasant about his laugh as he shut his car door and gave a mock salute. Amir was clearly up to no good, Mark thought, as the other man drove away noisily.

# 11

**OLD JAFFA**
**SEPTEMBER 11**
**2130 HOURS**

ON THE ANCIENT terrace of the Tarshish seafood restaurant, overlooking the fishermen's harbor in old Jaffa, a very troubled Natan sat across from the woman who was once his wife. Hanna's long, almond-brown hair emphasized her lovely oval face and chestnut eyes. She gazed at him now with understanding. She knew him well, and it hurt her to see him so distressed. Still he denied that anything was wrong.

"Look," she said at last, lowering her head to try to catch his glance. "You know you can tell me about it, whatever it is. We might not be married anymore, but I still have my clearance. What is it?"

"It's nothing. The usual attitude problem, that's all. One thing today and something else tomorrow. But it's still the same all the time."

"I'll never understand why you don't just quit that lousy place."

A waiter came over to their table at that point. He lit a candle in an amber-colored dish, and replaced the ashtray. "Would you care for something to drink?"

Natan nodded to Hanna.

"You go ahead," she said.

"I'd prefer just a beer."

"It's fine with me," she said. "I'll have a coffee."

Then they both ordered the catch of the day, with appetizers of hummus with tahina.

When hot pitas arrived with a large plate of assorted pickles, they started to nibble at once.

"I just can't get through to them," Natan said. "They think they're right about everything. And I'm talking about basic decency. I don't think that should be such a hard concept to understand." He looked at her wistfully. "Should it?"

"I've told you a million times, Natan. You come from a different environment. You don't fit here, you never have. You were born in the United States, educated there. You got your values there, and you'll never understand the way the men here think. They're on an endless macho trip, they think that it's expected of them. That's how they were raised and they can't change that."

"That's crazy, Hanna. Look, I was here as a kid. I spent my summers here. I was part of the youth movement. I belong here. I'm a Jew. Where do I belong if not here?"

"Yes, of course you belong here, *if* you become like the rest of them. But the moment you try to get them to see things your way, they shut you out, and then you start to eat at yourself. It's not worth it, I'm telling you. Get out, you can make it on the outside. Not like most of these nonentities you call friends. I don't think there was one of them who didn't try to land your wife in bed, when we were still married. And my, how they wanted to console me after we got divorced."

He stared at her.

"Don't worry," she said. "None of them made it. They made me sick. What a bunch of losers they are, this 'select few,' the 'chosen ones.' What a joke."

"It wasn't like that in the navy."

"Well, there you were with the cream of the crop, and you were young and so was everybody else. You were the front-line people. Those guys are usually the best. It's the ones who pull the strings and send guys like that to die who are the real jerks. And now that you're one of them, you can't take it."

"I never said I couldn't take it. Come on," he said, trying hard to smile, "let's just drop the whole thing. After all it's not that often I get to eat dinner with such a lovely woman."

"There's no need for that, Natan. You know I'll never come back to you."

"I know, I know." He nodded his head as if he wanted to brush away the whole conversation.

She went on. "Once the anger died, I realized I still liked you." He took her hand gently, but she pulled it back. "Let me finish," she said, a tear at the corner of her eye. Her voice was getting husky. "I wanted to find someone else to take your place, but it didn't work out. Then I realized I was trying to find another Natan and I know that's impossible. So," she wiped the tear away with her napkin, "what happens is that we'll always have each other, yet never really have each other. Do you understand what I'm saying?"

"I do."

"You know you're wedded to your lousy work." She smiled wistfully at him, then looked away.

The rest of the evening was more relaxed, as the two tried hard to keep the conversation safe. If Natan had hoped to unload some of his frustration and be consoled, it didn't work out that way.

After dropping Hanna off at what he had once called home, Natan drove around the sleeping city, thinking. He found he did so best at night, especially while driving. He eventually managed a few hours of sleep in his small apartment in the north part of Tel Aviv. At 0800 he was back at the facility and heading for the communications loft.

"Good morning, my friend," Natan said to Number Five. "What news of Nazir?"

"We made contact last night. It worked out great. He got back at about oh three hundred hours with the bait. Actually, she's there now. They should be getting up soon." He was smiling.

Natan turned on him. "What do you mean, they're back? I thought I told you to call me when he got back? Why the hell didn't you do that?"

The man seemed puzzled. He said, "Why, because last night, before everyone even got into location, Amir called and said you needed a rest. That we weren't to bother you unless something went wrong. Nothing did."

"What else did Amir tell you?"

"He wanted Number One to call him at his office. Something to do with personnel assignments."

"Did he make the call?"

"I don't know. My job was to give Number One the message, that's all."

Natan suddenly realized he was about to drop Number Five into the midst of power wrangling. He'd play a cool hand instead.

"Connect me with Number One, would you? I'll take it in my office."

"Right away." But as the man reached for the phone, they heard Nazir's low voice on the intercom.

"Wait," Natan said. "I'll talk to him in a minute."

Nazir spoke again. "Would you care for some coffee, my little flower?" He was speaking English.

"Sure, I'd love some." The girl's voice sent shivers down Natan's back. He punched the talk button and shouted through the open line at Number One. "Why the hell did you have to send Number Nine? Why her, for God's sake?"

"What the devil's the matter with you?" Number One was hissing down the line, clearly not alone at his end. "What difference does it make to you? Nine, Eleven, Fourteen? Would you feel better if it was Eleven? She's right here. Why don't you tell her?"

The line fell silent. All that could be heard now was Number Nine's voice, soft and persuasive. "You said you were going to make coffee." There was the sound of bed sheets rustling. Natan was furious. He stormed down the stairs, calling over his shoulder, "I'll take Number One in my office now."

"Sure, buddy." There was something friendly and sympathetic in Five's voice that had not been there before.

Once in his office, Natan stood for several seconds staring at the little yellow light flashing on the phone before he picked it up. "Why Number Nine?" He asked again coldly.

"Number Eleven was planned as the bait, but then I got a call last night from Amir, telling me to switch," Number One explained.

"I thought you were to take orders *only* from me."

"That order had nothing to do with your goals for the operation, so he had every right to give it. Besides, we were given to understand that you wanted it that way."

"You don't like me much, do you?"

"I don't get into that. What I care about is the job and my people. I know we're no more than pawns for the rest of you, so let's keep it that way, okay? After all, we're only numbers, right?" There was bitterness in his voice.

So, he wasn't immune, Natan thought. Staring through a tiny crack in Number One's facade, he could see a man agonizing over what he was doing, and how his people were being used.

Natan felt his self-control returning. "Can Number Five translate for me?" he asked.

"Yes. He's as good as Nine," Number One confirmed.

Natan hung up. He sat for a moment with his eyes shut, then went to his quarters where he took a cold shower and changed into a fresh khaki uniform. He would not leave again until this phase was over, he'd decided, knowing that meant he'd likely be there for quite some time.

He left a message for Mousa, who called back at once. "Listen Mousa," Natan told him abruptly, "I need to see you as soon as possible."

"Well, good morning to you, too," said Mousa. "What's up?"

"We're close to bringing the Fox in. If an opportunity arises, I don't want to be running around looking for okays."

"How shall I put it?" Mousa thought aloud. "Do whatever you want as long as you're within the guidelines I laid out for you. So in a way you have my approval. On the other hand if I were you, I would try and contact me before you do something. I'm usually available. Am I making myself clear?"

"Like Irish mist."

"Good, so you understand me then. I'll get down there when I can. At the moment, I can't leave the building. We're waiting for a special forum the boss called."

"Sure, but do get back to me. We need to talk."

A buzz sounded at Mousa's end, and he said "Now you'll have to excuse me. The master is calling."

# 12

**DAMASCUS**
**SEPTEMBER 13**
**1400 HOURS**

KARL REINHART had just returned to Damascus after a short visit to Paris. The trip had proved very informative, so much so that he had immediately started an investigation aimed at identifying and treating a leak in the Syrian security system. Karl's source in the Mossad had told him that they, the Mossad, had been cautioned about a Stasi officer working for the Syrians on a terrorist plot.

Karl didn't think he was in any danger of being identified. As far as BND, the German secret service, was concerned, he was dead. But he assumed that his file had been handed over to the Israelis, as BND was known to be a very close friend of the Mossad. Although he had prepared for such an event, and they would be getting a file full of information he had carefully compiled, he was still bothered by this leak. Karl had no intention of ending up on a slab, just because of some half-assed agent.

His cooperation with the Syrian secret service, the Muchabarat, was known only to a handful of people. He had been brought in at a very high level and given a temporary rank equivalent to the one he had held in the Stasi. Those who knew about him had known for some time now. So the fact that the information had reached the Mossad only in the last week made pinpointing the leak that much easier.

After spending several hours with the Muchabarat's chief of internal security, Karl determined that there were only two people who had learned about him just in the last week. Both had gotten the information at a special meeting the previous Thursday at the Ministry of Defense. Karl was furious at this, pointing out that it could have jeopardized an extremely important operation before it even got off the ground.

As things stood at the moment, Karl's source in the Mossad — one he was not about to reveal to members of a system that was nothing more than a leaking sieve — had made it clear that all they knew at the moment was that there was a German working for the Syrians. But they expected more information when their agent came out of Syria to meet his operator in Europe. The source also told Karl that the Israelis knew about the creation of a new terrorist group in Europe. Karl did not share with his Syrian friend the revelation that the Mossad had also been tipped off about a mole in their midst.

After reading the files of the two suspects, Karl easily picked Shaby as the leak. The other possible suspect had never left the country, so there was no way he could have been recruited by the Mossad. It was no secret that they did all their recruiting from their embassies, and they had none in Syria. But the man called Shaby had worked for several years in Europe as a diplomat.

The Syrian officer wanted to rush out and shoot the man, or at least arrest him. But Karl had different plans for Shaby, one of which he'd been working on from the moment he boarded his flight in Paris.

Karl wanted to know if Shaby's boss was back yet from his trip.

"I can check that by phone in a minute."

"Do," said Karl, checking a set of photographs which he then slipped into a heavy envelope.

"He'll be back in a couple of days," the Syrian said, after hanging up.

"Here," Karl handed the officer the envelope. "Have these delivered to Shaby's office with the instructions that he is to lock them in the safe until his boss returns. I want him to think they are photos of a Mossad mole meeting with his operator."

The Syrian's eyes narrowed. "Are they?" he asked.

"Of course not, but I want him to think that."

The Syrian was smiling. "I'll see to it right away, sir."

"Wait, there's more. I want you to arrange for Shaby to be sent to Holland for several months. He is to leave in one week, but he must know about it today, before the photos are delivered. Can this be done without arousing his suspicions?"

"Shaby has been sent on such missions before, so it will seem quite normal to him. It will be done, sir."

Karl saw no reason to explain to his Syrian friend that his source in the Mossad had informed him that part of their procedure was for an agent to communicate on a specific day of the week. Karl was hopeful that Shaby would be sending his message that very day.

Karl left the command building and drove for some time around the city. At about 1730, assuming Shaby to be on his way home, Karl parked his black Mercedes one block from the man's apartment building and slowly walked by it. He saw a car like Shaby's enter the parking deck beneath the building. Karl verified that the license number was indeed Shaby's, though he didn't stop or change his pace as he approached the entrance to the building. Still, he managed to get a good look at the man.

From the way the fat little man was moving, Karl knew he was tense and clearly had something on his mind. He was certainly in a rush.

Karl walked past without looking back. It wasn't until he passed a parked white U.N. jeep that he turned around and stared at the building. By then Shaby was already inside.

Things did hit a snag there for a time, he thought, but now everything was back on track — and maybe even running smoother than before.

# 13

**KFAR-SIRKIN**
**SEPTEMBER 13**
**1900 HOURS**

WITH HIS feet propped on the desk in his office, Natan was watching a television commentary speculating on the U.S. secretary of state's chances of pushing forward a new stage in the Middle East peace initiative. A couple of so-called experts were trying to decode bits of information as they built a house of cards on a constantly shaking table. There was a tap on his door. "Come on in," he called out.

Number Five entered without even glancing at the screen. Natan just nodded at him and said, "What a charade! They don't care if they're right, they just want to sound clever and besides . . ."

"Number One wants to speak to you," Number Five said. "Do you want to come up, or shall I transfer the call here?"

Natan turned the TV off with the remote and got to his feet. Looking straight at Number Five, he demanded, "What the hell's going on? You came all the way down here to ask me?"

"It's just that Number One wanted to give you time. You know, after that thing with Number Nine." The big man was clearly embarrassed.

"I'll talk to him from the loft." The words were out before Natan realized what had happened. These people who were so used to

working as a self-contained team had no idea who he really was or how far they could rely on him. To Number One, after his recent outburst, Natan was a loose cannon. He could cause damage at any moment.

"No," Natan sat down again. "Transfer the call to me here." He knew Number One would be talking on a more private line, and he would at least extend him the same courtesy. "I'll be waiting."

Several minutes later, the phone rang. Natan promptly pressed the speaker button. "Go ahead Number One. What's up?"

"We have a situation that I think you'll want to make use of."

"What sort of situation?"

"Nazir wants to take the bait for a weekend on one of the Greek islands."

"I thought he got what he wanted right there in the apartment."

"Well, not quite. She told him it was that time of the month, so she couldn't do anything, but by the weekend she'd be willing. Except that she'd already arranged with some of her girlfriends to take a trip to several of the islands. Although she'd love to have a good time with him," Number One started to laugh at this, "she actually said, 'I have to see the islands. I mean, what you've got is probably very nice, but those I can get back home in the States anytime I want. But Greek islands, man, those we don't have.'"

Natan started to laugh as it dawned on him that nothing — or almost nothing — had happened between Number Nine and Nazir. He realized now that what he'd felt wasn't jealousy, it was just that he'd worked with the girl briefly and he liked her. Of course, she was attractive too, but he felt more protective toward her than anything and he hated the thought of her being soiled by that jerk.

"So, now what do you have in mind?" Natan asked.

"I'd like to run something by you. We can get a team onto the island, then get Nine to take him for a short sailboat ride, and we'll grab him."

"It could work, but first we need the destination. When do you think we'll have that?"

"It's hard to say, but we'll get Number Nine working on it today. Talk to you later," and he hung up. Number Five came back at that point, and handed Natan a manila envelope.

"This just arrived by courier," he said.

The envelope, marked top secret, contained a series of personnel papers, each with a photo attached to the upper left corner and a small note referring to the present status of the person in question. There were about twenty subjects.

Natan read the cover letter that Mousa had sent with the documents. It explained that the files were of Stasi officers who could be the one Foul Play was referring to, based on the reference points Natan had asked for. From the notes attached, he saw that most were accounted for; either they were being shipped back to Germany from their hiding places in Russia, now that the former Soviet Union wanted a good relationship with Germany, or they were known to be working for the Chinese, who welcomed them with open arms as an asset they'd never believed they could obtain.

The most likely candidate seemed to have been an officer by the name of Karl Reinhart. In the Stasi, he had been head of the C/5 section that dealt with terrorists. However, he had committed suicide. A photo of the body was attached to his file.

It was hard to tell that the man was dead from the expression on his face; he seemed contentedly asleep. But there was no doubt it was the face in the file. Still, something about Karl's photo bothered Natan. He spread out all the files on the table so that he could study all the photos at the same time. He stood up at his desk and looked them over, comparing them.

"Come over here," he said to Number Five, who was arranging some documents on a long credenza by the window. "What do you see?" He pointed to the photos on the desk.

"A bunch of photos."

"Right, but is there something different about any of them?"

Number Five studied them more closely, then he pointed at Karl's photo. "He looks older than the rest of them."

"Exactly," Natan was excited. "That's right, the man is older." Smiling to himself, Natan sat down. "Thanks, Five, that will be all."

Number Five left the room looking puzzled. Natan went on examining the photos. All of the photos except Karl's had been taken in the same place: they all had the same background. His was different. And there was the age. All the other photos were of younger men, taken when they joined the Stasi. But Karl's photo was recent; his face looked much the same in the postmortem shot. Why would someone bother to update a photo in a personnel file — and why only his? Could it be that Karl was not dead at all, that the dead man in the photo was not Karl? Natan placed the other files in his drawer and went on staring at Karl's. He felt a rush of adrenalin, like a hunter spotting his prey. Or was it the prey suddenly recognizing the hunter?

Minutes later, Mousa called, just as Number Five came in with a second envelope containing a copy of a new communiqué from Foul Play, who was telling them to expect him shortly. He was to leave soon for Holland on official Syrian business, and he had a grand piece of information for Natan.

"So, did you get the copy?" asked Mousa, halfway through their conversation.

"Just now," Natan answered. "Let me read it." There was a short pause, then he went on, "The man has a photo of the mole. I don't believe it. That will be the best piece of information he's brought us yet."

"I agree," said Mousa, "and yet somehow it doesn't sound right. I don't know . . . . Tell me, do you think there's a chance he could have been turned by the Syrians?"

"There is always that chance. We might know more when we get the video," Natan said.

"I hope so," Mousa said. "I just have a bad feeling about this. Maybe it's the fact that he has something I want more than anything else just now. You know Avraham would give his left testicle for that photo."

"I'm sure he would, although I don't know if there would be many takers."

Mousa was not amused. "One more thing. In addition to this new communiqué, unit eight two hundred intercepted a coded fax to the Syrian embassy in Holland informing them of the arrival of a replacement for a member of the embassy who is ill. The man they're talking about is your boy; since we have his name flagged, they brought a copy of the fax in to me. So he'll be there on the twenty-sixth. I hope you'll have bagged the guy in Greece by then."

"Wait a minute! If we're going to get this photo of the mole anyway, why risk an operation with the Fox? We could keep on him and see what comes out. I don't think we should grab him now."

"Avraham wants to know more about the plans these terrorists have, so I guess we'll be bringing him in too. Where are you on that now?"

"We're waiting for him to make some final plans. Then we'll be sure."

"Don't over-complicate the operation. What we want is to get him to talk, then to dispose of him."

# 14

**KFAR-SIRKIN**
**SEPTEMBER 16**
**0900 HOURS**

As NATAN entered the green room in the compound, Number Five's voice greeted him on the intercom. "Natan urgently to the loft. Natan to the loft."

He headed for the stairs, halfway up calling, "What? What is it?"

"Number One wants you."

"Put him on."

Number Five pressed a button on the intercom and said, "Go ahead, Natan's here."

"You wanted a timetable," Number One said. "Here it is. They're going to the island of Zakynthos. It's a little out of the way, but there is a flight from Athens. It's not a heavy tourist location like Mykonos, though. He wants to leave the day after tomorrow, in the evening."

"What about Number Nine?"

"She doesn't know yet. I just heard it on the listening device now, as he told Halim. By the way, Nine is using the name 'Helen' now."

"Where is she, anyway?"

"Back at the hotel. I'm not telling her anything. That way, when he does, she'll react naturally."

"Sounds good to me."

"The guy is scared shitless about traveling. He thinks we're constantly on his tail. You have to listen to him. He really is scared."

"You know what they say. 'On the thief's head the hat is burning.' The guy may have good reason to be scared. Anyway, get his flight number and as much information as you can about his destination."

"Okay. Is that it?"

"Yes."

"Talk to you later." Number One rang off.

Natan was expecting Yegal, a Shaback officer and old personal friend from the army. They had done their officers' training together. Although Yegal was with the paratroopers and Natan from naval commandos, they both had to go through the infantry course, designed for all officers in the Israeli Defense Force. Even now, if Natan needed someone from the Shaback whom he could trust to do something out of the ordinary for him, he always called on Yegal. This particular assignment was even more delicate than usual, and so he could not fill Yegal in on the big picture.

When Number Five came to inform him that Yegal was waiting, Natan followed him into a small, well-furnished room. The visitor was let in through a separate door, since he did not have clearance to enter the facility, except for this "hosting" room. After a brief exchange of greetings, Natan got to the point. "Yegal, I need to break a man in about seven hours, and know for sure that he's telling me the truth. Can you do it?"

"Yes. I could probably do it in less if necessary, but there are always those people who take longer. It's faster with chemicals, though."

"No. We'll be returning him to his place of origin, where he'll be the victim of a fatal accident. There will probably be an autopsy and the time that passes between his questioning and the discovery of the body may not be enough for chemicals to clear. So we can't have any detectable traces or any signs of beating, torture . . . whatever."

"So, what are you telling me? You want me to sweet talk the guy? I'll be lucky to get *anything* out of him, even if he's a soft target. And suppose he turns out to be a martyr? Then, there would be nothing we could do. I mean, if I can't beat him, cut him, give him electric shocks, hold him under water or drug him, how the hell do you expect me to do it? Seven hours isn't long enough to drive him crazy, or scare him to death so he'll shit his pants. You're asking a hell of a lot, Natan!"

Yegal was clearly frustrated, but he knew Natan, and he knew that he would somehow get his way.

"Look," Natan said, "that's the way things are, and we're going to have to come up with something pretty fast because as far as I can tell, we'll have him sometime during the night of the eighteenth and take him back during the afternoon of the nineteenth."

"No way. I can't do it without hurting him," Yegal asserted.

"Wait a minute," Natan said, "I think I have an idea, Yegal." He stood up and started to pace the small room, mumbling something to himself as he dragged on a cigarette. Suddenly he turned to Yegal. "Sorry, my friend, but I have to go now."

"What about the help you wanted? You think you can handle this on your own?" Yegal sounded hopeful.

"Certainly not. You're not getting off so easy. I want you back here tomorrow at noon with some of your people. You'll be going on a trip."

After Yegal left, Natan reached Mousa on the phone. "We need to talk," he said, with determination in his voice that had been missing lately. Natan was taking charge. He had sat back as an expert observer up to this point, even though he realized things needed to be set up. But now it was time to move. Mousa caught the change of tone.

"What's up?"

"I have an idea for bringing the man in, but I'll need more people."

"I don't think Amir can spare any more," Mousa said.

"I need stand-ins. I don't need Amir's people. You can get me secretaries and clerks from some of the stations in Europe if necessary. I need bodies."

"This I have to hear. And if it makes sense, you'll have whatever you need. I'll be there in a couple of hours."

# 15

**ATHENS**
**SEPTEMBER 18**
**1500 HOURS**

HALIM DROVE Helen and Nazir to the west terminal at Hellinikon Airport. Nazir insisted they go by rented car, not cab. Though he didn't understand Nazir's reasoning, Halim was not about to question him.

Nazir had handed the money over as promised, and his instructions regarding the activities of the group, once they were all in Greece, were very clear. After Halim parked the car, he got out to help Nazir and Helen with their luggage. Until today, Halim had only heard about this woman, but when he'd seen her, he'd understood what Nazir had been talking about. She was absolutely gorgeous.

Their flight was to leave in less than thirty minutes. Most of their fellow passengers were in transit from Helsinki, on an organized island tour. As they approached security, Nazir turned to Halim. "My friend," he said in English, too aware that hearing Arabic made non-Arabs feel uncomfortable in an airport, "there's no reason for you to wait any longer. Just go and make sure everything is in order. I'll call you tonight from the hotel just to be sure."

"Well," said Helen, pouting a little, "I'm not so sure you'll be in the mood to make phone calls tonight, sweetie. Remember, you promised to show me what you could do in the . . . you know." She smiled at him fondly.

"Yes my love," he took her arm, then turned to Halim. "If I don't call right away," he winked, "don't worry."

Once they'd passed security, Nazir headed directly for the departure gate. He wanted to spend as little time as possible on view in a large terminal, since he was not unknown to certain secret services. He tried not to appear nervous as they stood near the gate, waiting to board. At 1530 the door opened and pre-boarding was announced. A steward ushered a woman in a wheelchair and her husband to the ramp leading out to the plane, then the rest of the passengers were allowed aboard. Soon they were all fastening their seat belts.

"I hate flying," Nazir confided in a low voice to Helen.

"You don't look as if you'd be afraid of anything," she told him.

"I didn't say I was afraid, only that I hate flying," Nazir replied.

As soon as they were airborne and the no smoking sign switched off, Nazir lit up. A few minutes later, he headed for the washroom at the back of the small turboprop. On his way, he briefly scanned the other passengers, most of whom were gazing out at the marvels of the Aegean.

Just before he reached the rear of the plane, he noticed three passengers who worried him slightly. It was probably nothing, he thought, but the three unshaven Arab-speaking men wearing jeans and T-shirts with Arabic slogans had not boarded at Athens. They must have stayed on board from a previous stop, he reasoned. But he still didn't like their presence. He could sense that they were trouble. He had to walk sideways to pass through the narrow aisle, and as he returned to his seat, he was about to light his second cigarette when all hell broke loose. There was screaming from the back of the plane, as well as the front. Nazir, who could see the fear in Helen's eyes, at first assumed the plane had a mechanical problem. Were they all about to plummet into the water?

He raised his head to try and see beyond the people who were now crowding the narrow aisle. It was then he saw one of the three he'd noticed at the back standing in the middle of the aisle, holding a large pistol above his head to make sure everyone could see it. The man was shouting something, but Nazir couldn't make out what above the noise of the other passengers. Then came a loud voice over the intercom, ordering everyone back to their seats. It was the third man. He must have moved up front when Nazir was in the washroom.

He was speaking in broken English. "Everyone sit down now. No play games. If you no listen, you dead for sure. Sit down! Now!" His message seemed to get through. There were terrified whimpers here and there.

The man went on, "We are the brothers of the revolution and we want not harm you people. We want our brothers free and to have money to put fuel into revolution of the Palestinian people." There was silence in the plane, as all began to realize they were being hijacked.

"What are we going to do?" whispered Helen, her voice trembling.

"Nothing. We are going to do nothing. Just wait and pray," Nazir hissed.

The other two men were now slowly walking down the aisle from the back, pointing their weapons at different people. The third man spoke again. "You give passports to my men. Do now!" he shouted. Hands clutching passports were seen almost immediately, and the two accomplices began collecting them. When the leader had all the passports, he stuck his gun into his belt. "Any Israeli?" he asked.

There was no reply.

Now the cockpit door was open. The leader was holding a string attached to something strapped to the pilot. He raised his hand to show the string. "If someone decide hit me, touch me, I fall to ground. This pull," he stared at the string, "pin from grenade. All cockpit go. Please, if someone want try, please." His smile was dead cold.

Next, he brought a microphone on a lead to the cockpit door. He shouted into the cockpit, "Is this on a channel Israeli can hear?" There was a response from the cockpit that Nazir couldn't hear, then the leader went on, shouting into the mike, "Israeli scum, can you hear me? This is brothers of the revolution. Come in."

There was nothing.

He repeated the call, and after several attempts, decided to speak Arabic. "We have a plane. We will kill passengers if you don't free our brothers." Then he went on to read a list of about twenty names.

"Who are you?" came a question from the ground.

"This is my location," he said. "You can see me on the radar. I will have plane turn to south in one minute you see where I am." He shouted something to the pilot, and seconds later, the plane started to tilt. At that, the man almost lost his footing, causing everyone in the plane to miss a heartbeat.

"Go to hell!" came the reply. "We don't deal with terrorist scum."

The leader was visibly furious, as he turned to the passengers and spoke again in English. "The names I read go to back! Now!" He read out six names, flinging down each passport as he did so. Nazir's name was fifth.

"Don't go. Just sit quietly," said Helen, holding onto his hand.

"They'll only come for me. It's better if I go," he said.

Once at the back, he was standing on one side of the washroom while the four ahead of him were on the other with the two hijackers. He couldn't see them, but was trying to figure out what the terrorists had in mind. The leader was speaking Arabic again to the ground controller.

"I send you a present from heaven every three minutes," he said, "starting three minutes from now. I not call you again, when you want me stop unloading the passengers, you call me." Then he said by intercom to the men in back, still in Arabic, "Start sending them down."

Nazir felt faint. He could feel the blood rush to his head and his knees begin to buckle. He was probably the only passenger who understood Arabic, and knew what they were up to.

Without warning, one of the hijackers flung the cabin door open, and as the plane began to vibrate, several passengers started screaming again. This time, it was harder for the leader to quiet them down. Then all the cabin lights went out and several overhead bins jettisoned luggage onto the terrified passengers. There was shouting from the back, then screaming, followed by a horrendous shriek. Nazir peered around just as the first passenger was thrown out of the plane's rear door. The man had tried in vain to hold on to the fuselage but one hijacker kicked him in the shin and he fell from sight. The terrorist then turned to the second passenger, pointing the gun at his head.

"No problems, no kicks," he shouted grimly over the howling wind. He was looking at his watch. "The next one go in two minutes," he said.

Nazir realized his time was running out. He was shaking and sweating, he wanted to vomit, and he tried not to defecate in his pants. He attempted to open the washroom door, thinking for a brief moment that he could hide, but the door was locked. In desperation he struck it repeatedly with his fist. The nearest hijacker heard him.

Walking over to Nazir, the man placed the muzzle of his small automatic at his temple. "What you do?" he shouted. "You go out this way." He indicated the open door, laughing as he did so.

"I'm a Palestinian like you!" Nazir screamed in Arabic. "I'm a fighter just like you, for the freedom of our land!"

"You," shouted the hijacker, "are going to be *part* of this land in a minute, so shut up, you pig!"

"Now!" shouted the hijacker with the watch to the one by the open door, signaling him to throw out the next in line. That passenger had been hit over the head and was lying face down by the open door.

"Listen to me!" screamed Nazir at the top of his lungs. "Listen, please! We're in the midst of . . ." With that, he fell to his knees, holding onto the man's pants. The passenger next to the open door was crying, begging for mercy as he realized what his fate would be.

Now the hijackers were lining up more passengers behind Nazir. Nazir was crying. He couldn't hold himself any longer and defecated in his pants, trembling uncontrollably as the next passenger was tipped out the door.

His very fear brought Nazir to his feet, and he pushed himself between the people behind him, running for the cockpit. Passengers screamed as he struggled by. He had almost reached the leader when the second terrorist, who was right behind him, grabbed him by the collar and pushed him to the floor at the leader's feet. Nazir managed to catch his breath as, staring up at the man, he started to beg for his life.

"Why should I believe you?" asked the hijacker in a soft voice, while Nazir tried to collect his wits. The shock of the relative silence in this section of the plane had a numbing effect. "How do I know you're not one of those . . . traitors who wants to sell us out for peace with the Zionist pigs?"

Nazir knew this was his only chance to save his life. The man clearly wanted to believe him, but he needed proof. He would have demanded the same, had the roles been reversed. "I'm part of an operation starting at this very minute," Nazir babbled. "I will tell you everything, everything, you can verify it. Please, please . . ."

The man nodded that he should go ahead, and Nazir spoke nonstop for at least fifteen minutes, laying out the entire operation and explaining what had been done up to that point. The victims of this operation were to be the traitors that the leader had been talking about: Nazir's terrorist group had as its target the Palestinian moderates at a crucial new round in the peace talks.

Staring into the man's face at the end of it, Nazir sought a glimmer of belief. He knew that his being a genuine Palestinian freedom fighter might not carry all that much weight with another faction, but still he prayed that it would.

Suddenly, there was a call over the radio, apparently from the tower of Ben-Gurion Airport in Israel, "Stop killing the passengers. Let's deal. Repeat. We will deal."

The leader signaled to his men to stop the executions and close the door. He then bent over Nazir. "And you, my friend," he said, helping him get up, "you go to the washroom and clean yourself up. I can't stand your smell."

Once Nazir was safely in the washroom, the third hijacker signaled the leader, who stepped into the cockpit. He turned to the man in the copilot's seat and said, "Well, Natan, I told you if he shit in his pants, he'd talk. Did you get everything you wanted?" Yegal raised an eyebrow quizzically.

"From the little that your man has translated so far, I think we got more than we could have hoped for," Natan told his co-conspirator.

"Like I told you," said Yegal, "there's nothing like real fear."

"Where is he now?"

"In the washroom. He'll be out in a minute and then we'll get him into a straitjacket so he doesn't hurt himself."

"Tell me something," said Natan. "How did you get this plane painted so fast?"

"I didn't. It was your friend Mousa. He chartered it from Olympic, I guess. We nearly had a snag, you know, when we came in to land. My friend over at Greek security was late coming on duty, and we almost had to do the gate switch ourselves."

Natan nodded, lighting a cigarette. "When you have Nazir in the jacket, let me know. I want to go out there and thank all the people who gave a hand in their first, and presumably last, active mission for the Mossad."

"Who are they?" asked Yegal.

"They're secretaries and office workers from several stations in Europe. They volunteered for this at incredibly short notice."

"Well, whatever they are, they were great."

"And who were the guys you threw out?" asked Natan.

"Wasn't that beautiful?" said Yegal. "They were some of my buddies from the paratroopers. They were set up with special hidden parachutes, like stuntmen use in the movies. You should have seen them. They were great!"

"By the way, Yegal, did you get anything out of him about a girl who was supposed to be coming out of Lebanon to help him coordinate and act as a go-between?"

"Yes, but what did you want to know?"

"I need the password that's to be used when picking her up."

"I'll see what I can do," said Yegal, heading for the washroom.

With all of the information in hand and a dumbfounded Nazir in a straitjacket in the back of a van, they moved swiftly from the military air base adjacent to the Ben-Gurion Airport to the Kidon compound. Once inside, Natan confronted Nazir for the first time. Without being a psychologist, Natan saw that the man had had a total breakdown.

He stank, having soiled his pants again when he realized what had happened. Now his eyes were glazed, his expression that of a man so fascinated by some horrifying scene that he cannot even blink. There was no point in trying to interrogate him further under the circumstances, and there was little need for it in any case. The sooner they could take him to his island destination, the better it would be. One of the combatants had registered there under Nazir's name, having been made to look very much like him. He had arrived with the real flight which had been diverted to another gate at the Athens Airport by Yegal's contact.

Once Nazir was taken to the island, he would have a diving accident. His body would be found by a tourist who would notify the police. At that point, Helen would place a call to Halim, telling him that Nazir was dead and she didn't know what to do. She'd ask him to come to the island or make arrangements to look after his friend's body. After she had placed the call, she'd be gone, and out of the picture.

Nazir was photographed, and they took his fingerprints. Yegal had one more crack at him, even knowing that all the information was in. He wanted to see if they could close some holes they had in other investigations, but nothing worked. Nazir's state of shock was just too great. He wouldn't talk at all. It was time for him to go and finish his vacation.

Natan was happy this particular part of the operation was over, although it hadn't uncovered the mole. The ball was back in Mousa's court. As far as he could see, it meant they would wait to see what Foul Play had in store for them and that would be the end of his involvement. He'd be glad to get back to what he was best at: working one on one, recruiting agents.

He still had more than two weeks of vacation left this year, too. Now that they had the total picture, Natan hoped he could get away. His last task was to make it all into a comprehensive report for Mousa, and he had no intention of delaying that.

# 16

**MOSSAD HEADQUARTERS**
**SEPTEMBER 18**
**2100 HOURS**

NATAN HAD almost finished writing his report when Mousa came into the library where he was working. "When you're done, bring the report over to the commanders' lounge on the fifth floor. I want to talk to you."

"Okay," Natan said. It had taken him longer than expected because of several last-minute details concerning Nazir's demise.

Several wrinkles had had to be ironed out of the original plan. At the eleventh hour, someone pointed out that it was just not logical for a novice diver like Nazir — who had mentioned in conversation with Halim that he'd be attempting it for the first time — to go out night diving. That had been the original scenario for the "accident," but it would make no sense, even to the least suspicious person. Number Nine — Helen — had therefore had to activate a backup plan.

She was to call Halim from the hotel where she'd already arrived and give him a message, ostensibly from Nazir, whose voice would be heard in the background. The voice had been taken off the tapes from the Piraeus apartment. Nazir was going scuba diving in the morning, she'd tell Halim, and he'd call him after that. So Nazir, who was still in the Kidon compound, was spared for several hours.

He'd be drowned in a saltwater tank there sometime in the early morning, wearing his full scuba diving gear. Its "malfunction" would be fairly easy to detect. An amphibious plane was then to transport Nazir's body, contained in a plastic bag filled with seawater, to the island. The body would be released into the water offshore to be found by a tourist in a rented fishing boat.

In fact, Number One fully intended to do some fishing while playing the tourist.

Natan and Mousa were alone in the dimly lit, club-like lounge. It was a favorite place of department heads and territory chiefs to sit and talk without the fear of being overheard by strangers, as it had the relaxing atmosphere of an exclusive clubhouse or hotel lounge. Soft music played in the background and, as he entered, Natan tried for a moment to place the tune, but couldn't.

Mousa greeted him with a big smile, indicating a comfortable-looking sofa. Natan sank into it, then bent forward and placed the folder containing his report on the table in front of him. Mousa went over to the bar, returning with two drinks. "You like tequila, right?"

"Right."

"So, it's one down and one to go."

"One to go?"

"The meeting with Foul Play for the information about the mole. After all, we didn't get anything about that from the Fox, did we?"

"No, we didn't." Natan sighed inwardly. "After what we've had going on for the last few days, that meeting seems so far away. Well, there's not much we can do until he's out of Syria. And once he is, there will be little fanfare. I mean, it's not like this last operation. It's a simple meeting. Or should I say that if the financing has been approved, it's a simple meeting. Has it?"

"Has what?" asked Mousa, trying to look innocent.

"Has the financing that Foul Play asked for been approved?"

"Yeah, yeah, no problem. Just get the photos he has with him. I'm going to send a passive defense team with you, just to secure the meeting."

"I don't see why you need to do that. After all, he's not a 'dangerous' agent. I'm sure I can handle him."

"It's not you I'm worried about. It's the photos. Don't you realize that these photos he's bringing are about the most important information we've received from the day the Mossad began? We've never had a mole before, have we?"

"No. Yes . . . look, you do whatever you want," Natan was tired. "But I don't want any team stuck up my ass. If they want to secure the meeting, that's fine with me, but tell them to keep away from me and from my agent. I don't want some asshole scaring him off."

"Don't worry, I'll send Dov. He'll run the protection. You two worked together before, didn't you? I mean, I always thought you were friends?"

"Yes, we are, and I'm sure he'll be great. But I want you to tell him that it's my agent and I call the shots. And I want it to come from you, so you tell him in my presence before we go. Okay?"

"You've got yourself a deal. Now, here's one to the great job you just did." Mousa raised his glass above his head, then tapped it to Natan's. "God, it was beautiful," he said. "That's one they'll study in the academy for years to come. As for holding the man here ready for execution like a live fish in a restaurant, that is sheer genius."

Mousa knew he was getting to Natan with this talk. The fact that a man was about to be killed in cold blood because of a technical decision made by Natan was something that would haunt him for a long time.

"Who will handle the counter-operation?" asked Natan, wanting to change the subject. He knocked back the shot of tequila in one fast gulp.

"It's not going to be that way," replied Mousa. "The chief wants us to let it be."

"What are you talking about? Let what be?" Natan nearly choked on his drink at that.

"Just the way you heard it. You have to admit it does make sense," Mousa said blandly.

"I don't seem . . ." Natan was still trying to clear his throat. "I don't seem to get the drift of what you're saying."

"Well, look at it this way. We're really getting someone else to do our dirty work this time — and on top of that, they'll take the blame. What could be better than that? I can't remember anything that good — except maybe the Iran-Iraq war — can you?"

"What on earth are you talking about? Do your ears hear what your mouth is saying? They want to kill the Palestinian moderates. That will put an end to any chance for peace in the region. The moderates are the only ones who can break the deadlock."

"Exactly. And what the hell do we have to gain from peace? I mean, we'd have to give up land, probably uproot settlements, lose strategic depth. Take a cut in the security and general military budgets. The Americans would probably cut back on aid — after all, we wouldn't be at war. The Jewish diaspora would feel less obligated to help. And after we'd gone through all that, they'd wait for the opportunity and just chuck us into the sea. The way I see it, we're better off the way things are at the moment . . ."

"What about a directive? I mean, Prime Minister Rabin will never sanction this."

"Rabin is old. He's looking for peace because he wants to suck up to the Americans. Besides, we need approval to do things. No one needs approval *not* to do anything, which is exactly what we are going to do, if you see what I mean. This will be just perfect."

The man Natan thought he knew had turned out to be someone completely different. He'd expected many odd things from Mousa over the years, and Mousa had usually delivered. But this was different. After trying for several minutes to digest it, Natan realized that although he had worked with Mousa for many years, he'd never actually sat down with the man and talked politics. Now, there was clearly no point in arguing.

"What if they decide to take out someone else, let's say some of our people? After all, we have delegations too."

"We're not just going to let them do whatever they want," Mousa said, smiling as if to comfort Natan. "We'll monitor them and make sure they do only what they're supposed to do. I mean, if they get some Americans along the way, who cares? It would make them even more unpopular. Who are we to stop them? But if they decide to pull a fast one on us, we'll be ready and we'll get them where it hurts." Mousa sipped from his drink. "It wouldn't be such a bad thing if they did get the Americans, after all. I think it's about time someone showed those arrogant bastards, who *think* they understand the Middle East, from where the fish pisses."

Natan, still coughing, got up from the deep sofa. So, he thought, the decision had been made and it was even out of Mousa's hands. There was no point in going on. "Well, I hate to choke and run," he said with a cheerfulness he did not feel, "but I'm still looking for someone to warm up my bed." He winked at Mousa.

"Go ahead, you deserve it." Mousa seemed happy to be chummy with Natan again. "By the way, since Foul Play's coming out next week, what have you got planned until then?"

"You know me better than that," Natan said. "Ever since I joined the Mossad, I don't make plans and I don't buy green bananas."

They both laughed.

As Natan was leaving, he said, "I've been thinking that I might just use a few days of my vacation — which I'm supposedly on now — and visit my family in New York." He pointed to the file on the table. "Don't leave that here, by the way. We haven't seen the face of the mole yet."

"When I do," Mousa growled, "he won't have one."

Up to now Natan had been able to rationalize just about everything that happend in the Mossad. The killings, the brutality — he justified everything as being necessary for the continual existence of the state. The rebirth — the so-called "old new land" that Zionism talked about. But this was different. This was like using a sledgehammer to kill a fly on your best friend's head.

He had always known that, in the Mossad, he was only cannon fodder. But as long as he could accept the cause, he could accept that fate. It was simple. Israel wanted peace and the Arabs didn't, therefore Israelis were justified in continuing to be warriors until such a time as there could be peace. Natan was as committed to this as the next person — *more* committed than many — and would shoulder the burden accordingly for as long as it took. But the plan Mousa had revealed was against everything Natan believed in. The audacity of these people! To build a barrier on the road to peace! That was sickminded. Natan could feel the rage building in him. He was ready to hand in his resignation. He would attach a letter, sending off a copy to the prime minister. He would come clean. He knew that if he didn't do that, he would never be able to face himself.

Halfway through the night, Natan was still seated at his kitchen table trying to word the letter so as to give it the most impact. He read it over yet again and at that moment, realized there was no point whatsoever in doing what he was about to do. The first thing his superiors would do would be to confiscate the letter and lock him up until this whole thing was over. Then and only then, would they let him out and discharge him from the service with an explanation that would discredit him forever. That way, they would shut him up. No. Leaving was not the answer.

Through the rage and fury, a decision had crystalized in his mind. It brought with it a calmness. He was going to take them all on. There was no going back for him. Natan would stop them if he had to do it with his bare hands — and there was an even chance he might have to do just that. If reason told him his efforts might be futile, he was still going to try. It was very clear to Natan that from this moment on, he'd be working both sides of a very high and dangerous fence. Falling off on either side would be fatal. But the most damning prospect he faced was working alone, without the Mossad support system.

Natan knew he would have to come up with a plan that would enable him to operate on the outside while still using the system on the inside. It was the only way, and as a theory, it sounded promising. But at this moment, he had no idea how to pull it off. He was going to plan this as if he had the Mossad behind him and then improvise. First, he would have to get someone inside that terrorist group in Greece. Someone the terrorists would trust, but who would not draw the attention of the Kidon team monitoring them. That in itself seemed miles beyond his reach. And it would almost inevitably mean trusting people he knew very little about and hoping for the best.

His time was limited. He wanted to get started before his planned meeting with Foul Play. He must move immediately, in order to succeed. First thing in the morning he had to take a lie detector test. That way he would be in the clear, since who could say if he would be able to pass one later.

### BEN-GURION AIRPORT, ISRAEL
### SEPTEMBER 19
### 1100 HOURS

EVEN BEFORE Natan had taken the first step in what he considered a rescue mission, he had already broken Mossad regulations. On this trip to New York, he had two sets of forged ID concealed in his attaché case. That act alone was highly irregular, to say the least.

He had spirited them out of his activity file in the Mossad's basement vault, where they were held for future use, having been prepared for an operation that was canceled and so, never used.

A clerk at the Al department drove Natan to the airport and before they entered the terminal, Natan handed over all his Israeli documentation, including his security pass and several ID tags, as well as his Beretta .22 pistol. All of that was placed in a plastic bag which the clerk sealed, both of them signing its paper flap. Natan would retrieve it from the Al safe once he was back in the country.

He was booked on an early El Al flight to Montreal's Mirabel Airport, leaving Canada shortly thereafter from Dorval Airport on an Air Canada flight to New York. That was Mossad procedure for any personnel operating in the United States. To enter direct from Israel was regarded as dangerous, operationally.

Although he was on a so-called private trip, Natan decided to follow the normal routine. His final destination was Washington, D.C. — something he had neglected to include on the travel plan he had handed in before he left. In Washington he would meet Syd Cooper. It would be good to see him again. It had been a while.

# 17

**WASHINGTON, D.C.**
**SEPTEMBER 20**
**1045 HOURS**

NATAN CHOSE the Sheraton Washington as a meeting place with his friend after arriving on the shuttle from La Guardia. Natan had stayed overnight at another hotel just across the street from it, the Omni Shoreham. Both were large hotels, favored by conventions, and somewhat discreetly located in parkland, well away from the hub of the nation's capital and the watering holes of its denizens.

This morning, Natan felt refreshed, having slept the sleep of the dead after his long journey. The day was sunny and warm, as he strolled the short distance to the Sheraton, enjoying a smoke. Casually dressed, he went to wait in the crowded lobby where young guests, many clearly heading for the tennis courts, jostled about in their varied gear. He had an excellent vantage point for watching taxis pull in.

At 1100 sharp, Syd stepped out of a cab. The man is like a Swiss watch, thought Natan. He was one man for whom Natan had a lot of respect, even if they didn't always see eye to eye. Certainly, Syd presented subjects to his readers the way they were and let them draw their own conclusions. Unlike so many journalists, he would not twist the facts to make a point or serve his own agenda. Once

Natan was sure that Syd had not been followed, he made his way over to him.

"Well," Syd said, smiling and clasping Natan's hand firmly, "Hello my boy. How's the world treating my pioneer?" Of average height and stocky build, Syd was in his early sixties. His tanned face was emphasized by his silver hair.

"The same way I treat the world, I guess," said Natan, giving the answer he always did to the question Syd always seemed to ask.

"So, what now?" Syd never had much time.

"Patience, my friend," Natan said. "Let's grab something to eat and I'll fill you in. You should learn to relax."

"Life's too short to relax. It's not like you can do it again if time runs out, you know. Or are you on to something I haven't heard of?"

"No." Natan was smiling. Syd had a solid quality about him that always made people feel good, secure. They went past the lobby area and over to the hotel's Courtyard Cafe. Crowded with delegates from a computer software convention, the restaurant's noise level would certainly drown their conversation. Natan actually had to lean forward as he spoke, so that Syd could hear him.

After they'd both ordered large burgers with everything, and a beer each, Natan began.

"Syd, I need your help," he said. "There's no one else I can turn to for this."

"So . . . what is it? You know I'll help if I can."

"First, you have to realize that you won't be able to use any of this in your column ever. You have contacts who can help me, and at this moment, that's what I need from you."

"Does this translate into lines of type?"

"You'll get that. In fact, I have a great story for you, whether you help me or not. But I must have your word that you won't use what we're about to discuss."

"Do I have a choice?"

"Of course. You can say 'no', and I'll give you something you can use, we won't talk about the other thing, and maybe I'll see you in another couple of years."

"This thing you don't want me to use. Could I get it on my own or find out about it from any other source?"

"Absolutely not. I promise you."

"Well, then," Syd smiled. "I can promise you that I won't use it."

"Great. I need you to connect me with a Palestinian whom you trust, who'd be willing to take a risk for the sake of his people."

"What are you talking about? How would I have such a contact? I'm just an old-time newspaper man, remember?"

"Syd, cut the spiel. I happen to know you have contacts. There's no way you could have written those features about the war in Lebanon from your desk in downtown Washington. And I know for a fact that you weren't in Lebanon at the time, so give me a break!"

"How do you know I didn't get my information from your people?"

"Because you're on the black list there, and no one would talk to you. Look, I need a favor, and I don't have time to play games. Will you help me or not, Syd?"

"What the hell's the matter with you? Not having time happens to be my line. Let's say I do put you in touch with someone," he lowered his voice even more, "how do I know he won't end up in a dungeon in Israel telling stories to Mousa Sadder, Sheik Obaid and old Vanunu?"

"Because," Natan shot back, "what I'm doing is outside the framework of my organization. Even the simple fact that we are meeting could get me in deeper shit than you can imagine. This is not some cheap trick to get a poor Palestinian into prison. That I could do on my own. And that's all I can tell you."

"You realize that anyone I might get for you will probably insist on having more information than this."

"Probably. But he'll need that information in order to help me. You don't."

"What makes you think that even if I do make the contact, the man will want to help you? After all, you're the enemy — or have you switched sides lately? Now that would be a great story." Syd chuckled.

"Very funny," Natan was getting edgy. "I can't force anyone to work with me, but if the man favors a peaceful solution to the bloody conflict over there, I believe he might help. All I need is a contact with those biases."

"Are you telling me you have a way to stop the violence over there in the Middle East?"

"No. But what I can do is prevent someone from irreparably damaging the peace process. That attempt is already in motion and I've realized that no one wants to stop it. If the violence is not stopped over there it will eventually blow up over here. Syd, for God's sake, don't ask any more questions. Just tell me, can you help or not?"

"Okay, okay. I'll make a few calls later on tonight. I might just have something for you in the morning. Is that soon enough?"

"Thanks. That would be just great."

"Don't thank me yet. I haven't done anything. Now what about this story you were going to give me?"

"Let's go over to my room," Natan suggested. "We can talk there without having to crane our necks across the table like this."

"Where are you staying?" Syd asked.

"At the Omni," Natan answered. "There's a back exit here on the lower level. The Omni's entrance is just across the street if we go out that way."

They finished their beers and Natan paid the check on the way out. "Lead on," he said. "You're going to love this story, my friend."

Once they were seated comfortably by the window in Natan's room, overlooking the hotel's swimming pool, Natan lit a cigarette. Syd opened a large yellow notepad and took out the fat black fountain pen he had been using since they invented ink, as he liked to say. Unlike the younger generation of reporters, he never used a tape.

Natan started at once. "Several days before the Camp David Accord was signed, President Sadat indicated his unwillingness to accept the fact that the Palestinian problem had not been clearly ironed out in the peace agreement." Natan got up and stood by the large window, moving the drapes slightly as he looked at the people in the pool. He went on.

"Sadat wanted the steps toward autonomy for the Palestinian people, based on U.N. resolutions two four two and three three eight, to be more specific and contain a binding timetable. Prime Minister Begin wanted that problem resolved at a different time, insisting that the question of sovereignty over the territories be left open.

"That, for Sadat, was tantamount to betraying the Palestinian people. He also had problems with the Israeli demand that Egypt guarantee Israel's supply of oil at a reasonable price, in exchange for the oil fields we returned to them, but he was prepared to concede that.

"As the time for signing the treaty drew closer, President Carter kept pressuring Sadat to accept the documents as they were, and he met with him on March fourteenth, nineteen seventy-nine in Cairo for a conversation in four eyes."

"In what?" Syd asked, looking up.

"In four eyes. It's an Israeli expression meaning that only the two of them were present. So, 'in four eyes,' you see?"

"Yeah, yeah. Go on."

"Well, in that meeting, the two leaders sealed their future. Carter convinced Sadat that this was a temporary situation and that it was imperative to get the accord signed. He then went on to promise that once he was re-elected, he'd push through a proper settlement for the Palestinian people. He promised Sadat it would be comprehensive and not vague or open to different interpretations as it was then. Furthermore, a proper timetable would be established. Sadat would, in fact, be helping the Pales-tinians in the long run, not betraying them, as he then saw it. With that promise in hand — and mind you, there was no witness — Sadat agreed to cooperate. President Carter then called Menachem Begin from the airport in Cairo and told him everything was settled. Begin told his cabinet about that call later the same day."

"Hold it right there." Syd was shaking his head in disbelief. "If the meeting was held in what you call four eyes, how the hell do you know what was said there?"

Natan turned from the window to face Syd. "After leaving the meeting, Sadat confided in his then prime minister, Mustafa Chalil, and in another minister who was totally opposed to the peace process. The prime minister was surprised that Sadat didn't get anything in writing from Carter, but Sadat told him he trusted 'Gh'imy.' The other minister, who fell to his death from a window in a Cairo high-rise several years ago, passed on the information to his Mossad operator . . ."

"What are you telling me?"

"What exactly don't you understand?"

"You just told me that this minister was against the peace process. Then you tell me he was a spy for Israel?"

"Right, Syd. So you do understand. This same minister was the one who sent the warning that got stuck on the way and didn't make it in time, revealing the exact timetable and strategy for the Yom Kippur War in seventy-three. To protect his cover, he was told to show himself as opposed to any negotiations with Israel. Having ostensibly taken that position, he had even better access to information."

"Okay, now I follow you. Do go on." Syd waved his pen.

"Now, because of his compromise with Carter, and realizing that Begin had no intention of bringing about a fair solution to the Palestinian problem, Sadat didn't want Begin to come to Cairo, and he would not go to Jerusalem. So the accord was signed in

Washington. It was several days after the signing that Begin learned of the promise made to Sadat by Carter."

"Just one thing," Syd was tapping his black pen on his notepad. "Why didn't the information come in earlier?"

"The Egyptian minister's meeting with his Mossad operator had to be well planned and very secure. At the time, no meeting was due until after the signing. Once the information did come in, it was immediately passed to the prime minister.

"Begin, who was already regretting having given up land for peace, now became extremely agitated at Carter. He feared that the president would fulfill his promise to Sadat and thereby cost Israel even more land. At that point, he called Yetzhak Hoffy, then head of the Mossad, and told him, 'Carter must not be reelected. It's a matter of national security for us.'"

"Did Begin give him any specific instructions?"

"Not that I know of. I understand that he was told to do whatever he could to prevent the re-election, short of killing Carter."

"Come on, man," Syd gestured in disbelief, and his yellow pad fell to the floor. "Are you telling me that the Mossad would kill the President of the United States?"

Natan smiled sadly. "So long as it goes through the proper channels, the Mossad would kill anyone. In fact they would probably have eliminated Carter, if not specifically ordered otherwise."

"I find that very hard to swallow." He picked the pad up from the floor, then asked, "How the hell do you know about this anyway? You were only a junior officer in the navy at the time. This is top brass stuff."

"The Mossad is like a hollow steel ball," Natan said, smiling at Syd. "Nothing gets out, but there are no secrets inside. If there is any 'need to know' kept, it deals with tactical information on specific operations, but in anything to do with strategy and policy, it's wide open."

Natan went on, "The Mossad at this time was involved in a deal to sell arms to the Iranians. Iran had already stacked up a large debt with Israel for various construction projects, as well as an unbelievable amount of asbestos for apartment balcony shades. All that, of course, before the Ayatollah Khomeini came to power — the debt, I mean. A plan was laid out to demand payment in advance for the arms, and once the money was in Israel, to announce that it would cover the existing debt. If the Iranians still wanted arms, they'd have to come up with a further payment." Natan lit another cigarette and started to pace the room as he talked.

"Who was running that operation?" Syd asked.

"It wasn't an operation yet, just a plan, because all attempts to make contact had so far failed. The Iranians wouldn't deal with Israel. After several weeks of working on plans, someone in Mossad headquarters happened to see a TV ad on the U.S. election, where someone had impersonated House Speaker Tip O'Neill. This inspired us to pretend to be Americans looking to strike a deal with the Iranians.

"We knew there was an ongoing dialogue between the Carter people and some Iranians in France, aimed at getting the U.S. hostages released. There was no point in our people trying to do the same. Instead, we would set ourselves up as being from the Reagan camp, and opposed to the hostages' release. Because Reagan was not yet president, he would need a broker to supply the arms. He'd use Israel, who would provide the arms from stockpiles and use the payment received to replace its depleted stocks. As someone put it, three birds with one stone, and one for later in a bush.

"Reagan's campaign manager, William Casey, was at this point to visit London for a day or so. That piece of information tied in beautifully with the plan. While there, Casey was invited to visit a wealthy Jewish man who was a Mossad helper. Casey was promised a large contribution to the Reagan campaign if he attended an unofficial meeting with another wealthy Jew at the man's villa outside Rome. While he was there, a look-alike — not perfect," Natan smiled, "but how many people knew Casey up close at that point? — had two meetings with the Iranians. One took place in Madrid and the other in Barcelona, where the look-alike 'Casey' initiated the talks that would go on after he had left, but were supposedly under his auspices, closing the arms deal.

"Because these 'Americans' had no access to Iran's frozen assets, not yet being in office, the Iranians had to pay for the arms up front. In addition, they were made to promise that the hostages would not be released before the election. This would effectively ensure that Carter would not be re-elected."

"But that's the so-called October surprise turned on its head!" Syd, leaning back in his chair, was now rubbing his chin and scowling slightly.

"Surprise, surprise!" Natan sat down across from him again. He gave a wide shrug. "That's the way it happened, and that's why nobody on the U.S. side knows what the *hell* happened. On the other side, you still have high-ranking Iranians who'll swear on a stack of Korans that they met with the Americans. And they're not lying, except that they met with Israelis posing as Americans."

"Now, how the hell am I going to prove that?"

"I didn't say I'd give you something you could easily prove, only something that took place. What I will do is give you the name of the man Casey met in Italy. But you'll have to take it from there. Just remember," Natan paused to look Syd straight in the face. "You alone have the story the way it really happened."

"What about all the stories about Bush here and Bush there?"

"Well, I guess Bush wasn't at the top of then Prime Minister Shamir's popularity list, nor that of the Mossad."

"The more I think about this, the better it gets," Syd's eyes had a twinkle now. "And you still won't tell me anything about why you want this Palestinian contact?"

"Not a chance."

"Okay. Well, I'll be getting back to the office now, and start working on looking up some people. I'm going to have to call them in Lebanon, by the way."

"Don't you have anyone here or in Europe?"

"I do, but how can they help you if they're outside the Middle East?"

"Stop thinking like a journalist, Syd. I don't need their contacts, I need the person."

"In that case, there may be someone here. Why don't we meet downstairs in the bar at five. I'll see what I can do meantime."

Natan asked no more questions as they shook hands at the door. If Syd came through with the right person, Natan's plan might move as swiftly as he hoped. Even so, he had never felt more alone than he did at this moment.

At 1650, Natan was watching for Syd from a corner table in the hotel bar.

"Mission accomplished," said Syd, as he sat down.

"So . . . you reached the man you wanted?"

"Yes. He's going to join us at the Sheraton bar at seven-thirty. How's that for fast service?"

"Fantastic. How about some dinner now? You can tell me a bit more about the man."

"That wasn't the deal, Natan. I don't mean dinner. But I promised you I'd try for this contact, not that I'd fill you in on him. I gave him a sketchy idea of you, and he was willing to come and listen. Clearly, he can't promise anything, but by the same token, I won't give you an advantage over him. All I'll tell you is that he's a Palestinian with family in Lebanon. He left there during the Israeli invasion of eighty-two. Any more details you'll have to get from him."

"Fair enough." Natan could see the sense of it.

Half an hour later, they walked up the street to a bistro-style restaurant. The food was good and the conversation even better. It was a long time since Natan had actually talked about world events with someone who had nothing to do with the Mossad. Hearing a fresh viewpoint was extremely important to him at that moment, as it helped reassure him that his own perspective was valid.

Shortly after seven, they walked over to the Sheraton and upstairs to the bar, where they took a table with a good view over the lobby.

"When Ibrahim comes, I'll introduce you. Then I'm out of here." Syd was starting to seem nervous.

"Why the rush?"

"I've got a column to get out, my boy, and since I can't write about your conversation with him, I'd prefer not to know about it."

"What if things don't work out? Can I call you at the office?"

"If I know you," Syd was smiling, "things will work out. But there's something else you should know. This guy is a good man. He's honest and he's fair. But I have no idea how much he likes Israelis. Probably not much."

"Well, I'm an American anyway, as you know," said Natan.

They smiled at each other in understanding.

"Regardless, I want to thank you," Syd went on, stretching out his short, firm hand.

"Thank me? For what?" Natan looked genuinely surprised.

"For trusting me, for calling on me, and last but not least, for giving me the scoop of my life. If I can prove it, that is." Syd's attention shifted. "Ah, there he is." He stood up and raised a hand to signal a tall, slender man in a light tan blazer. The man smiled at Syd as he came over, showing a set of perfect white teeth that gleamed against his dark olive skin.

"Hello, my friend," he said, reaching out to embrace Syd in greeting. "How good to see you again. You look great."

"Thank you, thank you," Syd replied, likewise hugging the tall man, and tapping him on the back. Although the newcomer was much younger than Syd, the two were clearly good pals.

"I appreciate your coming to meet us here," Syd said and turned.

"Natan," he said, "this is my friend Ibrahim." He then told the Palestinian, "Natan, a friend whom I trust. And now that I've introduced the two of you, I must go."

"Already?" asked Ibrahim sounding disappointed. "But we didn't get a chance to talk."

"Please, you two will have a lot to talk about, and I have a lot to do." He looked at each of them in turn. "Remember, if either of you should harm the other in any way, I'll never forgive you. You're both very dear to me, and I hope that in itself will help you get over some hurdles."

They sat quietly for a moment after Syd had gone. Natan spoke first. "I'm very grateful that you agreed to come."

"I agreed only to meet you and talk. The fact that you're Syd's friend doesn't give you an automatic bill of health. After all, the man has a lot of friends, so you'd better give me some details."

"Well," Natan began, "what we have is a threat to the . . ."

"No, no, I didn't mean that. I want to know who you are. And who you're working for. After that, we'll get to what you want of me."

"It's rather complicated."

"Only lies are complicated. I have the time. Please . . ."

"I'm an Israeli."

"I know that. Who do you work for?"

"I'm a member of Israeli Intelligence."

"You're Mossad?"

Natan hesitated. "Yes, I am," he said finally.

"And you expect me to work with you, although to me you represent all that is evil in this world? What the hell are you thinking of?" Ibrahim was getting to his feet.

"Please," Natan put out his hand in a conciliatory gesture. "Please sit down. If you want to leave after you hear what I have to say, then you must do so. But first, hear me out."

Ibrahim hesitated, and finally sat down, but on the very edge of his chair. It seemed he would not stay long.

"I'm from the Mossad, true, but what I'm doing now is not with their sanction. It's extremely dangerous for me even to be talking to you, never mind telling you what I'm about to say. All I ask is that you listen carefully, and then make up your mind."

"I'm listening."

Natan related the story as he knew it. He had decided not to leave out any information that could help Ibrahim understand the whole picture, but at the same time, if the man chose not to help, Natan knew he would have to kill him before he could pass the information to anyone else. Natan didn't like the options, but the stakes were too high.

At the end of it, Natan could tell that Ibrahim was engrossed with what he'd heard. The man sat in silence for several minutes while he assimilated the information. Then he looked straight at Natan.

"I must tell you that you are very convincing," he said, "and what you've told me rings true. But I cannot help you. I have a family that I had brought over from Lebanon and I am responsible for their well-being." The young man seemed extremely uncomfortable. "I can arrange for you to meet someone who could help you, though."

Natan felt as if the floor had just slipped out from under him. The circle of people involved was growing and there was nothing he could do about it. He felt like an amateur. "Who is this person?"

"A friend of mine who is well connected, and quite active."

"I don't need connections. I need someone to do something."

"Well, that's all I can do."

Natan stared at the man. "When can we meet your friend?"

"I could take you over to him right now."

Natan threw a twenty dollar bill on the table to pay for the drinks and stood up. "Let's go."

Ibrahim placed his hand on Natan's and said, "Wait just one minute. I'll have to call him first. We can't show up unannounced." He got up. "I'll be right back."

Natan let the man go and walked slowly behind him, keeping a distance. Ibrahim walked to a pay phone on the other side of the bar and punched in a number. Natan stood several feet away, and when Ibrahim noticed that he had come after him, he smiled but kept on talking. When he had finished, he hung up and walked over to Natan. "Someone will pick us up in a few minutes. We should wait at the main entrance."

This was really starting to get out of hand, Natan thought, but there was not much he could do. He could back out, of course, and try to forget the whole thing, but it was already getting late even for that. "Who will be picking us up?"

"My friend."

There was no point in arguing now. Natan had decided to take his chances. He realized that he was quite a trophy for any terrorist, but he had known the risks of going it alone when he started this. Less than ten minutes later, a white Chevrolet Caprice stopped in front of them. The passenger got out and shook hands with Ibrahim, then opened the back door and signaled them to enter.

"This is turning into a convention," Natan said grudgingly. "Who are all these people?"

"My friend sent them to pick us up," Ibrahim said, a little apologetically. "Don't worry. You are among friends."

"Whose?" Natan demanded.

"Are you coming or not?" Ibrahim asked him.

"What the hell," Natan said and entered the car. No one spoke, but several minutes into the drive, the passenger in front handed Ibrahim a blindfold, pointing at Natan and saying something in Arabic.

For the next ten minutes Natan wore a blindfold as they drove on. At that point he was amused, thinking that if they had wanted to grab him, he would have been sedated or dead by then. Presumably, he was being taken to someone influential, but what worried him now was that any of these people handling him could be active agents for the Mossad, if the individual they worked for was important enough.

The car came to a stop and Ibrahim gently helped him take off the blindfold. "We are here," he said as he opened the door. They were in a large underground parking garage and it took Natan several seconds to get used to the light.

"Please," Ibrahim said, waiting for Natan to get out, "my friend is waiting for you."

All of them walked away from the parked car in the direction of the elevator, but just before they reached it, the door of a parked limo opened and Ibrahim indicated that Natan should enter.

"Welcome to my little office," said a voice from the back seat of the limo, just as Natan was about to get in. The inside of the car was very dark, but a light above the speaker's head was bright and directed at Natan, making it almost impossible to see the man's face. "Please," the man said to Natan as he saw his hesitation, "do come in."

Natan entered the car and sat across from the man. Ibrahim got in after him and sat by his side, closing the door behind.

"Who are you?" Natan asked, not really expecting an answer.

"That is not relevant. Let us say that I'm quite involved in the region that you come from."

It was hard for Natan to detect an accent. There was something British in the voice and Middle Eastern at the same time. The man went on, "I am mainly involved in organizing aid for my people. I do not get involved in the mechanics of the region, if you know what I mean." The man drew on a large cigar which briefly glowed on his face. Natan could make out a pair of dark glasses and there was something familiar in the face, but he couldn't place it.

"Do you know what I need?" Natan asked.

"Not really. I only know what Ibrahim told me over the phone and what Syd had told Ibrahim before the meeting with you."

"So, you are the source Syd has," said Natan. "Why didn't he arrange a meeting for me directly with you?"

"Because he doesn't know me," came the reply. Natan could sense the man was smiling. "Syd thinks Ibrahim is the source."

"Where do you stand on the peace issue?" Natan asked, reaching into his pocket for a cigarette. Ibrahim's hand was on his before he could get the pack out.

"Slowly," Ibrahim said. "Take your hand out slowly."

Natan could feel something metal pressed against his ribs. Realizing what had happened, he said, "Only going for a cigarette."

"You can smoke later," said the man. "First of all, tell me the story from the top. And as far as the peace process is concerned, I think it should proceed. Peace is always good for enterprise, wouldn't you say? As long as my people want it, and feel confident they are dealing with someone who also wants peace."

Natan repeated what he had told Ibrahim before, and when he had finished, he leaned back in the deep leather seat of the limo, waiting for a reply.

"Let's say I believe everything you've said and that I want to help in any way possible. What would you want me to do?"

"I need someone to penetrate the terrorist unit. I need to know exactly what they're planning in order to stop them."

"And how would you expect me to do that? They're a well-knit team, aren't they? You can't just walk in from the outside and become a member. As a Mossad man, you of all people should know that."

"I do. But in this case, there is a window of opportunity, so to speak, though only for a short time."

"What do you mean?"

"The team is expecting a woman to arrive as its go-between. I have all the details regarding the real woman, but what I need is a substitute who will go in posing as the one they are expecting. Of course, the real one will have to be stopped. If that can be done, our substitute will be above suspicion."

"It will be extremely dangerous for the woman," said the stranger.

"I know," Natan confirmed.

"Why don't you just notify the authorities in Greece and have these people arrested?"

"First of all, they haven't yet committed any crime. Secondly, if we stop them that way, there will undoubtedly be another team available to do the job. One that we don't know anything about."

"I think I can help you. I only wish I trusted you!"

"How can I prove to you that I'm telling the truth?"

"Well, what I have in mind you might not want to do. I'm prepared to trust you as far as you will trust me."

"So, get to the point."

"I'll have someone meet you the day after tomorrow in Beirut." He scribbled something on a piece of paper.

Natan was thinking fast. Beirut was enemy territory, heavily policed by the Syrians. It was part of the "land of the dead". He would have to play this one very close to the wire, to say the least.

"Here," the man said, handing him the note. "Be at that address the day after tomorrow and we'll see."

"Do you have any idea how dangerous that could be for me?" Natan asked him.

Ibrahim was getting ready to leave.

The man said, "Trust me."

"I need to know that you'll help if I go," Natan insisted.

"You be there if you dare."

Natan leaned forward slightly. "Do you trust all these people you have around you?" There was a slight hint of sarcasm in his voice.

"No," the man said. "So I don't tell them anything, if that's what you're worried about. Except for Ibrahim, they have no idea who you are. Don't forget that I deal with a lot of people."

Natan looked at the address as he got out of the car. He was relieved at least that it was not in the Christian enclave of Junia, where there were so many Phalangists he had worked with.

He also realized that the man he had just met was one fast thinker. He had manipulated the situation so that Natan had lost his advantage, and what had been a potentially dangerous scenario for him had become a deadly one for Natan. And now he knew that he was about to take a step that he might live to regret — if live was the right word. But he was already in too deep. He had made the decision to see this thing through.

# 18

**BEIRUT INTERNATIONAL AIRPORT
SEPTEMBER 23
1100 HOURS**

THE FLIGHT to Beirut was long and exhausting, and by the time Natan got there, it was almost noon the next day. He was traveling on a high-grade false Canadian passport.

He wasn't planning to stay long in Lebanon: no more than two days if he could help it. He had contacted a Lebanese boat charter company whose owner he'd heard about from a Phalangist a while back, as someone who was occasionally involved in smuggling. If paid well, the man was said to be trustworthy, as long as you still owed him something. Natan had explained to the man over a very bad phone connection that he'd be there for only a short visit, checking out some diving sites. Smelling money, the man promised to have the boat and scuba equipment ready.

Disembarking at Beirut, Natan felt something he hadn't known for a long time: profound fear. The Syrian Red Berets were everywhere, as were heavily armed police. But even though the passport official seemed to regard him as unbalanced for having come to Beirut on business at all, he found the actual entry procedure easy enough.

What next amazed him was to see how life went on in spite of the visible ruin all around. Natan had decided to take a cab directly from the airport to the marina and the boat. He intended to use the boat as his hotel for the time he was in the city. His plan was to have Gamil, the owner, anchor the small vessel at a point he had marked on a map. That would place him some two hundred yards from the beach house where he was to meet whomever it was he was supposed to meet. Anchored there, he would be able to watch the house before approaching it from an unexpected direction: the sea.

When the yacht laid anchor, Natan changed into a swimsuit. Gamil, a big smile breaking beneath his huge black mustache, said, "You not often swim."

"Why do you say that?" Natan replied in a friendly tone.

"To swim, you must be in sun, and you white, no take sun."

"Well, what can I tell you? You're right. I haven't been doing this for a long time, but that's about to change." Natan knew he'd made a mistake, however small. And simple things are the ones that get you hung, he thought.

Sitting at the stern on a wooden ledge that hung from the deck, he was inspecting the scuba gear that Gamil had produced for him. From this vantage point, he could see several houses. Any one of them might be the one he was supposed to visit; there was no way of telling from here.

"So, you satisfied?" Gamil was looking down at him, holding two cups of coffee that smelled of cardamom.

"Yes, indeed. Where did you get this equipment, anyway? It's very good quality."

"So, you know this business, my friend. You want coffee?"

"I'd love one." Natan had to shield his eyes in order to see Gamil. The sun was shining directly in his face. Gamil stepped carefully onto the small lowered deck and handed Natan the cup. He put it down and went on inspecting the equipment.

Gamil said, "No, no. Don't let get cold. Drink hot, or you better drink water from sea."

Natan laughed and took a sip from the boiling coffee. The hot liquid scalded his tongue. "Shit!" he sputtered.

"You sip it like this," and Gamil took a noisy slurp from the rim.

"Now you tell me," Natan said, licking his scalded lips.

"So, you suck it in no touching cup. It cools in air. Try it."

Natan did. Of course, Gamil was right. With the exception of the noise, it was great.

It was several minutes later when Natan heard a sound just above the whooshing of the small swells that nodded at the side of the boat. Although faint, it was unmistakable — a sound he hadn't heard in a very long time. Soon he located the small dot on the horizon, gradually growing bigger. His heart pounding, Natan could feel his muscles stiffen. The Syrian patrol boat was heading directly toward them.

He and Gamil stood watching the growing gray image. This must be a routine check, Natan thought, but he'd have to act scared, like any other tourist facing such an intruder. With its two Styx missiles covering most of the deck, the boat, as it drew near, had a silhouette like a huge turtle. It was an ugly-looking boat.

"Bastards! Let me do talking," said Gamil between his teeth, as the boat pulled up beside the yacht, its wake causing the smaller vessel to sway heavily. A sailor in a gray uniform tossed a rope to Gamil, who caught and tied it to the yacht's bow. Now the patrol boat overshadowed them, and Natan could see several sailors toting MK 47 submachine guns staring down.

An officer spoke rapidly with Gamil, who then turned to Natan. "He want see you passport. Not worry, this okay."

Natan scrambled onto the deck, smiling up at the officer who regarded him with no expression at all. This was only the second time that he'd come so close to a vessel of this type. The last time had been during the Yom Kippur War when he and his team were on a demolition mission into the northern Syrian harbor of Tripoli to blow up several of them.

Now, as the officer checked Natan's papers, no one moved on

board his boat. Even after he'd handed them back to Gamil, who then released the rope, there was no movement. All eyes were on Natan. At last the officer touched the brim of his cap as if to say good-bye, then signaled the bridge. A large plume of smoke belched from her exhaust pipes as the boat started to move slowly away from the yacht.

The relief Natan felt at that moment could not be measured.

Gamil, smiling, still facing the boat as it veered away, muttered in Arabic, "May the bastards rot in hell, and the spirit of Lebanon haunt them forever."

"What was that?" asked Natan.

"Nothing, my friend, just wish them luck on sea." He was still smiling as he turned to face Natan. "So, what you think you find here?"

"I'm looking for a sunken ship, so that I can maybe add Beirut to the tour."

"You not looking for treasure on sunken ship?"

"If I find one, I won't throw it back, but the real treasure is the endless stream of tourists who'll come to see the ship, if it's the one I think."

"That be good for business." Gamil was about to head back to the cabin. "There," he said suddenly, pointing to the beach. "There real treasure."

"What's there?"

"Women, on beach. Wait." He disappeared below, resurfacing a minute later with a pair of powerful binoculars, which he handed to Natan. "Look."

This was an unexpected opportunity, and Natan took his time scanning the beach. Gamil was right. The beach was full of people, particularly women in tiny swimsuits.

"How come they're dressed like that?" Natan asked, playing the part of the first-time tourist. "Isn't it against the religion here?"

"You have much to learn on Lebanon, my friend." Gamil was laughing loudly.

Natan scanned the beach again, taking in the houses lined along it. One house that he could see had received a direct hit — probably a shell fired from the sea. It appeared to be deserted, while in and around the others, he noticed activity.

He knew he would soon have to head for the beach and house Number 26, where he was expected. It was the word "expected" that made him hesitate. He could still turn around and leave the territory with no harm done. But once he entered that house, there would be no turning back.

"I'm going ashore," Natan told Gamil, getting up from the small deck. "Do you think you could get the diving equipment ready in about an hour, so I can make a start when I get back?"

Gamil was smiling. "You see something you like on beach?"

"More than one, my friend. Now, is it okay with you if I take the dinghy?"

"Go ahead. Just remember, if you want leave it, you must pay someone keep it for you or it not be there when you come back."

"Do they take U.S. dollars?"

"You joking. This Lebanon. They take as many U.S. dollars as you can afford give them, and more."

After changing into jeans and a yellow T-shirt, Natan headed for the beach in the small rubber craft.

From the deck of Gamil's yacht, the water had seemed calm, but at sea level Natan realized he'd have to row hard. The final fifty yards he did on top of a five-foot, foamy wave that landed him on shore.

Several little boys were there to cheer him on and help pull the dinghy further in. They were hoping to earn a buck looking after it for him.

"Mister, wanna me to protect your ship?" asked a skinny kid of about ten in a brightly colored swimsuit.

"Are you sure you can do that?" Natan was amused.

"I can keep safe," stated the kid. "Can you afford to pay me?" He lifted his chin in defiance.

"I don't know. How much do you want?" Natan really had no time for this little game at the moment, but he knew he had to endure, so as to be convincing as a Canadian tourist.

"How much do you have?" asked the boy.

"I'll give you five dollars."

"You shame me," said the youngster. "I'll make you deal. I watch for you for free. You pay when you come back."

Natan knew he was being suckered, but he decided to let it go. It impressed him, too, to see how the other kids fell silent when this one spoke.

"Okay," Natan said. "I'll be back in half an hour and we'll talk."

He headed for a narrow passage between the houses that clearly led onto the street where he'd see the numbers. It had to be one of five houses.

Once on the street, he could see the devastation. The houses had been neatly arranged up a slope, but there wasn't one that didn't bear scars of war. Some of them had clearly been rebuilt and destroyed more than once, as sections were in various stages of reconstruction, some already bearing new scars. On the street itself, traffic was moving at a steady pace. Natan was happy he didn't have to make his way to the house through the streets of Beirut, but could just pop up in front of it. This being a popular beach, there were food vendors on both sides of the passage leading down to it. Not having eaten for some time now, Natan was tempted by the smells of cooking to order a lamb kebab. But when two Syrian soldiers walked up to the vendor, he quickly decided against it.

The address he was looking for was adjacent to the direct hit he had seen from the sea. The house was fairly large, with a red tile roof and arched windows reminiscent of the Turkish days. The building seemed extremely well preserved and a fresh coat of white paint gave it a festive look. The number was prominently displayed on the oak door, so although there was no reply when he knocked, Natan had no doubt that it was the right house.

He waited for several minutes, then walked around to the back of the house, facing the sea. The back porch was raised about five feet off the beach and had a rusting metal railing all around with a small opening to the left and a set of open metal stairs. From where Natan stood at that moment, his view might have been of a beach somewhere in California. As he slowly turned the corner and saw more and more of the large marble-floored balcony, an ornate white cast-iron table with a glass top came into sight, followed by a pair of tanned legs. As Natan climbed the stairs, he could see the owner of the legs more clearly. Her body was perfect: tanning oil glistened on smooth, silky skin. He hoped that she would have a face to match.

"Excuse me," he said in a friendly tone, not wanting to startle the woman.

She turned toward him slowly, elegantly, meeting his gaze. Natan couldn't have imagined a more attractive face. Dark, luxurious hair framed a light olive complexion. A sense of wisdom shone in her large green eyes. Natan suddenly realized he was staring.

"Do you speak English?" he said.

"What is it you want?" she answered with a slight British accent.

"I'm looking for Ibrahim." That's what he had been told to say.

"Ibrahim is not here," she replied, leaning back again and replacing her sunglasses.

"But he told me to meet him here," he insisted.

"Ibrahim is in Washington, who are you?"

"Someone he promised to help. But I'd better be going. Unless you have a message for me, there's no point in wasting your time." He had turned away when she said:

"What's your name?"

"Why?"

"I'm just curious. Do you have a passport?"

"Yes?"

"Can I see it?" There was a little smile on her face.

He drew out his passport and handed it to her. She looked at the photo, then at him as she handed it back. "Nice," she said. "What is your real name?"

Natan was uneasy. He was not used to being the one questioned, nor was he comfortable as the victim in a cat and mouse game. "Is there a reason for all this?" he asked her.

"It's possible. Well?"

He hesitated, finally coming to the conclusion that if this was a setup, they could have picked him up the moment he entered the yard. "Natan. My name is Natan," he replied.

She stood up and walked over to him, smiling. Offering her hand in a firm grip, she said, "My name is Nadin. Ibrahim told me a little about you. He asked me to help you in whatever way I could, if you showed up. Although he was quite sure you wouldn't." Indicating a pair of tall French doors that led into the house, she said, "Please come with me."

He followed her into the cool dark of the house. She had a feline grace when she moved, slow and silent, yet with agility. Natan thought her perfection itself, as he walked in the wake of her scent.

"Have a seat, and help yourself to a drink. There's a selection in the cabinet over there." She pointed to a long mahogany side-board. "I'll just go and change into something more suitable."

"You don't have to dress on account of me," he said, smiling. She returned his smile as she left the room.

He felt secure enough now, but a sense of urgency still nagged at him. He had to be back at the boat within the next hour and out of the country within forty-eight hours. Seated here in this cool room, occasionally glancing at the bright blue sea as the thin sheers blew in with the breeze, Natan felt very much at odds with the situation. It was all so amateurish, so unprofessional, so dangerous. Anything could go wrong and, of course, the more complicated his involvement, the more things there were to go wrong. Or suppose he was arrested for something minor like aggravating a Syrian soldier. That would require no effort at all, since the Syrians were such a nervous bunch in Lebanon.

Then there was Gamil, who might inform one of his many masters about this strange Canadian. Before he'd had a chance to do anything, the information could reach the Mossad. They had Lebanon saturated with agents and informants. They'd just put his alias on the computer and bingo! There he'd be, as large as life. He helped himself to a tequila and knocked it back in one quick gulp, hoping it would numb the tips of his nerves. If nothing else, he had to appear to be calm and in control.

Though she seemed to have been gone for a very long time, she took only a few minutes. She'd changed into the traditional house dress called a galabia. Of white cotton, the dress had an embroidered neckline with a brocade pattern of red and gilt threads covering most of the bodice. Nadin sat on a wooden chair across from him. She took a piece of Turkish delight from a small glass bowl on a table beside her and bit into it, daintily licking the remnants of powdered sugar off her lips. It was hard for Natan to take his eyes off the long slit up the side of her dress that revealed her perfect legs.

"So, what is it you want?" Nadin asked.

"Didn't Ibrahim fill you in?"

"No, I was only asked to help you if you showed up — which, as I told you, was regarded as very doubtful. So what is it you want?"

"I need your help to prevent an assassination."

"Of whom? And by whom?"

"A delegation of Palestinian moderates who will attend the peace talks, by a terrorist group."

"A terrorist to one is a freedom fighter to another."

"Well, these are people few would regard as freedom fighters."

"What makes you think I'm not one of those few?"

"If you were, I'd probably be dead by now. But look, if you are prepared to help, let's just get down to business."

"Before we do — if we do — I want you to know there's something about you that bothers me. It bothered the man who sent you too. You seem to think that because the target of these so-called terrorists is Palestinian, we should be extremely grateful to you for trying to help. We should therefore bow to your command and do whatever you say. Let's get things straight. I don't give a damn about this delegate or that one, be he moderate or extreme."

"Why?" Natan asked, perplexed.

"Because, I don't believe they'll succeed in doing anything, not even delaying the final inevitable and bloody battle. But, for the unlikely chance that a miracle takes place and they manage to prevent that battle, forcing your obstinate government to act in a rational way, I'll do whatever I can to help. But not as your little lackey."

"All I'm asking is that you help me prevent the act of assassination. There are no hidden agendas and once this is over, we'll each go our separate ways. Do we have a deal?"

"Let's start, and then we'll see how things work out."

"No," he said, "that's not good enough. You can tell me you don't want any part in this, and I'll leave now. But if you say you want to help, I have to know you're committed. This is not something you can start and then decide you don't like it. So, what do you say?"

His attention was suddenly drawn to the window as he spotted the red berets of several Syrian soldiers.

"Don't worry," Nadin told him, "that's a routine patrol that passes by here every hour or so. They like this particular beach because of all the women tourists in their bikinis. Now look," she continued, straightening in the chair, and looking directly at Natan. "How do I know you're not setting me up for something where you'll use me against my own people? After all, you *are* Mossad." He cringed as she said the word. It was not one he wanted to hear — especially on Lebanese soil when surrounded by Syrian soldiers. "You people are not famous for your honesty and good deeds toward the Palestinians, are you?"

"I came here, didn't I?"

"That only proves that you trust us. How can I be sure I can trust you?"

"I don't know what to tell you, but I'm running out of time. Suppose you think about it, and I'll come back later tonight."

"I'll help you." There was determination in her voice. "Just remember that if you double-cross me, there won't be a place on this earth that you can run to. Or that you'd want to run to."

He nodded, smiling at her as he got up and headed for the door. He paused, then turned to face her. In a slow and almost inaudible tone, he said, "I appreciate what you're willing to do. I am in your debt, and many others will be, though they may never know it." He paused again. "Now I have to get back to . . ."

"I saw your little boat."

"That's my cover for being here. Just so you know, I'm diving for a shipwreck."

"So, are you searching for treasures?"

"No, a site for a special diving tour. I'll be back tonight then, if it's okay with you?"

"I'll be here."

As he was leaving, Natan handed her a piece of paper. "If you have time this afternoon, please see what you can find out about this girl. We'll need that information later."

"Very well."

"Just don't draw attention to yourself with the questions." He was already half regretting having asked her to do it. Gathering information without making waves was something she couldn't possibly have learned. Very few people get that sort of training. "On second thought . . ." he began, reaching out for the paper again.

"Don't worry," she said. "I do know something about surveillance, and how to obtain information without making a mess."

"Where did you learn that?"

"From my father."

"And who might your father be?"

"I'll tell you all about that tonight."

He could see that Nadin was amused. She must have thought he already knew.

Natan got back to the beach without incident. He could see the kid standing over the dinghy, though from where he first spotted it, it looked more like a beach blanket than a rubber boat. As he approached, the kid waved at him.

"*Aha-lan we sah-lan* (hi, and peace be on you), boss. I have guarded your boat. Now that you are here, I can be on my way."

The dinghy was flat as a pancake. Someone had deflated it.

"What the hell are you talking about? What happened here?"

"I have no ideas, boss. You asked me to make sure that no one was to taking the ship."

"But what happened to the air?" Natan's temper was rising, but the sight of a patrolling policeman calmed him down instantly.

"I was to take care of ship, nothing about air. You owe me nothing, so bye, bye." The kid gave him a cheeky look, and sped off down the beach.

"Wait! Where the hell can I get a pump?" Natan had caught up to him.

"I can rent you a pompa for maybe twenty dollars American?" The kid was smiling and so were the others who now surrounded them.

"I'll give you twenty-five, but you do the pumping."

"Thirty."

"Deal."

Within minutes, the dinghy was ready and Natan handed the little bandit his money. The kid bowed his head and said, "*Merci, Ktir.*"

When Natan finally got back to the yacht, Gamil had all the

diving equipment laid out, ready for him. Rowing back out had been extremely difficult, so he rested for a few minutes before donning the gear and going down.

The wreck was almost directly under the yacht, but he spent about twenty minutes inspecting it, thinking that would be time enough to convince Gamil that his purpose was legitimate. Just before surfacing, Natan filled a red float with air from his tank, sending it to the surface as a marker to which he'd later attach a buoy.

He felt safe under the water, but he knew that time was running out and he would soon be back in the country of the dead.

# 19

**BEIRUT**
**SEPTEMBER 23**
**1800 HOURS**

AT ABOUT 1800 hours, Gamil moved anchor to a small marina at the northern corner of the bay. Once they'd moored, he invited Natan to join him for dinner, but he declined, explaining that he'd met this chick on the beach and was taking her out.

Gamil laughed. "You fast one, my friend. Just you not get more for what you bargain. This not safe city, so no good on you own. Canadian worth much money. You want I go with you? Just make you safe. Then I come take you back. What you say?"

"Thanks, but I think I can take care of myself. Don't worry about me."

"My friend, after you paid me rest of money what you owe me, I not worry. Now, you most important man I know."

"I thank you for your candor, but I still know how to take care of myself."

Gamil was clearly upset. He spat out a sequence of curses in a low voice that was just audible to Natan, though supposedly not meant to be. "You not want maybe pay me now?" he grinned slyly.

"And become worthless to you? Don't even think about it. You'll be paid when we're through, and not a moment before. Now, please excuse me, I have a date with a very beautiful lady, and I don't want to be late."

Natan jumped onto the pier. Dressed inconspicuously in his jeans and a dark blue T-shirt, he made his way to the end of the dock, then headed toward Nadin's house. Now that he knew the house, he decided to walk along the beach, avoiding the streets of this Muslim quarter, which was known to be a rough neighborhood. He wanted especially to avoid the police and military patrols.

The house was about two miles from the marina, but Natan found himself there faster than he had expected. It was still light, although the sun was about to vanish at the edge of the darkening waters. It left just a glistening trail leading to the glowing horizon.

The French doors off the porch were open, the sheer curtains rippling in the sea breeze. The light within was cozy and inviting, a safe haven in a potentially hostile environment. Taking the stairs two at a time, he approached the door.

"Hello. Anybody home?" he said, brushing the sand off his feet and putting on his loafers.

"Come on in." Nadin's voice was unmistakable, soft yet slightly hoarse.

Natan entered, then froze in his tracks at the sight of a huge dark man standing in the corner. His hands were folded on his chest, his bald head reflecting the light from a crystal chandelier.

Natan took a step back, ready to make a hasty exit. He hated surprises.

Nadin spoke up quickly. "Don't worry, he's a friend."

"You should have told me he'd be here tonight. Who is he?"

"A friend of my father. You could call him my bodyguard, though he's more than that. He raised us." She smiled at the man, who reminded Natan of the genie from Aladdin's lamp. "Bassam looks after me and my brother Nabil. You have nothing to worry about. Look, you've trusted me so far. Go the extra step."

"Does he speak English?"

"No."

Natan remained by the door. "You have to make me a promise," he looked directly at her, a stern expression on his face. "Never again bring someone to meet me without telling me first. Promise me that."

"I promise, and I'm sorry. But when you asked me to get that information, you didn't really think I'd go out personally to check it, did you?"

"In fact, I did, but that has nothing to do with it," he said, entering the room at last.

Bassam stepped forward. It seemed he was ready to protect Nadin, but she said something in Arabic that made him step back. She then ushered Natan to a chair, seating herself across from him.

"Would you care for a drink before dinner?" she asked.

"Yes, please."

"Tequila?"

"Yes."

She got up to get the drink, then gestured to Bassam, who left the room.

"I hope you didn't send him to get his friends?" Natan inquired jokingly.

"No. He's gone to set the table for dinner."

"So tell me, who is your father?"

"You probably know him, at least by reputation." She handed him the glass.

"Al Danna is our family name, and my father is called Catib." Chin raised, she was clearly proud of her father.

Natan almost dropped the glass.

"You don't mean that you're the daughter of Abu Nabil," he sputtered.

"That's the name he is better known by, yes."

"Holy shit! Of all the people in the world, you have to be the daughter of its most dangerous terrorist!"

"My father is a freedom fighter. He didn't ask to be thrown into this war. All your people had to do was leave him alone."

"I'm sorry, but the man is a brutal murderer."

"Please! You have no idea who my father is or was. It's easy for you to pass judgment. What do you know about fighting for freedom? You were handed freedom as a birthright."

"Not exactly," said Natan. This was neither the time nor the place to get into an argument of this kind, but he couldn't help himself. There was something very strange about this situation. Why was she willing to help? He had to find out. "We weren't born to freedom. We had to fight for it, remember?"

"Fight? Do you call Dir Yasin a fight? Wasn't that a massacre?"

"That was done by a marginal organization. Nothing like that happened on a regular basis. Not like what Hadge Amin al Husaini's bandits did."

"Don't give me that crap! The leaders of your so-called marginal organization are the ones in power today, while the offspring of al Husaini are striving for peace. As for my father, I don't agree with his methods or I wouldn't be helping you, now would I? But I can understand him. Do you know that my family had over six thousand acres of orchards in what you call Israel that included orange groves in Ashkelon Yavnah and Kefar Saba? All of that was taken away from us. So tell me, what would you do in his place?

"The house he grew up in, overlooking the sea in Jaffa, had twenty rooms. It's now a police station. One day he was an honorable citizen and the next he was a refugee. So don't tell me how you fought for your freedom! Because you got it on the backs of others. But, enough. It's time to see what can be done for the future. I still don't believe there is a real chance for peace, but it mustn't be said that we didn't try. Can you understand that?"

"Yes I can. But try to remember this. My people also lost everything they had in the Holocaust and had to start again."

"Why are *we* being punished for the Holocaust? We didn't cause it, but somehow we still end up paying for it. In a way, we are also victims of the Holocaust. That, we cannot alter, you and I." Nadin fell silent.

"Will Bassam tell your father about me?" Natan wanted to know.

"No. He doesn't report to him, only to me. In fact, my father isn't talking to me at all these days because he thinks I'm wrong. That's what he tells everybody because, for one thing, he believes that way I'll be safe from whatever fate awaits him."

Bassam came in to announce dinner. Following Nadin into the dining room, Natan felt as if he was in a surreal dream. He was as far out on a limb as he had ever been in his life — probably as far out as anyone could get. And if he fell off?

The table was laden with local delicacies, from a large bowl of savory rice with chicken to the traditional eggplant in tahina. As he started to eat, Natan realized just how hungry he was. They ate in silence for several minutes, then he asked her, "What did you find out about the name I gave you?"

She nodded to him as she wiped her lips with a white napkin. "Bassam checked the address. The family living there is a fairly large one. Five brothers and one sister. They are Palestinian, originally from Haifa. Was there something else you wanted to know?"

"Only if the girl is still at that address."

"Yes, she is."

"She's our ticket into the organization that is planning the assassinations."

"Tell me more."

"Well, to make a long story short, she's the niece of a man who, until recently, headed a small organization that has assembled for the purpose of assassinating the moderate Palestinian leaders. I'm referring to those who are willing to negotiate with Israel under the auspices of the U.N.

"Her uncle had it set up for her to go to Cyprus and be a go-between for his small team. He chose her because he could trust her, and because it's a situation where a woman can operate without arousing as much suspicion as a man. He had made all the arrangements, and was about to send someone for her when he had an accident — a diving accident, in fact — and died."

"How convenient," she said.

"You're very suspicious," he said, smiling.

"Shouldn't I be?"

"Well, it's not a bad trait in the present circumstances, I suppose." He went on, "The man left behind, who's the second-in-command, is expecting her. He thinks the messenger actually went to her and that she's now on her way."

"So, how does that help us get in? Are you going to get her to work with us?"

"That wouldn't be a bad idea if we had the time."

"So what then?"

"You will take her place."

"But, but . . ." She was clearly shaken. "What does she look like? I mean, they will find out right away that I'm not her. I don't even know what her uncle looked like."

"None of the people you'll be working for has ever seen her, or even heard of her, so we're safe there. As for her uncle, I'll fill you in on that, so there's no problem."

"Suppose she shows up? I mean . . ."

"We'll have to get her out of the picture, maybe hold her here . . . have Bassam keep her so that she can't leave. She'll come willingly enough, thinking it's her uncle's associate calling. She has no idea that her uncle is dead. And her family won't miss her because he's set it up so that they're to think she's at the Sorbonne in Paris . . ."

"If you know all that," she pronounced every syllable with care, thinking while she was talking, "why don't you and your people just go in and stop these guys?"

"Because I've learned that the killing of the moderate Palestinians fits the agenda of my people just as much as it does that of the Syrians."

"Are you telling me you can't get them yourself before they do this?"

"Nadin, I can't even come close to them. My people have them under surveillance just to make sure they don't decide to change their target at the last minute and attack an Israeli one.

"I want you in there so that I can stop them when the time comes, but there's no point in speculating on methods at the moment, with the little information we have. What's crucial now is to get hold of the girl here, and then get you on your way to Greece."

"Do you know what the messenger is supposed to tell the girl?" she asked.

"Yes — and I've got it written down in Arabic, just to make sure."

"I suppose Bassam could get her and keep her here." She leaned back in her chair and looked at Natan. "Now isn't it lucky we have him all of a sudden?" She had a point to make. "I mean, didn't the big Mossad man think about this before? What if we didn't have Bassam?"

"I hope you don't think you're the only person I know in Lebanon?" He hoped his bluff would hold. "But since he's here, there's no reason to involve any more people. And by the way, I don't have anything against Bassam. All I said, and I'll repeat it, is that I don't want to be surprised like that again. It's not healthy for me and it's definitely not healthy for the one who's doing the surprising."

"Fine," she said, "I'll go and ask him. After all, we're taking him for granted. He might just say no."

"Are you going to tell him the whole story? Or did you do that already?"

"I haven't told him anything. Only that you're a friend from the States. But if you want his help, you'll have to come up with a plausible story, or else we will have to tell him the whole thing."

"Let me think about this for a moment." Natan stared out the window. From where he sat, he couldn't see the moon, only its broken reflection riding the shallow waves to shore. "You tell him that I . . ." he was drumming on the table with his fingers . . . it was not supposed to be like this. He was spoiled by the Mossad apparatus that had pampered him for years, solving such problems as cover stories on the spot. And well documenting it. All he had to do was learn the details. Now this. "Tell him," he went on, "I work for the CIA and that I need your help because I'm doing this on my own to save a Palestinian leader."

"But I thought you didn't want to tell him the truth?"

"I just don't want him to know that I'm Israeli. Trust me on this one. Now, why don't you call him in and ask him?"

As it turned out, Bassam was eager to help.

After going over the details at length, Natan summed up what they were all going to do during the next few hours. He would return to the yacht, leaving for the airport first thing in the morning. There he'd meet Nadin, who would call Athens from there, and ask Halim to pick her up on arrival at Hellinikon Airport. Natan stressed how important it was that Halim see that her flight had come from Lebanon.

Halim would take her to the apartment where she was to stay and start collecting information. Natan had not told her that the apartment was bugged, because he didn't want her to act unnaturally there. But he did warn her that such a thing was possible, and that she must not use the phone in the apartment nor the one in the restaurant downstairs. Natan instructed her to contact him after several days there and leave a short message. He gave her a number in Paris. In case of an emergency, she was to call immediately.

"After you call," said Natan, "go to the Palace Athens Hotel on Syntagma and register under the name of Madeleine Marcus. Go up and wait in the room." He was writing the names down on a slip of paper for her. "I'll call you in the room, and tell you what to do next." He handed her the paper. "Memorize those names and the Paris phone number, then destroy the paper. Okay?"

She nodded.

Natan reviewed procedures until he was sure Nadin understood the logic of it all. Bassam was next.

He asked Nadin to translate what he was telling the man word for word and verify that there could be no error in identifying the girl. The last thing he wanted was a case of mistaken identity. Bassam, in turn, explained that he would keep her in a special cell beneath the house. It seemed that she would not be the first person to spend time there. Natan was not to worry: after all, if the girl was to get away, Nadin would be in danger. Bassam would never permit that.

It was close to 0200 when Natan left the house. Refusing Bassam's offer to escort him, he told them that he was a big boy who could take care of himself. Minutes later, he regretted that decision.

There was nothing concrete at first, but tension had sharpened his senses to the point that he was sure someone was moving in the shadows of the boardwalk behind him. It was a clear night, but in places the half moon created inky shadows. He had no choice but to keep on going and hope he could deal with whoever was following him.

He did not let on that he'd noticed anything, yet all Natan's concentration was on whatever was happening behind him. That, and keeping an eye on the waterline so that the low, rippling waves would wash away his footprints almost as fast as he made them.

A sudden blast of blinding light completely stunned him. He put up his right hand to shield his eyes.

Natan heard a voice shouting in Arabic, "*Tahal edak, tahal edak.*" Getting no response, the man spoke again in broken English. "Handsup, handsup."

Natan stopped dead, his mind racing. Was he being kidnapped? They would have just knocked him over the head or jumped him. If the man he still couldn't see wanted to kill him, he could have done that already. It must be either the police or the military doing a patrol.

"What do you want? I'm a Canadian. What do you want?"

"Passport," came the reply, and now he could see the outline of the man's submachine gun as he extended his hand for the passport.

Natan closed his eyes tightly to get used to the dark again. Then he took out the document and handed it over. The man held it in one hand, shining his flashlight on it with the other. With the light off his face, Natan opened his eyes.

What confronted him was a fairly short Syrian soldier who seemed to be on a patrol alone. From the way he was handling the passport, the man was clearly not worried about Natan trying anything. His weapon was slung over his shoulder.

The soldier placed the passport in his shirt pocket and gestured for Natan to follow him. This confrontation was apparently not going to end in a simple good-bye. The Syrian must have thought he had some sort of prize to bring in.

Natan took off his wristwatch and, still standing in the same place, handed it to the soldier as a bribe to let him go. The man stared down at the handsome gold watch, but shook his head in refusal.

"Well, that's just too bad," said Natan in a low voice that the soldier had to cock his head to hear. By now, his hands were on the automatic weapon, but Natan was certain the safety was still on. Deftly, Natan tossed his watch onto the sand just behind the soldier, who turned his head to follow its arc just as Natan had hoped he would.

He leapt at the soldier, hands outstretched, and pulled the man toward him. With his left hand on the soldier's chest, Natan used his right to grab the man's helmet by the rim just above his eyes and yank it to one side with a sudden powerful jerk. The popping sound of the man's neck cracking was loud in the stillness.

Natan was leaning over the body retrieving his passport when he was again caught in a sudden beam of light.

"Holy shit!" he said aloud, reaching for the AK 47 that was still attached to the dead soldier.

He managed to undo the safety and cock the weapon, pointing it at the light and huddling as close as he could to the body, which formed a partial shield. He was about to fire when he heard a familiar voice.

"I no tell you, you most precious man I know at moment?" It was Gamil, who now aimed the light up at his own face so Natan could see him more clearly. "Not forget watch," he said, picking it up and handing it to Natan who was now on his feet.

"You good," Gamil said, smiling in obvious satisfaction. "But maybe you not know these guys walk in pairs. They smart, not like some Canadian I know who want to go alone. Maybe now you thank me for I come."

"What happened back there?" Natan asked, pointing in the direction from which Gamil had come.

"I watching you whole time. One soldier walked to you — you no see until he in you face — but the other take cover in shadow of boardwalk. When he see you attack his friend, he want shoot you head off. I do what friend do, even if friend no trust me with rest of money. I cut soldier throat. It lucky he no have finger on trigger and gun go off. That bring more company for sure!"

"Well we'd better get rid of the bodies, and get the hell out of here before some other soldiers show up. Can you swim?"

"Why you ask?" Gamil seemed apprehensive.

"What we can do is drag the bodies into the water, take them out a bit, then weight them with something and let them sink. We can swim from there into the marina and avoid the patrols."

"I help get bodies in water," Gamil told him. "You swim to marina. I walk. No reason me not walk."

"You can't swim, can you?" Natan didn't wait for his reply.

"Let's get bodies in water then."

By the time Natan was out waist-high, Gamil had reached him. He was towing the other soldier by his collar. The cut to the man's throat was clean and deep, a testament to Gamil's experience with such work. In his other hand, he was holding a heavy iron pipe.

"Where the hell did you get that?" Natan asked, moving backwards into deeper water.

"From railing."

"We'll slide the pipe into their shirts. That will keep them down long enough. And it seems that the low tide never goes beyond this point."

It had been well known for some time that a dead body in Lebanon didn't really draw that much attention. When it was a soldier, there were many suspects, and some might even be punished.

This sort of killing as such did not bother Natan. As far as he was concerned, the man he had killed was an enemy soldier doing his duty. During his years in the navy, Natan had sent many like him to their early reward.

"Now," Natan faced Gamil in the water, "can you or can't you swim? Because if you can't, I can get you to the yacht with no problem. If you go walking along the beach all wet, you'll be picked up for sure."

"So what? Even they pick me up, they let me go in one minute. I Lebanis, remember?"

"Fine, but what happens tomorrow when they find the bodies and they remember stopping someone on the beach who was soaking wet? Come on, use your head, man, no matter how you feel about the water."

Gamil saw Natan's point and for most of the way there was no problem. They went in slightly deeper, but could still actually touch bottom. Natan went ahead in case of any deeper spots, where he'd have to help Gamil keep his head above water.

"I no learned swim," said Gamil, "same my father before me. He say, good sailor not know swim. He never abandon ship. He do his best because his life depend on it, too."

At the very last leg, they had to move further out from the beach, as light was just starting to break over the mountains. Gamil promised not to panic as Natan held him under the chin and dragged him the way he would carry a wounded man. They noticed patrols several times, and waited for them to pass, treading water.

Once back at the marina, they lifted themselves onto the dock, Gamil first. He was extremely happy to be out of the water, and they both boarded the yacht just as night turned into a pale, early day.

"What this all about?" asked Gamil, half an hour later as they sat, sipping the fragrant hot coffee he had prepared. "You no give me that bullshit about diving tourists. The way you kill soldier, you are no travel agent, my friend. Agent, yes, travel, no." Before Natan could answer, he went on. "I want in, I have experience in this thing. I not want money. I got plenty money."

"What, then?" asked Natan.

"Passport. Real passport. That all. So I can get out of Lebanon and stay out."

Natan didn't want any more people involved, but at the same time, he did need Gamil. For one thing, he couldn't be in several places at once and he also wanted someone who could translate from Arabic. But he'd have to set it up so that Gamil wouldn't know his true identity. Natan knew that Gamil would work for just about anybody, and could never be trusted completely. On the other hand, Natan thought, whom *could* he trust in this lousy situation? There was something he had to know, though. "What is your problem with getting out of here? You have money, you could buy a passport."

The big man nodded. "I want place let me in, not bad papers I need look over my shoulder. You know what I mean."

"I think I do. I know there is more to it than what you're telling me but I'll take you on," Natan said finally, "under one simple condition."

"What you want?" asked Gamil without hesitation.

"You don't ask me who I'm working for until I get approval to recruit you officially. For the time being, you'll be paid only expenses. I have to get all the paperwork in place and you must realize that it's not just up to me." Natan was playing it out to the end. "I mean, I can recommend you, but someone else will make the final decision."

"I told you, I have lots of money. I give you some if it help. But what passport?"

"That will be arranged. It might just be Norway." Natan wanted Gamil to work for him, but he had to figure out just how to recruit him. After all, he was still an active case officer, albeit on unofficial business at present.

"And," Natan went on, "you can keep your money. I don't need it."

They planned how Natan would contact Gamil, who'd be staying, from September 27, at a small hotel in Paris. There would be no need for him to wait indefinitely in his room for Natan's call, as he explained.

"So long as you check with the desk for messages every few hours. That way, I can leave you a message saying when I'll call again and you can be there."

Natan was fairly satisfied that he was beginning to have a team in place, even if it was no match for anything the Mossad could put together — or even the terrorists, for that matter. But he was confident that at least he'd made the best of available resources in an incredibly difficult situation.

# 20

**BEIRUT INTERNATIONAL AIRPORT**
**SEPTEMBER 24**
**0910 HOURS**

ALTHOUGH BEIRUT International Airport is only a few miles south of the city center, it took Natan about an hour to get there by cab. The lime green Mercedes taxi seemed in perfect shape, apart from several bullet holes in the rear passenger door, but a military roadblock on Ramlet El Baida held traffic back for over a mile. The driver, clearly not a patient man, turned into rue Venezuela, a street familiar to Natan, who had led a small raiding party there in his navy days. Then the cabbie made a right on avenue Camille Chamoun and headed south at a crazy pace.

At the intersection of the airport road there was another roadblock, this time by the Lebanese police. Each car was searched, though not very thoroughly, so that in ten minutes they were at the terminal. Natan spotted Nadin, waiting on one of the side benches. She waved to him, looking really elegant in a smart gray travel suit. She is just too beautiful, he thought. She didn't look like the type of woman Halim would expect Nazir's niece to be. Halim would be expecting a student type, and that's what he should get.

"I'm sorry," he said, "you'll have to change into something casual. There's no way the real girl would be dressed like that."

"I suppose I should have thought of that. I'll go and see what I can do." She took her suitcase and headed for the washroom.

While she was gone, Natan went to check in. His own flight to Vienna left about forty minutes after Nadin's.

She was waiting for him when he returned. She'd changed into a simple cotton dress and used its sash to tie back her hair. The loose dress helped obscure her figure, too, although there was little she could do to take the edge of beauty from her looks.

"You'll do," said Natan, "though I must admit you're still extremely beautiful."

"Well, forgive me for that." She was smiling.

"Did you make the call?"

"Yes, just before you came. He said he'd wait for me at the airport, also that he had some news for me. I tried to get it out of him, but he said he didn't want to tell me over the phone."

"Great. That means he doesn't want you to change your plans when you find out your uncle is dead. Remember to act shocked when you hear about it, but don't overdo it. You weren't all that close to him."

"Don't worry. I know what to do."

"Do you know if Bassam got the girl?"

"He did, and he's here. He just went to get my ticket."

"What?" Natan felt the blood rush to his head. "What do you mean he's here? If he's here, who's with the girl?"

"He told me he has her under control. Look, here he is."

Natan turned to see Bassam walking toward them. Clad in a grubby white cotton galabiyya, he was unshaven and looked tired. He handed Nadin her ticket and boarding pass, nodding slightly to Natan. "*Ah-lan wa sah-lan ya afendy,*" he said, giving the customary Arab greeting.

Natan, staring hard at the big man, was speaking to Nadin. "Ask him about the girl. Who is with the girl?"

She spoke fast. Natan, waiting for him to answer, didn't take his eyes off the man's face. Bassam smiled as he answered Nadin. Then he handed Natan a key.

"Everything is under control," translated Nadin. "The girl's in a place where she won't be found and he doesn't have to be with her all the time. He also asked me to remind you that he would never take a risk with something that affected me."

"What's the key for?"

"He said it's for a locker over there." She indicated a separate section of the terminal. "He said the number's on it and it's something for you. Sort of an amulet for good luck." Bassam nodded to them again, said something to Nadin, and turned to go.

"Ask him . . . hey, just a minute. Where the hell's he going?"

"He said he has things to do for someone else now. He hopes to see you again one day."

"What's this amulet business, d'you suppose?" Natan was worried. All at once he didn't like the idea of opening a locker when its key came from the man Abu Nabil entrusted with his children.

"I haven't got a clue, but you can be sure that he wouldn't harm you."

"What about the girl's papers? Do you have them?" Hearing her flight called, he suddenly thought of this important detail.

"Of course! Bassam brought them to me. He also had her photo replaced with mine. Don't forget, the man is well connected."

"I hope his contacts will be quiet about it, that's all." Natan desperately wanted a cigarette, but he'd have to buy some.

"Relax. Everything will be fine. Now, I'd better go if I'm to catch that plane."

"Remember everything I told you, Nadin. And most of all, don't try to be a hero. Take no unnecessary risks. If you think something stinks, it probably does. That's when you get out."

"Will do," she said, imitating his voice. He leaned over and kissed her on the forehead. She blushed at that and drew her head back. "That's not part of the deal, Natan. We'll do what has to be done and that's it."

"I'm sorry." He was embarrassed. "I only meant . . . oh, forget it. Now get going and take care."

She turned toward the security gate, then on impulse turned back to Natan, and reaching up, kissed his cheek. Without a word she walked away, disappearing within seconds into the crowd of people boarding her flight, leaving him totally disoriented. Natan realized he must still be smiling to himself when he saw strangers giving him odd looks.

Okay, he thought, feet firmly on the ground once more, time to see what the big boy left for me in the locker. I hope it won't explode, he thought, since that would really baffle headquarters. Suppose he got blown to pieces but they could still identify the remains . . . he could see it now. But he was on vacation. In Beirut?

Locker number 189 was the last one facing the wall. Good place, he thought. If it blows up, I get plastered to the wall behind me and hardly damage anything else. Natan hesitated for a minute, then inserted the key and turned it slowly, moving his body away from the door. When nothing happened, he stood to the other side of the locker, opening the door just a fraction, to run his fingers gently around the edge and feel for a trip wire or any other device that hinted of foul play. There was nothing, but by now he was sweating heavily. He never had liked bombs, though he'd had to handle them in the navy. He was convinced that such a device would go off in his face one day.

The locker was at about waist height, so that Natan had to bend down to look inside. At first, he couldn't comprehend what he was seeing. It was unreal. Then he retched, just managing to hold back. From inside the locker, a girl's face was staring directly at him. The eyes were wide open, and the expression of surprise was unmistakable. There was only the head, in a small wooden box set neatly against the back of the locker. A wire pulled up tightly just above the edge of the neck where the head had been severed explained why there was hardly any blood in the locker. A small note was attached to the wooden box, reading, 'close door do not lock.'

Bassam was clearly a man who took no chances. Natan wondered if Nadin knew, but imagined not. Had she known, Bassam would hardly have gone to all this trouble to let him know the problem was solved, Natan thought.

Standing there, he couldn't take his eyes off hers. She seemed to be staring directly at him. He slammed the door shut. He still felt nauseous and rather faint. He'd have to get some fresh air, but first he walked across the hall to the washrooms and thoroughly soaked his hair with water, taking the excess out of it with some paper towels. The cold water helped, but still he stepped outside for some air, coming back in just as his flight was announced. His hands were shaking as he paid for a packet of cigarettes.

The sight of that dead face haunted him all the way to Vienna, and he knew it would stay with him for some time to come.

He'd seen mutilated bodies in a military setting, but a battlefield makes the atrocities of war somehow acceptable to the human brain. What he saw today and the feeling that he was in a way responsible for it, was different.

Still, it was imperative that he turn his attention back to the operation that was now in motion. As the plane neared its destination, he began to analyze how he would handle Foul Play.

# 21

**A VILLA NEAR DAMASCUS**
**SEPTEMBER 24**
**1100 HOURS**

KARL REINHART, a tall, cold drink in his hand, was seated on a large, brocade-covered sofa. He was waiting silently as a servant cleared away the remains of what must have been a small party. There were a dozen or more empty coffee cups and two pieces of sweet pastry left on a large silver tray. When the man was finished, Karl signaled that he could leave.

"What I like about Ahmed," he told his companion, "is that he immediately understands my signals."

"Doesn't he have English or German?" The husky man seated at the other end of the sofa spoke with a Spanish accent. He leaned forward to pick up his drink.

"Not as far as I know, but still I prefer that he doesn't hear anything."

"How the hell do you know that the whole place here isn't bugged and your gracious hosts aren't listening in on us at this very moment?"

"One of my men sweeps this place every morning, so I can assure you that unless you've come here with a wire, there's no way anyone could be listening in."

"To be honest with you, I don't care if they do listen. I have nothing to hide. I mean, they've been perfect hosts to me, practically from day one."

"That's good to hear. But it's not the Syrians I'm worried about anyway. I happen to know they're riddled with agents working for the Mossad, among other organizations. The agents are the real problem."

"So what is it you want us to do? I mean, you've put together an impressive group here. I had the pleasure of working with some of them in the seventies. Others I've only heard about. This is a deadly bunch of people, my friend. So, what are we here for?"

"All in good time. For now, what I want from you is to help me set up a hit on a Mossad officer."

"This is some kind of joke, right?"

"No. Why do you say that?"

"Those guys are elusive buggers. Almost every time any of us tried to get one of them, we ended up on the run or dead."

"Well, this time it's going to be different. First of all, I don't want the man dead. It must not look as if I wanted to kill him. It will actually be a two-stage setup."

"Now that sounds interesting."

"It will be, but first we have a man in the basement who must give me some answers so that I can put it all together. I didn't want to do this on my own and knowing you, I thought you'd get a kick out of it."

"Shall we go?" asked Karl's guest, straightening his thick-lensed silver-rimmed glasses. He stood up and stretched, then followed Karl, who stepped into the hall and began unlocking the door of what looked like a small closet. Once inside, he started to descend a flight of stairs, calling back softly, "Carlos, just close the door behind you?"

"Very well, amigo. Is there light in this rat-hole?"

"Yes, once the door's shut."

The two men passed through a low-ceilinged section in the

basement, then came to a fairly thick metal door. It silently swung inward as Karl withdrew the key. They entered a small room about the size of the average elevator.

"Here," said Karl, handing Carlos a set of large goggles. "Put these on."

"What are they for?"

"There's no light in the next room. It's a technique we started using for interrogation a few years back. It totally disorients the subject and means that we can make his imagination work for us. If you make the sound of metal scraping against the wall, for example, you can see what he's expecting you to do to him. It's faster and more effective than anything we used before and you don't need that much in the way of instruments."

"Why not just use chemicals?"

"When you use chemicals, there's a drawback. You have to know the precise question to ask in order to get the answer. That's not always easy, as I'm sure you know. This way, when I activate the man's fear, he'll search in his mind for things that might interest me. What could be better than that? Just one thing, though. When we're in there, don't say a word unless I ask you. And then, always answer me with a yes. Is that clear?"

"Yes, I think I can handle that."

Once they had their night-vision goggles in place, they entered the cell. The goggles made everything appear as if lit in green. The size of the room surprised Carlos. It was easily seventy feet square and probably fifteen feet high.

In the center of the room, strapped to what looked like a dentist's chair, was the subject. Allowing for the distortion in vision that a one-color view creates, the man's face bore a terrified expression. His eyes were wide open in fear and he rolled them from side to side, searching for the source of the sounds the two were making. He could not move his head as it, too, was strapped to the chair in a specially designed harness.

"You see," said Karl, "our friend here is well fed." He pointed to an i.v. bag. "And he's been extremely cooperative, but I'm still not sure he has told us everything he knows."

"Please! Please! Let me out of this place!" The man's voice rasped.

"Now, now, we mustn't get overexcited." Karl walked over to the wall and took down what looked like a kitchen knife with about a fourteen-inch blade. He went over to the man in the chair.

"Well, Mr. Shaby," he said, holding the flat edge of the blade against the man's cheek, "much as I'd like to cut you up, I'm a fair man and I always keep my word. You'll remember I promised you that if you tell me everything you know, I won't slice you up slowly, starting with your toes. But you see, I have the feeling you didn't believe me. I'm afraid you thought I was just saying all this to scare you. It seems I must demonstrate to you that I'm actually serious."

Karl turned to Carlos. "When I brought him here, I did snip one of his toes off, but that was done with a pair of cutters. I suspect it wasn't quite as painful as he anticipated it would be." He kept on talking in a very calm, matter-of-fact way, completely ignoring Shaby's pleas and the man's babbling, as if he were inanimate.

"What I have here," he went on, "and I think you can feel it on your cheek now, is a fairly large bread knife. Now, as you know, a bread knife has a serrated edge, so that when I cut your toe, I'll actually be sawing if off. That will be a slightly longer process than last time, but it will give me and my friend here much more pleasure, and it will certainly give you much more pain."

Shaby was screaming now, the pitch of his voice rising as Karl adjusted the chair to bring one of his legs up to a comfortable working height. Now the man was struggling to free himself, his naked body writhing, testing every strap. Only the heavy padding of the straps prevented him from tearing his skin.

"Please, please," he begged. "What do you want to know now? I told you everything. Everything! What do you want from me? I'll do whatever you want. Please, please, *please*!"

Karl walked around the chair, placing the knife on Shaby's stomach, then allowing the saw edge to touch his penis, as he spoke. "I want you to describe Brad to me again, and don't leave anything out."

For the next few minutes, Shaby talked. He had described the man he knew as Brad, and now he did so again. By the time he had stopped, he'd described how the man dressed and walked, even mentioned that he used the expression "no problem" all the time.

"Well," said Karl, "like I said, I'm a fair man. Let me think about this for a while and we'll decide what to do with you. Come on," he said to Carlos, "we're going out."

Once they were upstairs, Carlos said, "That was amazing. How long has he been in there?"

"About twenty hours, but he thinks it's been much longer. You see, we have a tiny white light that can be adjusted so that it gets stronger, then fades again. It creates the illusion of light coming in from the outside, so that he thinks he can tell or count the days. In fact, we just keep speeding up the process so that by now he's going through a 'day' in four hours. I'm going to bring him out of there later today so that he can do a composite of this Brad."

"Who's Brad?"

"He's the Mossad case officer who runs our friend Shaby. The one I was telling you about. It seems that Shaby passed on some information to this man that could endanger me and my work, as well as the man I have in the Mossad." Karl started laughing. "If only I could see their faces when they get the information I'd planted for . . ."

Carlos opened his eyes very wide. A broad smile spread across his face. "You have a source inside the Mossad?"

"Yes. I've had him for a long time, too. More than ten years."

"Jesus Cristos! Ten years, and now you tell me?"

"I wouldn't be telling you now if I didn't have to, but I need your help. I want you to work with me on this one. And believe me, there are others like it."

"What are you talking about?"

"This operation is only the beginning, Carlos, just to make the first customer happy. After this, the sky's the limit. You see, I have people everywhere from the Pentagon to the Bundestag, but I need a large sum of money to get things started. And a base that we can call home."

"Well, count me in. I take it you do realize that as time passes, this country will cease to be the gracious host you think it is now. After all, it's coming closer to the Americans, since there's nowhere else to go."

"Well, we'll be leaving for Libya soon. After that, we'll run things from Europe, or even the States. But for now, let's deal with the present business. What I want is to set this Brad up so that they think he's the mole they're now after. That way, they won't find my man."

"How the hell have you managed this anyway? I always heard the Mossad gave lie detector tests to their people on a regular basis."

"Trust me, my friend. This one is working for me." Carlos chuckled at that.

"I'll fetch some wine," said Karl, returning moments later with a bottle of chilled Moselle. Karl took his time explaining to Carlos exactly what he wanted done. At the moment, he could not leave Syria and handle the operation himself. But, as he put it, Carlos had been out of the game long enough now that very few people would recognize him. And he had undergone certain minor but excellent plastic surgery. Karl knew he could trust Carlos, if only because they were two of a kind. Both were outcasts of systems that had gone wrong.

# 22

NATAN ENTERED the building in a rush, still pinning the security tag to his shirt as he got into the elevator. A minor accident had caused a traffic jam, and he was twenty minutes late for a meeting with Mousa.

As never before, Natan felt insecure in the building. A guilty conscience, perhaps. Would Mousa see through him? Would he guess that Natan was hiding something? Whatever made him think he could get away with such a thing? Now, it all seemed so stupid, so unplanned. Reaching the office, he grabbed the doorknob, and wrenched the door open.

"Well it's about time." Mousa raised his eyes from the newspaper he'd been reading. Natan was standing in the doorway, out of breath. "Is someone after you, or what? What the hell's the matter with you?"

"Nothing. It's nothing. I just got stuck in traffic on the way here and I thought you might have left, so I ran. That's all." Natan stepped into the room and dropped into a chair.

"So, what's new, pussycat?" Mousa tried to appear cheerful. "How was your trip? Did you get any rest or was it all sex?"

"A little of everything." Natan was doing his best to sound

convincing. He knew that from now on he would have to be extremely careful when dealing with Mousa in particular. At the same time he could sense that something was wrong.

"So, what is it you wanted?" asked Natan.

Mousa held up a piece of paper. "We got a communiqué from Foul Play. And the video came in, the one we took of his apartment house."

"Is he clean?"

"I went over it myself," Mousa said, "and from what I can see, he was. I'd let you have a go at it, but I don't think there's anything there."

"What can you see?"

"The man comes home normally. He walks to his building, and there's no special activity around the place. Everything seems completely normal. Incidentally, that agent of yours is an ugly son of a bitch, isn't he? How the hell did you go out on the town with him when you were recruiting him?" Mousa was almost cackling over that.

"All this joking. Have you been drinking or something?"

"Fuck you, you little bastard!" Mousa was on his feet. "Don't you ever talk to me like that again, or I'll pull your balls off — right out your throat. What's the matter with you? Suddenly you can't take a little humor?"

There was something decidedly off-key about Mousa today. He was holding something back, Natan thought. And he'd have given his right hand to know what it was.

"So, what did Foul Play have to say?" Natan tried to get things back on track after several seconds of silence during which Mousa continued to glare directly at him. Mousa sat back in his chair. His voice was cold. "We'll get to that in a moment." He paused and lit a cigarette. He didn't offer Natan one. "You'll be leaving for Amsterdam in the morning. You'll be met at the Schiphol Airport by Mayer Alon. Do you know the guy?"

"Sure. We worked together in Paris way back when."

"Good. He'll take you to The Hague and drop you off at the . . . have you ever been to The Hague?"

"Several times. I can't say I know the place well, but I can find my way around. After all, it's not that big."

"He'll drop you off at the Dutch Trade Center on Spui. From there, you'll clean yourself, because you know that he's the shits where security is concerned. You'll go to a safe house about one block from the Mauritshuis Museum. The man over at Providers is waiting for you, so when we're finished, you'll go to him and get the information you need about the apartment."

"No problem."

"Your man will come to the Syrian embassy in The Hague on the twenty-sixth. That's a Sunday."

"Isn't the embassy closed on a Sunday?"

"What I mean is, he'll come to the city on that day, and he'll contact us in the way you had set up with him. Which is what?" Mousa was staring at Natan. He took a deep drag on his cigarette as he waited for his reply.

"Well," Natan said, "he has a number to call in London and leave word of where he can be reached. If everything is okay, he'll ask for Brad. If there's a problem, he'll ask for Danny. The number is one of those automatically routed to Clandestine Communications, so the message can be forwarded to me at the safe house by way of a blue box. He's not regarded as dangerous, so the meeting can take place within a few hours or even less."

"So you say," Mousa eyed him blandly.

"What is that supposed to mean?"

"In his last message," he handed Natan the paper, "as you can see, he's said he won't meet with you alone, but that you must come with another person. He wants it to be someone from the embassy whom he can recognize. Listen to this: he prefers the military attaché and he even calls him by name, as you can see."

"What the hell is this all about?"

"Why ask me? He's your agent, buddy boy, and for some reason he doesn't trust you."

"What are you talking about? Why shouldn't he trust me?"

"Listen," Mousa pointed at Natan and his voice grew louder, "all I know is that your agent has photos of the mole in the Mossad. Now that he has those photos in his grubby little hands, he refuses to meet with his case officer unless someone else is present as insurance. Now, you tell me what the hell is going on!" Mousa waved his hand theatrically as Natan started to speak. "On second thought, don't bother. Let me tell you what's going to happen, and if you're smart, you'd better make damn sure that things go exactly according to my plan."

Natan got up abruptly and made for the door. Mousa had stopped talking, and was now glaring at Natan's back. As he grabbed the doorknob, Mousa shouted at him. "Where the fuck do you think you're going? I haven't finished with you yet."

"Well, I've finished with you. I don't need this kind of shit. I have better things to do."

"You goddamn well get back here and listen or . . ."

"Or what? You'll cut my balls off? Well, to hell with you! And if you want my balls, you'd better come and get them. But make damn sure you don't get fucked in the process. I'm going to have a little chat with Amos and bring him up to par on what the hell is going on here. As head of operations, he can have someone else meet with Foul Play and get those photos."

"You're crazy. What will that prove?"

"That way, you won't have to worry about me getting my hands on these photos that you imply are of me. Am I correct?" Natan had opened the door and was already out in the hallway as Mousa lunged across the room and grabbed his arm.

"Don't you walk away on me when I'm talking to you, mister! If you don't like what I'm telling you, then you prove me wrong. But you never, *never* walk away." Mousa slammed the door behind them and walked back to his chair. Natan lit a cigarette.

"Okay," Natan stayed by the door, leaning on the wall, "so what the hell do you want?"

"I want you to do your job without sobbing like a baby. I want you to go out there where the real problems are and solve them. Do you think you could do that?"

"Is this a trick question, or what?" Natan was furious. "For years, I shit fucking cubes for the Mossad, flushed my marriage down the toilet, put my life on the line every day for the bloody Mossad, and now you clearly think that I'm a bloody mole. And you have the nerve to ask me if I think I can do my job?" Natan stepped closer to Mousa, pointing at him with his cigarette. "If you think I'm the stinking mole, shoot me! If you're not sure, make up your mind! But until then, you get the fuck off my back if you want me to do my job."

"Can it be that you've worked here all this time, Natan, and still don't understand how things are done? You are a case officer and you will do what you are told because if you don't then you become the enemy. Since you began as one of us, that makes you the worst kind of enemy, so get this through your head, right now. As far as I'm concerned, there is no way that you could be the mole, but I don't count for much when the proof hints otherwise, so what I have to do is double guard. If you are not the mole — and I assume you're not — then maybe someone wants to set you up. If you are the mole, then your life is very near its end. What the hell would *you* do in such a case?"

"What about the lie detector?"

"Something must be wrong with that piece of shit. If it had been working well, God knows, this mole should have been found by now. We all take the test often enough. Do you catch my drift? Will you do this the way I've planned, and cut the arguments?"

"Could we just get to the point? I have other things to do."

"No you don't," Mousa paused briefly. "I've declared Foul Play a dangerous agent and . . ."

"You've done what?"

"Natan, the man wants to meet with the military attaché. As far as I'm concerned, he wants to do something we hadn't planned. So we take precautions. Of course, we'll have to make up a story for the attaché, so that he doesn't clue in to what the hell is going on."

"Why don't we get someone who looks like the attaché?"

"I thought about that, but the problem is that Foul Play might know the man. After all, your friend did serve as a diplomat."

"But if we bring him in on the route, why do we need the attaché? After all, he'll be in our hands and only later will he get to see the man. Meantime we'll have the photos and we can get to the bottom of this."

"But what if he's playing a trick?" demanded Mousa. "Suppose he doesn't bring the photos, but says he'll get them only after he's seen the man? There's no way I'll take a chance on that sort of thing happening."

"What the hell," said Natan. "We'll do it your way. Will that be all?"

"Yes. The security team will meet you at the apartment to go over the plan. Everything should be ticking like a Swiss watch by then."

"No problem. By the way," Natan looked away from Mousa as he lit up again, "what's happening with the Kidon team in Athens? You didn't tell me — or is it just that you don't want to leak any information to the mole?"

"Don't fuck my brains," said Mousa, trying to raise a smile. "All is well. They're getting ready to do something, but probably not for a week or so at the earliest. The Fox's niece arrived there yesterday, I think." He paused. "Yes. She came in from Beirut to be the go-between for them. I told Amir to tell the guys to keep a close watch on her in case she leads us to someone really big. But for now, there's nothing new. They'll probably all be fucking her in a day or two."

Natan's expression changed before he realized it. But Mousa inferred something else from it.

"And no, we're not going to take action to stop them from doing our work for us, Natan." Mousa tried to soften the edge on his voice. "You know this is not personal."

"Like hell it's not," snapped Natan. He was tired and extremely tense. He didn't want to mess things up with a case of bad attitude. All he really wanted at that moment was to get out of the building.

After seeing the man from Providers, Natan headed for the academy on the other side of the compound, and the screening room there. He wanted to watch the video that had come in from Damascus. Things were starting to get hot. At least he knew that Nadin had arrived safely in Athens and been accepted as what she claimed to be — even by the Kidon team on surveillance. And in a day or two, Gamil would be arriving in Paris.

Natan was happy to find the projection room empty. Once in the room, he slipped the tape into the slot on the wall, grabbed the remote control, and pressed *play*. A red light lit above the large screen, flashing above a sign that read "enter classification." Natan punched the key on the remote and the red light outside the door went on as it locked automatically. This was a top secret showing and until deactivated, the door would remain locked.

From descriptions of the building Shaby lived in, Natan had no problem recognizing it. They had certainly placed the jeep well, he thought. People were walking along the street, passing by the camera. Some stopped to look into the jeep, unwittingly right at the camera.

From what Natan could see, there was no active surveillance around the building — not that he could see all sides of it, but when surveillance was going on and the subject was not at the location, there was always something you could pick up over a period of time. Here, there was nothing.

Natan ran the tape on fast forward up to the point when he saw Shaby pull in to park and get out of his car. He seemed to be in a rush, probably wanting to get his broadcast over quickly. Shaby had always complained about having to broadcast. He was scared shitless by the prospect of being caught red-handed.

Once he'd entered the building, a slim, tall man who was clearly European passed by. He was wearing a white suit. For a split second, something about him bothered Natan. Although the man walked up to the jeep and passed it, Natan had the impression that he stopped just beyond it to turn and look at the building. But it wasn't there on the film.

Natan ran it again and again, just that section. As he watched, he became less confident that there was anything to it. So what had made him think the man stopped? After an hour of reviewing that small section, he marked a tiny area of the screen with an electronic pen and asked the computer for it to be enlarged. It showed the edge of a chrome roof rack on the car parked ahead of the U.N. jeep with the hidden camera.

When that detail was run on its own, enlarged, onto the whole screen, the picture was a bit fuzzy, but Natan could see that the man in the white suit did stop, then turned to watch the building, standing just behind the U.N. vehicle.

Natan picked up the internal phone. It rang for about two minutes before a voice asked, "Yes?"

"Are you the training equipment operator?"

"No, I'm his helper, but I'm on duty tonight. Who wants to know?"

"This is Natan Stone. I'm in the projection room and I need some technical assistance. Can you come up here, please?"

"I'll be there in a few seconds."

"What's your clearance?"

"Top, red. I have to work with a lot of raw data, you know."

Natan sat back in his big red vinyl chair, tapping his cigarette into the ashtray in its arm. All twenty seats in this small projection room had come from an old passenger aircraft. Where the Mossad had gotten them, he'd never known, but everyone loved the room.

At the assistant's knock, Natan released the door. "So what can I do for you today?" the technician asked. He was a cheerful twenty-five-year-old.

Natan explained that he wanted the enlarged section of film to run on a separate monitor at the same time as the regular picture was running on the large screen.

"Okay," replied the young man. "What we'll do is open a corner, or window, on the big screen that will show the motion in the enlarged area. You can move this window around if it happens to obstruct the view of something on the big screen. It's a program called lens. The instructors use it a lot to prepare films for class and to perfect blue movies." He chuckled to himself at that.

"What?" Natan had been only half listening. "Just get on with it, would you?" He was edgy now, impatient.

"Okay, okay, no need to get mad." The technician opened a panel in the wall and pulled out a keyboard to make some entries. Then he handed it to Natan. "Here. You can do whatever you want. The menu is on the screen now, and it practically runs itself."

"What if I want a print?"

"Freeze the picture on the frame you want and then type 'print'. The copy will come out of this slot." He pointed to a small tray mounted flat against the wall.

"Thanks. And sorry for snapping at you."

The young man smiled as they shook hands, and was out of there just as fast as he'd come in.

Once Natan got a handle on this new technology, he could see that the man in white definitely had turned back toward the apartment building. Maybe there was no surveillance on it, but someone was surely interested in Shaby. Natan's first instinct was to call Mousa. But in a flash of insight that created a picture as clear as the one on the screen, albeit with several pieces missing, he realized there was no way that Mousa could help here: he might even be part of the problem.

Natan froze the picture of the European in the white suit as he approached the jeep and called up a print. What he had just seen raised a new and more difficult question. In meeting Shaby, would he be walking into a trap? And if so, whose?

# 23

**SCHIPHOL AIRPORT, AMSTERDAM**
**SEPTEMBER 25**
**1200 HOURS**

NATAN WALKED out of the Arrivals gate at Schiphol with a small carry-on suitcase and a suit bag. He spotted Mayer waiting for him, just beyond the gate. That idiot couldn't be trusted to do one thing right, Natan thought. Here he was coming off a flight where someone might have followed him or recognized him — and there was Mayer, like a sitting duck, waiting to be burnt too. But Natan knew there was no point in getting angry at Mayer. The man just wouldn't understand. The only reason he was in the field was because his father was a Mossad veteran who had once headed the Masada department. No one wanted to mess with him, so they let him slide.

"Hello, Natan, how are you?" Mayer walked toward him, both hands outstretched. At least he was wearing a well-tailored suit and his hair had been neatly trimmed. Quite a transformation from the way he'd looked in Israel.

Restraining a curse, Natan said, "Hey, Mayer, let's get the hell out of here. There are too many people around. Where's your car?"

Mayer pointed to the southern door, then led the way to a parked white Escort. With Natan's luggage in the trunk, Mayer opened the passenger door from the inside.

"What the hell is this?" Natan demanded, pointing at the diplomatic license plate.

"What's the matter?"

"You came for me in a diplomatic car?" Natan was dismayed. This was too much, even for an idiot like Mayer. "Are you crazy? Where's your operational car?"

"I had a problem with it this morning, so I took one from the embassy. Why?"

"Forget it. Where are the papers you have for me?"

"What papers?"

"The ones sent to you in the diplomatic pouch from headquarters."

"Oh, those. They're at the safe house." Mayer was whispering now.

"So you went with this car to the safe house?"

"I was only there for a few minutes."

"Mayer, listen to me now. Once you park a diplomatic car at a safe house, it is no longer safe. Do you see?" Natan was not expecting a reply. "Do you know if the team has arrived?"

"No. They're only due this evening."

"Good. So, you go to the apartment and get those papers, then go and register at the Pullman Hotel under your real name and wait for my call. I'll tell you what to do then, but until I call, please don't do anything. Is that clear?" Natan was almost begging. "And don't go back to the embassy."

"What about the car? Should I change it before I go back to the apartment?"

"Don't bother. It's too late for that now."

"What about the team? I'm supposed to pick them up here."

"Just go and do what I told you. I'll take care of the rest. Now, please open the trunk so I can get my stuff."

Natan took a cab from the airport to the center of Amsterdam where he called Mousa to report the situation. Absolutely incensed, Mousa promised at least four times during the conversation to kill Mayer as a favor to his father, whom he admired and respected.

"You call me back when you get to The Hague," he told Natan, "and I'll have a new address for you. I'll direct the team to you there when they call in to confirm arrival."

Natan had come to take the rapid repair of problems in the field for granted. His short trip to Beirut and what was still to come only served to remind him of how reassuring it was to be part of a well-oiled machine. If only the machine played fair.

The train ride to The Hague only took about half an hour. Natan called Mousa from the station for the address and details on the new safe house.

It was a single dwelling and quite elegant, facing a canal that overlooked the beautiful Zuiderpark in this loveliest of Dutch cities.

The door had been left unlocked for Natan and he smelled fresh coffee as he entered the old house. He followed his nose into a large wood-paneled kitchen where brass and copper pots hung on one wall over a chopping block. The entire house appeared to be tastefully furnished and, knowing the taste of the people who handled these things in the Mossad, Natan thought it must have been acquired that way.

He poured himself a cup of coffee, sitting down to look at some business cards from various countries that had been left beside the coffee-maker. These actually showed phone numbers in The Hague, disguised as international ones in case they fell into the wrong hands. One was a transfer station through which Natan could call Israel or anywhere else in the world without the call being traced or even logged onto the phone number of the safe house. As for activating a safe house, Natan knew that by heart, the basic principle being not to change anything or do anything that might draw attention.

Natan next took his luggage upstairs. On one side of the landing was a master bedroom and on the other, facing the park, a large living room, its handsome French windows letting in ample sunlight, even through the sheers that covered them.

The place is certainly attractive, Natan thought. Not that he'd be spending much time there. He wouldn't be alone for long either, as the security team would soon start to trickle in.

For the moment, as far as he knew, all was well, but with no direct link, an element of uncertainty remained. What if the terrorist team had discovered they were being observed and had changed their location? There were so many ifs. Worst of all, he knew he had to put that situation aside for now and handle the problems at hand.

Natan lit a cigarette and poured himself a glass of Dutch gin. He sat down on an elaborate sofa and rested his feet on the adjacent coffee table, watching the people in the park. Lost in thought for a time, he suddenly heard the front door open. On his feet at once, he went over to the landing.

"Who's that?" he called down.

"It's the fucking tooth fairy. Who do you think it is?" Dov was like a breath of fresh air for Natan — a real professional with little interest in politicking. Not that he'd ever act against the system.

"Great to see you, you son of a bitch," Natan said. "Where are the rest of your people?"

"Don't tell me you've forgotten already? You know we never enter a safe house in a group." Dov was smiling as he walked up the stairs. He might have been hitchhiking across Europe in his faded jeans and striped T-shirt. He had his blond hair neatly brushed to the side, a black knapsack over one shoulder.

"I like your cover," said Natan.

"What cover?" Dov looked around. "Did you ever see me wearing anything else?"

Natan chuckled as they went into the living room. "So, who's with you this time?" he asked.

"The old team, you know them. There's only one new man and he's great. You'll get to meet him in a while."

"Where have you come in from?"

"We were in Brussels on the rotation. With this semi-freeze that's been imposed, we're about the only ones active. Everybody else is more or less on vacation just now." Dov then seemed to be looking for something. "Where's your gun?" he asked.

"What gun?"

"The one you got with the house. What's the matter with you, Natan? Now that I'm here, I have to keep it. You know the regulations."

"Oh, that. It's probably in the panel above the stove, where they left it. You know I never take them out. What the hell would I do with it? Shoot my way out of a police trap?"

"You're an idiot, you know. What if it hadn't been me coming in, but a Palestinian, say, out to get an Israeli intelligence officer?"

"I was clean when I got here. Now get off my case."

"Just remember what I told you maybe a thousand times: the fact that you were clean doesn't mean everybody else was. This house might be burnt and we don't even know it. What if someone that serviced this place from the embassy didn't clean himself properly and brought a tail with him? From that moment on, the other side could be monitoring the house, just waiting for something like this.

"So, my friend, if I find out that you didn't take the weapon the next time you're in a safe house, I'll turn you in. But only after I've beaten the hell out of you. I swear, Natan, I'll do it!"

Dov took out a city map that looked similar to the one Natan had bought at the station. He then walked over to the windows and drew the heavy side drapes, shutting out most of the light. After switching on the large chandelier, he produced a chrome-plated flashlight and, from his wallet, a small plastic disc. "Now let's get down to business," Dov said, placing the disc over the flashlight glass. He directed its beam at the map, which suddenly seemed to be covered with glowing markings.

"What the hell is this?"

"We just got it from Technical. It's a new system, so that we can carry an operational map without having to conceal it. I have here every detail that can help me with the present operation, including several good security routes." He indicated a small zigzag just near the Panorama Museum. "I think this will be good for the job we have to do. I can clear this agent in about fifteen minutes." Dov was smiling. He clearly loved his work, and was one of the best at it. "There are several directions we can take after you secure the package he's bringing. There is a package, right?"

"Yes, he's supposed to bring one, but he might not. That means setting it up so that he can fetch it, if necessary. We'll really have to play this one by ear," Natan said.

"I hate it when an agent brings a package, or when he's supposed to go back for it," Dov shook his head, then said, "but, okay. If there's something that doesn't feel right, we can extend the route to here." He pointed to the second zigzag on the map. "To tell you the truth, I don't think we need that, but since we have this guest from the embassy taking part, we want to make sure that everything is perfect."

"What about the locals?" asked Natan, meaning the local police and security services.

"Don't worry about them," Dov shook his head again. "If they should stumble on us during the operation, I have some contacts there, from the courses we gave back in Israel at the academy. Besides, we have a man ready to contact the head of their service if something goes bad."

Natan had been taking it all in methodically when suddenly he jumped up, grabbing the phone.

"What is it?" Dov asked, rather surprised.

"I forgot about Mayer. I told him to go and wait for me at the

Pullman in Amsterdam. I was to call him with instructions, but I forgot."

"That dumb ass, I'd like to forget about him myself."

Natan relayed his call to Mousa's office and passed on the information about Mayer. Mousa was satisfied that for the moment, the man was in a hotel room waiting for a call.

"This is the first time in a long while that we don't have to worry about him doing some damage," said Mousa. "So let's leave him there for a while, okay?"

"He's all yours now," Natan answered. "As far as I'm concerned, you can leave him there until the end of his stint in Europe."

By 2000 hours, all the team had arrived at the house. They were busy reviewing plans, making sure everything was in place and that everyone knew their job. A local Jewish car dealer had lent them several cars, so there was no need for rentals, which was always a good thing. They broke for dinner at 2130, but continued to discuss the operation at the big kitchen table, where they ate. By 2300, everything had been verified and they headed to their various rooms to get some sleep.

# 24

**THE HAGUE**
**SEPTEMBER 26**
**0700 HOURS**

THE NOISE the team members made preparing breakfast was not something Natan could sleep through. And the combined aromas of coffee and bacon and eggs frying were slightly nauseating to him. He could feel his temples throbbing — the result, he thought, of too much of that Dutch gin last night. It had helped him fall asleep, though.

After a shower and shave he dressed in jeans and a sport shirt and headed for the kitchen. They greeted him with a big cup of coffee, followed by a hearty plate of bacon and eggs. He started to feel better.

"In the land of the herring," said a tall, dark-haired fellow of about thirty with a North African accent, "they stock the place with food like we were in the United States. What's the idea? Could anybody tell me that?"

"Give us a break," said a redheaded woman who was busy making more coffee. "You'd complain about anything — unless we brought your mother along to do the cooking."

"Leave my mother out of this. Although come to think of it, that isn't a bad idea. What about it, Dov? Let's get my mother to cook for us," he grinned, adding a vast amount of sugar to his coffee.

"Anything change since we went to bed?" Natan asked Dov.

"Not that we know of. Anyway, you're the one who does communications. We just follow orders."

"Right," Natan said sarcastically, and made a show of hurrying to dial the local relay number.

Mousa was on the line almost instantaneously. "What?" he asked.

"I'm phoning to find out if there's anything new on the arrival of that package?"

"No, nothing yet. But about those photos you'll be receiving, I want you to bring them here on the double. Once you have your hands on them, just come straight home."

"What about the bonus our man wants?"

"The go-between from the embassy will be arriving there with an attaché case for you. There may be more than Foul Play wants, but pay him whatever he asks for. Just make sure that he signs for it."

"Well, aren't you generous today? When will this messenger be here?"

"He should have been there already. Maybe he took a longer route or something."

There was a ring at the door and Natan turned to Dov, saying, "Would you get that?" Into the phone, he said, "I think that's him. Just a minute." Looking down the hall, he saw a man with an attaché case who was brought into the kitchen to join them. "It's him," Natan told Mousa. "Okay, so I'll wait for your call."

"Talk to you later." And with that Mousa hung up.

Dov handed Natan the case, looking at him as if he expected an explanation.

"It's bonus money for the agent if he brings me what he's supposed to," Natan told him.

"I see. Why the hell don't we ever get a bonus?" Dov demanded. Everybody started to giggle at that.

"Go work for the Syrians, and you'll get one," Natan said.

Now they were all laughing.

Natan took the case upstairs to his bedroom and locked the door. The case was filled with U.S. currency: he estimated three hundred and fifty thousand dollars, give or take a few thousand. There was no way he would let that money get lost, no matter what happened.

He emptied the cash into his own small suitcase and started to fill the attaché case with paperback books from the shelf by the bed. Using the small stationery kit he always carried, he glued a series of fifty dollar bills onto a piece of black crepe paper he'd unrolled. He used this sheet to cover the books. At a quick glance, the impression was that the case was full of money.

If things turned out differently from what Natan anticipated, he'd give Foul Play his money. Otherwise, he had a far better use for it.

Late that afternoon, at about 1730 hours, the phone rang. Natan, in the middle of a backgammon game with the redheaded woman, was suddenly the focus of attention. All eyes were on him as Dov nodded, handing him the receiver. The tension in the room was almost palpable.

"Yes?"

"Kid?"

"Yes." The voice on the other end was distorted, but Natan knew it wasn't Mousa. It was from the message center in Clandestine Communications and was probably Mark, but he couldn't be sure. As long as the owner of the voice knew Natan's code name and had come in on this number, there was little to worry about.

"Your friend just called. He can be reached at five eight two eight one nine. I will repeat. Five eight two eight one seven. Did you get it?"

"Thanks. When did he call?"

"About five minutes ago. I told him you were out, but would be back in ten, and that you'd call him right away."

"Okay, we'll take it from there." The line was abruptly disconnected.

Mark gave Natan two different numbers: the first was a coded number and the different value of the second gave the key to the code. Natan quickly worked the number out, then turned to Dov. "I'm going to place the call in about five minutes. I'll tell him that I'll call him back in . . . What? Say, half an hour? How long do you need?"

"Make it forty-five minutes," Dov said.

Natan dialed the number.

"Bel Air Hotel. Good day."

"May I speak to Mr. Shaby?"

"One moment, please." Seconds later, there was a buzzing sound on the line, then a click, and Shaby answered.

"Hey, how are you?" Natan greeted him.

Shaby recognized the voice at once. "Well, hello Brad. How are you?"

There was a slight hesitation in Shaby's voice that bothered Natan — even though he'd used the name 'Brad,' meaning all was well. But for the moment, Natan could only play along.

"Thank you, my friend," Natan responded, "I'm well, and how are things with you?'

"*Inshallah* (thank God), all is well."

"There are a few small matters I must take care of before we make our arrangements, my friend. Allow me to call you back in an hour or so. Just stay where you are, okay?"

"Fine fine, *ya ahi* (my brother). But you *will* bring the other man, yes?"

"Yes. He'll be there."

"I'll wait for your call then."

"See you later." Natan hung up. To Dov, he said, "Do you have a photo of him?"

"Yes, and we'll be on him the moment he comes out of the hotel."

Dov then spoke to the others. "Go, go, go. You, over to the Bel

Air and wait for him to come out. We need to know if he's clean when he leaves the hotel. You know what to do."

The young man he'd designated left without a word. Then the others left, at several-minute intervals. Fifteen minutes later, only Natan and Dov remained.

Nearly half an hour later, the first man called to tell them he was in position outside the hotel. Then a second call came in to confirm that there was someone seated in the restaurant, with the rest of the team in position outside.

"Well," said Dov, as he hung up, "you can call your man and tell him to get going."

"What about the military attaché?"

"He'll be waiting for us on the way to the meet," Dov said. "Don't worry, it's all taken care of. You just bring the bonus and I'll handle the rest."

Natan ran upstairs, returning with the attaché case which he opened slightly, so that Dov could see.

"Holy shit!" he cried. "If only we could make that sort of money being honest!"

"Not a chance," Natan said. "Let's make the call."

This time, Shaby sounded distressed when he heard the meeting was to take place somewhere other than at a hotel. "Look," he said, "what's happening? Are we really going to meet or not?"

"Yes, yes. Of course we are," Natan assured him. "I want you to meet me at a restaurant on Hogewal street at the corner of Zeestraat. It's a small place, but you'll have no problem getting there. Just take a cab."

"What's going on? Why don't we meet at a hotel like we always did before? Why this restaurant thing? Is something the matter?" Shaby sounded more and more agitated.

"What's the matter with you, Shaby? Are you getting cold feet or something?" Natan's voice had lost its softness. "What is all this anyway? I told you we're meeting in a restaurant and that's what we're going to do. Is that a problem for you? Is there something you're not telling me?"

This was Natan's chance to sound a warning for Dov, something he could not do otherwise without arousing suspicion. He placed his hand over the receiver and said, "I don't like this. Something smells wrong." He spoke to Shaby again. "You know there's no way I'd let anything happen to you. But if you're holding something back, I can't be responsible for the consequences."

Dov looked worried and began to eye Natan oddly. He signaled him to cut the conversation so that they could talk, but now Natan seemed to be indicating that there was no need for that.

"Do you have a piece of paper and a pen?" he asked Shaby.

"Yes."

"Write down the name of the restaurant." Natan spelled the name out slowly. "Now, are you ready to leave?"

"Yes, I'm on my way."

"Good. See you shortly."

"See you," said Shaby and hung up.

"Something's wrong," Natan said, seeming uneasy.

"What do you mean? Don't you have a code word when something is wrong? I mean, that's only basic, man."

"Dov," Natan was clearly troubled, "I only wish this were a simple matter of a goddamn code word."

"Well, then, I suppose all you can do is meet the man and see for yourself. At least you'll know he's clean when you do."

"There is another option," Natan countered.

"Really? What's that?"

"Cancel the whole thing. It just doesn't smell right. In fact, that's what I'll do. Listen, you get the team back from the field. I'll call the restaurant . . . " Natan fell silent, seeing that Dov hadn't made a move. "What the hell's the matter?" he demanded.

"Nothing, except that what you just said is not an option. Mousa said that this meet would take place by hook or by crook, and that's what's going to happen, so let's step on it. We have a long way to go, and we're running out of time."

"What do you mean 'Mousa said'? I'm the officer in the field. I'm the only one who can make that call and you know it. If I say we call it off, we damn well do." Natan was about to pick up the phone.

"Not according to my orders," Dov told him. "And because of their unusual nature, I got them in writing. Signed by Mousa, king of the universe, and endorsed by God. Mousa told me you might want to call this off. So how about if we stop this power game and get moving?"

Natan had no choice but to go. It was obvious to him now that Mousa thought he was the mole, since he'd anticipated his wanting to abort the meeting. Even if Natan had suspected it from the beginning, when the team was called in to secure the meeting, he now realized that Mousa wanted to create a situation in which the photos that Shaby was bringing would get into his hands no matter what happened or who paid the price.

Dov parked the white Audi by a phone booth, got out quickly, and went over to the phone.

The car was so close to the phone booth that Natan could hear Dov's side of the conversation. It turned out that Shaby had been seen leaving the hotel. He was alone and had taken a cab, just as Natan had told him to do. There was no special activity after he'd left: no speeding car, no sign of someone signaling another person.

One of the team members was now on his way to pick up the military attaché and meet Dov and Natan at a designated place. There Natan would transfer from Dov's car to the one carrying the attaché.

Several minutes later, a call came in, relayed to the phone booth. It was the team member who had followed Shaby's cab from a distance, reporting that there was no tail. And the cab had also checked out clean. It wasn't a plant. The man told Dov, "I had my car washed and let me tell you, it's shining."

"Okay. Now, are you going to that other place you were telling me about?" asked Dov. Clearly satisfied with the response, he said, "I'll see you later." He turned to Natan. "Get ready to call your man again," he said. "Give me five minutes so my people can be ready again."

"What about the restaurant he's in now?" Natan asked.

"I had someone watching it before you even gave Shaby the location, so we know it's clean. Now we know he came clean, anyway."

Shaby was seated in the restaurant as they spoke, waiting. He had no idea that the unkempt character seated near the phone was actually there to watch him. He was far more concerned with the couple that had entered the place after him, although in reality, they were tourists.

"Okay," Dov said to Natan, "now it's time for you to call Shaby and send him on a second little trip."

Dov and the team were satisfied that Shaby had not brought a tail with him to this point. Natan, on the other hand, was certain one was out there. How the hell were they doing it? There was no way to bypass the system unless Shaby was cooperating with the other side and was wired. Natan felt a shiver run down his spine. That was it. He must be wired.

As certain as he felt about this, Natan knew there was no point in talking to Dov, who was now operating in automatic mode. Nothing would make him change his plans: as the man said, he had a note from God.

Natan dialed the restaurant from the adjacent phone. After several rings, a husky voice answered.

"Do you speak English, please?" asked Natan, though he knew the answer already, as they had checked.

"Yes, yes. What can I do for you?"

"I was supposed to meet a gentleman there about now, but I

can't make it. Could you call him to the phone, please? His name is Shaby, Mr. Shaby."

Seconds later, a surprised-sounding Shaby was on the line. "Hello? Who is this?"

"Sorry to do this, but you'll have to come and meet me somewhere else."

"What's going on? This is ridiculous."

"I'll explain it all when you get here. There's no time now. Please listen carefully. It's for our own safety."

"So what is it you want me to do now?" Shaby sounded tired and tense.

The man was scared, Natan thought, far more than he should have been. What the hell were they planning? Who were they? Natan knew he must concentrate now, so he momentarily brushed those thoughts aside. He focused on the paper in his hand and was beginning to read the directions when he heard Shaby mumble something.

"What did you say?" Natan snapped.

"Just . . . is everything okay? I mean, we never had to do all this before. It's . . . it's . . . "

"Everything will be fine. Just listen and concentrate on what I'm saying, and we'll meet in no time."

"Go ahead."

"When you leave the restaurant, turn left and walk for one block. Then turn left again and walk for one more block. At the corner, you'll see a large building that looks like a castle. Turn right there and go for two blocks, where you'll come to a traffic light. Turn left at the light. I'll be in the seafood restaurant at the corner. I'll just go over that again . . . "

The route was simple, but if anyone was following, the team could pick them up, as they were already in position. As Natan hung up, a silver BMW 750 pulled in beside them with two members of the team in front. They were accompanied by the military attaché, looking nonplussed in the back seat.

Dov said to Natan, "You're leaving in a minute, but I just want to hear from my man in the restaurant that Shaby didn't call anyone after he finished talking to you. If he didn't, we're all clear to go, and I'll let everybody at the office know that the party is on."

The call came in several seconds later. "Okay," Dov nodded, "it's clean. Just remember not to move until we give you the all-clear sign, once we know he got to the new place clean." He turned to the driver of the BMW. "You make sure they don't go in unless you get that signal."

"Yes sir!" The young man said, and they all started to laugh. Even the nervous-looking officer managed a slight smile.

Natan got into the back seat of the BMW. "Hello. You must be Brigadier General Gilboa?" They shook hands.

"Yes," the attaché replied. "And you are . . . ?"

"Just a friend," Natan smiled. "After all, what's in a name?"

Before long, they were parked some two blocks from the designated restaurant. Shaby should be there in about five minutes. So far, things were going well.

"When we go into the restaurant," Natan turned to the officer, "you're not to say a word. If the person we're about to meet asks you a question, don't answer it. Just smile at him. I'll introduce him, but after you've stated your name and rank, keep quiet. Is that clear?"

"Yes it is. Could you just tell me why the hell I'm here?"

"Not really, but as you know, we couldn't proceed without you — and we do thank you for helping us out on such short notice."

Outside the car, Natan could see the youngest member of the team, standing by a small scooter. At first glance he seemed to be trying to repair something on it. In fact, he was carefully watching a spot somewhere down the street that he faced. Moments later, he turned toward the parked car and then tugged at his shirt collar with both hands as if straightening it. With that, he got up from his crouching position. That was the all-clear signal they were waiting for.

The man at the wheel adjusted the side mirror with his left hand and drove in the direction of the restaurant. Half a block away from it, he told Natan, "We'll wait for you here. The boy will soon be inside." He was referring to the youngster they had just seen on the scooter, who looked much younger than his twenty-four years.

"We're also watching from all directions. Once you're finished in there, if you want to take your contact somewhere else, we'll pick you up at the door. There's a secured hotel room ready."

"Okay. But if we don't want the ride, we'll just walk by the car as if we don't know you."

"No. We must pick up the brigadier general. If you want to go off with the agent, that's fine, but we'll need Brigadier-General Gilboa and the package."

"Alright," said Natan. "See you when it's over."

"And if there's trouble, it's every man for himself," said the driver.

"So what else is new?" the second team member said as he lit a cigarette. The officer and Natan got out of the car.

"What sort of trouble do you expect?" The attaché, almost a head taller than Natan, leaned down a little, so that no passers-by would hear him.

"You're a military man. You know things can go wrong. If I knew what they were going to be, I'd make sure they didn't. But there are always things you don't foresee. Right?" They stopped at the entrance to the restaurant. "Don't worry, okay? And remember, not a word."

The large dining room was dimly lit. Paneled in dark wood, it had a nautical decor, with paintings of sailing ships in gilt frames hung here and there. Brass ships' lanterns hung on ropes from heavy wooden support beams.

There were about thirty round tables in the place, all with white damask tablecloths and candles in hurricane lanterns. Most of the tables were occupied, the patrons casually dressed.

Natan spoke to the head waiter. "We'd like a table for three, please. I think our guest is waiting for us at the bar."

"I'll have a table for you shortly, sir," the man nodded. "The bar is this way."

They followed him into an even darker, crowded room where a highly polished wooden bar dominated almost one entire wall. A jazz group was entertaining — noisily, at present.

Shaby was seated at the bar, but on seeing them enter, he immediately approached Natan. His complexion looked gray. No sooner had Natan made the introductions than the head waiter appeared.

"Will you want to stay here or do you want to be seated right away?" he asked.

"We'll eat now," said Natan, wanting to get out of the noisy bar.

Their table was under a painting of a tall ship in a storm. The head waiter gave them each a menu. "The *Ober* will be here shortly," he said, and returned to his station by the door on the other side of the big room.

"Who will be here?" asked Shaby nervously.

"The waiter. *Ober* is Dutch for waiter," Natan said.

"Did you bring the money?" Shaby wanted to know.

"What's the rush? Is everything all right?" Natan demanded.

"Fine. Everything is fine." The little man was sweating. He seemed very anxious. He kept shifting his gaze to look at the door over the officer's shoulder. Natan was sure that Shaby was expecting something to happen, but what? The tension between them was palpable.

"What's the matter, Shaby?" Natan pressed him. "What the hell's the matter with you? You ask me to come with this man. I have. You're meant to have some photos for me. So where are they?"

Shaby pulled out a small package, placing it on the table in front of him. "Who's he?" he said, looking at Gilboa as if he'd just seen him for the first time.

"The attaché you wanted me to bring. For God's sake, Shaby, I just introduced him!"

"I-I couldn't hear you in there."

"Okay, okay, take it easy. What the hell's going on here, anyway?"

Shaby started to breathe faster. He was gasping for air now and could only stammer, "A m-m-man came and g-g-got me." His eyes were scanning the room in fear. "A German I-I think, I-I'm n-n-not sure but he spoke good English. I'm just d-d-doing what he told me to."

Natan had been right from the beginning. They had to get out of there. If there was time.

He grabbed Shaby's package. "We're leaving. NOW!" he told Gilboa and rose, pulling the man with him.

Before he was even on his feet, there was a loud noise from the main entrance and several figures dressed in gray uniforms burst into the room. They all wore identical smiling clown masks. At first everyone stared at them, bewildered. Then one of them fired a burst from his submachine gun into the large dimmed chandelier that hung in the center of the ceiling. A million bits of crushed crystal burst into the air, as the huge fixture crashed onto a table, pinning several people underneath. With that, patrons started screaming. Everyone wanted to get out, away from the shooting. People panicked, trampling each other in the attempt.

One of the men standing by the door fired a short burst into the air and shouted, "Down, down, everybody down!" He fired a second volley, but this time it wasn't aimed at the ceiling. Most of the people dove for the floor. Several were hit and fell. One couple kept running. A masked man who was about to enter the bar area turned and fired at them, catching their backs as they almost reached the door.

Now, a third man pointed at the table where Natan was slowly sitting back down. "There," he said, aiming the submachine gun at him. Natan instinctively hit the ground as a barrage of gunfire slammed into the wall behind him. With that, all the masked men opened fire and several people at adjacent tables who'd taken refuge underneath were sprayed by the bullets and slammed against the wall. There was blood and shattered glass everywhere.

Shaby was on the floor next to Natan, staring at him in horror. It took Natan a second to realize he was looking at a dead face with a small black hole in its forehead. The men kept firing as they drew closer and closer to where Natan lay on the floor. Bits of wood from the shattered tables were flying everywhere now, bullets thudding into the walls and bouncing off the floor. As he tried to crawl out of sight under the table, Natan could hear Gilboa moaning. The attaché was bleeding from several wounds. Suddenly there was silence, as the gunfire stopped. Cries for help could be heard throughout the devastated room.

Natan raised his head, to see three of the clowns standing over him. One had picked up Shaby's parcel, the second was holding Natan's attaché case.

"Who are you? What the hell do you want?" Natan demanded. No one spoke, but one clown snapped a new magazine into his Uzi and cocked it.

It was all over, Natan thought. But imagine being killed by an Israeli-made weapon in the hands of the enemy!

He stared directly at the man with the Uzi, as if daring him to shoot. He felt anger, not fear. When a moan came from under the table, the man moved the weapon slightly to the left and fired right through it at Gilboa, emptying the whole magazine into him. Natan screamed out in anger and grabbed at the weapon.

The fourth gunman, who was standing behind Natan, hit him on the back of the head with a small club. He sank into unconsciousness.

# 25

THE HAGUE
SEPTEMBER 26
1400 HOURS

OUT OF THE FOGGY silence, Natan could hear sounds. At first they were very vague and far away, but slowly they seemed to get closer as the throbbing pain in his head increased. There were voices coming in through the haze from every direction, but one was familiar and very close.

"Can you hear me?" someone was whispering in Hebrew in his ear. All the other sounds were foreign and further away. He opened his eyes to a misty image leaning over him. He couldn't make out the face. "Can you hear me?" the voice persisted.

"I can hear," Natan answered faintly. He was still in a daze, then suddenly it all came back to him.

He opened his eyes wide. With the light came a sharp pain, but he recognized the face bent over him. It was Ilan, the youngest member of the team.

As Ilan helped him to sit up, Natan looked around the place. Police were swarming in, together with paramedics and ambulance attendants. They would each stand at the door for several seconds to take in the scene of carnage, clearly unprepared for what they saw. There were wounded people groaning in agony, some crying silently in total shock, and others clutching lifeless friends or relatives.

Natan turned to see Shaby's dead eyes still staring at him. As for Gilboa, he was on his face in a pool of blood, what was left of his right hand placed over his head as he'd tried to cover himself.

"Can you get up?" asked Ilan.

"I can try. My head hurts like blazes."

"We'd better try and get out of here," Ilan said in Hebrew. "Avoid the police if we can."

"What happened to the rest of the team?"

"I don't know. I was the man inside, and I haven't been out yet to see. The police and emergency people just got here. The whole thing happened so fast. They were in and out of here in less than two minutes."

"Who the hell were they?"

"All I could see was that they were a well-trained team. That they were after you and the people at your table. How the hell you got out of this alive, I don't know. Anyway, let's get moving."

Apart from a painful lump on the back of his head, Natan seemed to be alright. They were making slow progress toward the door when he suddenly stopped.

"We have to go back," he said.

"What are you talking about? What for?" Ilan looked annoyed.

"I want to check the agent."

"He's dead, man. Most of his head's gone. Come on, let's go!"

"No. I have to check him for a wire. He had to be wired. How else would they have known to come here? There was no way he had a tail, dammit!"

He pushed Ilan away and almost lost his balance, staggering back to where Shaby lay. Natan searched the body obsessively, though he noticed that the shirt had already been ripped. Running his hands over Shaby's remains, Natan was now also covered in blood.

"Where the fuck is the wire? Where the fuck is that fucking wire? They got the wire! Shit! They got to it first!" Natan was still ranting when Ilan grabbed him under the armpits and started propelling him toward the door.

"We have to get out of here," he hissed. "Leave that to Liaison. They'll get the information later from the police."

Natan stopped fighting him then and started to walk to the door under his own steam. A policeman stopped them. "A moment, please." He was directing people to the side of the restaurant where several paramedics were giving first aid to those who could walk.

"No thank you, we'll manage," Natan answered, and headed out the door with Ilan right behind. At the end of the block, he could see the parked BMW that had brought him here. Natan was not sure why it was still there. The security team were only geared for prevention, meaning that while they could try and keep you from getting into trouble, they were not capable of getting you out of it. There was no reason for them to stay once the shooting started, but this was no time to ask questions.

As he and Ilan approached the car, they realized what had happened. The driver was slumped over the wheel, a gaping hole in his temple. In the back seat, a burnt-out cigarette still hanging from his mouth, was the second team member, shot in the chest.

"God, they really did a job on us, didn't they?" Now it was Ilan's turn to be in shock as he stared at his friends. "How could this happen?"

There were three bodies beside the car, including Dov's. He lay on his face, several bullet holes in his back, as if he'd run to help — or had been trying to get away. Natan felt Dov's wrist for a pulse. There was none. He looked up at Ilan.

"I swear to you I'll get the people responsible for this, if it's the last thing I ever do." There was pain in his eyes, pain for what had happened, and because he'd have to leave them behind, to walk away from his dead friends. "Okay, Ilan, let's get the hell out of here."

Natan had to drag the young man by the arm. Ambulances and police cars were still screaming by as he hailed a cab about a block away and gave the address. The driver, noticing Natan's bloody shirt and face, asked, "What happened to you?" his eyes wide. "Do you want me to take you to the hospital? Do you need help?"

Natan smiled, wanting to calm him down. "No, no, just take us to that address, and quickly, if you can. We are okay."

"What happened back there?" the driver asked as he started to pull away.

"We were having dinner in the restaurant when some masked men came in and started shooting. You wouldn't believe it. They just sprayed the place."

"Do you know why?"

"I have no idea."

"Terrorists," said the driver. "The whole world is going crazy with terrorists. They have this stinking war in the Middle East and they bring their dirty laundry to Europe to wash in our streets with our blood. What the hell do they want from us?"

Natan and Ilan left the taxi about two blocks from the safe house. All Natan wanted to do now was get on the phone to Mousa and report what had happened, so that he could activate Liaison and get the bodies out of there as soon as possible — hopefully preventing an international incident. He could only contain the damage; there was nothing he could do for the dead.

Ilan insisted that they first do a check on each other to be sure they hadn't been tailed. Natan went along with it, realizing at the same time that they should have been more careful. In his present state, it just hadn't occurred to him that anyone would still be following. After all, they had gotten what they'd wanted.

Once in the house, Natan moved quickly. There was no time to lose. He had no idea what his adversary was planning, but he knew by now that he was good.

Natan also knew that there was a reason why he was still alive. He wanted to know what it was.

In five minutes, he had showered and changed. With his suitcase in hand and the pistol in his pocket, he headed for the kitchen.

Ilan was still sitting at the table, staring blankly out the kitchen window in shock. Now Natan saw that he had not escaped the blood either.

"Go take a shower and change your clothes. We have to get out of here in a minute."

Like a robot, the tall young man moved slowly toward the stairs.

"Move your ass! We don't have all night!" Natan shouted at him as he picked up the phone to dial the relay station.

"Mousa," he said, his voice dry as the other man came on the line.

"What happened?"

"Did anybody else call?"

"Yes, a few minutes ago. But I want to hear it from you. What the hell happened? Come on, man, don't hold back."

Natan noticed something odd in Mousa's voice. Odd, but still familiar. He'd pick up on it later, he thought. At the moment, he was so tense he could barely think.

He went on to relate the evening's events to Mousa in a flat, matter-of-fact tone, ending his report with what had happened at their table. "At the end they came over and shot Gilboa from close range through the table. Shaby was already dead. Then they took the photos. Actually I'm not even sure it was the photos because we never got to open the package. They took the attaché case with the money and then I got whacked on the head and that was it. Ilan woke me up and we got out of there. I know they killed at least three of the team, including Dov. I'm in the house now with Ilan. We will be out of here in about ten minutes. Now, what did you get? What about the others?"

"They got five all together. The rest are on their way home. I want you to leave now and go to Amsterdam. Call me from there."

"Do you have a clue who it was? Did you pick up anything?" Natan asked.

"It's too early for that. You know it takes time. But don't worry, we'll nail someone and make them pay. After all, we now have a dead diplomat to play with."

Natan suddenly caught that wrong note in Mousa's voice again. "Why Amsterdam?" he asked.

"There's still work to do. I'll tell you when you call. Now go."

"I'm on my way. Should I take Ilan with me?"

"No. Leave him in the house. We'll have him picked up."

Natan hung up. He picked up his bag, then walked upstairs. He could hear the water running in the shower. He went to the door of the bathroom and called out.

Ilan emerged, grabbing a towel.

"I made the report," he told the young man. "They've asked me to go on, but you're to stay here and wait. They'll pick you up in a while, okay?"

"Right. I'll see you back home then."

"Take care," said Natan. He hated to leave him there as he wasn't sure that the place was safe now. But those were Mousa's orders and for now, he'd follow them.

Natan's head was still pounding as he left the house. He'd decided to do a route just to check for a tail. If he had one, he'd know that the house was under surveillance and could warn Ilan. But he was clean. He caught a cab to the station, boarding the next train to Amsterdam. He'd be making several phone calls once he got there.

Once Natan's cab had turned the corner, a tall man stepped out of a parked Renault. He wore a gray uniform-like outfit and had a small black bag hanging on his shoulder. He made straight for the house Natan had just left and after tinkering with the door for several seconds, he entered. He left the building five minutes later and sped away in the car.

Natan had to find out what the hell was going on with Nadin, and then there was Gamil, who would be arriving in Paris the following day. He was extremely tired, yet his brain seemed about to boil over. Things were happening all around him that made no sense. And something was nagging at him, almost within reach, then gone again.

He kept thinking of the man in the video. The man in white. How the hell had he gotten onto Shaby? What had been his lead? There had to be a leak, but if he was in control, why did he let Shaby expose the fact there was a mole? Or did Shaby stumble on to it and the mole exposed the leak, closing the book on Shaby? Did he get to Shaby only after the leak took place? Why kill everybody in sight but not Natan? What did they want him for? Natan still had no answers, only suspicions.

Soon he was back in Amsterdam. Natan hailed a cab less than two blocks from the train station. He saw no point in doing a route now, as he had arrived clean and there was no way the other side could know he was there.

He'd chosen the Victoria on Damrak, a hotel he'd used several times before. It was also quite close by. Natan was aching for a soft bed as soon as he could get into one.

Seated in the corner of the cab's back seat, Natan noticed as they crossed a wide canal that another car had taken a very sharp turn after them. Whoever it was took the turn too fast, with tires squealing. The lights from the car behind shone right onto the driver's headrest. There was no way they could be after him . . . but maybe he should check, Natan decided.

"I'm sorry," he told the driver, "but I'll have to go back to the station. I forgot to pick something up."

"Yes sir. You want to go back right now? And you'll want the hotel after that?"

"Yes, so if you'd just wait for me."

The driver veered into a small street where he did a 180-degree turn, then headed back the way they'd come. The other car, a white

Opel, continued along the street by the canal without changing speed. Natan had no chance to see who was in the car. The next street corner was unlit and the suspected car was now out of sight.

"Stop! Right here!" Natan shouted then, startling his driver.

The man hit the brakes and the small cab came to an abrupt stop at the curb. Natan tossed him a fifty dollar bill and leaped out, calling back, "Thank you. Keep the change."

The driver just shook his head, as if saying, "Those crazy Americans," then sped back toward the station.

Natan found himself at the entrance of what appeared to be a warehouse. He leaned against the arch of a doorway, totally immersed in shadows. The moon cast a bluish light over trees and canal.

Natan focused on the road in the direction that the other car had gone. He froze when he saw the headlights and then the same car slowly reappearing around the corner. It was moving very slowly, as if the driver was searching for something. Once it had cleared the corner, though, the car picked up speed and disappeared in the direction the cab had gone. Natan was certain now that the car had been following him. But how could that have happened? How the hell could they have known that he was coming to Amsterdam? Only he and Mousa knew that.

Then it hit him like a splash of icewater. His own people were after him! But why? Was Mousa the mole, setting Natan up to take the fall and clear himself? He found that hard to believe, but he had to know. And as quickly as possible. If the Mossad had a team on him, he'd have to drop out of sight and try to run his private operation from a hideaway. There was simply no time to waste. The thought of being on their hit list was not something he wanted to dwell on. As a list, it never grew very long — and there was only one way to get off it.

He had to get out of Amsterdam, but first he must call Mousa. He had to be sure. Natan swung his bag over his shoulder and started off briskly in the direction of his hotel. Without the motorist's impediment of one-way streets and bridges, he estimated that he'd be there in less than fifteen minutes. He was headed for a semi-industrial area with plenty of shelter across the canal from the hotel. That would enable him to watch the hotel for a time without being seen. He knew there was some sort of boatyard there, on his side of the canal. He planned to use a pay phone at the boatyard, and see what was happening at the hotel as he was talking on the phone — especially if a team had been set against him. From now on, Natan would be very much on his own.

The streets were quiet, with just the occasional car — mostly cabs — going by. Before long, he found himself in the shadow of a tall Gothic church that overlooked the boatyard. Keeping in the shadows, he walked over and looked across the canal at the hotel. From where he was standing, he could see both the main entrance and a section of the side wall with a smaller door overhung by a neon light. If he remembered correctly, that was the street entrance to the hotel restaurant. There was a pay phone between the church and the boatyard. Natan dialed Mousa's number. The phone was answered on the second ring, then several seconds later, Mousa came on the line.

"I'm in Amsterdam," Natan told him.

"Where are you now? Have you settled yet?"

"Actually no," Natan paused. "I was on my way to the hotel when I remembered something I'd left here in a station locker the other day. I had to come back for it." Natan was thinking fast as he spoke. He didn't want Mousa to sense that he suspected anything, yet he knew that if Mousa's people were after him, he must already know about Natan's little trick with the cab. "I thought I'd call you from the station in case you were waiting."

"Yeah, yeah. Fine . . . what are you going to do now?"

"I'm going from here to the Victoria Hotel. What do you want me to do then?"

"Nothing. Just get a good night's sleep and call me back in the morning. I'll have instructions for you then."

"Okay, but if you need me in the meantime, I'll be at the hotel under my Israeli passport."

"Is that in the file?"

"Sure. By the way, what's happening in Athens?"

"Nothing new. It seems they're still waiting for orders."

"Did that idiot Halim get all his men in like he was supposed to?"

"We think so. We're not sure."

"Even with that kind of surveillance?"

"Well, since the girl came, they seem to be taking a lot more precautions. Actually one of the guys on the new surveillance team said that the girl reminds him of someone."

"Of whom?"

"Well, that's just it, he can't place her. But he was an officer in military intelligence, so he might have seen her photo in a file or . . . who knows? Anyway, we'll be getting her photo here to run through the computer for a match. If there's something going on, we'll find out."

"Right," Natan said. He leaned reflexively back as he saw two cars pull up at the hotel. Several men got out. Though he could not make out their faces or even their coloring, it was clear to him that they were taking position to set up a trap. Once he had told Mousa that he was going to the Victoria, they must have received the relayed message. And this setup was not for a kidnapping, as there was no car or van to pick up the subject — himself. They were setting up all to one side: that was so they wouldn't end up shooting each other.

They were going for an elimination.

"Okay," said Natan, "I'll call you in the morning. Oh, by the way, did someone pick up Ilan in The Hague? The man was in total shock when I left him."

"I haven't heard yet," Mousa said. "I should be hearing any minute, though. Everything's under control. Talk to you tomorrow." The connection was broken.

Mousa was lying to him, Natan knew, just as he now knew he'd been framed. That was why he hadn't been killed in the restaurant. It was all a setup to make him look like the mole. Mousa had clearly been convinced of it, so he'd given the order to eliminate Natan. But the mole could still be Mousa.

And if Mousa — or whoever was setting Natan up — could make it look as if he had been eliminated by the same group who did the job in The Hague, no one would have to respond to internal questioning by the Shaback or anyone else who might have heard that the Mossad had been harboring a mole. Instead, Natan would be found floating in an Amsterdam canal with a couple of slugs in his temple. Or so they had apparently planned.

Natan wanted to get a little closer, to get a better look at whoever it was they had sent after him. He felt much calmer now; he knew exactly where he stood as far as the Mossad was concerned, but they didn't know yet that he knew. He had managed to get a head start.

He moved stealthily along to the corner of the church and peered across at the hotel. The team had concealed themselves completely from anyone who might approach the entrance, as they expected him to do. Now he was peering through the window of a parked pickup truck further along the street, having made his way to it in the shadows. There had to be another person he hadn't seen yet — the one who would signal them that someone was coming and then identify him. Until he could see that person, Natan would not move from his present position. Suddenly he picked up a slight movement, not ten feet away from him. He squinted, trying to focus on the slender silhouette standing by a tree. It was Number Nine.

The bastard! Natan thought to himself. Of all the dirty, stinking things Mousa had ever done, this one really topped them all. For one moment, Natan was tempted to walk right up to her and tell her what was happening and that he was the wrong target. Would she listen to him? Not a chance, he thought.

Natan slowly crouched to the ground behind the truck, so that its wheels made a cover between him and Number Nine. Even if she were to look in his direction now, she'd see nothing.

"I'm in position," he heard her say, probably into a transmitter.

Once on the ground, Natan turned to try and devise an escape route. He couldn't stay there much longer. The trees would provide some cover, so long as Nine continued to focus on the hotel. Just at that moment a taxi pulled up at the entrance. Knowing it would engage the team's attention, if only briefly, Natan broke cover, walking fast along the grassy verge of the canal until he came to some steps leading down to the water. Roped to the dock was a small motorboat. Its Mercury engine was familiar from his navy days: he could probably take it apart and rebuild it with his eyes closed. There was a tarpaulin over the boat and after slinging in his bag, he used the canvas to cover the engine and muffle the sound slightly. After several minutes of tinkering, he pulled the cord and the engine roared to life. The small boat almost leaped out of its berth when Natan applied the throttle. Leaving a shimmering wake behind, he was on his way. For now, at least, he was out of the team's grasp.

"Why did you give him all that information?" asked Mark as Mousa hung up.

"What does it matter what you say to a dead man?"

"Well, he's not dead yet," said Amir, "and from what I heard about the man, it won't be all that easy, either."

"What are you talking about?" Mousa snapped. "It's your team out there. You mean to tell me they can't take out one unarmed, unsuspecting man in a friendly country?"

"The country may be friendly, but suppose Natan doesn't cooperate."

"But he doesn't suspect anything," Mousa countered.

"Are you sure we're doing the right thing?" Mark looked worried, for once. "After all, he's one of the best men we have. He's your friend, for God's sake. How can you be so sure he's the mole? We haven't even talked to him yet."

"You call that a friend? He sticks a knife in my back and sets up a whole Yarid team. What are you, stupid or something? Dov was his friend too, and where is he now? So what's to talk? The agent didn't want to meet with him alone because he had a photo of the mole and it was Natan. That's why he asked for a second Israeli, one he knew was not working for the Syrians. So — a secure meeting was set up, but now the only people there who knew about it, with the exception of Natan, are dead."

"What about Foul Play?" said Mark.

"Foul Play was clean, and up to the last minute, he had no idea where the meeting would take place. He was watched at all times and he didn't make any attempt to contact anybody.

"I'll be honest with you, after I talked to Natan on the phone from the safe house, I still wasn't sure. I thought, maybe the stinking agent was wearing a wire, so I just wanted the team to bring him in. Isn't that so, Amir?" Mousa looked to Amir for confirmation.

"That is correct," Amir nodded.

Mousa went on. "But when our people went to the house to pick up Ilan, they found him shot in the head. He was the one inside the restaurant watching. He probably saw something Natan thought he shouldn't have." Mousa turned away from them and stared out the window into the night.

"What?" Mark snapped. "You never told me that."

"Well, now you know." Mousa turned to face him. "And I bet Natan thinks that he's cleaned all the evidence and he can come back and laugh in our faces. We're not going to wait and have a full-scale investigation into the matter, though. Forget that. The man is dead. It's all over."

"I still think we should give him a chance to answer the accusations. We owe him that," said Mark.

"We owe him nothing. And that is final. I don't want to hear one more word about it, Mark. Do you understand me?"

"Yes." Mark's voice was low. He was staring at the floor.

"It's not easy for me either," Mousa went on. "He was my friend, too. We'll do it quietly, so we can bring his body with the others and no one will have to know his shame. That's what the chief wants."

"What if he gets away?" asked Amir.

"We'll find him wherever he is, and kill him. That's why we have a Kidon team out there."

Natan tied the motorboat to a small dock several miles east of where he'd found it. He was in a fish market that was just starting to open for the day. He'd thought at first of making his way to the airport and taking the first flight to Paris, but he feared that Number One would have placed at least one man at Schiphol as a backup in case anything went wrong. Natan knew they wouldn't attack him at the airport, but he preferred they didn't know where he was headed. Even so, they would no doubt alert all stations to be on the lookout for him, so that he would have to keep a very low profile wherever he went.

He ate a quick breakfast at a café and checked their phone book for the nearest car rental outlet. There was an agency about three blocks away and at 0800 he called to reserve a car. He drove to Rotterdam, where he caught a train to Brussels.

He called Gamil from there to say he'd contact him again later that day with instructions.

There had been no sign of a tail. With all the delays and the time he had to kill, it took him most of the day to reach Paris — a mere hour and a half flight from where he'd started. One thing he knew for sure: he was still clean.

Natan took the Métro to the Opéra station and changed trains there, getting off at Latour Maubourg. He walked to the corner of

Maubourg and St-Dominique, a small street leading into an old residential area of narrow streets, tall narrow houses, and small boutiques. He was hoping to get a room at a hotel he had used before, but had never discussed with anyone in the Mossad.

The hotel, Les Jardins d'Eiffel, was in a cul-de-sac called rue Émilie. It had a tiny reception area. The hall that led off behind it had a small inner courtyard on one side. The elevator and a luggage room were on the other. The only meal served at the hotel was breakfast, in a first-floor dining room that seated twenty at most.

They had a room for him and he went up to make several phone calls and change.

When he saw himself in the bathroom mirror, Natan realized how badly he needed a shave. If it was only a matter of appearance, it would be no problem, but it was much more than that. He was physically and mentally tired. In a matter of days, the magnetic poles of his life had shifted dramatically. Some of his best friends were dead and others were after him. Some people he would have considered his worst enemies were now his allies — at least he hoped they were. He pulled himself together. This was no time to mourn and dwell on what had happened. He had to make some calls.

He dialed a local number and let the phone ring twice. Then he hung up and redialed. At the second ring, a woman answered, "Oui, âllo?"

"Hi, how are you, my dear?"

"And you, chéri, are you in town?"

"Yes."

"When did you arrive?" Her accented English only added to the appeal of her husky voice.

"About an hour ago. Did anyone call for me?"

"No. No one has called. Are we going to meet, Natan, or are you just passing through?"

"I have the feeling we're going to meet, and have a good time too, only we won't be able to go out on the town this time."

"I have Paris all the time," she said. "It's you I don't have. When will we meet?"

"I'll call you back. Okay?"

"Okay. I'll wait for you." He had known Céline Roger for more than fifteen years. She had been a volunteer in an Israeli hospital where he was recovering from a wound he'd sustained during a special mission in Lebanon. Céline had come there in defiance of the embargo her government had imposed on Israel in the wake of the 1967 war.

Natan was unmarried at the time and she was something else. The "whirlwind of youth," she would call it later. For several years after that, they didn't hear from each other. Then one day a few years ago, they met by chance in Paris. He was already working for the Mossad and she was then at medical school. From then on, they would usually meet whenever he was in Paris, but he'd never spoken of her to anyone. He was now extremely happy he'd kept it that way. It was Céline's phone number that he'd given Nadin.

The Frenchwoman knew that she was only to take a message if ever such a call came through, and she loved the idea that he was involved in something that he could not tell her about. Discreet about such things by nature, she asked no questions.

After speaking with Céline, Natan called Gamil. He picked up the line almost instantly.

"Hello, my friend," said Natan. "I want to meet with you in about an hour."

"Where?"

"Well," Natan paused, "when you leave your hotel, go left into rue du Bac, then continue left until you reach a street called rue de Babylone. Make a right onto it and walk to avenue de Breteuil. Turn left there and in about two blocks, you'll come to the Bistro de Breteuil. Wait for me there. Did you get that?"

"I be there."

"Oh, and wait about forty-five minutes before you leave. It's not

all that far. If I'm not there by twenty-one thirty, go back to the hotel and wait for my call."

"Is problem?" Gamil sounded worried now.

"No problem, just precautions."

Natan quickly showered and shaved and was soon out of the room. The instructions he had given Gamil were such that the man would be going on a specific route and Natan could place himself somewhere along the way and observe him as he went by, to see whether he had been followed. Natan wanted to be very sure.

They met an hour later; as far as Natan could see, the man had come to the meeting clean. Natan gave Gamil a set of instructions for his role as go-between, which he would soon start to perform. They set up the phone and message codes they would need. Meanwhile, Gamil was free to do as he wished, but he must check with his hotel at least every two hours for messages from Natan.

Gamil was clearly enjoying himself and extremely eager to do things. For someone who'd come from Lebanon, most things were like a game, Natan thought. Just to be away from there must seem unreal.

Céline lived on the fourth floor of a lavish apartment house just off avenue Foch. With its high ceilings and heavy marble and gilt décor, the place looked more like a small wing of a palace than a conventional apartment, but then her father was in the arms business, leaving her with no shortage of money.

Natan had no sooner knocked on the door than she flung it wide open for him.

"Come in Natan," she said, smiling. She wore a floor-length sheer negligee of pale beige, trimmed with exquisite lace of the same color. Her chestnut hair was shoulder-length now. She really was an exquisite sight, Natan thought, pushing the door shut behind him and taking her in his arms.

They kissed hungrily and at length, then she shrugged out of

his arms and led him down the hallway. He followed her into her bedroom, where an open bottle of champagne was chilling in a silver ice bucket on the side table. She handed him a long-stemmed wine glass and held one herself as he poured the champagne. She sipped a bit, then placed the glass back on the table. Slipping off the negligee, she moved toward him. With that, she proceeded to undress him slowly, sipping champagne as she did so. Natan poured them each some more and, as he set down his glass, she wrapped her hands around him, caressing his body as she slowly slid herself down him until she was on her knees. Then the joy ride started.

# 26

**MOSSAD HEADQUARTERS**
**SEPTEMBER 27**
**1305 HOURS**

"COME ON IN, come in," Amos got up to usher Avy into
the room, closing the door behind him. He punched the intercom,
and notified the receptionist that he was not to be disturbed.

Amos was not in the best of moods, but he hoped that Avy might
improve it by shedding some light on what was happening behind
doors that he'd found closed to him for the first time in years. Avy,
a computer operator in Clandestine Communications, had information for him on some operation that was going on in Europe. The
operation itself, as everyone knew, was being run secretly by
Mousa, who was a close friend of the boss. It was confined to the
Masada department and as such, it was no skin off Amos's back.
But all that changed abruptly when an agent he considered to be
under his jurisdiction *and* an entire Security team were wiped out.

He, Amos, head of Operations — the most important department in the Mossad — had not even been informed of what the hell
was going on. They were keeping him in the dark. In the Mossad,
where lack of knowledge meant weakness, it was a slap in the face
that he could not tolerate.

Then Avy had called to say he'd found something that Amos
might want to know.

"So, Avy, what do you have for me?" Avy was soon being transferred to a clerical position in the London station. The transfer was because Mark had learned that he was one of Amos's clique and so wanted the man out of his department. But Amos had made sure Avy got a cushy job. He always took good care of his people.

"I was in the middle of transferring the file codes to the new kid who's replacing me when the information about the disaster in The Hague started to come in."

"What the hell are you talking about? You handle information from the land of the dead, don't you? The incident with the Security team was in Europe. Why was it coming through Clandestine Communications?"

"That's exactly the point. The information was from a Kidon unit that had been sent to Amsterdam. They were taken off a surveillance mission in Greece the day before the incident, and placed on standby in Amsterdam. After the massacre, they were dispatched to take out what the message called a mole."

Amos froze, his mouth slightly open.

Avy wasn't quite sure what to do. He realized he'd brought in a big one, but he couldn't quite quantify what he might personally gain from it.

Finally, Amos leaned forward, folding his arms on his desk, and staring hard at Avy. "I want to make sure I got this right," Amos said, his voice low. "There is a Kidon team out there now with instructions to eliminate a mole? Was that all?" Amos pushed, hoping for a bonanza.

"No, there's more."

"Okay, come on, don't wait for me to squeeze your balls. Talk, my boy, talk." Amos looked straight at him.

"Well, apparently the mole got away and now they don't have a clue where he is." Avy looked at Amos. "Mousa won't permit Mark to call for a 'red coat,'" he said, using the code words for a hunt involving all stations.

"Why not?"

"I'm not sure, but it's what Arik told me."

"Wait a minute. How come Arik is suddenly telling you things? I thought he was one of Mark's people?"

"Well he is, but I think he feels that something is not totally kosher, so he wants to cover his ass. It's always the little people that end up eating the shit when the bigwigs screw up, you know."

"Good, good." Amos was grinning. "Go on."

"Well, he told me that there had been this operation in Greece to make sure the terrorists who were under surveillance there didn't pull a double-cross and come after our people."

Amos wasn't sure what Avy was talking about, but he was not about to let him know that. The picture was becoming clearer the more Avy spoke.

"Did they name the mole?" Amos held his breath. This was something he didn't dare hope for.

"Sure. It's Natan, from Al."

"Very funny." Amos was not amused. His fair complexion seemed to turn a pale yellow. "I mean, you had me there for a second, Avy, but really, you don't . . ."

"I'm not kidding. It is Natan. I swear to you it's the truth."

"Who else knows?"

"Only Mark, Mousa, Arik, and a guy from Masada whose name I don't know."

"You're not going to tell anyone else about this, are you?" There was a subtle warning in Amos's voice.

"Why should I?"

"Good work. This will not go unrewarded." Amos walked Avy to the door with his arm across the younger man's shoulder. "Maybe I'll see you in London one of these days."

Amos shut the door and returned to his desk. This time, he was going to nail that creep Mousa, and that stupid asshole Mark, Amos thought. They didn't want a hunt? Well, he was going to give them one they wouldn't even hear about. He'd reel in that fucking mole and thereby guarantee himself the position of next head of Mossad. He'd been waiting for something like this for a long time.

He could see it all now: the man at the top forced out, handing the Mossad to him. The day was getting closer. There must be a God, he thought, grinning blandly as he lit a cigarette and proceeded to work things out in his mind. Amos then called in his secretary. "I'll be going over to the academy for an hour," he told her. "I want you to get me on the first available flight to London and book me into a hotel. Cancel all my appointments for today and tomorrow and reschedule them for later this week. Oh, and one more thing. Call my wife and tell her I won't be able to make it to dinner with her parents tonight. Say that I'll call her later on."

Several minutes later, Amos was out the gate in his car and on his way into Tel Aviv. He had to make a phone call that wouldn't be overheard. Time was a factor if he was to get Natan first, but he had the means.

Once in the city, he parked in the Klal parking lot just behind the Tel Aviv movie theater, then he walked several blocks to an apartment building. Amos let himself into a second-floor apartment, and headed straight for the bedroom, where he grabbed the phone and dialed a number in London. The call was answered on the third ring.

"I'd like to leave a message for Edgeworth, please," he said. "Tell him Fred called and he must call back urgently. I'll be waiting."

"Certainly, sir. I'll pass it on to him straight away."

"Thanks," Amos said and hung up. How he loved the British. So well-mannered, and everyone knew their place. Nothing at all like in Israel. Here he was, head of Mossad's most important department, one of the most powerful people in the land, and office workers called him by his first name. Yet if he were to demand a more respectful approach, they'd call him a snob or elitist.

When Admony had been boss, things had been a bit different, he recalled, and had started to get even better. But then came this slob Avraham, dragging the standards down again. Well, things would be different when he became boss, Amos thought, certain there was now a better chance of that happening than ever before.

The phone rang. Amos grabbed it. "Hello?"

"How are you, my friend?" Edgeworth asked.

"I'm fine," Amos replied, "but there's something we must discuss. It's related to the matter we were talking about the last time we met. Certain things have happened since . . . some I was not immediately aware of, and I need your help."

"I'd be delighted to help if I can. When should we meet?"

"I'll be there tomorrow morning."

"I do have several meetings in . . . well, you know what I'm talking about. After all, this is not official, is it?"

"No, of course not."

"I have a lot on my desk at the moment, you do understand?" he hesitated for a moment. "Shall we say . . . seventeen-thirty then, at the regular place?"

"See you tomorrow," Amos said, and hung up the phone. He left the apartment and headed back to the office. He knew he could count on Edgeworth. The Englishman had helped Amos a lot over the years.

# 27

**LONDON**
**SEPTEMBER 28**
**1730 HOURS**

AMOS HAD just arrived at the secluded house in Chelsea.
"A Scotch?" Edgeworth offered.

"Yes, please." Amos sank into the comfortable sofa, letting out
a short sigh.

"Is everything alright?" asked his host.

"It could be better, if you know what I mean."

"I think I do." Edgeworth handed him the drink and sat down
across from Amos on a high-backed leather chair. "How can I help
you?"

Amos gave him a straight look. "Let me say first that this could
prove to be just as important to you as it is to me." He sipped some
Scotch, placing the glass on the low coffee table in front of him.

"Can we involve my firm? After all, we could do much better for
you as an organization than I could do on my own, you know."

"No. We can't have MI5 asking questions. That would be like a
brush-fire. This simply can't go through the regular channels."
Amos opened his small briefcase, extracting a large manila envelope. He withdrew a number of documents and placed them on the
coffee table. "This is the man I'm looking for," Amos said, handing

Edgeworth a photo of Natan, attached to a sheet of paper. "This is a short summary of his file."

Edgeworth nodded. "And?"

Amos went on. "This man is, or should I say was, a mole in the Mossad. Another department is out to liquidate him at the moment, but I want him. I'd prefer to have him alive so that I could question him, but I'll take him dead if necessary. Either way, I need your help."

"Let's be absolutely clear on this." Edgeworth leaned forward, holding the file. "You want to get your hands on this man and, correct me if I'm wrong, you are a department head in the Mossad, with stations and all. What the hell do you need me for?"

"Because I can't activate my people to look for him. I'm not even supposed to know that he's been fingered."

"So what will happen if you catch him?"

"Once I've produced him, I'll clean house in the Mossad, getting rid of some thorns I've had in my side for a long time."

"And where do I come in?"

"The man is operating at the moment in Europe. You have unofficial contacts who could find him for me. Once you've located him, I'll take care of the rest."

"How long will you be here?"

"I have to go to Paris on my way back tomorrow, but meanwhile I can be at your disposal."

"I'll see what I can do. Just don't forget me when you're head of Mossad and I'm only a small potato for you." Edgeworth smiled slyly.

"You know better than that," said Amos. "Oh, and remember," he waved his hand, "the thing I was telling you about — that piece of information that came in on the terrorist team that wanted to hit a Palestinian target?"

"Yes, of course. We're still working on that."

"Well, apparently the leader of that team was kidnapped and eliminated by our people so that the terrorists wouldn't know we had a fix on them."

"Why didn't you tell me this before?"

"I only found out about it yesterday. You see, the mole was in charge of that operation, so he must have informed his masters by now. I have to assume that if they have anything to do with the terrorists, it's quite possible the hit won't take place at all."

"How did you realize the man was a mole, anyway?" Edgeworth sounded a little perturbed now, and when Amos took a moment to answer, he went on, "Look, you want me to drop everything for you but so far, you've held back on this. Now as far as I'm concerned, the whole thing could be a mistake and then I'd be the one with my ass in a sling. Come on, man, how do you know for certain that he's a mole? I really must know before I can take this any further."

Amos proceeded to tell Edgeworth the entire story, as he knew it, from Shaby's initial dispatch right through the bloodbath in The Hague, Natan's supposed murder of Ilan, and his subsequent escape. When he'd finished, Edgeworth walked over to the sideboard and poured them each another Scotch.

"The man is clearly a tough customer. Who do you think he's working for?"

"I haven't got a clue. That's one of the reasons I want the bastard alive — and it may also be a reason why someone else doesn't."

"You mean he might not be working alone in the Mossad?"

"It's possible, don't you think?"

"Yes, yes. Everything is possible. Right, then. I'll do what I can, though you know I can't promise results on the spot. But I'll do my damnedest. You can count on that." Edgeworth sat back in his chair and crossed his legs. "By the way," he smiled slightly, "I just wanted to ask you one more thing, Amos."

"What is it?"

"What are you people going to do about the terrorist team?"

"What do you mean?" Amos scowled.

"Why don't your people take out the terrorists?"

"What for? If they end up hitting some other terrorists who call themselves moderates, why disturb them? I mean, they'll be doing our work for us."

"You people play a dirty game, my friend," Edgeworth told him.

Smirking, Amos said, "Well, we live in a tough neighborhood."

"Which reminds me, what about this fellow you people kidnapped? What did you get out of him?" demanded the Englishman.

"Not much, apparently. The team hadn't received their directives yet, so he didn't know when and where the attack was going to take place. I don't have all the information on that. Can you believe it?" Amos sipped from the drink. "They were keeping me and the rest of the brass out for so-called security reasons while they let a mole in on the secrets." He shook his head in disbelief. "Well, they'll pay for that, every goddamn one of them."

"So, what now? Are you people at least watching the terrorists? I mean, what if they decided to hit another target?"

"We have a team watching them around the clock. Don't you worry about that. We won't let them out of our sight now."

"I'm glad to hear that, because I have my responsibilities too, friendship notwithstanding."

"It's all under control. Just get me that guy in the photo and you'll be a happy man, I can promise you that." Amos stood up. "I'll be going now. But I'll be waiting to hear from you."

"I'll be in touch. You said you're going back by way of Paris?"

"Yes. Just before I left Tel Aviv, I got a call from one of my case officers in the Paris station. It seems that an agent we shelved some time ago as useless called in wanting to sell us some information on how we could get our hands on Abu Nabil. It's probably nothing, but I told him to bring the man in so we could talk to him."

"How interesting," said Edgeworth, as they walked over to the door. "Do let me know if it amounts to anything."

"Like I always say, one hand washes the other, Edgeworth. You find my man and maybe I can send you Abu Nabil."

# 28

**PARIS**
**SEPTEMBER 29**
**1400 HOURS**

NATAN KNEW he had to keep moving, with the Kidon team on his trail. He and Gamil went by cab to a small airport outside Paris. Their destination was Athens.

Gamil had arranged the flight through a friend who owed him a favor from the "good old days," as Gamil called the time when he ran a prosperous business in drugs. Aboard the plane he cursed the Phalangists who drove him out of the trade.

"Bastards wanted take business. They not care about Lebanon. Made money same way I do, but not leave it in country. Say they patriots, but have Swiss bank accounts!" He went on griping for the greater part of the flight, which was mercifully short.

By nightfall, the two were in a hotel in Athens.

"Things are going to start in earnest tomorrow morning," Natan told Gamil. "You'd better get some sleep."

Natan was out in the cold again and he wasn't happy about it. In fact, it was much worse this time, as all the doors were locked. He found it difficult to sleep. It wasn't the stress or the tension, he knew, because he had slept under worse conditions. After all, a good soldier could fall asleep anywhere.

There was something different tonight: the arranged meeting

with Nadin was tomorrow. She hadn't called early, so things were well, but he kept seeing Nadin's face whenever he closed his eyes. He was worried about her, felt responsible for her. But it was more than that: he missed her. As strange as it sounded to him, it was true — even though they'd spent very little time together.

The next morning, Natan told a sleepy Gamil, "In a few hours, you'll be sitting in a small restaurant called Fatso's, a couple of blocks from the Hilton. When you get there, order something to eat," Natan smiled. "I guess I don't have to tell you that."

"No," Gamil yawned. "With food, you trust me, okay! So, I in restaurant, I eating. What you want me do? I know you not bring me from Beirut to taste food."

"True. You're going to the restaurant to meet a lady. I'll describe her to you but regardless, she'll have a green cotton carryall about the size of a telephone book with her. The lady is Lebanese, so you can choose whichever language you want for making the contact."

"I use English"

"So long as you feel comfortable. When you see her, you're to ask directions to the American Embassy. If she says she doesn't know, but she can direct you to the British Embassy, you have the right girl. You can then tell her that Kevin sent you and that she is to call this number from the main post office in Omonia Square. Is that clear, my friend?"

"You think I stupid?"

"No. If I did, do you suppose I'd work with you?"

"Tell me, lady I meet named Nadin, yes? One you see night we meet on beach?" Gamil raised one eyebrow and leaned across the table.

"You son of a bitch! You knew all along!"

"You bet, when I see you go to house of daughter of Abu Nabil! I watch you first time you go to shore with dinghy."

"Well then, if you know what she looks like, you'll have no problem identifying her. But you must still go through the routine, since she doesn't know you — or is there something else you want to tell me?"

"No, nothing. But this not to be very dangerous, what we do. I mean, how dangerous it be if you to put Nadin in it?"

"What do you mean?"

"If I telling daughter of Abu Nabil do something, believe me, I be sure it safe for her. Or I not want her father to know what I look like!" Gamil laughed.

"Well, I guess I'm in really big shit then, since she is in a very dangerous situation indeed. Now that we're together, though, I'm sure you'll do whatever you can to minimize that danger. Am I right?"

"You bet. So, what in name of Allah we doing here?"

"The deal, if I remember correctly, wasn't for you to ask questions, but to help me out in return for a passport, right?"

"True."

"Well then, when the time comes, you go to the restaurant and pass the message. Is that understood?"

"Yes."

Gamil left around 1130. Natan went out shortly afterward and hailed a taxi. The driver of the yellow cab had a set of traffic rules all to himself. Natan only wished that he could call on this driver whenever he had to shake someone off.

On the other side of town, he entered a small restaurant that he knew had a working phone, as he'd called earlier that morning. After ordering lunch, he told the waiter that his name was Kevin and he was expecting a phone call. The man seemed to appreciate the effort the tourist made to talk to him in Greek, as well as the ten-dollar tip. He replied in very good English, "Sure, Mr. Kevin. It will be my pleasure."

"You speak English. Why didn't you tell me?"

"You seemed to be having such a good time torturing our language, I didn't want to be the one to stop you." The waiter smiled jovially as he went to take another order.

The phone call came half an hour later. It was Nadin, her voice quavery. He could tell right away that something was wrong.

"Nadin, what's the matter?" he demanded.

"I have to meet with you," she said. "Someone will be coming in tomorrow with the instructions for the operation. It's to take place in the next couple of days. I must talk to you."

"When are you expected back?"

"Not until later tonight. I told Halim that I was going to stay out at the Plaka tonight and that he shouldn't wait up for me."

"Are you at the post office in Omonia Square?"

"Yes, that's where the man you sent told me to go."

"That's great. Can you see out from where you're standing?"

"Not much, wait a minute." There was a pause. "Yes. Okay."

"Well, there should be a big Coca Cola sign on the side of a building. Actually, it's almost the size of the building which is . . ."

"Yes, I can see it, it's right across the square."

"I want you to go to that building in about half an hour. Until then, I'd like you to browse in the cosmetics shop at the left of the post office. Can you do that?"

"Yes. Alright."

"When you leave the shop, don't cross the square, though. Go around counter-clockwise and stand by that building for not more than ten minutes. If I'm not there by then, go back the way you came, and into the cosmetic store again. I'll call you there."

"What's going on? Why can't you just come over here and pick me up?"

"I want to make sure it's safe."

"Don't worry. I know the people I'm working with, and I know they didn't follow me, so relax."

"You don't know the half of it. Trust me, Okay?"

"Okay. See you soon."

Natan had no time to finish his lunch. He handed the waiter two twenty-dollar bills.

"That should take care of the tab, but I have to run. Keep the change."

He was already out the door, grabbing a taxi almost immediately. "Syntagma Omonia," he said to the driver and placed a twenty on the seat next to him. "I need to get there yesterday."

The driver clearly got the message — the more so when he saw Natan holding a second bill. What should have taken almost half an hour took less than fifteen minutes. After a perilous passage through narrow side streets, they screeched to a stop in Omonia Square.

Unfortunately, Natan found himself on the east side of the square, opposite to where he should be according to his plan. "Damn," he said through clenched teeth, and started to run. He had to go one block parallel to the square, since it would be folly to run through it. If someone was following Nadin, he would run smack into them. Instead, he had to work his way around until he got to the other side and a building he knew there. From its second floor stairwell, he would be able to see almost the entire square, except for where a few short palm trees blocked the view.

He still had time, but he wanted to be there when she left the store so that he could see if anything was happening. When he reached the building, he ran up the stairs, breathing heavily. Every cigarette that he'd ever smoked seemed to have come back now to haunt him. He got to the window in time to spot Nadin walking out of the store. There was no one on her yet. With her long, shapely legs beneath a short, close-fitting skirt and her hair swinging prettily as she walked, she stood out in the dwindling crowd. Most people were leaving the business area now for lunch and siesta.

Natan would wait until she turned the corner and disappeared from his view. If there was a tail, that was when it would expose itself.

So far as he could tell, she was clean, and now he couldn't wait to get to her. He took the stairs down two at a time. "Nadin," he called, waving at her from the open doorway.

She smiled, walking over to him, and stopping just inches away. He had a powerful urge to embrace her, but instead he took her hand. "You look great. How are you doing?"

"Thank you. Fine, I think." Her wide green eyes glittered like emeralds. He could drown in them, he thought. Just then, the sound of a loud explosion reverbrated behind him. Responding through reflex, he grabbed Nadin, pinning her with his body to the wall inside the entrance. There was no way he was going to let anything happen to her. Only when he turned did he realize it had been a car backfiring in the square. Natan smiled at her apologetically. She gave him a rueful smile in return.

"Let's get the hell out of here," he said.

"Where can we go?"

"There's a place I'm sure nobody we're worried about will go to. Come on." With that, he hailed a taxi.

Natan had always thought the Likavitos Hill the best point from which to see the city. Without the smog that covered Athens during the day, the view could have been breathtaking, as it once was; these days it was spectacular only at night.

He helped Nadin out of the car, telling himself to stop feeling like a kid on his first date. After all, she was at this point still a pawn in this operation. If he let his emotions get involved now, he could scrap the whole thing and go home. Well, not *exactly* home, he mused.

They walked into the park, which was deserted except for couples necking here and there on the wide lawns. They chose a wooden bench set close to the trunk of a big, old fig tree. The shade gave an illusion of coolness and the smell of the rotting figs on the ground was sweet. As they sat, Natan saw Nadin staring at the ground behind the bench and blushing. The ground there was almost completely covered with used condoms.

He turned to her, smiling. "I'm sorry, but this is a place where we'll be safe. It seems that most people here have been safe!" They both laughed, and he went on, "This place is used at night by the youth of Athens as their open bedroom. It's like one big orgy."

"I'd rather not see it at night, then."

"No problem," he said, "you won't. So, what's going on at the apartment?"

"Nothing at the moment, but as I told you on the phone, the word is that tomorrow the man with the instructions will be arriving. Then we'll be leaving for wherever the job is to take place. Now, you said that we should be careful. But all the people . . ."

"I was talking about my people. The place is bugged and they're watching it at all times. The Mossad is practically sitting on top of the group."

"So, they're a party to this assassination that's about to take place?"

"I thought you understood that?"

"I know it, but I still find it very hard to believe."

Natan went on to question her about the group. He wanted to know what every one of them looked like and what weapons they talked about using. What did they do in their spare time? Who was running the show? An endless stream of questions with even more resulting from some of the answers. At the end of it, he almost felt that he knew the terrorists personally.

When a young couple arrived, taking the other end of their bench and starting to neck vigorously, Natan said, "Come on, let's find some lunch."

At the end of a winding path, they came to a restaurant with a wide terrace overlooking the entire city. They sat at a small round table, next to the stone wall that bounded the terrace. A breeze from the west was starting to break up the smog over the city.

"So, what are you going to do when you have all the rest of the information you need?" asked Nadin.

"I intend to do my best to stop them, but I can't be more specific than that just yet." Natan took a photograph from his pocket and showed it to Nadin. "Have you ever seen this man?"

She stared at the photo. "No, I don't think so."

"No problem. I had to ask, though."

"Who is he?"

"I think he's the man behind all this, but I can't be sure. And at the moment, I have no way of finding out. Forget it for now. Here's what we do next," he began just as the waiter brought their order. The man set down their plates of grilled fish and salad, then poured their wine. Natan smiled fondly at Nadin. When the waiter had left, he went on, "I can't come near you because they're watching your moves, as you know. On top of it, they're after me, so we'll keep using Gamil as a go-between, if that's okay with you?"

"I don't have a problem with that. He seems like a good man. Do you trust him?"

"No further than I can throw him, but at the moment I have no choice. I need someone and he's it."

"I wish you'd told me. I could have found someone for you."

"Things have changed considerably since we last met, but don't you worry. We'll get it done."

"What you need is a guardian angel," she said.

He smiled. "True, but they're fairly hard to come by and anyway, the one I want has another job to do just now."

# 29

**ATHENS**
**OCTOBER 1**
**1145 HOURS**

THE PHONE was ringing. Only Nadin knew that Natan was at the Hilton under the name Kevin Douglas. He grabbed the receiver.

"We're leaving for France in a few hours," she told him. "It's going to be at a place outside Paris. That's all I know at the moment."

"How did you get the information?"

"Halim received these instructions at a meeting. We're to leave everything behind, weapons and all."

"Are you okay?"

"I'm fine. What about you?"

"No problems. So you know what to do?"

"Yes. I'll call you as soon as I know anything new."

"Who did Halim meet with?"

"I don't know."

"Is there a timetable of some sort?"

"Halim said only that it might take place next Friday. We still don't know who the actual target is."

"Did he tell you this at the apartment?"

"Yes. I know what you're thinking, and I'm sure you're right. Anyone listening in now will know as much as we do."

"The men in the group, do they know they're going to hit Palestinians?"

"Sure. They knew it almost from the start, but you must realize that they regard these moderates as traitors — people who are selling out."

"What do you think?"

"For me it's easy. If the Mossad wants them dead too, that can't be good for the Palestinian cause. It's that simple."

There was silence on the line. They had nothing more to say, yet neither wanted to hang up. It was as if they were holding on to each other. Natan broke the silence. "So, I'll be waiting for your call. I seem to be doing a lot of this lately."

"I have to get back now," she said. "I'm with those who are leaving sometime tonight. The others will go in the morning."

This was starting to be very difficult for Natan. He didn't want her to go. If anything should happen to her, he knew he'd never forgive himself.

"Nadin," he said, "I wish I could come up with something that wouldn't put you in so much danger."

"I appreciate what you're saying, Natan. I can assure you that I'm in far less danger than you think."

"What's that supposed to mean?"

"Let's just say that I have a guardian angel watching out for me at all times."

"What are you talking about?" But as he said it, Natan suddenly got the picture. "Wait. Don't tell me! Does that angel by any chance look like he came out of Aladdin's lamp?"

"My lips are sealed, except to say good-bye and hope to see you soon." She was gone.

Within minutes of Nadin's second call, which simply confirmed Paris as their destination, Natan was out of the hotel and in a cab on his way to the airport. If the group was leaving the city that night, there was still lots of time for him to clear the airport before anyone following the terrorists got there.

Natan reached Paris in the early evening and made several calls from a phone booth at the foot of the avenue de la Grande Armée.

A surprised Gamil said he'd be on his way to Paris and the same hotel as before, just as soon as he hung up. In reality, that probably meant the next morning, with Gamil able to do errands by about noon.

Natan walked from there to Céline's apartment in avenue Foch. The key was where she always left it for visitors, as she'd told him on the phone. She was going to Provence for several days with a man she saw from time to time, so Natan could stay at her place for as long as he wished.

"I'll be away for almost a week," she'd said, "but if you're still there when I come back, I promise we'll have great fun."

"Fun," he smiled to himself. Some fun. So many things could go wrong. Little things. Suppose he'd missed Céline, for instance. After all, it was her number that Nadin had. They did have a backup number, but even so, he should have checked earlier with the Frenchwoman. He'd been sloppy.

Still, his luck had held so far. Not that luck was a thing he'd ever really counted on.

# 30

## AMERICAN EMBASSY, PARIS
## OCTOBER 1
## 2100 HOURS

"I'M HOPEFUL," said Major Dennis West, "that the information regarding the location of the meeting is still a secret. There's always the chance of a leak, of course, but I think we've handled it well enough up to this point."

The forty-five-year-old marine major was in charge of security. Clearly uncomfortable in a suit he had to wear in this role, he leaned forward now, across his desk.

"We can really only assume that, as you know," said a chubby little man who sat facing him. Gilbert Duval, known to his friends as "Ashtray," was the French liaison officer working with the Americans. His many years' experience in Arab countries made his input invaluable.

"Could you be more specific?" Major West was not comfortable with the concept of joint ventures. He would have much preferred a clear American operation with the French assisting only when called on. But because of the special nature of this whole affair, it was not going to be that way. West was responsible for the security and well-being of the Israeli delegation, while Ashtray was to look after the Palestinians. Yet even though this was to be a secret set of negotiations outside the official agenda of the peace process, it was clear to some strategists at least that it was not a well-kept secret. While very few people knew the exact time and location of the talks, the fact that they were indeed taking place was now known in certain diplomatic and security circles.

Neither delegation was official, rather both were carefully selected teams of moderates willing to sit together and try to find a pragmatic solution to the situation, despite the unending hostility and mistrust on both sides. Once they reached a workable solution, they were to prepare a paper outlining their proposals and also indicating the most strategic pressure points that the U.S. president and European community could apply on all sides, with the gains to be made by those who could accept the proposal. In short, they would be the ones to break the deadlock.

Clearly, the officials of the two sides in the conflict would not view such action as positive because it would afford the big powers an intimate view of the problems; they might even attain an understanding of the situation that they'd never really had before, and so bring about a solution — even peace — to this perpetually troubled region.

"Allow me to explain, Major," said the Frenchman, sending up a dense cloud of Gauloise smoke that made the big marine squint.

"We must assume that at least some delegates have mentioned these forthcoming talks to their friends. The so-called doves — or as you call them in the United States, bleeding-heart liberals — are not really appreciated in that region, as you probably well know." He paused.

"So, any respectable intelligence agency — and most of the countries in that region have fairly good ones — will try to recruit someone from the relevant delegation. I can tell you with some certainty that the secret is not really secret, except of course, for any information we've not yet given the delegations. And always assuming that our own organizations are clear of leaks. And who can say that for sure?" the Frenchman shrugged, smiling sadly.

"I can assure you that our people are not spies," Major West snapped.

"Exactly my point," Duval went on. "Even if your organization is totally clean, it still would make no difference if mine was not. Isn't that so, Major?"

"So, what are you telling me?" The American was becoming impatient.

"All I'm saying is that we should expect the worst. Personally, I would have preferred this whole thing to take place in Italy if possible, or Belgium, as far away from my jurisdiction as possible."

"Well, that's good to know, Duval. But since they are meeting here, what I must establish is what sort of security you can give my delegation, and where you propose they stay?" West wanted this meeting back on track.

The Frenchman casually lit another Gauloise, cleared his throat, and went on.

"We'll give you whatever you ask for. And I recommend that you keep them in a safe house here in Paris — one where we can arrange to have fairly large forces nearby. Our Palestinians will be in a château out in the country, guarded by a special police unit."

The meeting went on for several more hours. It was early Saturday morning by the time all the problems were ironed out — ostensibly, at least.

The delegates were to arrive in Paris on October 3. There was still much to do. Everyone knew that if anything went wrong, the outcome could be disastrous. Some people in the State Department had told the president that it would be safer to leave things as they were, because any wrong move could open a Pandora's box. But the president was adamant: apart from anything else, a solution to this particular problem would secure his place in history.

After the meeting, Major West entered the embassy's communications room in its basement.

"Yes, sir?" The young marine duty sergeant sprang to his feet.

With the same massive build and close-cropped brown hair, he might have been West's clone.

"Have this coded and sent right away to State," the major said, handing him a summary of the meeting. "They're waiting for it."

# 31

**MOSSAD HQ, TEL AVIV**
**OCTOBER 2**
**0900 HOURS**

"LOOK, I DON'T give a shit if he's not here," said the soldier. "I was told to bring this over and hand it directly to him. If we wanted somebody like you as a go-between, I wouldn't be here."

"So what is it you want me to do?" asked the sentry at the gate of the Mossad compound.

"You? Nothing. Unless you know how to use the phone. If you do, call the duty officer."

The guard was not used to such an attitude, but he wasn't about to start something, either.

"Hello?" He'd dialed the duty officer from the phone just inside the gate. "This is the front gate. There's a guy here from unit eight two hundred with something for Mark Heller. He won't leave it with me and he insisted I call the duty officer. Could you come down here and take care of this?"

"Can you put him on? I'll authorize him to enter. I'm not exactly dressed to come down there at the moment."

"I'm sorry, but you can't authorize it unless you're here to bring him in with you. Regulations."

"Fine," said the duty officer, clearly annoyed. This was turning out to be a great day in the sack and he was not going to have it spoiled. Less than an hour ago, he'd picked up the wife of a colleague who was on assignment in the Far East. She had come to use the pool at the academy, but after a little persuasion she joined him in the secured section and they were just drying off from the pool when the call came in.

"Tell the man," he said, "that he should get comfortable. There's something I have to finish before I can get there."

"Will it take long?" asked the guard, watching the arrogant little soldier uneasily.

"It's something you're not supposed to rush," he answered, watching the woman's breasts emerge from her bathing suit. She finished drying herself and lay back on the bed.

"I really have to go now. See you soon. Tell the man to wait." He would call Mark now, the officer thought, and then attend to his colleague's lovely wife. He called Clandestine Communications and had the duty officer there call Mark at his home and pass on the message.

## 1100 Hours

As Mark pulled up to the gate, he lowered his car window. "So, where's the schmuck with the papers?" he asked the guard.

"Over there," the man said, pointing at the soldier who was by now asleep in his little Renault.

Mark walked over to the small car. "What is it you have for me that couldn't wait, so that I got dragged here on a Saturday?"

The soldier was startled awake. "Who are you?" he wanted to know.

"I'm Mark Heller. The man you insisted on handing the documents to, remember?"

"I'm sorry, but can I see some ID?"

Mark drew out his identity card. "Is that okay with you? Can I have the papers now, or do you want to do some gene testing to verify my identity?"

"I'm just doing my job. God, you people are really something."
"You bet we are. Now, the papers please."

Several minutes later, in his office, Mark opened the envelope. There were two pages, one of them a covering letter from a friend of his over at 8200. Headed, "The most advanced deciphering and electronic information shoot-down unit in the world," it began:

> Dear Mark, I'm sure you'll be extremely happy to have been dragged from home on a Saturday but as you'll see, it was necessary.
>
> The following page is a copy of a document that was transmitted several hours ago from the American embassy in Paris to Washington. It seems to be extremely important. It also relates to your company, so there was no choice but to call you in.
>
> As you know, the level of sensitivity of this shoot-down is not only in its contents, but in the fact that it *was* shot down. The following page contains all the information regarding a secret conference to be held in Paris and the locations of the delegates by name, as well as designated responsibilities. It was signed by a Major Dennis West, U.S. Marines, in charge of embassy security and security of related matters.

Mark saw no point in sending the copy down to the Paraphrasing Department for rewriting, as there was not much there. He decided to do it himself, and within the hour, he had it ready. He would have it sent to the Paris station and all departments to whom he thought it would be relevant. He placed one copy in his office filing cabinet and then called Mousa, who happened to be at home.

Because he headed Operations Security, Mousa was one of the few Mossad members to have a scrambled phone line at home.

Information had to be relayed to him so that he could take control at any given time.

"Did you send it out yet?" Mousa asked.

"No. I was just about to, but I called you first."

"Good. Kill it. Inform only the Paris embassy in brief. Can you imagine what would happen if the French and the Americans got wind of the fact that we knew about a terrorist cell working on an operation that's to take place on French soil and we didn't warn them?"

"I don't even want to think about that, Mousa. Okay, I'll destroy it. See you after the weekend."

## ISRAELI EMBASSY, PARIS
## OCTOBER 2
## 1145 HOURS

"ISRAELI EMBASSY," said the girl on duty at the switchboard. She sounded bored, understandable on a sunny fall day in Paris when the shift she had gotten was not the one she wanted.

"This is Isa. I want talk to David."

"I'm sorry, sir, but the embassy is closed. There is no one here."

"You not understand," said the man, his voice growing louder. "This is Isa. I want talk to David."

The girl realized that it must be a code. "Just a minute, sir," she said, punching the names into her computer. She looked at the screen, then threw a small switch on the intercom.

"Gill?"

"Yes."

"There's a caller on the line," she said into it. "I think he's one of yours. His message is Isa calling David. Do you want me to transfer him to you?"

"Just a minute." She could hear that the man she had called was now at his computer. He typed the message and a number showed up on the screen, 32975. "Pass him to me," he said finally.

"Mr. Isa, I'll pass you to David now," and she clicked the phone over without waiting. She didn't like the guys in Shaback who received these coded calls. They were arrogant, and then there was the way they treated her and all the other secretaries: those guys couldn't keep their hands off a female, it seemed. Just because they were in charge of the embassy security, they seemed to think they were little gods.

Gill had taken the call in his office on the second floor. He was not a big man, though he appeared to be when seated.

"Where are you calling from?"

"What the matter? You forget how say, 'Hello, how you'?"

Gill droned, "Hey, how are you? Where are you calling from?"

"Paris. I come back in morning."

"When can you come to the embassy?"

"You kidding me! Why no you just put bullet in my head?"

"Look, I don't feel like playing games. The person who wants to meet with you asked me to tell you that I am to arrange a meeting in the embassy."

"And what about someone see me come in?"

"We can look after that. So what's it going to be? I don't have all day."

"I think about it. Anyway I have something must do first."

"We'll be waiting for your call."

Gill was pleased the call was over. The man sounded strange to him. There was nothing in his file, although there is seldom much in the files that the Shaback hold for such cases of "call-ins" for the Mossad. He'd go down there to check the files, also the ones in their offices in the basement and spend some time with the duty officer. He notified reception that he was going to be at number fifty-five if anything came up.

After the murders in The Hague, most stations and embassies were on absorption alert, ready for an attack at any time. Not that it was easy to maintain the level of alertness that was called for when there was just not enough manpower, and people had to double- and triple-shift.

Roly, the station chief, was on duty today. With five case officers and a staff of almost ten people, he ran the biggest of any Mossad station. He was not alone, as Gill discovered.

"Excuse me," Gill said. "I didn't know you were busy."

"Don't worry about it. Come on in," said Roly. "This is Amos, a friend of mine from Israel."

"Pleased to meet you. I hope you're having a good time."

"Indeed. I have a great host here."

"Was there something you wanted?" Roly asked.

"Yes, there was a message for you." Gill stared at Amos for a second as if silently asking whether he could speak in front of the stranger.

"Go ahead," Roly urged. "I told you he's a good friend of mine. He's from the office, too."

"Well, that guy who was in town and wanted to meet with someone . . . he just called again. He's back."

Roly leaned forward, clearly interested. "And?"

"I told him the meeting would have to take place in the embassy and that I'd arrange a safe entrance for him."

"What did he say?"

"He said he'd think about it and get back to us."

"That's the dormant agent we were talking about," Roly explained to Amos. "Thanks, Gill. When he calls again, would you pass him to me if I'm here, and if not, to the duty officer at the station?"

"But the regulation says that I have to handle the subject until the contact is renewed and the security classification reestablished. At the moment, he's regarded as very dangerous."

"We don't have any arguments about procedure, Gill. All I'm telling you is that when this man calls again, you're to transfer him to the station."

"But, I . . ."

"What's the matter with you? Shall I make it clear?" Roly was now on his feet. "When the fucking man calls, you transfer the fucking call to me, or I'll make life not worth living for you." He smiled. "Is that clear now?"

Roly was someone who had to be obeyed or he'd go through this instant transformation into the worst bastard Gill had ever known.

"Okay, okay. So I'll do it your way."

Roly was still smiling, showing a row of slightly yellowing teeth with what looked like very bad bridgework. "I knew you'd see it that way. Like we say in the office, one hand washes the other."

Once Gill was gone, the other two men went into an inner office where they both lit cigarettes and poured themselves some coffee. Amos had taken a copy of the report that had just come in from Israel regarding the setup of the secret meetings in Paris. Though it was against regulations to take documents of such high classification out of the building, as the department boss, he could do as he pleased.

"I'll be at my hotel, so call me if something new comes in — or if anyone needs me," he told Roly.

# 32

**PARIS**
**OCTOBER 2**
**1400 HOURS**

NATAN PICKED up the phone on its first ring. He'd become extremely tense, just waiting for the call. "Yes," he said, keeping his voice even. The last thing he wanted to do was to give Nadin the feeling that he was not in total control.

"We've settled but I don't know exactly where we are."

"Where are you calling from?"

"It's a small shopping center about five minutes from the farmhouse we're in. It's north of Paris. I don't know the area, though, so I can't give you proper directions."

"Can you get to this shopping center with no problem?"

"Well, one of the men drove me here, and I'm doing the shopping. He's waiting for me in the car."

"Could you get back there again later today?"

"I think so. I'll forget something on the list they gave me. Then I'll have to come back."

"Better to say you left something in a store in the mall and go back for it. Otherwise, they might take you to a different center."

"So what do you want me to do?"

"I must know where you are, as well as where you're staying.

I'm quite sure you've been followed to where you are now, so just act normal."

"What if they saw me dial? They could get to you." She sounded frightened.

"Don't worry," he tried to calm her down. "Even if they had my number, they couldn't get to me. I'm not physically where the number is. I took some gadgets with me when I left, thank God, so don't you worry. As soon as I can, I'll be sending you a special brooch that I want you to wear or keep with you at all times. Will you do that?"

"Of course."

"Another thing. When you come back later today, bring a sketch of the route from the house to the mall."

"That I can do," she said assertively, although she had now begun to feel as if she were being watched. "Do you know what they look like?"

"Who?" he asked.

"The people following me, so I can watch for them?" she said.

"Don't even try. Don't turn your head, or they'll suspect that you know they're watching. We can't afford that now. Do you understand?"

"Yes, but it's not easy."

"I know, but forget about them. After all, they're not there to harm you. Only to observe, so relax."

The conversation lasted several more minutes. Nadin seemed to be getting very nervous. She was starting to come unraveled, Natan thought, and he didn't want to pressure her any more than was absolutely necessary.

"Is there a sign in the booth with a phone number on it?" he asked.

"Yes. Right in front of me."

"Read it to me," he said, and she did.

He let her go, saying again that she must return to the mall later that afternoon. Gamil would be there to take the sketch from her, and give her the small brooch that would enable them to trace her if necessary. Before hanging up, she gave him as good a description as she could of how to get to the farmhouse, in case anything went wrong. She also told him the names of two of the stores in the mall. One was a record store, and that was where Gamil would go.

By 1600 that day, Gamil was at the mall waiting for Nadin. Natan had traced the stores and by phone, he got directions to the mall from Paris. It was near a town called Marines, northwest of Paris on route D/915. Finding it turned out to be fairly simple for Gamil.

Natan had told him to meet the girl in the record store. He gave Gamil a small package for her. She would give him a note. They were not to discuss anything but the records and they must not stay together for more than a few minutes. After the meeting, Gamil was to call a number and leave a message there, then go back to his hotel and wait for instructions.

Nadin entered the record store at 1614. She started to look at various albums, moving slowly in the direction of Gamil. When she came along next to him, she smiled at him politely.

"May I help you, Madam?" he asked, with quite a good French accent.

"Yes," she told him, "I'm looking for a particular song by Adamo called, 'Tombe la neige'. Have you heard of it?" She handed him a piece of paper, as if it contained the selection she was talking about, and he looked at it with interest. He then reached out and selected a record which he handed to her with the small package underneath. Thanking him, she walked to the counter with the record and handed it to the salesclerk, casually placing Gamil's tiny package in her pocket.

He left the store ahead of her, returning to his rented Renault Five for the drive back to Paris. On the way, he stopped at a garage to make a phone call and buy a Coke from their vending machine. It would take him over an hour in the traffic to get back to his hotel.

## Israeli Embassy, Paris
## 1610 Hours

"This is Isa. Give me speak David, please." It was the same voice again, thought the receptionist, transferring the call to Gill.

Gill told the man on the line to wait a moment. David was expecting his call. Then he buzzed Roly. "Your man's on the other line. I told him that David was expecting the call, so do you want to get on the line or what?"

"See if you can get him to come here."

"I'll be right back to you."

Gill pressed the flashing button on his phone and told him what Roly had said.

"I told you too dangerous I come there. What if someone see me?"

"Where are you calling from?"

"A pay phone. Why?"

"Do you have any reason to believe that it's bugged?"

"Why bug phone in middle of Gehenom, what you say nowhere?"

"Okay, and we know this line is also clean. I can guarantee that. What I'm telling you is that we're having a confidential conversation at the moment, so if you do what I tell you, there's no reason why anyone would see you come in here."

"Why you no sent someone to get me?"

"I'm sorry, but that is against regulations."

"What you want me to do?"

"I want you to take the Métro from wherever you are to the Franklin Roosevelt station. You'll come up on the avenue Montaigne. Cross the Champs-Elysées and go north on avenue Matignon for about two and a half blocks. There you'll turn left onto a small street called Rabelais. You'll see the embassy. You can't miss it. Now, don't worry about the French gendarmes. They won't stop you. They're more for decoration. Are you with me?"

"Yes, yes, go on. I still not see how you know I safe. Anybody can see me come in."

"You have nothing to worry about. We will make sure that you're clean. When will you be here?"

"In one hour."

"See you then, my friend."

Gill hung up. On the intercom, he called his security people whom he had already placed on standby. He then let Roly know that his man would be there in an hour.

"Fine," Roly said. "You take him to the silent room and call me. I'll join you there."

"Okay." Gill sent his people out to the street to take their positions for an incoming dangerous agent. If he was not clean, they would notify their boss, and then it would be up to him to do something about it.

When the man arrived, he had to go through two security checks, before he was led to the small room known as the silent room on the second floor. It had no windows and the only furniture was a small wooden table and three wooden chairs. It was called the silent room because it was bug clean, although monitored, and soundproof. If Shaback had to question a suspect, the room was ideal. It resembled almost every interrogation room in Israel; that in itself was a point of pressure for many.

The man had been seated there for several minutes before Gill entered the room. "Is everything okay?" he asked.

"I think so, but I know for sure when I go out and have head shot off."

"You have nothing to worry about. You're in safe hands now."

"Sure, I know the hands are safe, but me?"

Gill spoke into the intercom. "Anytime now would be fine."

"I'm on my way," said Roly. He was with them in less than two minutes.

"Hello, Mr. Gamil," he said on entering, "I'm David and I'm really glad you could make it."

Gamil got up to shake the tall man's hand. "Everybody David around here," he smiled. "I glad my name not Goliath."

They all chuckled at that. "Could you please leave us now?" Roly asked Gill and the guards.

Gill nodded and signaled the others to follow him. Although they left the room, it was monitored from several spots in case an individual became difficult during interrogation.

"So my friend, is there something you would like? Maybe something to eat or drink?" asked Roly, acting the gracious host.

"No. I fine."

"How long do we have to talk?"

"I'm in middle of something," Gamil told him, "so I no have much time."

"Does this have to do with any terrorist act? I mean, is there something we must do right away to prevent casualties, if you see what I mean?"

"Yes, I understand, but is nothing immediate. I have something else for you."

"Which is . . . ?"

For the first time in a very long time, Gamil was scared. He could feel the power that Roly generated and he was also very aware of being in enemy territory. Could he get out in one piece? He would have to play it cool, but his palms were sweating and he could feel a slight tremor in his whole body that he couldn't control.

"I want make trade with you," Gamil told Roly, "but first I need know if I get what I want from you."

"What is it you want?"

"I want be citizen of European country. I mean real citizen, no with fake papers, like I can get too. And some money, yes."

"Of course. Well, what you want is not out of the question, depending on what it is you have for me."

Gamil leaned forward at that and lowered his voice. "I can give you daughter of Abu Nabil. What better bait for getting man himself? He love his daughter very much, everyone know that."

Roly's expression did not change. "Where is she?"

"In the neighborhood."

"What is she doing here?"

"She belongs to terrorist group soon doing job here in Paris."

Roly got up so fast that his chair flew back with a crash. Gamil stared up at him in surprise.

"You told me there was no terrorist attack imminent and now you tell me that Abul Nabil's daughter and her pals are about to do one. What's your game, Gamil? Don't play with me! I don't have time for that."

"*Ya sidy*, the terrorists is not for you people. They go after Palestinians."

"What the fuck are you talking about?"

"Look, I working with guy I met in Beirut. Contact man for terrorists, I think. He using me do things for him. He not go close to terrorists, I not know why. But he promise get me passport and citizenship. I see way this guy work, I not sure he can get it. He loner. And he work with Abu Nabil's daughter, so I worry who this I work with, so I came to you. If you want the group, that fine with me. It same price for one or all. I throw in guy from Beirut if you want."

"You'd sell him just like that? You'd probably sell us just as fast."

"Well, I hope you not think I come to you because I good Zionist. I not even Jewish." He took a packet of cigarettes out of his pocket. "I smoke?"

"Go ahead. So what's your timetable?"

"I have to make phone call soon and go wait instructions at hotel room."

Roly got up. "You wait here. I'll be right back and we'll see what we can do. I'm not the man who makes the decisions, so I'll have to speak to someone."

"Oh, yes," Gamil looked over at him. "I want also two hundred thousand dollar. Small bills please."

Roly smiled at him and walked to the door. "Should I send in some coffee?"

"Please do, and if you have some cardamom, I be in your debt."

"I'll see what I can do," Roly said, and left the room.

Gill was waiting for him. "There's something you have to know." His tone was urgent.

"What?"

"My men on perimeter observation just told me, Gamil was followed. They were good, too. They cut away at the end of the road, probably spotted our people."

"Do you have any idea who they were?"

"No, but from the way they worked, I would almost say they were working for me."

"Shit. This complicates things, doesn't it? If it was his people after him, he'll probably be dead as soon as he hits the street. Look, I'm going to call someone in. You make sure everything is okay with him, get him some tea and I'll be back in a few minutes."

Roly went back to his office and called Amos, giving him the rundown on what was happening. Amos said he'd be there in less than an hour. The man must be held until he got there. He also ordered Roly not to breathe a word to Gamil about having been followed.

## 1910 Hours

Amos and Roly conferred quietly outside the silent room.

"So, you're positive that he was followed?"

"That's what the Shaback man says."

"Well, I guess we'll just have to get as much out of him now as we can. We won't get a second chance at him. He's a dead man once he leaves here, I'm sure."

"Should we tell him that he was followed? That might scare him and make him more cooperative, since he'll want our protection."

"No. He'd more likely start to bargain for his personal security and want all sorts of guarantees from us. He'd link the information he has to the guarantees. No. What we want is for him to be happy for the moment, and give us all the information he has in return for his demands. We'll bargain over it, of course, but we won't make it all that difficult for him to get what he wants. Then we'll send him home."

"But they'll kill him for sure."

"So what? Do you want to take him home with you? You can keep him if you want, but after all, he's just a stinking Arab traitor. So let's go squish us an Arab." The two of them laughed aloud.

Gamil was extremely cooperative. He knew what he wanted and he was willing to sell anyone he could to obtain it. In a little over an hour, all the information had been passed, including that Gamil thought the terrorist team was under Israeli surveillance. Which is why he met the girl outside the surveillance ring, and the main reason he thought they would be interested.

Amos then asked Roly to leave the room briefly. He showed Gamil a photograph of a man, holding it in such a way that the cameras scanning the room would not pick it up. "Do you know this man?"

"Sure. That's the man I meet in Beirut.

"Thank you, my friend," said Amos, smiling with satisfaction. "You've just earned a substantial bonus. Where will you next meet him?"

"I must to call him at this number." Gamil handed Amos a small piece of paper with a Paris number on it. "Then wait my hotel room for call."

"Well, we'll not keep you any longer. David will bring you the advance we were talking about and we'll have someone drive you away from here. But do call me back, once you've spoken again with your man, so that we can go on with whatever it is we've started. You know, the passport and all, okay?"

"You bet, *ya sidy*."

After a manila envelope with the money was given to him, Gamil was ushered out of the building to a parking lot at the back and asked to lie low in the rear seat of a big Peugeot, so that they could drive him away from the area without risk. As well as the driver, a second man was seated next to Gamil in the back, holding a small gun at his head. For a moment, Gamil thought this was going to be the end for sure: the two would kill him and take his money.

He was still waiting for the bullet after the car had stopped. But then the driver came around and opened the door.

"Last station, my friend," he told Gamil, who stared out blankly at the street, not recognizing the place.

"Where this place?" he asked.

"Saint-Denis. You know, where all the whores are," said the driver. As he closed the door, the man in the back said to Gamil, "Yes, my friend. You should feel right at home here."

Gamil heard them start to laugh, and seconds later they were gone.

# 33

**MOSSAD HEADQUARTERS**
**OCTOBER 2**
**2110 HOURS**

THE PHONE on Mousa's desk had been ringing for some time before he reached to answer it. Things were moving rather fast on several fronts and tonight he was stuck in the office far later than he'd anticipated. At this hour, he was almost positive the caller was his wife.

"Yep," he said, finally picking up the receiver.

"This is the Security duty officer. Can I speak to Mousa, please?" a man's voice asked.

"This is he. What do you want?"

"I need to talk to you urgently. Could I come up to your office?"

"Sure, I have nothing better to do. When?"

"I'm at our lab right now, in the basement, so . . . just a few minutes, okay?"

The young man arrived almost at once, and was clearly eager to talk.

"Right," said Mousa, "now, where's the fire? What the hell is suddenly so urgent?"

"As you know," the security officer began, "we've taken over surveillance of the terrorists from Masada since they moved to France from Greece."

"Get to the point."

"Well the girl, the one that joined the team from Beirut . . ."

"What's his name's niece?"

"Yes. She left the farmhouse today with one of the men and went to do some shopping at a mall not far from there."

"So?"

"Her escort stayed in the car, so the leader of the surveillance team sent a foursome to follow her. In the mall she made a phone call, bought a few things, then went back to the farmhouse."

"This is fascinating. Is there any point to it, or does it just go on this way?" Mousa demanded impatiently.

"Please bear with me. Several hours later, she went out again. This time, the surveillance leader went in with six because he assumed there might be a contact. After all, she was brought in as the go-for.

"She entered a record store at the same mall and gave a note to a man who handed her a small package. Our people say the exchange was done as if by amateurs playing spies. Two of the team followed her back and the other four took the man. He headed back to Paris, stopping once to make a phone call. They couldn't get the number." The man paused. He had Mousa's attention now.

"He then drove into Paris and parked his car near the Clichy Métro station. They all went in after him, and almost lost him once. But two managed to tail him when he changed trains. He got off at the Roosevelt station, and went straight to the Israeli embassy."

Mousa almost fell forward in his swivel chair. "What did you say?"

"He went into the Israeli embassy."

"What is this, a joke or something? What the hell are you talking about? The Israeli embassy? Who the hell is this guy? Where does he come from?"

"We don't have a clue. All I can tell you is that he was expected, because he had a welcoming committee. Our people think they were spotted by the embassy security, but they didn't stick around to find out for sure."

"Did he meet with someone? What was he doing?" What he'd just heard had thrown him off.

"I was coming to that. We weren't the only ones following him. There was one other person there. That's why my people had to keep a distance. They were lucky the tail didn't pick them up. It seems he was good, but not that good. He was on the girl in the beginning, and then he took the man."

"Did the idiots from the embassy see that other guy?"

"I doubt it."

"Did the embassy people see that your people left?"

"I think so, but I can't be sure. You know how these things are. You can never be sure what someone else has seen."

"So it's possible that the other tail stayed and the people in the embassy don't know about it?"

"It's more than just possible, but I can't be sure. Like I told you, I would bet that they don't know."

Mousa was deep in thought now. This was not a simple situation. Finally, he grabbed the phone. "Get me the Paris station," he shouted into the mouthpiece. "Who's that?" he barked when the phone was answered in Paris.

"What's the matter, can't you say hello?" came a metallic response. "Who is this?"

"This end asks the questions," said Mousa.

"It's Roly here. Who are you?"

"This is Mousa. Who was the man you brought in this afternoon without getting clearance from Operations Security?

"It was a dormant agent who revived himself. What's the big deal? We worked according to procedure."

"Did you know he had a tail?"

"Yes."

"Thank God! So you still have him there?"

"No. He left a while ago."

"What! Do you know who the tail was?"

"No, but I guess they were yours, or you wouldn't be on the phone, right?" Roly's voice dripped acid. There was no love lost between field personnel and security brass.

"Right," Mousa whispered. "But you didn't know that before, did you? Did you also know there was a second tail?"

"No. But you'll have to take this up with my boss. He was here and approved the operation firsthand."

"Amos is there?"

"Yes, my friend. Are you happy, now that you know everything is under control?"

Mousa decided there was no reason to start an argument with a subordinate who had received approval from his boss. Instead, he asked, "Is there something special that made this dormant agent want to wake up?"

"Yes. He brought in something we hadn't been warned about until today, that there's a terrorist team here in Paris planning an attack. I understand that we are not one of their targets. He also said that there's a woman in that team acting as contact and that she's relaying information to someone outside the team's location."

"Is that all?" Mousa asked, grinding his teeth.

"I gather all this was known to you people back there in Wonderland, but you didn't think it necessary to tell us out here in the real world. Right?"

"What are you talking about?"

"You knew these terrorists under Abu Nabil were planning an operation against some Palestinians but you . . ."

"What did you say about Abu Nabil?"

"Please don't tell me you didn't know that. It didn't seem to surprise Amos, so why should it surprise you?"

"I'll level with you. Roly . . ." Mousa began.

"Now you want to level. I don't need that sort of leveling." Roly's voice was getting loud now. "You stay away from me and my people.

I'll give you what I think is important for you to know in order to do your job, and nothing more. Do you understand me?"

"You little pisser. Who do you think you're talking to?" Mousa was about to explode.

"I'm head of the Paris station. I get my approval from Amos. With all due respect to your position as head of Security, you are not out in the field. You were never a case officer. You have no idea what it takes. I'll tell you what I think you need to know. For anything else, call my boss. The girl doing the delivery is the daughter of Abu Nabil. Her name is Nadin. Now, if your people are on an operation in France that I've not been informed about in advance, just remember this: I'll blow the whistle on them anytime we think we see or hear something. Then you can deal with the French, because Liaison will not be there for you either!"

"Roly," Mousa was livid, "you are going places, but not the ones you want to go to. You are an idiot, do you hear me? I'm calling all support units back to base, so if you happen to need any surveillance set up, you can use your precious case officers to do the job."

"You can't do that! It's not your private fucking army!"

"Watch me!" Mousa slammed down the receiver. The duty officer in front of him sat motionless. He had never seen a Mossad officer wield so much power or use it in such a way.

Mousa glared at him. "You go back to that office of yours in the basement and bring me the charts of all, and I mean all, active operations in France, including the ones scheduled for next month. And I want all the requests that other stations have put in for the support teams. Then I want a full new schedule with no teams working in France until further notice, except for the team that's on the terrorists at the moment.

"You'll prepare a letter to all stations that they are not to expect support in France in the near future because of security problems in the country. And all assistance to the Paris station must be cleared through me, and I do mean all assistance. Furthermore, you'll prepare a list of ongoing recruitment activities in France that involve our units, and notify them that we are withdrawing our support until further notice."

"But . . ."

"Did I ask you for your opinion?"

"No."

"Then get going. I don't have all night." The young officer was out of the room as fast as he'd entered it.

Mousa slammed his fist on the table. "Shit!" He then grabbed the phone and when his call was answered, said just one word: "Rom."

In seconds, Avraham was on the line. "What is it?"

"We have a situation. There's a player in the wrong place at the wrong time and it doesn't make sense."

"Talk to me."

"That thing we have going on in Paris?"

"Yes?"

"Well, it appears that the girl brought in from Beirut is not who we thought she was. She's the daughter of Abu Nabil."

"*The* Abu Nabil?"

"It seems so. It could mean several things, one of which is that he's running the operation. I doubt he'd use his own daughter, but we can't be sure. She might be there without his knowledge."

"But that makes even less sense," Avraham said.

"I don't know what to tell you. I'll get Amir and his people on this but for the time being, I'm closing off France for all operations."

"Do you think that's necessary?"

"Yes, I do. In fact, I've already called for the orders to be drawn."

"It's your ass in the sling if this backfires. You're on your own."

"I know that. We need to talk, though, because something doesn't smell right . . ."

"I have a late meeting tonight, but we can talk in the morning. I'll call you when I come in."

There was nothing more to be said, now that the boss had

spoken, and Mousa wasn't about to aggravate the situation further. He'd received what he wanted: a confirmation for the muscle he'd pulled on the French station. He was going to flex that muscle, too. If he had to break the station completely, he would. And he'd make sure that everybody knew that.

Most of the night was spent signing letters and reassigning operations to other stations. When all the paperwork was in place and orders were being rushed around the world, Mousa was ready to leave. But there was one more thing he had to do.

He reached the head of the department in the Shaback in charge of security in the Israeli embassies around the world. The man was groggy when he took the call, but promised his friend to handle his request immediately.

Before Mousa went in to meet with Avraham in the morning, he had already reviewed the videotapes from the Paris embassy of the meetings with the newly-revived agent, Gamil. Mousa had received the original tapes and was able not only to see what was happening in the room from several directions, but also to hear what was said — something the security people at the embassy were not allowed to do, in order to allow conversations with agents to be kept secret.

When Amir came in, Mousa filled him in on what he had to know and then had him direct the Kidon team to Paris.

# 34

NATAN HAD been trying to reach Gamil for some time now. Finally, the man answered, but he sounded very tense.

He was reluctant to tell Natan what had happened. All he would say over the phone was that he had met Nadin and gotten the paper. He also confirmed that he'd given her the package, and said he was fairly certain that he hadn't been followed. Natan arranged to meet with him an hour later.

After hanging up, Natan immediately left the apartment so that he could get into position and watch for Gamil. He had no intention of waiting where the man was expecting to meet him.

Fifteen minutes after the meeting was due to start, Gamil had failed to appear. However, there was an alternative meeting place, three hours later, so Natan headed back to the apartment. With an hour to spend before he had to go out again, he bought a pastry at a shop across the street to have with a cup of coffee up in the apartment.

But the moment Natan went in, he sensed that something was wrong. As he put his hand on the light switch just inside the apartment door, he felt the cold contact of something metallic at the back of his head, and then the door slammed shut behind him.

A deep voice spoke to him slowly, with a Middle Eastern accent. "Please don't do anything that would make me use this gun."

"Who are you? What do you want?"

"Turn on the light. But move slowly," said the voice. The intruder must have stepped back slightly. Natan couldn't feel the gun barrel anymore, though he hadn't heard the man move. Natan flicked the switch, illuminating the crystal chandelier in the foyer.

"Now you can turn around," said the voice. Natan did as he was told. He was not going to fight someone he couldn't see, and there was no point playing games with anyone who had a gun pointed to his head. Natan's relief was overwhelming. Facing him was Bassam.

"I'm sorry to have frightened you like this," the big man said. He placed the gun on a table next to the phone, then raised his hands slightly to show that they were empty.

"How the hell did you find this place? And since when do you speak English?" Natan challenged.

"I have spoken English since I was a child. As for the address, I got it from Nadin, who thought you needed a guardian angel."

Natan started to move into the living room and Bassam followed.

"You are very stupid for a Mossad man, my friend," he said then, "or maybe we all have far too much respect for that organization."

"What are you talking about?" Natan sat down on the sofa.

"You have employed a man by the name of Gamil?"

"What else has Nadin told you?" Natan was becoming concerned.

"She didn't tell me even this, although she should have. Let me explain something to you. Nadin's father is a close friend of mine, albeit somewhat misguided. And now, the first time that Nadin has ever gotten involved with an Israeli, she is placed in greater danger than she has ever been in before.

"Did you know that after Gamil had left Nadin today, he made a phone call and then headed straight for the Israeli embassy?"

Natan was on his feet at once. "What did you say?"

Bassam calmly went on, "I said he went directly to the Israeli embassy, where he stayed for several hours. Then he was taken by two security people from the embassy in a car and let out elsewhere in Paris. After that, he called you and went to his hotel."

"How do you know all this?" Natan had sat down again and was now lighting a cigarette, trying to assess the damage that Gamil might have done.

"I followed the bastard."

"We have to get him and find out what he told them."

"That's easy. He told them everything he knew, and then some. He told them who Nadin really was, and when someone showed him a photo of you, he identified you as the man he was working with."

"Where is he?"

"In the bathroom."

Natan opened the bathroom door and turned on the light. Gamil was slightly submerged in the tub. His eyes were still open. His mouth seemed to be gasping for air. There was still fear in the dead eyes. His huge mustache, floating straight up from his top lip, broke the surface of the water only slightly. His hands grasped the sides of the large marble bath. The water was murky and tinged with pink.

"You have to stop doing these things!" said Natan over his shoulder at Bassam. "I thought you said you disapproved of violence?"

"I don't think you understood me properly. I'm not at all opposed to violence when it comes to taking care of your own. What I'm against is planting a bomb at random, where anyone might be hit: the way your army does when it throws a bomb into our refugee camps."

"What was the point in killing him? I could have used him for a diversion or something."

"That was one of the reasons I got rid of him. You still think the way you did when you had the whole goddamn world working for you. Now, my friend, you are on your own. Although if you so wish, I will be more than happy to work with you."

Bassam explained that he had several more people working with him and that they were watching Nadin, following her wherever she went. He knew that the Mossad was watching the terrorists, but he and his people were on the outside of the surveillance — and they were fairly good at it, he assured Natan.

Bassam and his men, it seemed, had been trained in both the Soviet Union, by the Seventh Directorate of the KGB, and in what used to be East Germany, by the subversive support unit of the Stasi.

"Germany?" asked Natan. "You said Germany?"

"I did." Bassam raised one bushy eyebrow.

Natan fetched his small suitcase from the bedroom, withdrawing a couple of photographs from an envelope. "Have you ever heard of a man by the name of Karl Reinhart?" he asked.

"Certainly," said Bassam. "He coordinated all our training and support systems."

"Is this the man?" Natan handed him the photo taken from Karl's file.

"No. I've never seen this man before."

Natan then handed him the other photo. The one of the man in the white suit taken in Damascus. "How about this man?"

"Is this some sort of game? This is Karl."

"I knew it. I *knew* it!" Natan was excited. He looked straight at Bassam. "Now, you are sure, yes? This is extremely important."

"Oh, that's Karl alright. He's the Master. Or was. The poor bastard killed himself in Leipzig."

"Why do you call him 'The Master'?"

"For a while, I worked with him," Bassam sighed. "It was when we were doing the groundwork for the world liberation network. It was his idea. He was still a junior Stasi officer then, but he had imagination. Everyone wanted to work with him and at the same time, everyone feared him. I mean groups ranging from the Baader-

Meinhof terrorists in Germany to the Weathermen in the United States. And all of our own fringe groups."

"How do you know the man is dead?"

"I was in China a while back, setting up a weapons deal for Abu Nabil, when I ran across several people I knew from the Stasi. They're now working for the Chinese: they can be assimilated into the West more easily than Chinese operatives, you see. Well, one of them told me that just before the Berlin Wall came down, Karl's wife, who was once a prisoner of the Stasi — she'd been in a play that satirized the regime and he'd had to interrogate her . . . that's how they met, seems he really fell for her, got her out and they were married — anyway, she was one of the first group to escape the East through Hungary. She left him, taking their five-year-old boy with her, and that devastated him. When the Wall actually fell and they were starting to arrest Stasi people, he locked himself in his apartment and shot himself in the head. They found him splashed all over his sofa."

Natan placed the photo in front of Bassam again. "Look at this photo one more time, would you? You've no doubt this is Karl?"

"Not the slightest."

"What if I tell you this photo was taken less than a month ago in Damascus?"

Bassam started to frown, finally glaring at the photo and nodding. "You dirty bastard," he whispered to the man in white. "You actually did it." Bassam's eyes narrowed as he looked back at Natan. "What has he got to do with all of this?"

"I can't tell you much, but I do know he's connected somehow to the source of the information we got regarding the pending terrorist attack."

"My God," Bassam suddenly placed his hands over his head, "we have to get Nadin out of there fast."

"What are you talking about? What happened?"

"I just realized that if the Mossad knows about Nadin and who she is, they will probably grab her to get her father. We have to get her out." The big man headed for the door.

"No." Natan blocked his way. "They won't let you near her. We can't do anything yet. We need to cut across the Mossad people on the outside, then handle the terrorists. Otherwise, she'll be dead before we get halfway there."

"So . . . we just sit and do nothing?"

"No. We must stall the Mossad."

"And how will you do that?"

"By offering them a bigger slice of the cake. You'll call the Israeli embassy . . . did you get Gamil's code for contact?"

"Yes. He said he used the name Isa and had to ask for David." Bassam looked hard at Natan. "Does that sound right?"

"Yes, but we can't be sure until we try. Do you think you can imitate Gamil?"

"That not be hard," Bassam said, smiling. "He also said he was to have a meeting with one of the bosses sometime later today."

"Did he say who?"

"He said they were all called David and that this particular one wanted to meet with him, but didn't want the rest of them to know. He also said that this same one was giving orders and was probably the boss. He gave me the time and place of the meeting, too. He was trying to persuade me that he could be valuable to me."

"Here's what we'll do. You'll call the embassy several minutes before the scheduled meeting with this David. Use a pay phone and give the code. They'll hand you over to security, you tell them you don't have much time. You're leaving the country because things are getting too hot, but you'll be back for the money, or you'll call them again."

"What money?"

"He must have been promised money, and there's no way they'd have given him all of it, so we can be quite sure he's owed money. Then you tell them Abu Nabil is arriving in a day or so. That way, they won't make a move on Nadin. There is no way they would risk the chance of grabbing her father."

Bassam nodded, happy with the plan.

Natan went on, "Tell them that you think someone is on to you, then hang up. Go to the rendezvous that Gamil had planned and see if you can grab the man he was supposed to meet."

"How will I know the man?"

Natan closed his eyes. He was trying to concentrate. Bassam was silent. Natan said, "Okay, here's what you do. Have one of your men call the restaurant when you are there, say, five minutes after the time of the rendezvous, just to be sure the man is there. The caller should ask for David. Your man will probably not come to the phone, but will more likely get up and leave. After you grab him, check his papers. He is sure to have Israeli diplomatic papers."

"What do you want me to do with him?"

"Bring him here, if you can manage it, but don't harm him. And arrange to have Gamil's body dropped into the Seine."

"I'm on my way. Where will you be?" Bassam asked.

"You can call me here, but I have a way to pick up your call no matter where I am."

Bassam nodded. "I'll be back in a little while with someone to move your friend from the bathtub."

"Just do me one favor," Natan said. "I do want to talk to this man you'll bring back. See if you can keep him alive long enough for me."

Bassam nodded and he was gone. There was no time for Natan to explain to Bassam why he really wanted the man from the embassy, nor was there any reason at this stage to do so.

Natan knew that whoever it was had some ulterior motive not to share his knowledge with others. Arranging a meeting outside the embassy on his own was highly irregular, so that Natan could only guess at what else the man might have kept from his Mossad colleagues. He had to find out not only what they knew, but what had been kept from them, in order to assess the situation properly.

Though he was not happy about ordering a kidnapping, Natan saw no other way to gain the edge he needed.

# 35

**TEL AVIV**
**OCTOBER 3**
**0900 HOURS**

OREN, AVRAHAM'S aide, ushered Mousa into the office, and closed the door quietly behind him. Oren always adopted a peculiar skulking behavior around Mousa. Now he took a seat at the far end of the long table, fussily attending to his papers.

"The Kid is in Paris and I have no idea what he's up to," Mousa came straight to the point.

"How the hell do you know where he is? Last time we spoke, you were still looking."

"Amos interrogated a self-revived dormant agent in the Paris station yesterday, and the man told him he was working with someone who brought him from Beirut."

"Well?"

"When Amos was alone with the man, he showed him a photo of Natan. The agent positively identified him."

"What the hell was the Kid doing in Beirut?"

"Like I said, I have no idea what he's up to. All I do know is that he must be stopped."

"So stop him. What are you waiting for?"

"Paris is not a small place, but the Kidon team should be there by now, so we'll see what happens."

"Keep me informed. Do you think he's the mole?"

"He's the best candidate I have."

"Well if it's not him," Avraham said, "we can always find the right man after the storm subsides. But at least it will appear we cleaned house. What else do you have?"

"The agent also said that Natan was working with a woman in the terrorist team, and that she is Abu Nabil's daughter."

"Abu Nabil's daughter?" Avraham was on his feet, his expression furious. "You're telling me she was in the terrorist team and we didn't know it? What the hell is the matter with you people? Terminate the Kid! Get rid of that asshole! And bring me the girl!" He stared down at Mousa. "Don't you realize that she could bring in her father?"

"I had, but we can grab her after they do what they came to do. That way, we have it all."

"You're playing with fire, my friend, just remember that. You have her now in the palm of your hand." With both hands flat on the table, he leaned across to Mousa, speaking very softly, but making sure he was being very clear. "If you lose her, you personally will pay for it. So you think about this, Mousa. It's up to you. As I said, keep me informed. I also want to know the moment the Kid is dead. Is that clear?"

## PARIS
## OCTOBER 3
## 1115 HOURS

BASSAM WAS several minutes early for the meeting that Gamil was to have had with the Israeli. Not having seen the man he was supposed to meet didn't help. Nor did the fact that he wasn't Gamil. But Bassam had a plan in mind.

The meeting was to take place in a small café several blocks from the Eiffel Tower. Bassam got there early, as Natan had instructed him, and he'd brought one of his men to make the call.

They were going to follow the man, after he left the restaurant, and grab him at the first opportunity they had.

At 1130 precisely, a man entered the café. He sat in a corner watching the street, but several minutes later when the waiter called for a David, the man got up and left the place without even ordering. Bassam and his man followed him the short distance to the Hilton hotel, where he stayed for over an hour. When they spotted him coming back through the lobby, he wasn't alone.

Amos was leaving the hotel after meeting with Edgeworth. The two shook hands. "I want to thank you again for coming to Paris," said Amos.

"Any time, my friend. The information regarding Abu Nabil's daughter will be extremely helpful. I guess I owe you one again," Edgeworth smiled.

The two men parted company near the main entrance, Edgeworth heading back toward the elevators.

Amos had walked about two blocks when a large black car with tinted windows slowed down, stopping slightly ahead of him. A husky, well-dressed man in his early thirties got out of the back of the car and was about to cross into a store when he turned, apparently talking to someone in the back seat. By now, Bassam's number two man had almost closed the distance he'd kept behind Amos and was right behind him. When Amos was across from the open car door, the well-dressed man stepped sideways, causing Amos to tilt toward the door, while the man behind him pushed him into the car, getting in behind him. The other man closed the door behind them and entered the front seat of the car which immediately sped away.

In the car, Amos found himself staring down the muzzle of a large, gleaming revolver. He was not about to struggle, nor did he speak. Before long, the car entered an underground garage, from where Amos was led up the back stairs to Céline's apartment. Bassam tied his hands and feet, then wrapped him with ducttape, leaving only a small slit for his nose. He placed him on the bathroom floor, after making sure he first got a glimpse of Gamil's body, which was still in the bathtub, before he taped over his eyes.

Bassam sent two of his men back to keep watch on Nadin. They were to return that night and remove Gamil. "Who knows?" Bassam told them. "You might have to deal with two bodies by then."

Shortly after Bassam's men had left, Natan returned to the apartment. Hearing the key turning in the lock, the big man drew his gun.

"Shit," said Natan as he entered the room. "What is this? A new way to say hello?"

"I got your man. He's in the bathroom."

"What! Is he still alive?"

"Of course he is. He's just taped, Lebanese-style."

"Are you sure he won't die?"

"Positive. He can't even harm himself."

"Let's see him then," said Natan.

When he realized that Gamil's body was still there, Natan shot a look at Bassam. But before he could say anything, the big man shook his head. "I didn't have the manpower to get rid of the body. I needed them to follow this jerk."

Amos was wrapped very much like a mummy in the silver tape. The very sight of him made Natan itch all over.

"Are you sure this is the right man?" Natan demanded.

"Yes, he's your man alright." Not wanting Amos to hear, Bassam leaned over and whispered something in Natan's ear.

"Are you sure?" Natan asked again, his voice rising toward anger.

"They shook hands and he went back upstairs, I imagine, while your friend here went out for a walk. Then he came for a drive with me and my people."

"You're sure about this?" Natan felt a cold sweat chilling his body. "Time to see his face," Natan said. He was extremely anxious, if apprehensive, at the prospect of finding out who it was.

"Are you sure you don't just want us to kill the man and be rid of him?"

"No!" Natan snapped. "I need this one."

Bassam began to rip the tape from Amos's face.

Natan was even more surprised than Amos. For several moments they just stared at each other, not saying a word. Amos spoke first.

"Let me out of this thing, you bastard. I'll break every bone in your fucking body, you lousy traitor! How long have you been working for that scum, Abu Nabil?"

Bassam moved to strike Amos over the head at that, but Natan signaled him not to.

"What the hell are you talking about?"

"These punks that grabbed me are a newly formed unit of the Mossad, are they?" Amos was furious. He was used to getting his way and even now, he could still shout. "You're making a big mistake, Natan. You are going to pay very dearly for what you've done. I suppose you're going to kill me now, the same way you killed young Ilan in The Hague."

"What are you talking about?" Natan slowly unwrapped more of Amos's body from the tape, leaving just enough on so that he couldn't move his hands or his feet.

By the time Amos was finished relating the story of recent events as he knew them, Natan had begun to realize that someone had been setting him up, and everybody had been more than happy to buy. Now the motive was clear. Whoever was behind the operation against the moderate Palestinians wanted the Mossad to run in circles, for the simple reason that they thought the Mossad would interfere.

Natan stood up and lit a cigarette. He was thinking. From the floor, Amos was still shouting, "Get me out of this, you asshole. I'm talking to you, big fat baldy." Bassam was ready to shut him up.

"It's not going to work, Amos."

"What the hell are you talking about? What is all this? Are you trying to pin something on me? Is Mousa hiding in the next room? And if not, then what the fuck is going on here?"

"Who did you meet with at the Hilton?"

"Edgeworth. He's an acquaintance of mine from MI5. I've known him for years."

"How did you meet this Edgeworth?"

"That is none of your fucking business!"

Natan drew a sharp pencil from his pocket and bending down, he placed the tip in Amos's ear, then held it up gently. "You know the drill," he said. "One millimeter for every two seconds of silence. In three minutes I'll be writing notes on your brain. Think about it, Amos, what have I got to lose? We're on your time now." Natan nudged the pencil slightly.

Amos decided to talk. "When I was a junior case officer in the London station, I had a meeting with an agent in a safe house. At that time, we used to bring them to safe houses." Amos was sweating and there was a quiver in his voice.

"The agent was a new recruit and I didn't have all the routine set up yet. Several minutes into the meeting, the police broke in. They thought we were IRA or something. They wanted to take me in, but just before they did, Edgeworth, who was at the time MI5 liaison to the police, came in. If they had taken me in at the time, my career would have been over. You know the regulations." Amos stared up at Natan, wanting a confirmation.

In reply, Natan pushed the pencil slightly further into the man's ear. "Don't stop talking," he said.

"Edgeworth took me aside and we had a talk. I proved to him that I was not IRA and that, in fact, I was Mossad. He released me and made sure there was no mention of what had happened. We became friends after that and over the years, he helped me with information and I helped him. It was sort of a private liaison, and it worked out well."

Natan placed a photo in front of Amos. "And this is Edgeworth?"

"Yes, that's him."

"Do you know where this photo was taken?"

"How the hell should I know? Where did you get it?"

"In Damascus, less than a month ago. This man is ex-Stasi. He's the one Foul Play, the agent who sent in the communiqué about the mole, was talking about. And you, my friend, are the mole."

As Amos realized what had happened, he started laughing in a strange, broken way. Then he began to cry.

Natan felt for the man. Amos was the mole alright, but he hadn't even known it. For that reason, he hadn't failed a lie detector test. He was the perfect mole: the last one to know it. He had been brilliantly duped. It was imperative now for Natan to know what Amos had told Karl at their meeting.

"I told him everything," Amos said. "Even the new stuff that Gamil brought in."

"What exactly do you mean? What did Gamil bring in?" Natan's voice was cold, level.

Amos poured it all out: the information about Nadin and the fact that he had assumed the terrorists were to carry out an Abu Nabil operation.

This meant that Karl, if he was the man behind the terrorist activity — and Natan had little doubt now — would know Nadin was a plant. He would realize that she was working for someone else outside the Mossad — someone who was probably not about to let the terrorist operation take place. Nadin was undoubtedly in great danger now, with Karl perhaps contemplating her demise. Nadin's only protection at the moment was her father's reputation.

When the phone rang, Bassam picked up the extension.

The conversation was in Arabic, but Natan heard Bassam repeat Nadin's name several times. He then hung up and turned to Natan. "Nadin was called to a meeting at the Hilton, where we picked up our friend here. Two of my men followed, and saw her leave the hotel with a man whose description fits Karl.

"One man followed them to an apartment building, but he couldn't tell which apartment they entered. He didn't see her leave the building, but the man who looks like Karl did leave. He passed on the message that the team at the farmhouse seemed to be getting ready for something. They were loading suitcases and various things into several cars."

"They're on the way to the hit," said Natan. "It must be starting now. We have to get to Nadin and get her out before it's too late." For several seconds, he stood immobile. It was all beginning to happen, but he wasn't ready. He couldn't be in several places at the same time. He had to get to Nadin, but he also had to stop the terrorists.

"What's the address where they're holding Nadin?" he shouted to Bassam. It proved to be a sidestreet just off Grande Armée, less than ten minutes away. Natan took a small device from his bag. "I hope she's wearing the brooch I sent her with Gamil. That's the only way we'll find her quickly." He turned to Bassam. "You'll have to notify the French police about the terrorists. Get them out there to stop them, if they haven't left yet."

"I can't do that. They'll never believe me." Bassam was adamant. "You know how they treat Arabs. Besides, they know me. If I go to them, I won't soon get away!"

"I can do it," said Amos. "Please let me do it." There were tears in his eyes. "I had no idea that I was helping the other side, you know that. I love Israel, but I'm a dead man anyway. What have you got to lose?" He then started to speak to Natan in rapid Hebrew. "Don't leave me like this. I've devoted my life to my country. You know I fought in all the wars. I never turned away from danger. Please let me prove myself, and maybe vindicate myself."

Natan stood by the door. The man had been duped and now he wanted a chance to vindicate himself. That was something Natan himself wanted. He also needed someone the French would listen to and trust. And there was no time. Amos was probably the best one for the job.

"Let me kill him," said Bassam, advancing toward Amos, who was still partially bound.

"No. Untie him," Natan said.

"What are you talking about?"

"I said, untie him. Give him the address of the terrorist team."

"You're crazy," Bassam told him.

"Do it, man! We don't have all day!" Natan shouted, walking over to Amos as if he was going to do it himself.

"Very well, but mark my words, you'll be sorry." The big man untied Amos, cursing in Arabic the whole time. Then he handed him a piece of paper. "This is where they are."

"You won't regret this," Amos said to Natan. And to Bassam, "It's alright. I know where they are. Don't worry, I'll handle it."

"When you've dealt with that," Natan told Amos, "wait for me under the Arc de Triomphe. There's a series of tunnels there leading in all directions. Wait for me in the center. There is much more to be done."

"Okay. I'll see you there," Amos called. Natan picked up his small case, and he and Bassam headed out.

"You're crazy, you know," Bassam said, as they left the apartment. "You should let me kill him, or he'll get us all killed."

"You don't understand," Natan replied. "The man was duped. Trust me on this one." Bassam looked skeptical.

Outside the building, they walked over to a white Peugeot. Natan put his case in the trunk as Bassam spoke to the driver in Arabic. The man got out of the car, put on a black beret and walked down the street. Bassam nodded to two men who were seated in the back, then took the driver's seat and they set off.

"What was that all about?" Natan asked.

"There was something he had to do for me," Bassam said, "that I can't do."

Once he was alone, Amos pulled the last piece of tape off his leg, cursing. He picked up the phone and dialed the Israeli embassy, at first intending to have the man in Liaison notify the French authorities exactly as Natan had asked. But while the phone was ringing, he managed to calm down a little, and his head started to clear.

This was the end of his career in the Mossad, the end of any dream of ever becoming the chief. On top of all that, he could very well find himself imprisoned for treason for the rest of his life. He knew he wasn't a traitor, but who would believe him? Natan? The man running around with a bunch of thugs from the Abu Nabil team? Terrific. Natan would be his witness. What a joke!

"Israeli embassy, may I help you?"

"Give me extension seventy-one."

"Hello," came a flat voice after two rings.

"Black one, one, nine, five," Amos said.

"One minute, please." The man at the embassy was punching something into the computer. He came back on the line. "Who do you wish to speak to?"

"Connect me to the Owl. The one in the big tree."

"Right away." He waited for several seconds.

"What is it?" came an impatient voice over the phone.

"Mousa?"

"Who is this?"

"Amos, I think I found what you were looking for."

"What are you talking about?"

"Don't play games with me, Mousa. Aren't you looking for Natan, the fucking little mole?"

"And if I am, how come this sudden cooperation?"

"We're on the same team in the big picture, after all. Do you want the man or not? I can get him myself, but I thought that since you have a team out there already, you might as well do the job."

"How did you learn about this?"

"Let's say I have a source in Clandestine Communications, okay?"

"Where is Natan now?"

"I don't know. But he'll be in the tunnel below the Arc de Triomphe in a while. Is your team in Paris?"

"That's none of your business. How did you find him?"

"That, my friend, is none of *your* business." Amos smiled to himself as he hung up the phone.

It was all taken care of. All Amos had to do now was wait and see what would happen. Something in Mousa's voice had bothered him, though. They never had got along, and were always trying to screw each other. Since this was hardly the time to take chances, he called the embassy again and this time had them connect him to Amir in Masada.

Amos went directly to the point. "When your people find Kid, is he to be taken or eliminated?"

"Eliminated," said Amir. The fact that Amos had asked was reason enough to give him an answer. Amos was one of the strongest people in the Mossad, so if he knew about this, Amir was not about to fight Mousa's battles. Besides, it was Mousa who had ordered Natan to be eliminated.

"Well, if anyone should decide to change that order and have him taken alive, I'm officially overriding it. He must be eliminated."

"My team is positioned now anyway," Amir confirmed. "They got their orders just seconds ago, then all communication was cut. Those orders are now irreversible."

Amos smiled to himself as he hung up the phone. He'd done it. There was still a smile on his face when two large hands grabbed his head, one holding his forehead and the other pulling hard on his chin. He might even have heard the cracking sound of his neck just before everything went black.

The man let Amos's lifeless body drop to the floor. He adjusted his black beret and left the apartment as quietly as he had come in.

# 36

## PARIS
## OCTOBER 3
## 1600 HOURS

NATAN, BASSAM, and his men drove past the apartment building that stood on rue Brunel, parking around the corner. A tall young man wearing a short-sleeved khaki shirt and black trousers came over to the driver's window. Once he saw it was Bassam, he spoke.

"A group of people left the building about five minutes ago. One of them was a man I saw with the one who brought Nadin here. Since I'm alone, I couldn't leave, because if they took her out of the building we'd lose her. So I didn't see where they went. But they got into a van."

"Well done," said Bassam. "Now wait for us in the entrance. Is there a problem getting in?"

"You need a key, but if I wait around for a few minutes, I can get in when someone leaves."

They waited in the car until they saw him go in.

"How come he speaks English to you?" asked Natan.

"Because he doesn't speak Arabic. He's from New York. We also have a diaspora that cares, you know."

Bassam turned and spoke to one of his men in Arabic. The man nodded and turned to open the trunk while the others with Bassam made their way to the building. The man who was the largest of the bunch took out a big black tote bag. He swung it over his shoulder and followed them. The man leaned forward to offset the weight of the bag, holding it tight with both hands.

The young man held the front door for them and they all slipped in quietly.

"Where could she be? This is a bloody big building," said Bassam, keeping his voice low.

Natan turned on a small device he'd taken from his pocket. A set of small LED lights blinked at the front of the gadget and he pressed a small yellow button on the side, like a switch on a flashlight. There was a low buzz.

"Great," he said. "She's in the building, or at least the device I sent her is."

Bassam pointed to a door that led to a narrow staircase, beside the elevator door. "We'll wait for you in there. You find the apartment and then come for us."

Natan nodded and started down the hall. But he could soon tell that the source of the signal was not on that floor.

He returned to the staircase and they all went up one floor; it wasn't there either. For the next twenty minutes, they advanced one floor at a time. The signal was getting stronger.

"I found it," said Natan at last, entering the small stairwell. "It's the fourth door on the right, but we'll have to be quick. There's no point in knocking on the door or anything like that. What we must do is enter fast, take out whoever is in there, and make sure we don't hurt Nadin."

Natan prayed they hadn't harmed her. He swore to himself that he'd kill every last one of them if they had. He only hoped that they saw her as much more valuable to them alive.

Bassam said something to the large man with the black tote bag. He placed it on the floor and opened it to produce an impressive array of weapons. Each of them was handed a weapon. Natan took an Uzi pistol with a silencer, and two thirty-five bullet clips. Much more than he really needed for this, he thought — or hoped. The others carried Ingrams and large pistols. Natan explained what he wanted them to do, and then started slowly for the door. He felt almost comfortable in the role now.

The others moved into position on both sides of the door, while Natan braced himself against the door across the hall. Once they were ready, he slammed at the apartment door, opening it wide with one hard kick. Finding himself in the middle of a large, empty room, he kept his body low, making the smallest possible target for anyone wanting to shoot at him.

The rest of them entered behind him and scanned the room, each with his back against a wall. There was no one in this room or the next. Natan dreaded entering another room and finding Nadin dead.

Finally, in the furthest corner of the apartment, he found her. She was tied to a large bed in a spread-eagle position. Her mouth had been taped with an adhesive bandage. When she saw him, her eyes lit up. He walked closer to her, still looking around in case a surprise awaited him. But it was all clear.

Natan gently removed the bandage from her mouth, trying not to hurt her. He could smell her fragrant skin and was tempted to lean over and kiss her. But he held back, as Bassam was there next to him, untying her hands and legs. With her mouth free, she started to talk, though it was difficult for her at first.

"The man they call Karl, he's the one whose picture you showed me the other day in the park."

"We know," said Natan.

"He called Halim to say that the attack would be tomorrow."

"Tomorrow?" said Natan. "I thought they were getting ready for it today."

"They are."

"Nadin, what are you saying?" Natan thought she'd gotten confused.

"Listen to me." She was speaking slowly now. "The attack will be today. I'll tell you in a minute how I know. But Karl told Halim and the other members of his team that it would be tomorrow. Do you understand now?"

"Okay. What else?" Natan asked.

"He then told Halim that a Mossad unit might try to knock them out, so they should get ready to defend themselves if necessary. He said the Mossad people would come dressed like French police. He said also that his sources were very good, and that they should fight and then get away. They must not be taken prisoner, because the Mossad team had instructions to kill them and would do so, no matter what."

Natan sat down next to her on the bed. She went on, "But this Karl has another team. And they are on their way to kill the delegates. They're on their way to set up and they will attack after dark tonight."

Natan could hardly believe what he was hearing. Karl had created a nightmare situation. "I overheard him giving this other team their instructions in the next room," Nadin went on. "They wanted to keep me for later, so they could bargain with my father for a huge ransom. They listened to tapes in Hebrew, and seemed to be trying to imitate words that sounded like orders. Then Karl told them to try it out and they started shouting at each other. They sounded just like a group of Israeli soldiers. Then he told them that while the police and everybody else was involved in taking care of the 'fucking Arabs,' meaning Halim and his men, they'd be finishing off the moderates at this villa where they're staying."

"It might just be a trap, you know." Natan was still somewhat skeptical. "I just can't believe that he'd go over the plan in a place where you could hear him."

"Don't forget, he had no idea that I understand German. Anyway, that's all I know. They're to attack at ten tonight, and they plan to make sure it's spectacular."

"Where the hell is that villa, I wonder? Well, no one's going to tell us." Natan thought for a moment. "I know! I'll get Amos to bring Mousa into the picture. He can stop them. After all, having a group of Palestinians kill another group is one thing for public relations. But to have a team posing as Israelis do it is another story."

"They were constantly referring to a big map they had. It might still be in the other room. And what happened to Felix?"

"Who's Felix?"

"The man Karl left behind to guard me. Didn't you people deal with him when you came in? He can't have just left."

They were suddenly very uncomfortable, knowing there was a Felix somewhere. As for a map, they could find nothing. The place seemed to have been totally cleaned out. Natan decided it was time to leave. Even if he couldn't find out where the delegation was staying, it would not be a problem for Amos and Mousa to find out. It wasn't so critical, and there were still hours before the attack.

Bassam ordered his men back to the car and was himself halfway across the large outer room when Natan heard the shots. The big man who still carried the empty tote bag was hit just after he'd opened the door. The man behind him managed to jump to one side, and was now face down on the floor, trying to crawl fast out of the room.

Natan reached the outer room to see Bassam facing the door, his back to Natan. He seemed to be reaching out, wanting to grab something. The submachine gun bullets were coming from the outer hall, hitting Bassam in the chest and stomach and splashing out his back, splattering bits of bone and flesh forward into the room. Bassam was still standing, but his back seemed to be exploding outward.

Before Natan could fire past Bassam at the gunman in the hall, the gunman turned his fire on the young fellow who was making his way across the floor. At that moment, Bassam's huge body fell to the ground with a thump, giving Natan a clear view of the attacker. Nadin came up behind Natan, but he pushed her back, delaying his aim. Now everything seemed to move in slow motion,

Natan's split-second delay enabling the terrorist to fill the crawling young man's back with lead.

Natan raised the Uzi to his shoulder and fired a burst directly at his enemy's face. All of the nine-millimeter bullets caught the man on target, blowing the back of his head onto the wall behind him and into the half-open door across the hall. Natan stepped over the body and with his foot, slammed open the door opposite. He rushed into the apartment, crouching low, in case other members of Karl's team were there. No one was. But he found video equipment, a military-style transmitter, and a pile of papers. This had been Felix's hiding place. He probably saw them come in. But now that he was dead, Karl's timetable might change. Since he no doubt would check with Felix every so often to verify that all was well, he might decide to move the plan up when he got no answer. Why else would he leave the transmitter behind?

Nadin entered the apartment seconds later, as did the other man who had survived the attack. "Bassam is dead," she said, fighting to keep the tears back. Her voice was quivering.

"I'm sorry," Natan said. "There was just no way to see it coming. But we have to get out of here." He handed his Uzi to Bassam's man. "Here, put this in the tote. The police will probably be here any minute."

Nadin had picked up a folded map. She and Natan opened it out, revealing heavy markings and arrows that pointed to one location from three directions.

"That must be it." Natan quickly refolded it. "Let's go, now."

With Bassam's man at the wheel, they were just pulling away when the police cars started arriving in the next street. Sirens wailed louder and louder as other cars joined forces.

Natan told the driver to move out very gently, rather than take off as he might have wanted to. As they continued to move slowly through the heavy traffic, Natan tried to make sense of the scribbling on the map. Nadin was seated next to him in the back, tears for Bassam rolling down her cheeks. She kept looking up at the roof as if hoping to make them roll back, finally dabbing at her eyes with a handkerchief.

"That's probably where the delegation is staying," she said, pointing to a small cross on the map. "You see, it says *Schlag*, which means 'hit' in German." She then pointed to another marking on the map. "That's probably where they'll be coming from."

"Something doesn't seem right," said Natan. "The points where you think the assassins are coming from are too far from the target. I mean, look at this. If the target is this small place called St-Rémy, then the team is coming in from three places on the other side of Paris: Chavenay in the west, Coubron in the east, and Cordon in the south."

Nadin leaned forward to study the map again. "They all have a small airport. Look."

Natan peered at the map. "You're right, dammit! He'll bring the assassins in at the last minute from the air. Stop the car!" he told the driver. Natan had to repeat the order, and the car pulled sharp right, tires squealing. The driver behind honked repeatedly and swerved to the left, barely missing them. As Natan hopped out, he was treated to a grand repertoire of French curses from drivers all around him. And when he opened the trunk to extract his small case, they all began to honk.

"What are you doing?" asked Nadin. She was alarmed now.

"Have him drive you to the airport at Orly and wait for me there," he said. "It's a safe place, but if I'm not there by midnight, or I haven't paged you by then, get out of the country. Go wherever you can."

"But what will you . . ."

"Don't waste time. If I need help, I'll call you. Stay near the Air France ticket counter on the main level. And here," he handed her the case. "Keep that for me. If I don't show, there should be plenty for you to get away with. They'll be after you. You know that."

She was almost whispering to him now. "Okay, but you take care of yourself. I don't want to lose you, too."

She was so beautiful, and yet he knew there was only a small chance he'd see her again. He'd probably be dead by midnight. Still, he couldn't bend down and kiss her full on the lips, as much as he wanted to. He turned and walked away. Minutes later he disappeared in the maze of the Paris Métro system, on his way to a rendezvous with fate.

# 37

**MONTIGNY- LE- BRETONNEUX**
**OCTOBER 3**
**1730 HOURS**

IN A SMALL building at the end of a gravel runway, Karl was seated with several of his men. Outside was a blue and black Dufin helicopter that bore the insignia of the French police. Except for Karl, the men inside the building wore the light khaki uniforms of the special anti-terror unit of that force. Karl had rented the helicopter and two more like it several days earlier, and some of the men were busy painting and sticking on the proper striping and insignias to match.

"So, let's go over it one more time — just to be sure you've got it all," said Karl. "Tell us again what's going to happen," he asked of a large, bearded man who looked like a wrestler in a tight uniform, "and remember, there can be no going back. We might even have to move it up slightly, because I can't get an answer from Felix."

The forty-five-year-old giant with the neat blond beard had a heavy Bavarian accent. Better known in terrorist circles as "the Sergeant," he'd served for a time in the Congo as a mercenary.

"First," he said, hands behind his back, "we'll wait to see what's happening with the terrorists over at the farmhouse. The police should be arriving there shortly, and since they think the police are really the enemy, there will be a small fight. Several news networks will have been informed about that and so, the media will cover it. Since it will be assumed that the terrorist group had come to attack the Israeli delegation, there will be a commotion.

"We know from one of our sources in the French police — an old friend from the Legion — that in the event of such an emergency, a helicopter squad will move in to take the Palestinian delegation away to a new location, just in case. That way we are assured they will not be at a high state of readiness. The helicopters will come in from three different places. One or two from each, and more than enough to get all the delegation out.

"We have two more setups like this one, as you all know, located halfway between the helicopter bases and the target. When the call for a location change comes, we'll be ready in our helicopters here and in our other locations. As the rescue helicopters pass overhead . . ." and with that he pulled back a canvas from a box containing four Soviet-made shoulder-launched anti-aircraft missiles, known as frogs " . . . we will shoot them down with these. They are at every location."

"There is no chance they can get away. Don't forget that they will not be taking evasive measures. After all, who would shoot a missile at a police helicopter near Paris? They would have to be mad." Everybody roared with laughter. All present were old hands at this, but they were tense nonetheless.

The big Bavarian went on. "We also have the frequency that the rescue helicopters will transmit on, so we'll be able to listen in.

"Once we've destroyed them, our helicopters will take to the air, continuing on their routes. We will resume communication with the police center as if nothing had happened. After all, we will be on the line monitoring beforehand. As the 'friend or foe' transmission system that all aircraft use to identify themselves, we won't need that. We're not landing at an airport.

"It's possible that no helicopters will leave from one of their locations, or that more than one will. That will make no difference to us. And while the explosions will be seen, by the time they're reported to the proper authorities and then checked, the whole operation will be over."

At that, Karl turned to a small man seated in a canvas chair. "You go on from there."

This man, known as Topo, or "Rat," in Italian, was a member in good standing of the Red Brigades. He was here as a personal favor to Karl, who had helped him in the past with such activities as kidnapping and the murder of Aldo Moro.

"Well," he didn't bother to stand as he spoke, "once we're in the air and in control of the radio bands, we'll approach the compound from three directions and prepare to land the choppers around the main building. We'll order the security on the compound grounds to secure the perimeter, removing them from the main building, and then we'll come in for the kill.

"With the choppers still hovering for a fast getaway, we'll enter the villa and kill everybody inside, except for several guards whom we'll only wound, and make sure they hear us speaking Hebrew. We can do just about anything in the building, because the three hovering helicopters will cover any noise."

"Excellent," said Karl. "Then, when we're back out of sight, we'll fly low to the collection points, dispose of the helicopters, and go on about our business. We'll meet again in Damascus in thirty-six hours. Good luck, and happy hunting!"

They all answered, "Happy hunting!"

Karl was satisfied that everything was in place. Yes, it was going to happen. He knew it. He could almost taste the blood, and he loved it.

# 38

**MÉTRO STATION, CHARLES DE GAULLE-ÉTOILE
OCTOBER 3
1730 HOURS**

THE MÉTRO WAS the fastest way Natan could get to the Arc de Triomphe. Believing Amos was with him on this one, and having most of Karl's plan in his hands, gave Natan a sense of security.

As the train stopped, Natan opened the door and started to run. The place was crowded, but he managed to reach the street quickly. And right there was the floodlit arch, encircled as always by an endless stream of noisy, honking cars. Natan inspired some honking himself when he veered into the parade of vehicles, running between them like a matador in a ring full of mad bulls. Number One spotted him first.

"The fool is going to do the work for us," he said to Number Nine, who was seated on a large motorcycle, dressed entirely in black.

"He'll make it, don't worry." She seemed certain of this.

They stood there watching as the fish made its way into the net. This — and the failed attempt on him in Amsterdam — was the only time the team had ever had to hit an Israeli, someone they knew. It wasn't going to be easy, although they'd been assured he was a traitor. The plan was simple enough.

Natan was heading for the entrance to the pedestrian tunnel

leading under the Arc de Triomphe when they jumped him. Number One had allocated five men to do the job, but it turned out to be more than they needed. In less than two minutes, they had nabbed him and led him to the edge of the road.

Number Nine and another motorcyclist managed to clear the way for a black Renault van that slowed down with its side door open. They practically tossed him in, then clambered into the van behind him. Another two were picked up by the motorcycles which had now opened up a getaway path for the van.

They headed along avenue de la Grande Armée in the direction of the Bois de Boulogne. The van didn't slow down until they were deep into the woods and clear of anyone who might have followed. Number One had managed to transmit a message while they were still moving. "Dead. I repeat, dead," was the confirmation he'd received to proceed, so he turned off the radio. He knew what he had to do.

Natan had been bound and gagged. He was shaking his head, trying to get the dirty cloth out of his mouth. Number One moved closer to him, then pulled the cloth away with one sharp yank. Natan first spat and then stared directly at Number One.

"Would you like to tell me what the hell is going on? I was promised help to prevent a catastrophe and this is what I get. What the hell is this? Some sort of joke?"

"I'm sorry, buddy, but it seems that your time is up. Once everybody's here, we're going to have to carry out our orders. Nothing personal, you understand."

"No, I fucking don't understand."

When the van door opened, they all seemed to be there. Natan knew they were just obeying orders, but that didn't help his predicament.

"Can I say something, before this goes any further?"

"Go ahead," said Number One, making a gesture of acquiescence.

"I have no idea what they've told you about me, but in a very short time there is going to be a hit on some moderate Palestinians who are willing to . . ."

"What the fuck is this?" said Number Four. "Are we supposed to listen to this guy? He's a goddamn traitor. Let's get this over with and get the hell out of here!"

"He's right," said Number Two. "The police could be closing in. After all, we grabbed him in full view of a lot of people. Let's damn well . . ."

"What's going on here?" asked Number One. "I'm still in charge and I said the man can talk. So shut up and listen or go piss on a tree. But don't stop him again." —

Natan went on. "They want to make peace. What if I said that you were helping to destroy the future of our country you so love? At this moment, there is a conspiracy being played . . ."

"That's enough," said Number One. "A conspiracy is it? We've all heard *that* one before. The men are right. We have a job to do. Sorry, buddy, you took the wrong turn and you hit the train."

"You said he could talk," interrupted Number Nine, stepping forward. "Look, we were on the bike and there was no one behind us. We have the time, I know. Let the man finish."

There was a silence that Natan was not going to let slip. "They're playing a savage game out there, using you to cover things up so no one will ever know." Several of the team were shaking their heads in disbelief. "Listen to me." Natan went on, raising his voice. "Just because they give you a number and treat you like a robot, is no reason to become one. Do you know what they really sent you to do? Do you really believe killing me is your real mission?" He smiled mockingly. "What you were sent to do is kill a real chance for peace. Yes."

Number One turned to Natan again. "What the hell are you talking about? You sold out and now you're trying to sell us this bullshit about doomsday. I don't buy it."

"If I'm a traitor, why do you suppose they didn't even consider bringing me in? They could court-martial me and shoot me. You could get me back to Israel alive, but no, they want me dead. Did you stop to think why? Can't you see what's going on? You were following terrorists. Why didn't anyone stop them? Why are they still out there? Think, goddammit, think."

No one said a word. They all just stood there. Number Three, who'd wanted it over quickly, was staring at the ground, kicking the gravel with his heel. Natan was making sense. They let him go on.

"What's the problem? Now that you've caught me, you can kill me anytime. Before you were numbers you were Israelis: proud, honest, loyal idealists. Look at us, what has become of us? From Zionist dreamers we've turned into warriors and fighting robots. We pray at the monuments for our dead. We worship the dead rather than the living, promising ourselves Masada never again. Shutting ourselves off to the cry for peace. The marble monuments are full, they don't need more names. You're being used by people who do not care about you one bit. They have an idea in their twisted minds of a country that stretches across lands we do not need. That's what they want and we fuel their madness with our blood."

"Let's say," said Number One, "let's say we don't eliminate you. We'll still have to bring you in."

"In fact," Natan lowered his voice, "I don't really care what you do to me. All I know is that there's a terrorist team out there at this moment, headed by an ex-Stasi officer, that will assassinate the Palestinian moderates — wiping out our only hope for a peaceful solution with our Arab neighbors. They are on their way, with the blessing of your bosses. And guess who will be blamed for the attack? Israel.

"I don't know what they've told you about me, or the reason they've given that you should kill me. But let me tell you this." Natan knew this was it. He would either be dead in less than five minutes or he'd have the best support team anyone could ask for. "You have a chance to do something good and real for your country.

Help me stop them. I'll be with you every step of the way, so if you decide to kill me after all, you'll be able to do it any time."

Natan looked at each of them in turn. He felt that some were with him, but he needed them all. They'd had their orders and to disobey them, they would all have to agree. He knew he'd done his best to persuade them, now he lowered his head to wait.

Suddenly he felt a hand on his shoulder. Number Nine was standing next to him. "My name is Tamar, and I believe you. I think most of us do."

Number Three took several steps back. "Number One, stop her! This is ridiculous! What the fuck does she think she's doing!"

Number One faced the men. "My name is Eli," he said, "and I believe him too. Something about this whole operation stank, right from the beginning. Come on, you know I'm right. Anyway, what the hell do we have to lose? If he's lying, all he's bought is a couple of hours at the most. We are off the air anyway, and they think the man is dead. I say let's give it a try. I don't feel right about killing him anyway. This is one order I'm refusing to follow. I have no authority to make you join me. This is a decision each one has to take for himself."

Number Five leaned over the door of the van. "I agree. It would be better to take him to Israel for trial. Why do they insist we kill him?" He turned to Natan. "By the way, my name is Elbaz."

It wasn't long before they were all seated around the map, plotting what would probably be their last operation. Even Number Three joined in. "I disagree with you people," he grumbled, "but I won't go against you. We've been through too much together. I'm going to keep an eye on the traitor, though."

Natan smiled at him with understanding. They knew they would face a court-martial for not carrying out the order to kill him, and that it would be held in secret. But Natan had a solution for that potential problem.

If they managed to eliminate the attackers, they would surrender to the French police as an Israeli team, part of Operation Lion of Judah designed to save the delegates. This exposure would prevent the Mossad from closing accounts with them in secret, and they'd return to Israel as heroes because no administration would ever admit that it was willing to condone the assassination of a moderate Palestinian delegation. As for Natan, things were still unclear and he would have to play it by ear.

# 39

AVRAHAM WAS seated on his high leather chair and Oren, who had just joined him, sat next to him. They were both transfixed by one of the television monitors on the wall across the room.

A seemingly endless stream of police cars were converging on a farmhouse. The TV cameraman had to run low to avoid being shot, while the sound of rapid automatic weapons fire could be heard over the excited voice of the announcer.

A similar picture appeared on a second monitor, then another, and then CNN. All networks were interrupting regular broadcasting to bring in this breaking news: a Palestinian terrorist group had been surprised by the police in a small farmhouse outside Paris as they were preparing to attack the Israeli delegations to a secret round of peace talks being held at an undisclosed location. The commentators offered little on the talks, as there was very little known. But they all kept repeating that the secret talks were not really a well-kept secret. If they had attracted little attention, it was because of their low-ranking delegations.

Minutes later, there was a commotion as the French special police units had started to storm the house. There were several explosions, then a fire, and the house went up like a torch. Two figures came running out in flames and were wrestled to the ground by police. Then there was a second series of explosions, after which it was hard to determine what was happening.

## PARIS
## 2130 HOURS

"CAN YOU hear anything?" asked the man holding the frog missile to his shoulder.

"He should be overhead in about ten seconds," shouted the Sergeant over the sound of the helicopter engine into the small mike he had attached to his helmet. "Be ready."

The noise level on the ground was so high that they couldn't hear the incoming chopper. Suddenly its blinking lights were visible.

"There he is!" The Sergeant shouted, pointing skyward. "Fire! Fire!"

Two missiles left the ground almost simultaneously, their wake of smoke glowing as their rocket engines rapidly burned themselves out. They climbed slowly into the sky, gaining speed as they sought the slow chopper. Like two glowing fingers, they reached for the flickering lights. For a split second they disappeared into the black silhouette of the helicopter. Suddenly a thunder overcame the noise on the ground and a bright orange and blue glow lit up the dark sky for several seconds. Then came an odd silence, followed by showers of debris that lit up the dry wheat field, starting a series of small fires. Within seconds, the stand-in chopper was in the air. This exact scenario repeated itself in two other locations outside Paris.

The police controller on the outskirts of the city who had a voice channel open to the rescue helicopters noticed that something strange had happened. At first, he thought it was a problem with only one helicopter: a second or so of communication loss, and then he was back on the air. But when the same thing happened with all three, he attributed it to a radio disturbance. After all, they were in touch, with everything going according to the contingency plan.

Minutes later, the three helicopters were approaching the compound. Using codes Karl obtained from his source, they notified the police guarding the compound of their intention to lift out the Palestinians. As the guards were expecting them, approval was instantaneous. The three helicopters joined into a single formation passing low over the perimeter fence. Karl, in the lead helicopter, noticed a van that seemed to have crashed into the fence, with several policemen standing around it. Within seconds, they passed the grove covering almost the whole half mile of grounds leading from the fence to the main buildings.

The helicopters hovered overhead until the commander of the police guard unit had notified them that his men were in place and it was safe for them to land. Which meant for Karl that all French police on the ground were concentrated on the perimeter away from the main building. Karl tapped the pilot on the shoulder, pointing his thumb down; following the lead of the first chopper, they all descended, now hovering less than two feet off the ground.

Forty-five minutes earlier, Number One had skidded the van into the fence just around the corner from the main gate. In seconds, all but Number Six had managed to jump the fence, using the van roof as a platform, as the fence was only nine feet high. Once they were all in the grounds, Number Six, now in the driver's seat, leaned on the horn. Guards from the gatehouse were at her side in seconds. Since they had the driver and there was no visible damage to the fence, the police felt things were under control.

Not sure exactly what they were getting into, Natan and the team were happy to discover that the grounds had no elaborate security system, but relied almost entirely on the perimeter guards. The Palestinians and the two French guards who were in the main building were surprised and terrified at the sight of the Kidon team. It took Natan several minutes to calm them down, bringing them into the picture. The French guards were bound hand and foot, then moved with the Palestinian delegates to the second floor, out of harm's way.

"Why are you doing this?" asked a woman delegate.

"Wouldn't you save an Israeli who wanted to make peace with you?" asked Natan.

Her face lit up. "It is a hard road you have chosen, and so have we." She swiftly scanned the faces of the other delegates who had stopped halfway up the stairs to listen. Given the circumstances, they were all extremely calm. She turned back to Natan. "It's a new road, too, we're taking, that no one has taken before. Although it's very old, it's also very new. I wish you luck."

"Believe me, I'll need it. Now please, we are running out of time."

Number One positioned his people and gave Natan a loaded handgun. "We'll need all the firepower we can get."

"Just one thing," Natan said. "Did you report me as dead?"

"Sure. You were there."

"If things work out the way we hope they will, I'd prefer you left me that way."

Number One smiled. "No problem. It's good for my reputation, you know."

The choppers hovered several feet off the ground at first, as the men poured out, each group lining up on both sides of each entrance. As soon as they were satisfied that the grounds were secure, the chopper pilots touched down, leaving their rotors idling, ready for a fast getaway.

Number Four and two of the other Kidon members lined themselves up to take control of the pilots, once the attackers entered the building. Karl was standing between the main entrance and the one to the right, not visible to anyone except two of the three assault leaders. They were all waiting for his signal to storm the building. From his source in the French police, Karl was assured that there were only two guards in the building, but when there was no sign of them, Karl assumed something must be wrong.

He signaled the Sergeant by raising his hand and then tapping himself on the top of his head. That was to activate the contingency plan calling for only one team to enter the building, leaving the other two as backup in the event of a trap.

The Sergeant kicked in the door and rolled in a stun grenade. Seconds later, a white blinding flash of light filled the open doorway. Assuming all inside were temporarily blinded, the Sergeant, followed by his men shouting instructions in Hebrew as planned, stormed into the building.

Number One and his team at the top of the open stairwell had backed out of sight as the grenade was thrown.

Finding no one there, the Sergeant and his men raced for the staircase. Before the first one could grab the railing, Number One and the rest of the team opened fire. Like marionettes whose strings were suddenly severed, the group fell lifeless to the floor.

Hearing only one burst of fire from within the house, Karl took it to be his people doing the shooting. He signalled the second team in.

Their entrance caught Number One and his men by surprise, but he opened fire with his submachine gun, taking out the first two mercenaries, then diving to the floor to avoid the hail of bullets coming his way. The newcomers didn't manage a long stream of fire, as the team members still at the top of the stairs took them out as soon as Number One was out of their line of fire.

When he heard machine gun fire from the outside, rising above the helicopter noise, Number One ran to the main door and stood to one side, his back to the wall. Natan gained the other side of the doorway and stopped there.

Number One shouted across to him, "There can't be many left."

"Should we head out?" asked Natan.

"No, let the guys outside handle it. There's no point getting killed because of impatience. Once my men finish the scum off, they'll call us out."

As he finished speaking, they could hear Number Four outside shouting, "It's all clear, we got them all."

After the second team had entered, Karl realized something was definitely wrong. He was on the point of breaking cover to run for the chopper when he heard a barrage of gunfire slamming against the wall, rattling his third team to the ground. At first he thought it was the French police coming in from the direction of the main gate. He stayed put long enough to see the three men running in from behind the choppers, then he noticed the pilot slumped halfway out the open door, face down, body dangling lifeless. The men started to shout something in what sounded to him like Hebrew. Realizing no one had noticed him, he decided to stay put.

"Now," said Number One, "is a good time to go out, and time for you, my friend, to get lost."

"Thanks. After you."

"And how will you get out of here?" Number One was already halfway out the door.

"I'll take one of the choppers. We flew them in the Navy." With that, Natan pointed in the direction of the main gate. Headlights of what seemed to be a jeep were heading their way. The two made for the nearest chopper. Its blades were whirring loudly.

Karl waited until the two men reached the chopper before sprinting toward them, firing his pistol as he ran.

The noise of the helicopter covered the sound of gunfire and none of the other Kidon team members had spotted Karl. Number One grabbed Natan's arm and as suddenly, slid to the ground. The man seemed bewildered, blood gushing from his neck. Seconds later, he was dead.

A bullet slammed into the fuselage beside Natan, and he wheeled to see Karl running at him, screaming like a madman and still firing. As several bullets smashed into the chopper's side window, Natan swiftly raised his gun. In his sights, he knew, was Karl Reinhart, a man who was also "officially dead". Killing him would merely set the record straight. Natan squeezed the trigger twice. Karl staggered and pitched to the ground, the top of his head blown away.

The jeep was closing in fast. With no time to waste, Natan climbed into the chopper. In seconds, he was airborne and out of the compound. He knew the team could manage now. As for him, he was on his way to Nadin. Mentally plotting his course, he suddenly realized that the dials on the helicopter's control panel were starting to go haywire. He was heading down toward the treetops: Karl's bullets had penetrated the fuselage and damaged the chopper. Karl might have the last laugh yet.

Natan struggled with the controls as he tried to reach a small clearing, but the chopper's angle as it approached the open space was too steep. Natan braced himself and pulled as hard as he could on the stick. He almost cleared the trees, but the tail caught in one and the rear blade spattered into a thousand metal shards. The chopper broke into three sections, crashing in a crumpled heap. Fuel was pouring out of the ruptured tanks, covering the mangled remains.

A small bush softened Natan's fall, for he had been thrown from the chopper by the same jolt that crushed it. Though he was more than thirty feet from the wreck, he was almost totally covered with fuel. He guessed an explosion was seconds away, and one spark would turn him into a living torch. Shaken and sore, Natan rose to his feet and limped away from the clearing as fast as he could go.

At the compound, the remainder of the Kidon team had their hands up in the air, as the French police swarmed around them and the remaining helicopters. They saw Natan's chopper go down, then several seconds later they heard it explode and watched the sky light up briefly.

"So, he's dead after all," said Number Five softly, shaking his head.

When the explosion came, it had knocked Natan flat, but did him no other damage.

Now he was seated in an old Citroen Deux Chevaux that he had flagged down on the road nearby. The elderly driver was headed into a small town only minutes away. All Natan wanted was to get to a phone and call Nadin. There was no way back, not if he wanted to live. And since he was already "dead," starting a new life would be much easier. And how ironic, he thought: the dead have no future, yet he would have no past.